SAVE OUR SOULS

Ford forced his hands against the g-forces in order to cover his face. The Seng continued to shake, metal screeching against metal and buckling all around him. A sharp thud struck his head and with it came the realisation - he had no idea what was going on.

"Hull breach on E Deck," Mason yelled, "bulk heads dropping."

Ford didn't care. There was no one on E Deck.

His father's words rang in his ears, 'One step at a time, that's all you can do', words Ford tried to live by. Keeping one hand over his brow, he opened the life support controls, cutting the pipe's feed. The purple deluge promptly slowed to a trickle.

A forth collision, followed by a fifth. With each crash, the violent shaking diminished until it was no more than a distant vibration. The remaining cameras showed the object rolling along the spine, bouncing between cargo pods and smashing them free. Almost, exactly as Ford predicted. Most of the damage had been buffered by the pods. The ship at least, had a chance. Then, everything went black: lights, cameras, complete inaction.

SAVE OUR SOULS

By Leighton Dean

Leighton Dean

First published in 2018 by Leighton Dean

This paperback edition published in 2018 by Leighton Dean

ISBN – 978-1-98055-250-5

For Cliff and John,
thanks for stirring my imagination

ONE

J ian Seng, having travelled past the last outpost eleven months previously, lumbered through the long emptiness of space. Jian Seng was a three hundred and ten year old break bulk cargo ship, constructed in the orbital ship yards of Mars. Her Martian origins being reflected in the slight crimson tint on her hull plating. She was enormous, stretching over three kilometres from bow to stern. Most of this was taken up by a cylindrical spinal corridor from which spurs of cargo pods were attached. They spun around the tunnel, providing gravity to their cargo. The staffing areas were granted gravity by artificial generators at either end. At its rear, or stern was the engineering section, containing a block of fuel tanks, coolant silos and the main propulsion unit. At the front or bow of the ship were living quarters, stasis pods, shuttle bay, infirmary and the bridge.

She'd been built to last generations but wouldn't win any beauty contests; her once gleaming plating now looked scarred and pocked. Sure, the smell of oil and grease persistently clung to her halls and her subsystems were rerouted into knots, but the grisly leviathan carried a secret regenerative remedy to all her failings, the love of her crew. To those thirty-five men and women, Jian Seng wasn't just an out-dated labouring vessel, it was their home.

"Screw this, let's get some coffee." Ford would argue his case until his cheeks ran as cherry as his hair, "We've been at this, what? Two hours already?" His anti-gravity jacket did little to ease his back as his working space was so damned tight he couldn't bring his elbows above his chest. He'd said the job had taken two hours already, it felt more like three. But the job needed doing. Being part of the five person duty crew meant regular diagnostics on the ship, including frequent checks of the thirty other crew members sleeping in stasis, but it was still a pain. Why he'd thought it was a good idea to return to such a toiling existence, he couldn't recall.

His sister Rebecca, better known as Becca, paused to check the time on her omni-glove, "Fifty two minutes Ford and we've done three beds out of ten. Mason's still running diagnostics on the bridge systems. We'll have a break in an hour as scheduled."

"You're a cruel boss sis."

"You know I don't like doing this any more than you."

"I really doubt that." Ford muttered under his breath, his sister certainly had the better deal. She stood at the foot of a bed, holding a data pad.

The last thing Ford expected to hear next was the proximity alarm. A piercing shrill which no part of the ship escaped. It sounded for two seconds and repeated after a one second interval. Ford slid out from under the bed and looked to his sister. Her lake blue eyes stared at the display monitor mounted on the wall opposite. The lights dimmed on the second sounding and emergency beacon lamps flashed red along all walls urging them to the bridge.

"When's the next drill due?" He asked, knowing the last one had only been conducted last month.

"Not until the next shift rotation," she answered, remaining focused on the wall display, "This is real."

On the third screech; Rebecca dropped her data pad, "Come on." Her auburn pony tail whipped around as she vanished from the room before the beacon lamps had chance to wash the room red. Ford grabbed the side of the stasis bunk and climbed to his feet, slapping his jacket's chest controls and turning off the anti-gravity field. He chased after her, kicking Becca's fallen pad across the room on the way out the door.

Becca wasn't far ahead, disappearing around corners seconds before he caught sight of her again. The siren continued to scream its warning: something was going to hit them. On the fourth turn Ford grabbed the pipe-work and swung himself around, keeping his momentum. He landed closer to Becca, but she'd always been faster and by the time they took the next corner she was already breaking ahead.

They were now at the bow of the ship and with the last corner behind them they only had two decks to climb. Ford knew reaching the bridge would only be the start of it. The Jian Seng was massive; her scanner array was able to pierce the void for thousands of kilometres. The chance of anything colliding with them should have been next to impossible and yet something had clearly got through. Something that was too close for the navigation computer to avoid. The deflector turrets were designed to blast rocks out of the way, but the Seng wasn't a military vessel. Her targeting systems wouldn't be able to lock onto something moving too fast or too small.

Becca leapt onto the junction ladder, landing about half way up and climbed from sight. Ford mimicked her actions, "Why isn't Mason on the comm?" he screamed between klaxon beats.

"I'm not psychic," she screamed back.

Ford couldn't remember the last time he'd rushed a ladder climb, and it told. His calves burned and his chest tightened. By the time he'd reached the desired deck, he was out of breath and Becca was out of sight. He jogged down the corridor and entered the bridge; Becca was already seated at her terminal and fastening her safety belt. Mason was sat in the Captain's chair, his terminal pulled across his lap. The room was tiny, only six metres in diameter, with five articulated chairs set in a diamond formation. Ford grabbed the nearest seat available and let the system identify him, a klaxon screech later and the terminal's touch screen arranged itself to Ford's personal configuration.

"No I haven't seen anything." Mason answered the unasked question,

"Can we kill the damn klaxon?" Ford snapped, while attempting to study the telemetry in front of him.

"I don't have anything either." Becca announced as Mason silenced the alarm. The sound of which was instantly replaced by a high pitched whistle inside Ford's ears.

"Readings suggest something is definitely out there." Ford commented. He couldn't visually see anything and the readings on his screen made little sense but he wasn't willing to dismiss it. The Seng knew something was out there, it just couldn't tell him what or, "Where are you?" He mouthed the words, tapping against his screen, oblivious of the conversation continuing between the other two.

"There's nothing on the lanes." Mason offered, "I ran an invasive scan but everything came up blank."

"Well something tripped the alarm." Becca said, before starting to relay their route and speed via comms to whomever or whatever might be out there. "This is the commercial transport, Jian Seng..." she continued to relay their route and speed, all by the book procedures that Ford had little concern for. The persistent ringing in his ears whistled higher in pitch until he could hear nothing else.

"Anything?" Mason asked,

"Ford? You got anything?" Becca asked, loud enough to attract Ford's attention.

"What?" He snapped, trying his best to ignore the tinnitus.

"Have you got anything?"

"No." His screen was a mess of contradictions. He doubted he'd make sense of it even without the ringing. Ford took a breath and trawled through the event log, right back to the initial alert. There it was, lasting just over a second but it was there, out in the black and coming right at them. He adjusted the ping against their own velocity and trajectory, "Check bearing three-three-zero, mark one-five." he said, putting the data into his own scanner and following the line.

"Still nothing." said Mason and Becca agreed.

"Same here..." Ford mouthed. He stared into his screen, willing the object to reveal itself.

"Maybe it's a sensor ghost?" Becca asked,

"I think I nearly had a heart attack." Mason replied, hand on his chest for comic effect. As ship's First Officer, Mason wasn't all that bad, too casual at times, especially with Becca. They'd all grown up together on this tin can, so a level of familiarity was to be expected. But his casual nature was a fault for one in command and it was all too eager to reassert itself when they hadn't confirmed an all clear.

Ford licked his lips, sucking at the inside of his cheek. He'd re-calibrated the sensors not two days ago. Addressing Mason he asked, "Have you changed any of the sensor settings?"

"What?" Mason asked, "No, of course not." a little more insulted at Ford's question than he could hide, "Running a diagnostic on them now." he spat, tapping his terminal.

"Bridge, what's going on?" Crudge's voice called over the intercom.

"Stand down Chief." Mason said, "I'll update you when we know more."

"Where is Jo?" Becca asked,

"Running manifest audits."

"Pull her back." said Ford,

Mason pondered on the statement a moment, pensively rubbing the six week old beard he'd cultivated during his duty shift, "Mason to Jo, I need you to drop what you're doing and get back here."

Her reply was immediate, "I'm already on my way, still in pod twelve."

"This isn't right." Ford was speaking to himself now, the world outside his screen a hazy dream.

"Guys..." Becca started to say in urgency. She had no need to finish as Ford saw it too, right along the trajectory he'd calculated.

One solitary object, heading right at them, "Got it." He said, his fingers raced over the screen but too slow to gain a lock on it before it vanished, "What in the hell?"

"Could there be something wrong with the sensors?" Becca asked,

"Diagnostic is running." Mason reminded her,

Without looking up from his screen, Ford replied, "I don't think so. If there was something wrong with the sensors the contact wouldn't be this precise. Sensors have found it, whatever *it is*, twice already, and both times travelling along the same path." He brought the two points up, lining them up in correlation to their location and sent the image to their stations, "See, it's coming in - and fast."

"So, what you're saying is, it's cloaked?" Mason asked,

"Don't say that." Becca snapped,

Not one for superstitions, Ford answered "If they're pirates we'll know soon enough."

"Ford!" Becca's tone was one he'd heard many times down the years. Scathing and scolding.

Ford was too busy recalibrating the scanners to acknowledge his sister's objection. Saying to himself, *if I tweak them back a bit...* PING, "Got it." It was big. Too big for the Seng's sensors to have let it get so close, but then, as quick as it had appeared, it was gone - *something that big just can't disappear.* "Gone."

"Ford..." Becca said, "What do you mean, gone?"

"Yeah, it's not like it has anything to hide behind." Quipped Mason,

"Funny." Ford complained, just as his sensors pinged, *back again old friend.* Ford's fingers, ready this time, "Dammit." He yelled as it vanished, "I can't get a lock."

"Can we dodge it?" asked Becca,

"Crudge, give us some more engines." Mason called to engineering,

"You already have everything I've got." Crudge replied,

"What's going on?" asked Jo from her current position.

The Jian Seng was too big a target to miss and the object would hit them in just over one minute. Ford jabbed his controls, running several simulations while running the math in his head. He wasn't judging the scenario of avoiding the collision, which Mason was hoping for. To Ford, that way of thinking was a waste of precious time. The object was too close to avoid and instead he looked to reduce the incoming damage.

"Jo, we're about to be hit, where are you?" Mason replied,

"Outside cargo pod twelve."

Ford's best possible outcome was to barrel roll the ship. Force the UFO to the underside of the bow, avoiding the antenna stacks along the top of the ship and let it hit the cargo pods. In Ford's head, the cylindrical warehouses would cushion the blow and break away from the ship; hopefully taking the object with them. Better to lose the payload than the ship... "Wait, where?"

"Outside Pod Twelve." Mason repeated Jo's position.

"She's still in the spine?" replied Ford, the anxiety in his voice clear.

"Yes... I am. Why?" Jo picked up on it,

Crudge was secure in the engineering section at the stern. The bridge along with the crew in stasis, were secure at the ship's bow. Joanne was now stood right in the middle of the spinal corridor, just one tube surrounded by cargo. Ford closed his eyes, cursing under his breath, "Jo, get the hell out of there, quick." He said urgently, while plotting the ship's rotation. He craned his neck around and spoke to Mason. "The best I can do is angle the ship for a glancing blow. It will hit the underside of the bow and the first row of pods." *Hopefully, then it will bounce off.*

His plan was as solid as he could make it. The belly of the front section was shielded by a maze of corridors and domestic quarters, Ford didn't mind writing off someone's bed as collateral damage. Best case scenario, it would glance off the hull plating and head off into space. Worst case scenario the object wouldn't bounce, but hit the pods at such an angle it would sever the spine. Admittedly, both the engineering section and the front section could act as life boats for up to six months, but they were at least nine months away from the nearest rescue... Realistically, the result of the collision would be somewhere in between. Either way, it was still the best possible solution for survival for everyone except Jo. Ford held his head back, watching Mason arrive at the same conclusion.

"Jo, this is Mason, get out of that corridor now. That's a direct order. Get to control. Don't hang about." Then he said, "Ford, get it done."

"It's going to hit section one or two as she gets here." Ford said, swinging back around to his terminal.

Mason, rethinking his last command to Jo said, "Jo, belay my last order - get to engineering."

"Are you sure?" her voice shrill, fear hidden beneath her anger. It was going to be a long run but she could make it. *She had to.*

"Ford?" Mason asked,

"Stern."

"Jo, head to Crudge."

Ford keyed in the commands necessary to barrel roll the ship, nearly smashing the panel when he jabbed the execute button. The information went directly to the engines and a copy to Crudge's terminal so he could monitor the progression. Once executed there was nothing to do but wait as hundreds of manoeuvre thrusters ignited in unison across the ship, rolling her anti-clockwise at an achingly slow pace. It was the first time Ford noticed his hands shaking.

"Is this going to work?" Becca asked,

"I hope so." Ford said under his breath, following the data running up his screen. Hope was all they had now. No ifs or buts, this was worst case scenario.

"Where are you now Jo?" Becca asked,

"Coming... up on... twenty-two." She sounded stressed and exhausted; Ford couldn't begin to imagine how scared she must be.

"Keep going, you'll make it." Mason said encouragingly, drawing Ford's eyes off the clock. Jo wasn't making good time. Ford guessed she'd only make it as far as twenty eight before the thing hit. Mason must have known this; meaning his officer training had kicked in. Out of the five of them Mason arguably took this job the least serious. But when he put his mind to it he always got the job done. Even if he leaned on his faith in the *Trinity* too much. But now, Mason's voice brought Ford as much comfort as his misguided religion.

"Engineering's secure." Crudge's voice came over the comm, sounding as stalwart as ever. Ford would be hard pressed to find anything that shook the Chief's mettle. "Manoeuvre is exacting as requested."

"Strap yourself in old man." Mason cracked, clicking in his own seatbelt and reminding Ford he'd not yet fastened his own. He pulled the strap across his chest and missed the socket on the first attempt; cursing they'd not upgraded to automatic belts. He used his second hand to stave the first from shaking. Ford's trembling brought with it the memory of a cold breeze and he instantly recalled the frozen wastes of Otzu. He crouched alongside his squad, rubbing the chill from his gloved hands before Becca shouted, "Ford, strap in!" He snapped back into the pilot's chair, dismissing the memory and clicked his belt into place. He'd escaped death on Otzu, he wasn't about to get swatted like a bug on his first outing.

"Ten seconds, hold on to your butts. This is it!" Mason called out his readings, as he tapped his commands into his terminal. One by one, the bridge's terminals lit up with views from the Seng's exterior sensors. They had front seats to the disaster of the century.

"What is that thing?" asked Becca,

It took Ford a full second to find the object; a foreboding doom given physical form, lumbering toward them from the black. It didn't look so much a ship, but as a large frozen spear spinning toward them. It shimmered against their flood lights. Stars rippled behind its icy transparency.

Ford tapped the terminal's frame, knee jerking up and down. The whistling in his ears had faded. It was a small but significant favour from the 'verse. But in its place came a whisper of words, spoken in rhyme from behind Ford. A poem begging for forgiveness, Mason had taken refuge in the Trinity's prayer.

Ford envied Mason in his belief that the Trinity were watching over them. But to Ford, the thought of three living Gods sitting in their Cathedral of Glass orbiting Earth gave little relief to their immediate horror. So he looked to himself instead, steadying his knee and stalling his fingers. One eye on the approaching spear, the other on the clock and when it came in range: he fired the deflector turrets.

Becca shouted, "Grab hold of something Jo."

Ford closed his eyes, willing Jo to reach her goal - no matter how impossible it was. But in his heart he knew it was too late and despite hope's best wishes the object was on them.

The deflector volley lit up the spear's glimmering hull with silent explosions. Short ranged Kren-class Torpedoes, with enough punch to impede the most insistent of space debris were no more destructive to the object than rain hitting a tin roof. Ford tapped his screen again, targeting the remaining turrets. Within a second all of the guns were spent and still the leviathan rolled forward. Mason's prayer whispered in Ford's ear and in that moment something inside Ford died. He'd been lying to himself the deflector turrets would be enough to save them. It was pure folly. They were about to be hit and they still hadn't finished their manoeuvre. They were short by ten degrees.

The giant craft crashed into the underside of the Seng's bow. Astern of the crew quarters. It slammed into the power distribution nodes and several of the sensor feeds instantly went blank. Ford's belt pulled tight across his chest just as a ceiling pipe burst, showering the bridge and its occupants in liquid coolant that appeared purple under the red emergency lamps. The floor bounced again, flipping Ford's stomach. Bile raced up his throat. His mouth opened to vomit, but the foul souring taste of coolant filled it instead.

Ford forced his hands against the g-forces in order to cover his face. The Seng continued to shake, metal screeching against metal and buckling all around him. A sharp thud struck his head and with it came the realisation - he had no idea what was going on.

"Hull breach on E Deck," Mason yelled, "bulk heads dropping."

Ford didn't care. There was no one on E Deck.

His father's words rang in his ears, 'One step at a time, that's all you can do', words Ford tried to live by. Keeping one hand over his brow, he opened the life support controls, cutting the pipe's feed. The purple deluge promptly slowed to a trickle.

A forth collision, followed by a fifth. With each crash, the violent shaking diminished until it was no more than a distant vibration. The remaining cameras showed the object rolling along the spine, bouncing between cargo pods and smashing them free, almost exactly as Ford had predicted. Most of the damage had been buffered by the pods. The ship at least, had a chance. Then, everything went black: lights, cameras, complete inaction.

Ford's heart beat like a drum, a soundtrack to their misfortune. Everything had ceased, vibrations, chatter, the incessant praying, even the sound of breathing was absent. He was alone but for the constant thumping in his chest, ba-bomb, ba-bomb, ba-bomb. Darkness pressed against his face, cold fear pumped in his veins and after what seemed like an eternity in limbo, but in reality only seconds later the emergency lamps returned, bringing with them a fresh hope amongst the carnage.

Part of the ceiling had collapsed onto the right side of the bridge. They were lucky. If anyone had been sat there they'd have been crushed. The debris smothered two terminals. If the rest of the ship had fared as luckily as the bridge had... maybe, just maybe they'd have a chance. Ford shivered, cold lingering in his bones. He had nothing but his adrenaline, ba-bomb, ba-bomb, ba-bomb.

The sound of clapping was unexpected and Ford jumped in his chair, once again pulling his belt tight. Nothing else had broken, nothing else had gone boom. It was Mason, clapping his thanks, "Good work Ford." he said, releasing his belt and walking unsteadily to Ford's station to rest a hand on his shoulder, "You saved us."

Ford mustered a smile, but refused to tempt fate any more than Mason just had. Right now, congratulations were unfounded and superfluous. They had no idea if Ford had actually saved them or simply delayed the consequences. He tapped Mason's hand, giving him a nod, "How's your heart?" He asked, trying to lighten his mood.

"Nothing a bottle of Kentucky can't remedy." Mason replied, patting Ford's shoulder.

Ford leaned across Mason, checking on his sister. She raised a thumb in his direction, distracted. Her face contorted, brow pitched down, working her terminal. Which if it was anything like Ford's was dead, "I've no communications."

"Most damage was to port, under the bow, the arrays are fine." Ford said, more in hope than knowledge.

She glared at him, "And yet I still don't have any."

"Then get it back." Mason ordered, with more than a degree of irritation in his voice, "Or is there someone better qualified I need to rouse?"

"No, Sir." She spat,

"We need to get a damage report." Ford said, trying to remember the emergency protocols. He knew there was a QWERTY keyboard behind his screen, but a fog of indecision blocked his path to turn the damned thing on. *One thing at a time.* He unclasped the secondary keyboard. When Mason's hands grabbed hold of his head, Ford flinched.

"Stay still." Mason ordered, "You took a hit."

Ford pulled his head away, bringing his hand up in objection to Mason's amateur medical opinion, "I'm fine."

"You're bleeding."

He brushed Mason away. "It's nothing, the scalp bleeds a lot." He had no idea where he'd picked up that little gem. He touched the growing lump. It stung but otherwise was fine. Besides, they needed the damage report more than he needed medical care. He smiled as he remembered how to activate the keyboard. As the terminal loaded up in safe mode he breathed more easily. Resting the keyboard on his lap, he typed his queries. Jian Seng replied, sending data scrawling up his monochrome screen. The damaged sections were three, five, nine and twelve continuing into the spine before the final collision ended in contact with the engineering section. Unfortunately, that particular collision had rendered the ship's internal sensors inoperable. He'd have to repair damage to the diagnostic system before learning more. Still, at least none of the bow's critical systems were hit.

Static erupted from the speakers and all of the bridge stopped to listen to the distant, alien voice.

"That Crudge?" Mason asked,

His question spurred Becca to her console, pulling a corded microphone to her mouth, "Crudge?" Static, nothing but static blurred over the comms, "Jo, that you?" Yet more static. Becca clicked the microphone, repeating her questions while tapping commands into her own keyboard, "Looks like the internal line was severed somewhere between two and three on the spine."

The pods rotated around the spine in clusters of three, held in place by what was dubbed a cargo pod collar, "There's a breach before the third collar." Ford announced, before relaying the rest of his damage report.

Mason's facade dropped, nostrils flaring as he sucked oxygen into his brain, "Ford, prep a duck for launch. Becca, concentrate on getting the comms up and running. I'll launch a buoy and divert command privileges to Operations and then wake Bounette and the Captain from stasis." A sound plan, Ford agreed. Disaster Recovery dictated the ship's Captain, in this case Ford's father to be woken as a priority - if the emergency systems hadn't automatically done so. Dependant on the situation the ship's Doctor and the rest of the sleeping command crew were also to be roused from stasis.

"You got an omnitool?" asked Becca, crouching next to her console podium.

Ford checked his tool belt, "Here." He passed her the required item, removed his belt and went to stand. It was a mistake. "Woah..." failing, he sat back down with a bump.

"For goodness sake Ford, wait a moment will ya?" Mason said with a sigh of irritation, "On second thoughts, don't move till I tell you to."

"I can walk." Insisted Ford,

"Clearly." Mason replied with sarcasm, "Tell you what. Take five, then go wake your dad and the doctor. You'll need to see Bounette anyway. The ducks can wait until I've launched the buoy."

"Shouldn't we all head up to operations? We can take a look from there. The more information we can give the Captain the better." Ford replied, rubbing his head.

"We will, in time." Mason agreed, "But first we need the ducks ready for launch so we can reach Crudge. Once we have the Captain up and about, then we'll discuss options."

"We don't know how much time we have." Becca slipped in,

"Running head first into this won't help." Mason reminded her, pressing a finger to his lips.

Ford understood his meaning: other than the spine, there wasn't another route to engineering without heading outside. To do that you needed one of the three tug boats, which the crew affectionately called ducks. As a primary tug pilot, it fell to Ford to prep them as initially ordered. But as much as Ford refused to admit, he wasn't up to the task. He couldn't be sure if he'd reach the stasis chambers without stumbling into a wall, "I'll get on it." He said, grasping the chair and fighting the head spin until he found his feet.

"Guys," Mason added, "I don't want any half-baked rescue plans until we know how much of a problem we're dealing with. If you come up against something you can't easily remedy, then report it in. We'll decide what's happening once we have the command crew together."

"What if it can't wait?"

Mason turned to Becca who was back on form and speaking with authority, "I'm not saying don't do anything, I just don't want any of us getting ourselves killed needlessly. I'm sure Jo and Crudge are fine and are waiting for us."

Becca nodded, her big lake blues finding Ford and sharing his understanding. Just keep your wits about you and don't do anything stupid and at least one of those names belonged to a dead person.

***

This wasn't supposed to be hard, Ford reminded himself, as he stepped into the stasis room and picked up the discarded data pad. Becca hadn't had time to close the file down. To think, just seconds before the alarm went off he was bitching about how boring the shift was. The tick list was still present, just as she'd left it. He pressed close on the pad and set it down on the shelf near the door. He knew he was procrastinating but couldn't help it. Waking the Captain up was one thing, waking his Father was all together something else.

"Hey dad, it's me." He spoke aloud, "Sorry to wake you up early, but I totalled your ship." *Our home.* He shook his head, cursing his earlier dizzy spell from preventing him from doing what he really should have been doing – prepping Huey for launch. If they managed to survive this catastrophe the insurance his dad had on the Jian Seng would be swallowed up by the courts. If they could cobble half of what the Seng was worth, it would be a miracle. Ironically, if his father was registered devout they would have gotten enough to buy another ship. Actually they would already have a better ship, one that could have avoided the collision in the first place.

But his father was not devout; he was the opposite - a heathen. There would be no funding available to him, not that he would ever ask the Church for a bail out. Captain John Dahl avoided the Church at every opportunity. So no matter how Ford spun the event in his head, it came down to the fact that he had destroyed the family business. A business Ford never wanted in the first place, a fact his father understood all too well.

Opposite his father's bunk was Second Officer Gail Faraday, the bunk he'd been working on when the alarm went off. He crossed the path between them and crouched at its side. The circuit tray was still open and needed securing. He slid it back in and thumbed the lock closed,

"Mason should be down here." he grumbled and stood, *time to face the music, time to wake the old man*. The bunks were usually set to open at the beginning of the shift rotation and their stasis field would switch off two hours before. This allowed the occupant to rouse naturally as the lamps inside the tube gradually brightened, mimicking sunrise. To bring someone up manually was just a matter of overriding this procedure. He typed in the command at the terminal at the bunk's foot.

Strip lights running down either length of the bed flickered to life, revealing his father. Captain John Dahl still slept; the emergency automation protocols had failed to wake him, but Ford knew that even before he'd entered the room. John had a thick head of auburn hair, with more than a few grey streaks and an almost entirely grey beard. His hands rested on his hairy stomach, he wore nothing but his jockey shorts and the plethora of tattoos he'd picked up over the years.

Ford pressed his thumb and index finger together and checked the time stamp that appeared on his omni-glove, even with the overrides there were still protocols which needed to be adhered to. Many of the drugs pumped into the body during stasis bore similarities to hallucinogens, helping to maintain a dream like state whilst sleeping. Coming up early meant the drugs needed to be flushed out first or risk waking to a psychedelic morning from hell. Ford keyed in the necessary command and then headed to the Chief Surgeon's bunk, repeating the process.

Jake Bounette was smooth; not a mole or a birth mark as far as Ford cared to investigate. He didn't know the doctor all that well as the man had joined the crew during Ford's sabbatical. Ford had worked one shift with the man, but in that short time he had known him, he'd found Bounette quite fun to talk to. Bounette had a penchant for pot stirring which was fun to watch (there wasn't much in the ways of entertainment when you're stuck on an overgrown tin can for months on end). Crudge's daughter Natalie had liked him enough to take his name. Also, he wasn't a spacer. He hadn't been born in space, which the majority of the crew had been. He was a landlubber, planet-born. He'd told Ford where he'd grown up, some little town in the south of France which Ford had quickly forgotten. Earth; being a core planet to the Holy Trinity still had conscription. Bounette had joined the Church Militant's medical service. Ford related to that, being the only other on board to have served, albeit not in the same military.

A hissing sound from behind; turned Ford around. The magnetic seal on his father's bunk disengaged and the lid lifted. Ford walked tentatively over, not wanting to attract any premature attention before he could run the report through his head one last time. His father's eyes blinked as they adjusted to the bunk's lighting. He breathed a deep, waking breath followed by a loud cough. "What's going on, what's the emergency?" John Dahl had been Captain of this vessel for the entirety of Ford's life and knew the procedures better than he cooked breakfast. So, the direct and to the point question came as no surprise to Ford. His father pulled the tubes from his arms, searching Ford's face for answers, "Boy, don't make me ask twice."

"We've been hit."

Before his Captain's instincts clicked in his fatherly dispositions took precedence, "Are you okay? Is Becca?"

"I am, we're both okay." As soon as he'd confirmed this information, John Dahl's facial muscles relaxed. Ford grimaced; he was relieved to know his father's first concerns were to his children. It was a side of his father he'd rarely seen growing up and not at all since his mother passed. Hearing your ship had been hit was a lot to take in without having it thrust upon you straight from stasis, so Ford remained quiet, waiting for the inevitable questions.

John sat on the edge of his stasis bed and asked quietly and calmly, "How bad?"

In way of an apology for any misinformation, Ford pointed out he'd taken a hit to the head before reporting the damage as best he could remember; it wasn't quite verbatim. John listened without reaction, not even when he learned of Ford's injury. This was the cold, stoic man Ford had expected to wake. Even after Ford finished, the Captain said nothing, taking his time to digest the information.

After a few sloth paced moments, John asked, "What exactly happened?"

Ford gave him the abridged version of events as his father stood up, limiting his own role in events. He informed John that he was at the helm and that there was no chance of avoiding the collision. He knew Mason would give him a full report when he had the chance. There was little point in giving excuses now, not when they were against the clock.

"I take it Becca is working comms?"

"Yes Sir, she is the comms officer."

His father produced the sharp, disapproving look which Ford knew so well and said "Don't be flippant, boy." He then shook his head; what he was thinking at that precise moment Ford could only guess at. And what he guessed wasn't complimentary. "Hand me a robe." John said.

Ford grabbed one from the wall's inset wardrobe, returning passed it to him.

His father nodded in thanks, "Is everyone else okay?"

"Mason's launching a buoy. We've not had contact with Crudge or Jo since the collision, everyone in stasis checked out fine. I'm also thawing out Bounette."

John fastened the robe's belt around his waist, "Crudge was in engineering?"

Ford nodded his head, "Jo was in the spine." seeing his own fears reflected in his father's brown eyes.

"Okay." John said, "Any indication of foul play?"

Of course there is. The chances of a collision were astronomical and his father knew that or he wouldn't have asked. John had once told Ford 'never feed fear to your crew, necessary or otherwise', on some level that sentiment could have been responsible for the superstition of never saying, 'pirate', "It has to be considered, Sir. But there is no evidence either way."

"No evidence?" John scoffed, "You know the odds of two ships crashing into one another out here?"

"Sensors couldn't tell what it was that hit us. I saw it for a split second on the cameras. It was a massive ship, maybe, but I couldn't tell you for certain if it was being steered or not." That latter piece of information was irrelevant, for something to hit with such precision it was foolish not to consider intent.

"Okay." His father said, "Come here."

Ford obeyed, unsure whether to raise his arms for a hug or not. His father placed a hand on Ford's shoulder, slipping up behind his neck before splaying flat against the back of Ford's head and pulled it forward. His father's other hand rubbing softly over the bump, "It's not that bad."

"No." Ford confirmed, "Just a small one."

His father released him, "Okay, at ease." the authority of Captain in his voice beginning to return, "Mason is launching a buoy, you say?"

"Yes sir."

"Good." His father scratched his beard, "If we can't contact Crudge, we need Sharon." Ford nodded in agreement, she was the Second Engineer and someone Ford selfishly wanted to be part of the team.

"Jake should be waking up anytime now." Ford added, tilting his head in the direction of the Doctor's bunk.

"Good, get Natalie up and about too. We'll need someone who knows life support."

Ford nodded, trying to remember in which of the stasis chambers he could find Natalie's Bunk. Then deciding it would be far better to allow Jake Bounette wake her instead.

"I'm going to get dressed." His father stated, "Inform everyone to meet in Ops in fifteen minutes."

"Yes sir"

John grabbed Ford's shoulder again, "It's going to be alright."

"I know dad." Ford said, unable to match the confidence in his father's delivery.

"What time is it by the way?" John asked, dropping his arm.

Ford checked the back of his hand and pressed his finger and thumb together, "Oh-Four-Twenty-Four."

"Make sure Mason has a full report with him."

"Yes, Sir."

***

"How did he take it?" Mason asked, looking over his data pad at Ford while thumbing some buttons on the wall.

"How'd you think?"

"Well, I'd wager it wasn't strippers and champagne."

With a laugh Ford replied, "Your money's safe, he'll be about ten minutes. Did you get a duck prepped?"

"Didn't get a chance, had some issues launching the buoy. We'll roll it into the meeting."

"Probably for the best, didn't fancy getting your ham fists all over Huey anyway."

"Hey, these are the hands of an artist."

"That what you tell my sister?"

Mason shook his head in dismissal, "Shut up and come take a look at this."

Ford rounded the central table, its holographic interface dormant, black as ice. Most of Operations was in the same way. The wall computers to his right were dark but without visible damage. On the opposite wall the blast shutters were raised and the view stretched along the top of the ship down to its distant tail, "Holy shit." He said, continuing his route around the table to join Mason against the transparent wall.

"The magnification system is bust, but if you look hard enough you can make it out." Mason said, pointing to the tail.

Ford followed Mason's *artistic* index, searching through the masses of uncoupled cargo pods to the stern. It took a moment to find it; the faintest of shimmers drew his attention to the large jagged icicle reaching out from their engine. It was lodged deep into the aft section, right where it met with the spinal corridor and right where Jo was heading... "Have you heard from her?"

"Nothing. Not from either of them." Mason said, his voice echoing Ford's private thoughts. The spinal corridor was no longer spinning and its barrel cargo, at least the ones still clinging to the ship were static. The spine had no power and a good chance of unseen hull breaches all along it, "It's not looking goo-"

"Cameras?" Ford changed the subject.

Mason shook his head, "All down. Hopefully it's a simple server reboot, but with our luck..."

Static burst from the speakers, "...you hear me?" For a split second Ford believed the female voice was Jo, laughing at their assumption of her death. But it was Becca, "I have internal comms up... I think."

Mason pulled a microphone from its hook, "Loud and clear Bec." He said, grinning, "You did good."

"Someone owes me breakfast." Becca replied.

"I'll cook." Mason grinned, "Once the galley is up and running. In the meantime, get your ass to Ops."

Not that Ford was an addict, but finding the coffee machine inoperable was momentarily the worst thing he'd experienced so far that morning. He rested his forehead against the vacant display and closed his eyes.

"Mace..." Becca's voice was scared and distant over the speakers, "Ford was right, we only have access up to section two of the spine."

Ford thought about Jo, sprinting along the spine toward the end of the ship, right where the giant icicle had hit. He'd been the one who sent her in that direction. He'd sent Jo running to her death. That thought snapped Ford's eyes open. He quickly turned around and locked onto Mason, "I..." Ford started but didn't know what to say, so instead he looked around the room for something to busy himself with.

Next thing they heard was the commanding voice of the Captain as he entered, "Gentlemen." If they didn't know John Dahl had been in stasis only ten minutes ago, they'd have sworn he'd been in front of a mirror for the last hour. His uniform was pressed, collar straight and his face betrayed no thought, no fear and no emotion. A talent Ford envied him in the here and now, just as he'd despised it equally during his youth.

"Sir." Mason stood straight, raising his hand in salute.

"Let's leave the formalities for now shall we." John said, closing the gap between the two men and wrapping his arms around Mason, "You good?"

"Yes Sir." Mason replied, exiting the hug and bringing the Captain up to speed.

By the time Becca arrived, the rest of the group had already assembled. Jake Bounette, unlike his Captain turned up dishevelled and irritable. He shuffled in, rubbing his temples and ignored everyone's welcome. Ford was sat at the Ops table and from behind him he could hear the tapping sounds getting louder and louder until it piqued Ford's interest enough to turn around. The Doctor was trying to get coffee from the dead machine and with each failing attempt he grew in rage, until finally he banged a fist against the button in defeat, cursing in French. He turned around, finding three bemused onlookers, "Quelle?" He asked, it sounded more like a threat and he quickly bared his teeth to ward off any comments. Many of the crew disliked him. The stories of his hot temper echoed though the ship's corridors. But currently, he was giving some much needed entertainment.

Next through the door was Sharon Greaves, Second Engineer. She dazzled Ford; her raven black hair was pulled into a ponytail, bringing full focus to her narrow face and lavish eyebrows. She'd tied the top half of her green overalls around her waist, with her layered grey and black vests showing off her athletic build. It wasn't the time, but Ford couldn't help but remember removing those overalls. They were on shore leave on Asturas, just prior to starting this voyage. Since that lustful encounter, they'd not shared the same shift rotation but it was something he intended to pursue if given the chance.

She greeted the room, spoke privately with the Captain and took up a position at the top of the table, crouching down underneath to get at its guts. Ford was pondering whether or not to go talk to her when Natalie Bounette, wife to the Doctor and daughter to Chief Engineer Crudge, entered the room. She skirted the table, half awake at first, but with each passing face, her eyes got wider until they were out on sticks, "Where's dad?"

"Engineering." John said,

Given the circumstances, Ford didn't think that was enough of an explanation.

"Is he okay?" She asked, whitened knuckles rolling on the table top.

John waved her over and put his arm around her in a fatherly manner and admitted, "We've not heard from him yet. But I'm sure he's fine, your old man is too stubborn to be anything else."

Bounette, still not feeling the urge to say anything, left his stool and walked up behind Natalie. He nodded to his Captain, who released her to him. Husband and wife hugged, whispering to each other in French. She was the only person on board who had bothered to learn the language. She was his wife after all. Bounette however, took it as a personal insult that the rest of the crew hadn't bothered. Or so Greaves had warned Ford during the crew's last supper together on Asturas.

When Becca finally jogged through the door Ford clapped, "Communications woman of the year." He said and as Mason, John and Sharon clapped with Ford, it was almost as if nothing was wrong. That was until Ford thought that exact thought. Then everything was wrong. He continued to clap, but his hands sounded hollow. Ford's smile became forced as he scanned the room - Natalie and Bounette had failed to join in. It was obvious why; the doctor's eyes were on his wife and her eyes were focused on the window and the darkness beyond.

"Great work." John said, waving his arms in the air.

Becca ducked, blood rushing to her cheeks and slipped in for a hug, "Thanks."

"Becca," Sharon called out, still obscured by the table, "Give me a hand here."

Becca obliged and John Dahl took the Captain's seat at the end of the table and repeated what Ford and Mason had told him. There were audible groans from the good doctor. The Captain then praised Ford, Becca and Mason for their efforts in keeping the ship mostly in one piece and giving them all a fighting chance.

Ford's cheeks warmed as his father used his name and wished he was under the table with Becca. However, as that wasn't an option, he found refuge from his embarrassment by gazing through the window. He heard his father use the word engineering and rejoined the conversation, glancing in Natalie's direction but avoiding any chance of eye contact. All he could think of saying to her were the very same phrases his father used, "We'll get him back, don't you worry." It was a meaningless platitude, because from her face, it was clear: worrying was all she could do.

The table hissed and whined, "Got it." Sharon said, pulling herself up, "Ford, would you do the honours?"

Thumbing the button on the side of the table cleared the blackness from the top, vertical lines drew themselves in green, horizontal in blue creating a flickering grid matrix over table and then vanished. A second later and a holographic image of Jian Seng flickered to life, hovering an inch off the table and taking up its length and width. It was patchy, it fizzled every three or so seconds but the image held, "Another small victory." John said as Becca and Sharon climbed to their feet, taking the nearest seats available, "And this is how we're going to survive. There's no magic wand, we can't expect any immediate rescue, not this far out..."

Bounette interrupted, "If at all." waiting for all eyes to turn to him before continuing, "I assume the collision knocked us off the shipping lane?" One hand rubbed his chin, the other settled on Natalie's arm. A man with powerful priorities, what he meant of course was: how far off course are we? And I'll be the one protecting my wife. When Ford looked up from the doctor's hand he noticed that all eyes were on him for an answer.

But he didn't have the answer; the ship's sensors weren't working. He shrugged his shoulders, looking to Mason for some support but only found a blank face staring back at him, waiting.

"Best guess?" asked his Father,

"Maybe, a couple of kilometres?" He said without thought, then feeling the slight vibration in the table he realised the engine was still running, "If the secondary navigation computer is undamaged, it would tell the engine to correct our course, I can't say if we're still moving but Damage Recovery protocols dictate the ship will attempt to right itself before going to a dead stop." He paused, knowing it wasn't enough, "Of course, there's no way of telling whether it is still functioning without getting to engineering. However, as the UFO pretty much hit us head on physics alone would suggest it would have slowed us rather than knock us off course." *And breathe...*

"That's a convoluted way to admit you don't have a putain d'indice." Bounette again,

"The buoy is programmed to sit on the shipping lane." Mason argued,

"Then triangulate its ass. We could be drifting hundreds, thousands of kilometres in the wrong direction."

"Calm your space boots Jake." John Dahl was the only person on board who called Bounette by his first name.

"I asked a simple question, it was your boy giving the slew of babble." Ford stared at him until the Doctor crossed his eyes, "No offence."

"None taken," Ford replied, watching as his father looked to Natalie for support, but she hadn't been listening for a long time. Her eyes pierced through the fizzling hologram, locked on the viewing window and beyond.

"The buoy's not going to help anyway; it will be weeks or even months before anyone gets to us." Bounette muttered, antagonising John further.

"We could send a prayer, the Church will respond in a couple of day..." Mason started,

"We're not devout." John said, he offered a simple grimace to ease the words and Ford instantly felt his father's pain. Bounette and Mason were tag teaming against him. To send a prayer, a focused beam signal to the Church was one of the luxuries provided to the devout. A benefit given to those who paid over inflated Tithe to the Church. But Mason was correct in that they could be rescued in a matter of days; the Church's technology surpassed anything else and bordered on the magical.

"Pour l'amour de baise - and whose fault is that?"

"Last time I checked you were a heathen also, Jake." John rasped, looking around the room, "When was the last time any of us used the Chapel? I didn't choose this life for you; you decided to join my crew." John settled his eyes on Bounette and held his gaze until the doctor turned away. Taking solace in silence and holding his wife close.

"It's still an option, I'm devout." Mason defended, "Gail Faraday, Tomos, Saburo, we have devout on board."

"But at what cost?" John asked, "The Trinity's love is anything but unconditional. I don't pay Tithe, and there would be a costly condition applied to this rescue."

"But we'd be alive John, we could work something..."

"Captain." John sounded tired, "Last time I checked, I was still Captain."

As far as Ford knew, John had never followed the faith and neither had his grandfather. They didn't believe in anything else, they didn't poke the beast and follow the path of the heretic. They just chose a different life, the heathen life, one where they made their own way in the 'verse and kept what they earned. For those onboard who were devout, half of their earnings went to the Trinity. They at least had it better than most, crewmembers didn't have outgoings. They didn't have to live planet-side where everything came with a price tag. True they had access to advanced technology and privileges, but they still had to pay for it. That was the reason why John Dahl couldn't stomach the Trinity and their conditional love.

John ran his hand down his beard, "I won't deny that I keep you and the others onboard for some shiny extras, the upgraded computer core and the ducks for example." He said to Mason, "But if we pray for a rescue then it's going to have consequences. Consequences that not everyone will be able to pay and when I say this, I want you to understand that some costs aren't monetary."

When Mason didn't reply, John scanned the room across the faces of everyone present. When Ford's time came he met his father's gaze and showed him support in his decision with a subtle nod. He agreed with him to an extent, to be rescued by the Church would mean swearing allegiance or to be left out here as they returned with only the devout. Ford knew his answer, he stood with his father. But he had issue with the ethics, his choice and father's choice would be imposed on the rest of the crew. They didn't have a say in the matter, they were all asleep.

"Right..." Greaves broke the silence, slapping her hand on the table, "We should wake some of the engineering pool. Take a duck and start repairs as soon as we can."

Glad of the change in subject, Ford took note and did the math, "What strain would that put on the life-support?"

"Kid's got a point." Mason added, "There's already six of us here, we don't know what state the generators are in, or whether Jo and Crudge are alive."

There it was Ford thought and like everyone in the room he avoided Natalie's direct gaze. They'd been discussing the collision like a crappy day at the office, but now in the eye of the storm, the gravity of the situation was as real to them as it had been all along for Natalie. The room went silent.

The calming tone of Captain Dahl broke the extended silence. "They're both fine, I suspect, probably keeping each other warm in the engine room."

"Ten. We can support ten with life support as it is" Greaves interjected, having done her own calculations.

"We can push her to twelve." The Captain rebutted,

"No, I'm sorry, but you're both wrong." Natalie shocked the room with her comment, "If we had full power then we could risk ten, but without knowing what state the atmosphere generators are in I wouldn't push it past eight. Anything over nine will just eat our air supply."

"You're the expert." Greaves said, knocking her knuckles against the table.

"We have nine already." Ford thought aloud,

Mason suggested, "We can all suit up; most of us are headed outside as it is. Keep the atmosphere generator for emergencies."

"I'd prefer to leave the suits as the last resort." Natalie said, "It's all well and good using them now, but if we need to leave quickly I'd prefer knowing I have a full tank." She raised her hands off the table, angling them up from her wrists which remained under Bounette's tight hold, "However, with a team outside, that would give us something to play with. Then when the team returns, if they're not on duty shift they can be put back into stasis. But don't wait until everyone's back inside before doing that, stagger the return. Keep the pressure off until we know for certain."

"If you're sure?" Asked her CO,

"I am sir. That gives us an additional one crew member we can wake if we suspect Jo and..."

"Okay." John cut her off before she could finish, "Mason, it's bedtime for you."

Ford had to wait for Mason's reaction before he was certain he'd heard his father correctly, "What? You can't be serious?" Ford closed his eyes, stretching his arms out along the table, certain his name was coming next. There wasn't as much need for a pilot as there was for an engineer. They weren't about to start flying the Seng and everyone else was at least rated proficiency in piloting the ducks. Hell, he'd been flying them since he was thirteen.

"I am." John replied, continuing to surprise everyone with his next choice, "You too Becca."

"What?!" Her voice was shrill, laden with injury and Ford couldn't blame her. He doubted anyone around the table would. The choice was beyond reason. She was the most experienced with the ship's communications systems. She'd just repaired the internal comms to the front half of the ship with nothing but an omnitool and common sense, and now she was being benched.

"Don't start Becca." John jumped in before she could continue, "You're both going in. We need engineers."

Ford felt his sister's eyes steaming the sweat off of his forehead, but couldn't bring himself to look at her. He wasn't surprised when she countered, "And Ford?"

If her eyes burned holes in Ford, they were nothing compared to the look their father gave her. He'd been on the receiving end of that glare more than his fair share in the past and did not wish it on anyone, let alone Becca who only wanted to help. He opened his mouth to support her. However, nothing came out. Fighting his father had never been his strong point and the courage to do so now was nowhere to be found. Instead, he closed his mouth and just gave his sister a glance. A supportive look, he hoped, but as her eyes lingered, it may have been construed as pity. She turned her head away, "He's not an engineer."

"Noted." their father said coldly, rapping his wedding ring against the conference table like a Judge would his gavel, "Once Greaves gets her team up and running, the first priority is to assess and repair the damage. Ford will taxi them to the engine section, dropping some along the way to attend any urgent breaches. Most importantly, I want a team in the engine room to assist Crudge. I don't want any heroics. We need to save the ship before we can save ourselves."

"I'll keep Natalie, wake-up Daichi." Greaves said, picking her team.

"Wake up Benjamin too." John added,

"That puts us back up to nine." Ford said, placing his head back under the guillotine.

"Nat?"

"I'd rather just one at this point."

John stared into a space a moment, "We'll risk it. Add Benjamin to the pot."

"In that case I'd like to wake Ed instead. Daichi's good, but Ed and Ben have a short hand that surpasses anything he could bring to the table." She replied,

"It's your team." The Captain said as found his next target, "Jake, get the infirmary ready to receive, just in case." Bounette waved his hand and nodded acceptance of the task. Then came the infamous Dahl clap. Two loud claps of his hands, signalling the end of the meeting. Ford slid from his stool, catching his sister's raging eyes before he left the room.

***

Ford hung around the hall between two doors, trying his best not to get in the way. The stasis bays were busy, Mason setting his bunk up for a deep freeze and Greaves warming up the new blood, bringing the reserves into play. True, he was supposed to be prepping the duck for launch, but neither Mason nor Greaves said anything. They, like him, knew he had a little time to spare. He only wanted to speak with one person and Becca hadn't arrived yet. Held back to speak with Dad, Ford could just imagine the tone and weight of the guilt trip he was hanging on her shoulders.

Greaves was fastidious, moving from one bunk to the other. Two engineers, the ones everyone was placing their hopes of survival on. Eddie the square jaw poster boy and his side kick Bennie, the Asian narcissist. They were an odd couple, but then it was hard for anyone to believe that Bennie could love anyone other than himself. But for whatever reason they had seen something in one another and made it work. It was also true in what Greaves had said about them, their short hand communication elevated their engineering abilities far beyond any other duo team onboard.

Greaves stood between their beds; legs slightly apart while tapping on her pad, watching their progress. She was probably doing her best to avoid eye contact, prompting Ford to realise he was gawping, he swung around, over playing his mannerisms and grabbed the opposite door's head jamb with both hands, "Everyone's taking it pretty well."

Mason looked up from a crouched position next to his bunk, "What you on about?"

"You know, everyone seems calm." He clarified, knocking his knuckles against the frame and stepping into the room.

"You're calm?" Mason asked, standing up.

"No." Ford admitted, frustrated at not explaining himself coherently, "I mean everyone's taking this in their stride." He took Mason's raised eyebrow as a disagreement, "I mean we're not running around like headless chickens."

"That's because we're safe." Mason said, lowering his data pad, "For now."

"Yeah right." Ford grimaced, "As far as we know the engine could explode in the next ten seconds." Then when his comment fell flat, "That didn't sound any good in my head either."

Mason nodded, fingers idling the small intricate silver pendant dangling from his neck; depicting the three phases of the moon cycle. Waxing signified the child, Nimrod. The full moon, the warrior Etana and Waning representing the sage, Ninus. It was their symbol, the sign of the Immortal Trinity. Ford didn't know how long exactly they'd been around, only that it was a long time. The scriptures put them back a thousand years at least. They weren't exactly immortal either; each of them lived extended lives and would eventually die. But when the grandfather perished he would re-incarnate to the child, while the child got bumped up to the warrior and warrior to the sage. And according to their scriptures they would precede over the human race until the end days.

They ruled from the Cathedral of glass on Luna, living Gods looking over their first creation, Earth. Hallowed be their names. They governed with not one church but two. The Church Triumphant was their carrot, which provided all the luxuries you could fathom. But it was The Church Militant, their stick, which reigned supreme with their warrior Templar, indestructible Saints and their attack dogs, the Inquisitors - all part of an unrelenting cruel force with superior technology, surrounded by mysticism. Those who feared the Church knew of the militant all too well and those who followed the Church, those like Mason, somehow managed to gloss over that violent, darker side of their faith.

"Doing you any good?" asked Ford, nodding at the pendant.

"The Trinity will see us through."

"Yup." Ford nodded, raising his hands up and suggesting toward their predicament.

"You don't have to believe Ford." Mason picked up on his insincerity, "Their will is carried out regardless."

"Indeed it is." Ford said through gritted teeth, remembering their will in full action. Only two years ago he'd fought against the Church Militant on the small mining colony of Otzu. A frozen wasteland, nothing more than a chunk of ice orbiting a Dwarf star, but the treasures beneath the icy surface had brought the mining rights of two rival companies to battle. For all of the wrong reasons, Ford had opted to leave the Seng and help his friend's family. He hadn't considered the consequences, or that the opposing company was devout.

"Yeah well, what I think doesn't matter anyway." Mason said, interrupting Ford's thoughts,

"What's that supposed to mean?"

"I'd rather not talk about it."

"Then when?"

Mason straightened his pose, pulled the creases from his top and glanced at the floor all the markings of a man working up to say something, "I think you're father benched me because I'm devout." He pursed his lips and held his gaze on Ford, who suddenly found himself on the back of his feet.

The thought had crossed Ford's mind as well, "I'm sure that's not the case."

"Well it sure feels like it. If I hadn't suggested praying..."

"It needed to be said." Ford offered,

"I'm not sure John would agree." Mason tilted his head back, stretched his jaw out and groaned, "I'm sorry. This isn't the time for this. Or religious debate for that matter. Please, don't let on to your dad, you know..."

"Hey, if you don't say anything, neither will I." Ford had no intention of reliving this conversation with his father, he held out his hand and they shook, "Besides. I should be the one apologising. I brought it up and shot you down."

"Still, I am sorry." Mason grimaced, "Your father may be a heathen, but he's a good man." Mason's hand took

Ford's shoulder and Ford could have sworn Mason passed some of his strength into him.

"I'm not hugging." He smiled, "But I could read you a bed time story, or sing you a lullaby?"

Mason shook his head, laughing as he turned back toward his bunk, "Sing? With your voice? You're cruel kid."

Ford smirked, but the curl in his lips faded quickly as he noticed Mason's deflecting eyes.

"I understand what your dad's doing..." Mason trailed off, eyes drawn to his data pad.

"But..."

"It's the right call, I'd like to think I'd make the same one in his shoes, but I don't like facilitating it."

"Definitely no lullaby then."

Mason chuckled, laughing the comment off as his fingers returned to the pendant, "Ford." He said, eyebrows encroaching on one another, "You know Bounette."

"The crazy Frenchman with the scalpel?" Ford jested,

"He has a shotgun under his bed."

"I thought that was a joke."

"I did too, until Natalie showed it to me."

"Wait." Ford held up his hands, "You were looking under Mrs. Bounette's bed?"

Mason rolled his eyes, "Yes, but not in the sordid way your mind works."

Ford grinned, "Everyone's mind works as sordid as mine."

"Shotgun?"

"Yes, please continue."

"It's all true," the gravity in Mason's voice didn't go unnoticed. There was a reason why everyone called Bounette the crazy Frenchman. He was crazy, well almost. Space travel isn't paradise, it's a nightmare. Anyone wanting to work deep space haulage underwent psychological scrutiny before they could even apply for the job. Kids call it 'Space Madness', Earthers call it 'cabin fever'. There are hundreds of stories, people going nuts, running around ships naked and murdering entire crews with nothing but their bootstraps and pair of pliers. The problem was that some of the stories were based on facts, albeit exaggerated. Doctor Bounette was supposed to have been certified borderline, which meant on normal circumstances he wouldn't have been allowed on board. But he was and that was why Ford and the rest of the crew disbelieved the rumours, "So watch your back." Mason said, snapping Ford back to the conversation.

"How is he here, exactly?"

"He has an extenuating circumstance." Mason raised his eyebrow, "And that particular extenuating circumstance, is Natalie."

Ford looked doubtful, "I can't see her telling you that, even if it were true."

"She didn't. Your dad did, all the command staff knows. Bounette has regular counselling sessions and takes a cocktail of prescription pills and potions. He takes so many you can hear him rattle when he runs."

Ford's smirk faded quickly, "Yeah, but allowed on board?" It still seemed far-fetched to Ford, who would have pressed the issue further if his sister hadn't stood in the doorway, looking right at him.

"What are you doing here?" She asked.

"I wanted to see you." He said, laying his hand on Mason's shoulder as he left him, "Before you went under." As he passed the doorway, he could see into chamber B. Greaves was talking to Ben Dykes, giving him the low down on the situation. He wasn't taking it well; he was as white as the robe she handed him.

"I'm not in the mood, Ford." Becca said before he got within three steps of her.

"Are you ever?" He fell into the routine of sibling argument too easily.

"Leave me alone." She really wasn't in the mood.

"Look sis, I don't want to fight."

"Then walk away." She pointed to the door.

"I..." She wasn't making it easy, "No, I won't."

"Then we have a problem."

"Why?"

"Because... I do want a fight." She hadn't looked at him yet, busying herself with her stasis prep. She was obeying the order at least, but clearly against her will, "Just leave, will you." Her voice was laced with venom and defeat, "Please."

"Look. Becca, I just need you to know that I'm not the little brother anymore." On paper he still was the little brother. But technically and chronologically he was now older, having spent years away from the ship while Becca slept in stasis meant Ford was now biologically older. Something he'd guessed had caused much of the friction between them after he returned.

"What?" Her fiery eyebrows butted heads above her face,

"Ever since I got back, you've been hamming up the big sister act."

"If you think that's what's wrong then you're dumber than I thought."

"Then what?" she'd already slammed him with running away, "Is it because of mum?"

"Can we please not do this?" She pleaded, staring at her stasis tube.

"Hey." He said, pulling her hand away from the tube and hugging her.

"You have no idea how scary this is." She said, then under her breath, "I may never wake up."

Her remark cut him down to size as he realised it wasn't about him. She was terrified. Big sis always the one in control and now being forced to relinquish it. Putting herself at the mercy of events she would not have any part in shaping. She, just like Mason, was being benched in the last ten minutes of a grand-final. Except; in this game if your team lost you all died, "Of course you'll survive."

"You don't know that."

"Becca." He said, holding her face in his hands, "You won't die in this tube." He thumbed away the first of her tears, pulling her head into his chest as she began to sob, "Dad really did a number on us, didn't he?"

"He doesn't understand." She said, pulling away and wiping her face, "We're going to need communications."

"I'm sure once we've secured the ship he'll swap us out."

She forced a smile, "If he has any sense."

The knock from the entrance called all of their attention, "Twenty minutes and the duck better be ready." Greaves stated,

"Two minutes." Ford said, raising his fingers for clarification.

Greaves produced her middle finger, "You have one, make it count."

"You're worse than dad." Ford said, but it went unchallenged. Greaves moved away from the door and out of sight.

"What..." Becca said, "Do you see in that woman?"

Ford shrugged, grinning, "I'm a masochist."

She shook her head, "You don't have a chance. You know that, don't you?"

"Oh really?" Ford smirked, "And you'd know all about unrequited love, wouldn't you." He rolled his eyes toward the only other person in the room.

"You're a dick." Her fist jabbed his shoulder, catching him off guard, and throwing his balance. He took hold of her bunk to steady himself.

"Touched a nerve did I?"

She raised her fists in front of her.

"Okay, time out." He smirked again, "Are we good?"

She nodded, "Yeah, we're good."

"You really have the better deal you know." He replied, raising a fist for Becca to bump.

"You'll be fine." She bumped his knuckles, "Thanks, for coming down. It means a lot."

"Don't mention it." Ford slipped past her hands and pulled her in for another hug, "I'll wake you up when it's all over, I promise."

"There are no mistakes..." Becca began the space fairing mantra,

"...in space." They both finished, before Ford added, "Sweet dreams princess," pulling her in for another hug; then to Mason, "You too dick-head."

TWO

F ord slid in from the top hatch, attached his suit's air
tank to Huey's supply tube and closed the roof. Huey's
controls were set up about him on a circular tabletop,
which ran along the interior of the vehicle. Ford flipped
the start up switch and the hull above his worktop
dissolved away. Effectively the top half of Huey became
invisible, albeit trickery through the use of sensors and
projectors. While the image allowed him a less
claustrophobic panoramic, it was still just a holographic
illusion and the inside of Huey's hatch, now appearing to
float above his head served as this reminder: he still sat
inside a metal sphere.

Huey's design, though practical, left little room for
stretching and there was absolutely no option to stand.
While running the pre-flight tests on the systems he peered
over his work station at the engine ring which ran around
the pod at its equator. Similar to his controls the ring was
able to run independently around the tug's exterior by
means of magnetic anchoring. He locked the engine ring

in place and to the group of engineers waiting outside the Jian Seng said, "Looking good."

"Time's-a-wasting." Greaves replied over the intercom.

Ford settled in his chair. The padding on the left hand side was flat, leaving his rump sitting on the hard frame. He made a mental note to get the seat replaced. Emergency rations were in the floor box, some ship made Billtong from first Chef Tabor. Mason complained it was over salted but Ford thought it was perfect. Some ice packets, water. Fire Suppression was standard, no need to mess with the lifesaving equipment. Spare oxygen canisters and emergency seal patches in case of a breach.

The only personal items he kept in the duck were his military dog tags; two small metal plates with his name, rank and the Trinity's three moon logo pressed into them. They hung over a rivet on the workstation and dangled just out of his knee's reach. Other than his baptism certificate, his tags were the only other evidence which proved he was a registered devout. His mother had insisted on both he and Becca being baptised. Ford's mother had always been the smart one. Being non-practising opened more doors than being a heathen and as much as his father argued against it, he was grateful for the extra tech he could purchase as a result. Ford had seen personal benefit on Otzu, having been provided Stenwich body armour along with the logo on his tags. He kissed the tips of his gloved fingers, tapped the tags for luck and began the launch sequence with a flip of a switch.

The tug bay's glow lamps dimmed and tinted orange. Ford spun his seat, looking around to ensure no one had wandered into the bay and was about to get hit by his demolition ball ship. It was all clear. Everyone was waiting patiently for him outside, or so he thought until he heard Greaves through his ear piece, "What's the hold up?" She said tersely, she did enjoy busting his balls.

"Keep your knickers on." He replied, avoiding the temptation to flirt with everyone listening. Another button lowered the giant mechanical swing arm from the centre of the bay's ceiling. It rotated, grabbing Huey with a magnetic clamp, lifting the duck from its re-charge station and carried it to the Primary Air-Lock, PAL. The work party had left using the personnel airlocks in the launch-bay's anti chamber.

The arm detached, leaving him at the mercy of the air-lock's ejection system. Four rows of brush wheels, using some kind of magnetic frequency Ford never bothered to fully understand, pushed Huey along the cramped tunnel until it reached the outer door. The inner door closed and sealed with a loud thump. Vents roared into action, sucking the air from the tunnel and the outer door opened, magnetic wheels pushing him the rest of the way.

Once ejected, the master overrides which prohibited him from using the thrusters inside unlocked and Ford brought Huey about to face the Jian Seng. Outside Huey, the engine poles extended making the ring more accessible to passengers. The outer airlock closed with a smooth and silent bite. To PAL's port side were four waiting engineers waving their free hands at him as he steadied his ship, ready for their boarding, "What took so long?" Bennie asked,

Ford lit them up with Huey's flood lamps, "Your mum wanted a goodbye kiss."

"I hope you're on antibiotics." Bennie said, clambering onto Huey with the others.

"Hold on tight." Ford said, flipping the switch and kicking on the main thrusters.

Around Huey clung Sharon Greaves, Natalie Bounette, Bennie Dykes and Eddie Tarris. With everyone aboard Ford pulled back on his stick, reversing Huey while continuing to face the front of the Jian Seng. Its massive size made it impossible to judge overall damage up close. He was no more than a flea on a whale's nose.

As he moved back however, allowing more of Jian Seng into view, the sensors flagged up the hull buckling with red circles. Each damaged area was catalogued and prioritised for analysis. He turned Huey clockwise until his systems confirmed he'd completed a 90 degree spin, now looking on the Seng upside down. Allowing his instruments to do the lion's share of the damage assessment, he began his trek upward to the bottom of the ship.

The ship was made of three sections, Head, spine and Engine. The head resembled a large malformed pear. The top half housed the antenna clusters which would allow them to contact the next outpost once they got it working. They were the reason he'd brought the Seng's belly to bear the brunt of the collision. He'd sacrificed the domestics and power distribution nodes for a chance to call for help. In the split second he'd had to make that decision he knew it would turn out to be the right one. The nodes were better shielded by domestics. As Huey rose over the belly of the ship, Ford assured himself he'd chosen wisely.

The damage was immense, a dark scorched channel gouged into the hull. Plasma fires burned and air was escaping from several breaches, "Saints save us." Bennie exclaimed.

Ford piloted Huey along the ship's belly, following the score marks and perforated hull plating. Reading the damage on his bridge terminal hadn't prepared him for seeing it first hand and it was a disheartening experience. Whole sections were torn open, exposing the inner hull shielding and in the worst cases the corridors inside. He knew that bulk heads had dropped, preventing their precious air supply gushing out of these holes. He'd taken basic engineering and somewhere in his mind a memory told him not to panic, but he couldn't avoid the gut pounding fear from seeing his devastated home, "Someone *please* tell me it looks worse than it is."

"It looks worse than it is." Eddie fired back,

"Oh good, I was getting worried."

"Cut the chatter." Greaves ordered, "Interior bulk heads dropped, all you're seeing is air escaping from compartments nearest the hull. It's just air we can't use anyway."

"But it's still going."

"They're micro fractures. It looks more than it is because the air is freezing on its way out."

Ford grinned, "So it does look worse than it is."

"I told you so." Eddie added, then a second later adding, "Sorry boss."

Ford's fear took full advantage of the silence which followed, wriggling in his stomach - nausea tightening its grip. This was only the lower decks, but from the amount of free floating cargo pods it was safe to say the damage wasn't contained here. True, there was nothing of importance in the spine apart from cargo and value as a transport mechanism to the engine, but if this damage was mirrored in the engines they'd have a heap load of trouble coming their way.

"That's a lot of overtime." Bennie finally quipped,

Ford breathed easy, gladder of the comment than he would admit, "Anyone need to drop off?"

"No, straight to engineering," Greaves ordered. "These can wait."

Looking at it, Ford disagreed. There was a lot of work to do. He also didn't believe they had nearly enough engineers aboard, sleeping ones included, to fix it all. They'd need at least a month birth at a repair station. But, he wasn't an engineer and concluded it was best not to disagree with the order, "Okay." He said, flipping the comms switch to include the Jian Seng's bridge, "Captain, do you read me?"

"Just about." The almost jovial voice of his father replied,

"I'm sending you a video feed, and the analysis report."

"I have them." He was no longer jovial.

"We're heading to engineering." Ford advised, rotating the banner switch to the Jian Seng's general frequency, "Crudgey, this is Ford, do you read me?" With nothing in return he modified the frequency, "Jo-Jo? You out there... Jo?" Nothing. He modified the frequency again, "Hello? Anyone read me?" Out of the port hole, he watched the front section fall away and the spine begin. The score marks continued to track the course of the UFO's path of destruction. Parts of the spear had broken off in the spine. Small reflective, almost translucent shards jutted out of the dull fabric of the Seng's hull.

The engineers began talking about it, using technical jargon in high tones of excitement which only alienated Ford further from the conversation. He didn't find it exciting; he'd seen the thing, the whole thing. It wasn't at all fun or interesting, it was scary as hell and something he had no intention of repeating. Ever!

He let them converse and carried on trying to contact Crudge, while keeping an eye on the dislodged cargo pods and chunks of metal ripped from the Jian Seng. Every piece of debris was a risk to his little duck. He spun his chair around and magnified his view of the dislodged pods, counting twelve dancing. There could have been more, but he couldn't perform any manoeuvres with everyone hanging onto the rail. What he'd seen was enough. With twelve dislodged pods and all the damage they'd seen so far, it meant the computer's damage report had been wrong. It was a lot worse.

The frantic banging against Huey's hull brought him to look ahead, "What?" Huey's flood lamps were pitched down, running along the underside of the spine. He flipped the light dead ahead as Eddie began making childlike noises. Directly in front and embedded into the engineering section was the object. A long, smooth intersection of what had been a far larger ship had stabbed itself into the end of the Jian Seng. The shimmering icy spear rose up, towering over the approaching tug. It was smooth, with no windows or etchings that Ford could see. Even with Huey's magnification the embedded ship revealed none of its secrets.

"What is it?" Bennie asked.

It was unprecedented and alien, mankind had been in space thousands of years and in not once had they made contact with another race. The Trinity's children were alone in the 'verse. The Church were the most technically advanced of all humans and even their ships looked nothing like this. Ford had never seen anything remotely similar, "Damned if I know."

"Ford..." Greaves said,

"Yeah?"

"How in hell did you not see that coming?"

"It..." He remembered back to the bridge, alarms blaring in his ears, information rushing up his screen. All of that wish wash garbage seemed distant now that he was looking dead at it. It was too big, far too big to have been missed by the scanners. There shouldn't have been any issue with locking on to it and correcting their course before it got near them, "I don't know." He pulled back on the flight stick, raising Huey as they reached the engines. He wanted a better look at the shard as they past.

"It's a ship." Ed commented,

"Really, I'd never have guessed." Bennie was quick with the put down. "But is it one of ours?"

"It's not corporate." Said Natalie, reminding Ford she was with them. She collected ships. As in, when she wasn't fixing the real thing, she built models.

"If it's not corps, then it must be Faith." Deduced Ed,

"You really are on fire today Ed." Bennie continued with the put downs, "You don't think anyone else in the 'verse can build ships?"

"There is no one else doom brain."

Huey rocked gently to some shuffling outside by its passengers, "Cut it out." Greaves ordered, and Huey abruptly stabilised, "Ford, bring us to Section Eight's air-lock." Ford wasn't paying attention, he was too busy watching the shard's top pass by, its structural fabric, be it metal or whatever, was bent and twisted. He could see right into it. Three rooms; empty - frozen by vacuum with one corridor leading deeper in, whatever this ship was - this spear wasn't all of it. The twists and tears were angled toward the rear of the Seng, consistent with its trajectory, indicating to Ford the rest must have sheared off from the impact inertia once the front end got lodged into the engine, "Ford?" Greaves voice,

"Yeah?"

"Did you hear me?"

"Sorry, must have been something wrong with the comms." He blurted, "Please say again."

She repeated her instructions, and this time he listened, "Gotcha." He swung Huey about and began their descent toward Section Eight's air-lock, a five metre tall by five metre wide service door. It opened into a corridor that led directly to the engine core, with nine emergency bulkheads along the way. Good for replacing large engine parts, better still for getting Crudge a speedy rescue.

"Bennie, I want you and Nat to head inside, find Crudge and assist him in whatever capacity he needs." Greaves dished out the orders, "Ed, once we drop these two off, there was a breach I saw at the base of the object I want us to take a look at." Ford listened in and couldn't help thinking and admiring how authoritative she sounded when giving orders. Then he heard, "Ford you can take us back once we've dropped Ben and Nat off."

"Aye aye," he acknowledged, slowing Huey's vector and bringing her to a stop. He trained the flood lamps on the air-lock, a large square that was cut in half by the door's vertical lips; each identical side had yellow and black hazard décor and arrows aiming away from the lips and a porthole window looking into the darkness beyond. The only difference was the control panel on the right hand door, just below the porthole.

Aside from the light from Huey's flood lamps the Jian Seng was in complete darkness, nothing more than a hulk of old metal, "There doesn't seem to be any power." Greaves said, "Ford we're going to hang around to make sure they get in."

"Understood." He said, placing Huey on automatic and setting up some systems checks to run in the background. Natalie kicked off Huey and glided the short distance to the giant air-lock. Bennie followed behind her. They both touched down, with only seconds between them, hitting either side of the air-lock's mouth. Nat clung to the left, Bennie to the right.

Ford listened to the sound of his own breathing in the silence of conversation, waiting for Bennie to alter his position slightly and open the door's control mechanism. Bennie tried the controls a few times, nothing, "No power." Bennie confirmed, using the indented hand placements to pull himself down below the door where the emergency override was located, "I'll work the manual." He followed procedure by giving a step by step of his actions.

Ford stowed his concerns for Crudge and Jo by thinking ahead of Bennie's actions. He would next open the panel, inside was a pump which gave just enough power to open or close the door. In a second or two, he was going to announce to the group that he would be working the pump, "Give it some elbow grease."

Bennie's free hand came up and although Ford couldn't be sure, it looked like the engineer was giving him the finger. "You don't have to hang about, we've got this." Bennie said.

"We'll wait until you're through the door." Greaves replied,

Bennie worked the pump, "Shouldn't take more than a minute to fully prime, but if you're sure you wanna hang around."

Ford twirled his chair around; his 365 degree view provided an equally vast and boring view. Black to the East, South and West with Bennie the Diva pumping away to the North. They were alone and the blackness was unforgiving. If they left them to open the door alone, they'd have nothing but their wrist lamps to light their work. Greaves was right to keep them here. There was nothing out there but a solitary gloom, a breeding ground of terror. It was as important to provide them light as it was to provide light hearted motivation, "Hurry it up Ben." He said, "Some of us have work to do."

"Ford, they don't need a cheerleader." Greaves said, not agreeing with him, "You'll have plenty of time to waste once you've dropped us off." That was true and also horrifying. He'd have nothing to do but wait, sitting in a ball while everyone else did important things. He may as well have jumped into a stasis pod; at least there he'd be able to rest comfortably.

"Yes, sir." He said, distracting himself with his terminal.

"Seriously guys, it's okay, you can head off." Natalie spoke up.

"No, we're good for now." Greaves repeated her sentiment, "This won't take much longer and I'd be happier knowing you're both inside." She added, picking up on Natalie's tone. Ford had noticed it too, but couldn't quite pin it down. Maybe it was nothing, but it sounded a little highly strung. Not surprising when she was nearing the truth to her father's fate, "I'm sure he's okay, Nat."

"Me too." Natalie said, in a quick, almost rehearsed response.

"Pump is primed." Bennie announced, "Nat, you want to move from there?"

"Okay." She said, following Bennie's path to below the door.

"Releasing the lock." Bennie announced, slapping the mushroom shaped button and setting off the ring of warning lights around the metal mouth. Slow and steady, the left and right halves of the door separated and the lock was opened. Huey's flood lamps lit the interior, showing no more than the inner door and the glass of its two portholes reflecting straight back, "Heading in."

Ford continued to watch Bennie and Natalie make their way to the inner door controls, "No power." She announced to no one's surprise. They were going to have to prime the outer door again to close it. Then repeat the procedure for the inner door, it shouldn't take too long, with two of them on the job each of them could prime a door simultaneously. Natalie glided to the inner door porthole and peered through, "Its dark, but I can see some small fires a way in. Looks like the ceiling cradle has fallen."

The ceiling cradle held the data and power cables which ran above the corridors for easy access, if it had fallen then the wiring would be all over the place. It could also be the reason why there was no power to the door. But if the corridor was also black then the problem could be far worse, "Cables are floating." Natalie added, "Doesn't appear to be any gravity, yeah I can see the cradle."

"We're going to prime these doors, you sure you don't..." Bennie started,

"Don't say it." Greaves interrupted, "Get priming."

They watched on as they primed each door, Bennie continued to give a beat by beat log of their actions until the outer door closed. Then Natalie took over, "Pressurising the lock." Ford heard the vents filling the lock with air before her comms cut out, and then waited with everyone else for the next update.

"Wait a second." Bennie shouted; his voice stern through Ford's helmet speakers.

"Inner doors opening." Said Natalie,

Orange winked through the portholes of the outer lock, "That was stupid." Bennie said,

"Do you mind?" Natalie asked,

Greaves shuffled her position on the ring, "What's going on over there?"

"Natalie's rushing." Bennie snitched,

"I'm going in." Natalie said. Under normal circumstances, Ford would have had a hard time imagining Natalie behaving in this way. But she was close to discovering her father's fate. The hours had turned into minutes and Ford could understand she wanted to skip the seconds.

"Jesus Nat..." Bennie again,

"Get off me." She snapped, followed by sounds of a scuffle. An unrehearsed dance between two imbeciles wearing air filled suits, Ford was disappointed he couldn't see it, "I'm serious Ben, get the hell off of me." There was another rustle of fabric.

"PEOPLE!" Greaves shouted, "I know we're all strung out, but acting like children isn't going to help." More rustling, less violent, "Can I trust you both to get the job done, or do I have to come over there."

"Yes sir." Natalie said, automatically responding to authority. Anyone with half a brain could determine she wasn't happy about it though.

"Aye aye." Bennie said, Ford placing an imaginary salute in his mind's eye.

Greaves took a deep breath, and said, "Good, can you get to the engine room from your position?"

"I think so." Bennie said, "It's dark, but it looks clear enough. Some wiring, debris. Natalie, wait..." He sighed, "For Pete's sake."

"What's happening?"

"Natalie just removed her helmet."

"There's pressure and oxygen." She defended, Ford admired her balls, but it was reckless of her to take off her helmet before a filter check was completed, "The air smells burned." She continued, "Electrical fires, I'm going in."

"That was royally stupid." Bennie murmured, just audible over the comms.

"Natalie." Greaves said, "Reel it in. That's an order. You'll be no use to your father running in blind." Her sentence hung in the air like a bad odour, another public scolding with the weight of their shared catastrophe on her shoulders.

"Yes, Sir." Natalie replied, her tone resentful as she pulled herself deeper into the ship.

***

"Quelqu'un putain me tirer dessus." Jake Bounette cursed in French, rubbing his scalp in the doorway of the infirmary, which in all sense of the phrase, was upside down. Cupboard doors hung slack with their contents spilt across the floor, and that was just the one room. He hated to think what the store room looked like. In fact, he wanted to turn around and walk away from it all. Even if he had the rest of his staff, it would still take a day at least to put things right and that was with Ross, who for reasons beyond Jake's ability of logic, loved cleaning. Oh how he would have traded one of the engineers for him right now. Hell, he'd have even settled for a cleaning 'bot.

"Jake?" Dahl called, reminding him he was on an open channel.

"Oui, John."

"Did you, say something?"

"I did." Jake swallowed his woes and stepped into the circular chamber of the infirmary. Sub rooms such as his office and the store room branched off the main one through circular doors. The only exception to this was the quarantine bay. A recess at the far end, segregated from the main chamber by a sliding wall of armoured smart glass. As it contained fixed furnishings such as a sink, toilet and bed, it stood out as the only area to survive the crash intact, "The infirmary is literally upside down."

He crouched, picking up a plastic box. The bio-patches which it had contained were scattered around his feet, "We did suffer a mid-space collision." John reminded him with a hint of sarcasm in his voice. Jake kicked the patches away, noting the four operating tables still fastened to the walls, then the broken glass. His eyes scanned the room for the culprit, finding one of the main ceiling lamps broken. "It's going to take me a week to clean this up." He really needed Ross.

"Don't over dramatise, Jake. You don't need to clean everything up." John's voice, ever calming, was falling on deaf ears, "Just get it ready to receive an emergency."

Jake knew different. The nature of an emergency was you didn't know what to expect. He couldn't put the room back to deal with every eventuality without putting it all back. He couldn't work like that, and he never expected his staff to either. Jake pushed his feet through the clutter, pondering how he could speed things along. He sighed,

"Okay, John, I'll do what I can." His voice carried the essence of dismal optimism, but he said it to avoid a confrontation with his Captain.

"That's all I ask."

Jake dropped once again to his haunches, reached under the table to his right and grabbed an upturned box. He settled the container on the floor, right way up and looked for a broom. Kicking his way through the ankle deep mess he reached the cupboard, finding the door ajar. He closed his eyes, knowing his future was not one of fortune and opened it fully. One by one he opened his eyes, "Typical." He muttered, the mop and bucket were still inside but where the broom should have been was an empty stand. He cursed in French again and fantasised about having Ross searching for the tool instead, but eventually and resentfully searched the room himself.

Jake hated looking for mundane things. As a scientist, he could lose himself quite easily in a biological quandary but pitting his reason against the illogical results of where something *should* have landed and where something *actually* landed was just another card in his already staggering house of frustrations.

He found the erstwhile broom in the last damned place he looked, in his office. How it managed to get out the cupboard, cross the infirmary and make a forty degree turn back on itself before stopping just inside the door he would never know. He lifted the plastic pole, bringing the head to his face and grabbed the bristles with his hand. By the state of it, he imagined the broom had visited most of the ship on its journey to his office. The head wobbled between his fingers and the shaft had several dents but at least he could use it.

He tightened the head and retreated back to the broken glass, brushing it up when he realised he only kept latex gloves, "John, do you have a pair of gloves?" He asked, "Thick enough to pick up glass." He corrected,

"Why? Isn't everything plastic down there?"

"Oui," he replied, expelling his exasperation with an audible exhale, "except the lamps, windows, and smart wall." All of which, were tempered and smash resistant, just not mid-space collision resilient.

"There'll be some in the hanger bay, but I have a pair in my quarters. Hang on. Stand by, Jake... say again, Ford?"

"It's a ship, stuck deep in the engine section." Ford's voice joined John's over the comms and set Bounette's mind racing. Another ship could mean other survivors. That could mean more injuries. Or on a more positive note, it could mean another infirmary, one which wasn't as messed up as his. But Jake Bounette wasn't an optimistic man and his negativity was all too quick to reassert itself. He expected two casualties, Joanne and Crudge. That was already a mission to undertake, but another ship could constitute a full crew needing attention. He wiped the beads of sweat from his forehead before they had chance to fully form.

"Does it pose an immediate danger?" John asked, bringing a whole new set of worries to the doctor. Radiation, disease, his grip on the broom tightened. Weapons, of mass destruction.

"Insufficient information at this point, dad" Ford again, "Greaves has split the team, Nat and Bennie have just entered the aft section. She and Bennie are investigating."

From what Jake learned from the crew, Ford was always eager to please his father, too eager in many of their eyes and in the limited time Jake had to get to know Ford, he didn't disagree. No matter what he did, Ford always ran it passed the Captain, even if he knew it would be a resounding no. Better to be warned off than told off. This was Greaves' call but his relay of the order was coming across like snitching rather than an update.

"Is it worth it?" John asked,

"We think so." Ford said, surprising Bounette as he tipped a tray full of glass and bandage flutes into the box, "There's a chance the aft section is losing atmosphere through it."

Bounette raised an eyebrow, was there a chance the kid was beginning to think for himself? Or maybe the rumours that Ford and Greaves were bumping uglies were true. Disinterested in the conversation which continued over the speakers, he dropped the tray into the box. Thinking of the crew had reminded him he needed access to their medical records, blood types, allergies etc. He didn't want a malpractice suit on top of having to clean this crap up.

"Whatever she thinks is best. Over and out." John said abruptly, snagging Jake's attention. John didn't convince easily, normally he'd insist on further deliberation, at least another six or seven questions in making sure they'd thought out the strategy before jumping in feet first. It was very unlike John to cut anyone off like that, especially Ford.

Bounette's finger hovered above the button on his screen. Once decided, he opened his mouth to ask his question, but just as he formed the first of his words - static filled the infirmary.

"....this is...UE...core...do you..." Bounette released his cheeks on realising he'd sucked them into his mouth while struggling to follow the dis-en-sentenced words. A man's voice, one he didn't recognise. His mind calculated the possibilities. It had to be another ship, maybe even the one which was buried in theirs. But there wasn't enough to go on. They were nothing more than incomplete words, floating to the surface in a bowl of static soup.

"This is the Jian Seng, please repeat." John replied,

More static, combined with a fluctuating pitch leading Jake to guess John was adjusting the frequency. It occurred to him that John hadn't intended on keeping him on the line. He hadn't been part of the previous conversation; it made sense John must have forgotten about him. Wouldn't have been the first time, recalling being sat at an unnamed bar on Titan nursing a Bloody Mary and waiting for the get together which had been rescheduled after he'd left the ship.

"UES Alba..." The words erupted from the static, "we...your...inmates..." the voice sounded distant, too weak a signal to be coming from the ship that had collided with them. Which was a silly observation to begin with, he noted, Ford would have been able to pick up that signal in the tug.

The static squealed to a halt and the words came as through clear as glass, "This is UES Albacore; we have your coordinates and are on route." Bounette breathed a sigh of relief. UES stood for United Earth Ship. It had to be a rescue vessel. It was only a matter of time.

"Albacore, this is commercial transport Jian Seng, do you copy?" John's question sounded concerned and in juxtaposition to the warming sensation Jake felt growing in his chest.

"This is UES Albacore; we have your coordinates and are on route." The message repeated, sounding clear and concise on the correct frequency, but lacking in sincerity. Jake began to understand John's concern. The message could mean anything, or nothing. They'd made no direct confirmation as to whom they were talking to. It could be a subspace comms ghost, lost between worlds meant for a disaster years previous. They could also be too far out for two way conversation, he wasn't a physicist so couldn't work out the distance and time it would take a message to get to them. His mouth became dry as paranoia grazed its icy fingers across his neck, nestling its hands on his shoulders. It could also be bait, fishing to ascertain whether or not the Seng had survivors.

John repeated his question; cementing Jake's concern his friend shared his fear. His legs begged him for mercy, their strength reducing him to unsteady shakes and he rested his backside on the edge of the desk. Jake pursed his lips, controlling his breathing before it had the chance to run as rampant as his heart. He reached into his desk drawer, pulling out a small box. He rolled up his sleeve, opened one of the wraps from the box and slapped a bio-patch onto his arm. Bounette shut his eyes, breathing in deep as the drug diluted his anxiety.

The Albacore's dead pan message repeated once more and he heard John's muttering from the bridge. He'd never heard John utter the words before, he just wasn't that person. Maybe, he thought, it was the drugs now coursing through him. John Dahl was not after all a faithful man, he'd left Earth to get away from it, but John's words were unmistakable, "Saints save us."

***

"Shine some light on this." Greaves asked,

She and Eddie had dropped to the base of the UFO and were assessing the damage to the Jian Seng. Ford, impatient in the silence of their assessment had launched Huey's drone: Archimedes. It wasn't anything special. It just had a set of small arms to move even smaller items out of the way. The one bonus was it had twin lamps and a central camera which would, at least, allow Ford to get close to the action. Not that he wished for more action. He just didn't like the idea waiting in the duck for infrequent orders like the one just received, "By your command." He replied, bringing Huey's flood lights down to Greaves' position.

Up close the UFO was just as impressive. It appeared to be almost organic in structure; there was no sign of any panel-joins, no rivets and no indication of how anyone could have built it. It was the furthest it could be from appearing man-made and if by some miracle of technology it was, Ford still had no reference for it and he'd been in space for most of his life. The beam from Huey's flood lights caused the surface to ripple, as if the light was a finger tracing the surface of a lake, "Is that happening or a trick of the light?" Ford asked, seeing Greaves' hand on the side of the ship through Archimedes' feed.

"It's not physical." Greaves replied, "Looks like a rainbow in oil."

Ford added, "Maybe it's some kind of cloaking system?" wondering if that's how it had eluded the Seng's sensors.

"Possibly..." Greaves was a gear head and didn't like projecting fancies, "Let's take a sample. Can Archimedes pick that up?"

"Sure can." Ford brought the little fella close enough for his thin robotic arms to touch the metal. A simple gesture on the remote controls and one of the claw hands folded back on itself, making room for a small rotary blade to slide forward, "You may want to back off."

"You expecting it to explode?" Eddie cracked, stepping back the same as Greaves. They all knew that cutting into the surface could cause shards or small debris to fly off, and you didn't want anything, no matter how small it was hitting your suit.

The spinning blade edged closer, Archimedes' transmission focusing on the area to be cut. It didn't need to be big, an inch or two squared. The blade touched down on the ship's surface, sparked and broke off, shooting out of camera sight in an instant.

"Wow!" Eddie yelled,

"You okay?" Ford asked, riding up over his console, peering out the view screen

"Yes." Eddie replied, "But that was too close man. It almost hit me."

"I did warn you..." Ford sat back down, "Sorry boss, a sample is out of the question." He brought up the diagnostic report, "It burned out the motor too."

"What can do that?" She asked,

"I wouldn't read too much into it, the blades are meant to cut pipes and cables. But I have used it on the Seng's hull. It should have at least made a mark."

"If it can cut the Seng's shield plating, what in the hell is this stuff?" Eddie asked,

"Aren't you guys carrying laser cutters?"

"Yeah, but..."

"But what?"

"You know it's built into my glove, what if it..."

"Explodes?" Ford turned Eddie's quip back on him,

"Guys." Greaves interrupted, "Come and have a look at this. Ford, I need your floods."

Ford turned Archimedes around until he found Greaves, standing well back from the hull. He then steered Huey into position, "What is it?"

"This." She said, stepping back and pointing upward along the UFO.

He followed her lead, bringing Huey's floods in the direction she pointed. In large print, English letters were almost legible in grey on the ship's side. There was damage, obscuring much of the word but Ford could make out most of the lettering, "What does it say?" Greaves said,

Ford, who could see the whole word, read it, "Centurion."

"One of ours?" Eddie asked,

"Unless there are aliens out there, who've just happened to also have created English." Ford jabbed,

"I meant Earth Alliance."

"Of course you did." Ford re-read the confusing report on his console, "Scanners still don't know what to make of it."

"Or maybe it's the Church, they have advanced shit." Eddie re-visited his earlier statement, "Could even be stealth?"

Ford nodded to himself, "Maybe, it would certainly explain a few things if it were. I've just never seen anything like this before."

"I'll put myself out there and say no one has."

"I certainly haven't." Greaves added,

Ford jabbed at his console, "Wait a second," there had to be some information he could use. Ford took a deep breath, his cheeks inflating as his breath escaped through tight lips, "I'm pretty sure the Centurion has pressure."

"How deep is it buried?" Eddie asked,

"I can't tell." Ford tapped some buttons, "Deep?"

"Anything else?" Greaves this time,

Ford wiped sweat from the back of his neck, "Like what?"

"Life signs maybe?"

"Greaves, Huey's a tug boat. I don't have all the toys." *Give me a break.* He tapped some more buttons, but the same illiterate crap came back. Huey just wasn't cut out for research, "I could harpoon it, try and drag it out?" He knew he was scrapping the bottom of the barrel; Huey's engines would burn out long before the Centurion budged.

Greaves thought about it for a second or two, "No, leave it be. If it's lodged in too deep you'll cause more damage." Greaves replied, "I think it's time to take a look inside."

Ford, who thought the idea reckless at this stage said, "You sure?"

"We have to do it sometime, if you and your instruments can't tell us what's inside then we need to get in."

"But there could be anything inside that thing."

"Exactly, if there's pressure, there could be survivors. There could be an engine core about to explode. We don't know what caused her to crash into us. There are too many questions and nowhere near enough answers..."

"I'll come with you." Eddie said,

"No." Greaves stopped him, "Head to the engineering. Help Natalie, I'll check this out by myself."

Ford shook his head, the plan was far worse than previously thought, "That's crazy, there's no way my dad would sanction that."

"We need to re-establish communications and make sure the Jian Seng is functional first, this could be a waste of time."

Eddie added, "Then let me go in. If Crudge is dead, they'll need a chief."

"Crudge isn't dead."

"Listen to the man." Ford agreed, unconvinced by Greaves' optimism.

"Eddie, you know the plasma drive as good as Crudge, you're better off helping Nat and Ben." She said, "Ford, I'm not about to do anything stupid. We have to see inside, and I won't be alone. I'll have Archimedes to keep me company."

Yeah, and all Ford would be able to do is wave Archimedes about, hoping for the best. He licked his lips, "You have brass balls Greaves."

"Give me a lift?" She asked,

"Anytime."

"Guess I'm leaving this party early then." Eddie said with a sigh.

"I'm sure the other one will be just as exciting." Greaves replied, raising her wrist to change channels before relaying the information to Natalie.

"We haven't gotten into engineering yet, there is a lot of debris in the corridor." Natalie returned.

"Eddie will be able to help with that." Greaves said, waving Ed away, "He's on his way, call if you need me, over and out."

"Yes, Sir." Eddie bowed out, waving as he engaged his suit's mediocre thrusters.

Ford was about to offer him a lift when Greaves called, "Anytime today, Ford."

***

Crudge pulled himself along the grate flooring, his knuckles white and his arms aching. At sixty-four this was one experience he had not put on his bucket list. Some time ago, he'd watched the collision unfold through his terminal's screen until one by one the external sensors winked out. Whatever that *thing* was that hit them, it had crashed into the front of the ship and knocked out the power manifolds. If it had glanced off the hull, then it wouldn't have been so bad. But the *thing* had rolled along the spine and hit the engine, destroying any chance of either end being used as an independent life-pod.

There were ways and means around this, but for arguments sake he conceded the loss, for now. From there, the damage had cascaded along the cargo pods, destroying four of them outright and dislodging more before stabbing the central corridor and breaching the hull. Emergency bulkheads had dropped either side of the breach, but the object continued to roll, perforating the corridor in several more places before hitting the engineering section.

That was where Crudge's fun began. He'd not bothered to count the explosions. None were large enough to rupture the engine core, but were enough to damage pretty much every other damned system they had. Even Crudge's chair, which he was fastened into, had been torn from the floor and thrown against the ceiling. When he'd come to he'd found his legs broken. Which was why presently, he could only pull himself across the floor toward a small fire and a light green box with a white cross stamped on its side.

It was just a few more feet away and right now he wanted that box in his hands more than anything in the 'verse. He hadn't cried since his wife had died eight years ago, but now, the pain throbbing through his legs was testing that resolve. He fought with his emotions and the pain, telling himself he wasn't about to let a little collision bring him anywhere near how low he felt when his wife, Natasha passed.

He reached for the box, fingers falling short by an inch, "Come on you old bastard." He dug into the grill, pulling himself closer before reaching a second time. The flame kissed plastic was soft to his touch and until then he'd not considered the fire burning on the wall, where the first aid box had once been. In a strange way he was lucky the fire burned where it had as the plastic hook may not have melted, the box may not have fallen to the floor and he would have had to struggle further to reach it.

Dismissing his irrelevant chain of thoughts, he snapped open the latches and opened the box's lid, pulled the morphine injector free and stabbed his thighs with quick, precise determination. Waves of relief pulsed through his legs, the pain washing away with each beat of his heart, "Feck you." He said in deep gravelly tones, wiping finger trails across the sweaty film on his face before rolling onto his back and staring at the ceiling, giving himself a moment to enjoy his small victory.

It was a small victory too. There wasn't an option to lay there forever, waiting to be rescued. The folks at the front of the ship would have their own problems to deal with. He'd expect a rescue, probably with some engineering back up to help him put the engines in order, but he couldn't wait for them. The wall fire was just one of many small electrical blazes, stealing his oxygen and raising the core temperature of the room.

The fire suppression system hadn't kicked in. Which in his mind; meant a problem with life support. It was a whole heap of problems, all pointing to him being neck deep in a pile of unmentionable at the ass end of space.

Reluctantly he forced his body to move, sitting himself up against an airflow pipe to better survey the room. The morphine was working; he couldn't feel anything, anywhere. Even the heat wasn't an immediate concern, only the long red slug trail of blood he'd left as he'd crawled across the room drew his mind to his next course of action, his legs. He'd need to find something to splint them with. He needed to tie them off to slow the bleeding or he'd pass out.

While he formulated a plan of attack for that problem, he continued looking around the room. Several pipes were streaming coolants and water, showering the south end. The damage was too high for him to reach, there was no way his old bones were going to carry his dead legs up the ladders to the gangways. He felt the urge to spark a cigar, one of the Martians he'd been saving. The morphine was good, he noted, re-focusing on the tasks at hand. He'd wait until things were a little more secure before delving into his tobacco stash.

It wasn't just the gangways he could no longer reach; the engine room was seven stories tall with sub rooms on each level. There could be any number of failings he couldn't see from his position, and it was a momentous ask of his crippled body to repair the whole room. What he needed was a diagnostic report so he could prioritise the jobs and work out the hows after the whens. Luckily, he came across the resolution to his leg problem while mentally planning his route to the engineering terminal. Unfortunately, he'd also glimpsed the silent alarm flashing red on its screen.

His grey eyes orbed, reading the large, screen filling words, 'Coolant System Failure'.

"That's not good, Crudgie me old mate" He informed himself. "However, first things first..." He rolled onto his front and began the arduous crawl to Control Station B. The single stack, podium style console no more than five meters away had taken damage to its metal facade plates. The wiring inside was now hanging loose. It took longer than he anticipated to reach it. Despite the morphine he was still struggling to move. Finally, he yanked the wiring out from under the floor space.

Taking his ever handy army knife from his pocket, he sawed through the wires, laying out one metre lengths along the floor next to him, four in total. He tied two of the lengths tight, one around each thigh just above the torn fabrics of his overall. The bones would need to be set, but he took a moment to marvel at his handiwork, announcing to the room he did not need the help of a filthy Frenchman.

He still needed a splint, luckily for him there was no shortage of bars and handrails which had fallen to the ground. As Chief Engineer, he made a mental note to bring up the lack of ship maintenance to his teams after the emergency had finished. Finding a suitable length, just longer than his legs, he used the third and fourth wire ropes to tie the pole between his useless limbs. It wasn't the sexiest splint but it would do the job, for now.

With his legs attended to and a rhino's dose of morphine pumping inside of him, it was time to attend to the next problem. The coolant system ensured the engine properly vented at intervals so the plasma didn't build up and over stress the containment conduits. The screens on all the operational terminals, displayed the same message: 'Coolant System Failure'.

The plasma from the engines was either not being vented efficiently enough, or more dangerously, not at all. The only difference between those two faults was how long it would take for the engine to overheat and explode, "And you only need a swift pair of hands, nerves of steel and the right tools to fix it."

Thankfully the 'verse had seen fit to leave Crudge with his hands, the morphine supplied his steely nerves. However, there was one small problem, his tool bag was yet to reveal itself and his army knife wasn't about to cut it. He snickered at his own pun, "What, it's funny." He said, reminding himself how much morphine he'd taken. From his position he looked first where he'd left the tool bag, the empty surface of his work station. From there his eyes looked around for possible landing areas for the bag, or at least, knowing he never closed the lid during his shift, some of its spilt contents.

He found himself assessing, yet again, the damage and his inability to reach the majority of the faults. Even with the pseudo confidence provided by the morphine in his veins, he couldn't convince himself that it was possible for him to treat all the faults and prevent the engines from overheating, "Natasha darling," He told his dead wife, "You got out at the right time."

Without even considering mitigating factors, the maximum threshold for plasma build up was ten hours. He couldn't say for sure how long he'd been unconscious, or how long it had taken him to crawl from where he'd woken. At that point, a piece of the gangway from the level above came crashing down and smashed into the deck, just where he'd been laying after his morphine injections. It was a sobering thought that he'd survived not once, but twice now and by sheer luck both times. But, with the falling debris came an idea - one that could solve the majority of his problems.

He crawled half the distance he needed to, before faltering with an exotic outburst of obscenities. He'd failed to calculate the added weight of the makeshift splint between his legs and that the knotted wires holding them together did their best to catch on the flooring grids. He cut the strands back as far as he could, pushing the knots in as far as they would go. He even considered giving up, what would be the harm in laying there until rescue. If they were all dead, then what would be the point in spending the last moments of his life struggling to fix something only to run out of air?

If it wasn't for the thought of Natalie, he may have done that. If she was alive and he had to believe she was, she'd be trying her damnedest to reach him. So, in turn, he would try his damnedest to get this end of the ship ready. The rescue team would be engineers, good ones. There wasn't any one of his team he wouldn't have with him right now, if only to help him walk. He'd interviewed each and every one of them and they were all assets to both the ship and to him. They were on their way and he'd see to it that they still had an engine to fix.

This was useless, he thought. Why am I thinking in circles? He reached forward with both hands, slipped his fingers between the grills and pulled his chest across the floor, his overall buttons clicked and clacked against the metal grill strips. If nothing else, this was good exercise for his wheelchair. He smirked, "Na." Refusing the idea to the room, "I'll have a powered one or some poor sap to push me around." He reached again, just a little further, "Or maybe some of those fancy robotic legs." He mused, anything to distract from the burning in his biceps as he pulled forward.

Just one more; one more reach, one more pull, and he could rest. He'd be on top of where he needed to be. The next grate sat above the deck's gravitational field distribution hub. Victory was within reach. He'd have the power to move about engineering without his legs, or exhausting himself. He refused himself the last respite and with a purple snarling face he pulled himself along the floor for one last time. His head dropped to the grille, a cool, welcoming reward for his efforts which he enjoyed for what seemed only a minute until he felt Natasha's lips on his cheek, "Just a bit further." She said.

His eyes snapped open, his vision was blurred. Yellow and orange blobs wobbled above him and with each blink the room took form. Electrical fires burned high on the walls, heavy black smoke gathered at the roof and filtered out into the sub rooms. His once pristine overalls were now slick with sweat. He coughed, taking in long breaths and focusing on the present. He knew he'd fallen asleep, but for how long? He pressed his thumb and finger together, noting the time but without reference he couldn't be sure how long he'd been out. The only grace he had was that he'd made it to his destination. With the flat head of his knife he unscrewed the grille's corners. Then, slipping the knife into its sheath, he grabbed the grilled tile with both arms, lifting it out. He rolled onto his back, holding the squared off metal above his head before throwing it as far away as he could. It rattled against the floor less than three feet from him.

When he rolled back, his head and shoulders hung over the open floor section. Below him, just past arms-length was a black hexagonal block, each of its six sides was connected to a black and yellow striped tube which extended out under the floor. The top face had a cover, protecting the controls. Lying on his belly, he stretched his right arm deep inside the open grate probing for the protector. Once open, only a tiny lever stood in his way from terminating the gravity in the entire section.

That was if the fail safes were still operational. They ensured if one junction was terminated, all junctions would follow suit. If they didn't then you'd be pulled toward the nearest gravitational field. That would be very much like falling, nay, exactly like falling but in the wrong direction. There was a deck above him and one below him, if both of them continued running then he'd be okay, he could hold onto the grate and lay between fields. If the one above him continued while the lower deck stopped, he'd fall right up. He stopped fumbling in the pit, taking a moment to check what was above him.

A plasma conduit, but he already knew that. The good thing was that he'd probably break his back instead of the conduit, "If there was another way, you'd be doing it." He reminded himself, rolling back into position and stretching his arm deeper, edging himself further into the hole. This was his best option. His only option and once he'd found that bar-steward of a switch his life would take a magnificent U-Bend for the better. If not, then he wouldn't be granted the time to regret it. He reached his left arm forward, feeling his legs lifting up behind him as he balanced his saggy gut against the metal flooring.

Sweat poured down his face, "Mother of a whore..." He snarled. His hand dropped, his breathing eased. *Maybe take a little break before I break my arm.* Breathing out hard, he licked his lips and rethought his strategy. His arm wasn't reaching deep enough because his body and head remained outside. He'd never touch the override if he continued holding back. If he pushed further into the hole, he wouldn't have the room to turn himself around or the mobility to pull himself out. He'd be trapped. But if he succeeded in pressing the switch, none of that mattered.

Crudge pulled his arm back out, rotated his shoulder and dove in as far as his torso would allow. It was dark; the flickering lights from the fires above caused shadows to dance along the black and yellow pipes. He stretched out with both hands, feeling around and finding the security latch. A good tug and it popped open; he reached for the lever and felt the rubber sheath almost instantly. He could feel his luck changing as he wrapped his fingers around it, "Gotcha." and yanked down.

Behind him; the engine room lamps flashed amber and his weight shifted immediately. He smiled, his plan was working. There was nothing, no pull from any direction. He was floating. The safety protocols had worked, his plan had worked, "About time." He said, pushing against the junction. He reversed out of the pit, floating feather-like until he grabbed hold of the grille. Another win, "If things keep going this good, I'll be done in time for supper." The thought of food rumbled his stomach; he couldn't recall how long it had been since breakfast. It didn't matter. There was no time for food, with the gravity off he could move freely and there was a lot of work to do.

***

Crudge's eyelids weighed heavy. Even without gravity, the strain he'd put on his arms in moving about had taken its toll and he was silently begging for a break, "No time for that sonny boy." Natasha's words in his own voice spurred him on. He worked slowly and methodically. Under the circumstances, it was the only way he could. Without gravity, spot welding was more hazardous than seducing a disgruntled hippo. He lowered the face shield once again. It was time to brave the fourth pipe fracture. He sparked up the torch, laying the steel bandage over the crack and began warming the edges.

The steel grew red and then yellow. He pulled the torch away as glowing balls of slag began floating away from the pipe. He leant to the left, watching the burning metal pellets redden as they cooled, floating past his face. He needed to be more careful.

"Dad?!" The voice was familiar yet alien; he'd dreamed of hearing it again but hadn't put much stock in hope over the last half hour. He'd been too consumed in ensuring his own survival, "You in here?" But there it was again, clearer now he'd tuned into it and unmistakably his daughter. From beneath his face shield he smiled, leaving his grip on the pipe go and extinguishing the torch as he scanned the room through his letterbox view.

"Up here." He said, realising it wasn't quite right. While her voice had come from below him, he was inverted. He raised the face shield, needing a better look at the room. Cables and tools floated aimlessly amongst the carnage, but he saw her almost instantly, breaching the main doors with another face he recognised and was glad to see, "Here." He repeated, waving in her direction. Natalie looked around the room until she found him, her eyes lighting up her face and his heart with it. She was more beautiful than his old brain remembered.

Natalie pulled herself through the portal, crouching against the wall and kicked over to him, gliding across the space between them with ease, while knocking the debris clear from her path. Father and daughter embraced each other and her warm lips pressed into his bearded cheek. His nose filled quicker than his eyes and he returned the kiss to her forehead, "I thought you were dead." He said.

She smiled, her eyes glistening with joy, "I thought you were."

Tears spilt, speckling the air between them with salted crystals. He waved his hand, dispersing them enough to give him a clear shot of her face. Her gorgeous, living and smiling face, "It's okay baby girl. I'm okay."

"For the record, I knew you were still alive." Bennie interrupted,

"Wait your turn." Crudge grinned, "There's enough hugs for the both of you."

Natalie laughed, the one she saved for his corny jokes, which meant he had to fight back the urge to start balling, knowing that if he started properly, there'd be no stopping him. He pulled her close, unsure if he would be able to let her go ever again.

"Like what you did with the place." Bennie said, appearing next to them.

"Well, I've had some time on my hands, thought I'd get on with that remodelling I've been putting off." Crudge spoke over Natalie's shoulder at him, "Feel free to join in."

"There's a lot to do." Bennie surveyed the spot fires, flames cascading along the walls like miniature waterfalls. Finally his eyes fixated on the blow torch Crudge was carrying.

"Aye." Crudge agreed, reluctantly releasing Natalie from his arms.

"Why are you using that?" He pointed to the torch, "You couldn't have run out of patches?"

He referred to the emergency seal patches, of which were kept in abundance. Just not in the immediate area. Crudge pointed up to the smoke's escape route, "I used what I had down here, but I couldn't get to the breather. The rest are up there." He noted Bennie's suit, "Feel free to get them, while you're at it you can get me a suit."

Bennie stared at the black haze clouding the ceiling. The smoke moved steadily through the open doors and into the rest of the deck, "Top deck still has gravity and air flow."

Natalie was less interested in what was above her, more so of who was in front, "What happened?"

That was Crudge's question, except that he meant the ship and not his legs which Natalie was currently staring at. She worked her way down his body, careful to avoid touching his most prominent damage, "It's nothing." He said, trying to ignore what he knew couldn't be ignored.

"Yeah right, looks like nothing." Bennie said, also staring at Crudge's legs.

"Dad?"

"What do you want me to say, we got hit, I got thrown. I've been busy fixing the cooling systems since."

"We need to get you to Jake." She said,

"There's too much to do."

"Don't argue."

"You turned the gravity off?" Bennie said, looking toward the open hatch, he was smarter than Crudge gave him credit for, "Because of your legs, you crafty bugger that's genius."

"Old men rule." Crudge admitted, giving the younger man a wink.

While Bennie laughed, Natalie pulled herself up to look her father in the eye, "You're still bleeding."

"Probably." He said, "But we should stop talking, there's a list of..."

"Dad, just stop it."

"I mean it. The Seng is in a far worse state than I am." He pointed to the main engineering console, "Check for yourselves. We've got less than an hour before she goes critical."

Bennie swam down to the terminal for a better look. Natalie however was resolute, her eyes never left his. Crudge knew the shoulder tap and point routine had failed, "You need to see Jake, dad, now."

As much as he'd been happy to see her, he was equally revolted at her suggestion, "Natalie, What part of ship go boom don't you understand?"

She glared at him in silence.

"How many have survived?" He probed, trying another avenue, "Because we need to make sure everyone gets out of this. If we can't fix the engine, which I'm not sure we can given that there's only three of us." He paused, "Why you two?" There were more experienced engineers on board, "Did Greaves make it?"

"She made it." Natalie spat, "But you won't unless we get you to the infirmary, you could bleed out. You may have already lost too much. Look at you, you're white as a sheet, dad. You're shaking, you should be resting not welding."

"Don't be such a child. I'd be unconscious if I'd lost too much blood. Where's Greaves?"

"She's checking out the other ship." Natalie said, before giving him the bullet points of the events leading them to engineering. With each point she revealed his interest grew and her stubbornness faded. "There was pressure leaking from the contact point, they'll join us as soon as they can. But then..." he should have figured there would be a *but*. "You're going back to the front with Ford."

"Another ship?" he asked, she nodded.

"We need to work out a route for the coolant..." Shouted Bennie, reading the console, "...run a vent test and iron out any issues as soon as possible."

Crudge took a deep breath; his praise for Bennie's smarts was short lived. The old man licked his dry lips wanting desperately to sound diplomatic, "What the blasted hell do you think I've been doing?"

THREE

A rchimedes led the way, tilting down and aiming its lamps into the hole to which it descended. Five meters above, Greaves clung to Huey's harpoon winch with Ford controlling both descents from the tug, which was positioned directly above the tip of the Centurion.

"It's like dangling a thread down a straw." Ford commented, noting the distance between Archimedes and the surrounding walls. He'd corkscrewed up the ship during their ascent but had found no other entrance except where it had sheered at its tip. He'd protested once more when he'd seen the jagged metal teeth, each one able to effortlessly shred Greaves' suit. With just one metre to go before she reached the mouth, he checked Archimedes' camera feed.

The gnarled metal glinted back off of the drone's lamps, flaring the screen, "Damn."

"Please don't say that." The first inklings of concern in her voice breaking through the surface.

"No, it's just this ship. It's blinding the cameras." It didn't like being studied.

He glanced at the auto pilot's readout, they were holding steady. The winch was lowering her two centimetres every second. In less than a minute her feet followed Archimedes into the pipe, "Don't move."

"I know."

"I'm serious."

"I know." She repeated; her breathing heavy but controlled, "Just check on the drone."

His eyes moved from her screen to Archimedes in a blink - nothing but lens flare. If the rest of the ship was made of the same stuff, and why wouldn't it be? The drone was going to be useless. He went to Huey's ventral cameras, and saw that Greaves was now central to the tunnel's gapping maw. Ford breathed a little easier, because from his earlier vantage point it had looked as if she'd never squeeze through. Now with her in perspective he saw that she had at least half a metre around her. He glanced back to the drone's telemetry screen and called out, "You'll be fine once you pass the threshold."

"Just keep her steady," she replied, "I don't want any of your antics."

"You love my antics." He said glibly, keeping one eye on the ventral camera and a second on the telemetry.

"Not right now I don't."

She was passing the threshold at an agonisingly slow pace. The winch could have done more, but they were both in agreement that slow and steady was best until she got past the risk of being torn apart. He checked the drone's camera again, the same useless lens flare greeted his eyes, "The camera's not much use inside, you're going to have to direct me."

"What's wrong with it?"

"The interior's reflective; I'm getting flare back on the vid-feed. Don't worry, the sensors are working and I've got full telemetry coming through." He looked back at the ventral vid-feed in time to see Greaves' head disappear into the ship.

"I'm in."

"Are you getting any flare?"

"Yes." She paused, "I've turned my lamp off, Archimedes' light is enough. Looks like I'm in a corridor, I've a walkway running parallel to my descent."

"Understood. I'll keep his lamp on as long as you need it, but if you want a second set of eyes I'll try the night vision."

"Okay."

"Until then you're going to have to tell me what you see."

"I understand."

Ford waited an agonising moment, "Do you see anything?"

"Dammit Ford, just hold your horses a second." There wasn't much else he could do, so he checked the drone's screen. Archimedes was five metres below her and still hadn't come up against anything. According to its sensors, the area they were in was a couple of metres in diameter with a few recesses, as far as the data went, he'd have to agree with her assessment, "The walls are coated in soot. It's crystallised."

"That's where the flare is coming from then." He said,

"There's a lot of fire damage." Said Greaves,

"She did crash."

"Idiot."

Ford rolled his eyes, "You had a different opinion on Asturas."

"That, my boy, was a onetime deal."

"That hurt."

"You'll get over it; you're a big boy now."

"You know it."

"You have a one track mind, Ford."

"Yes." There was no point in denying it...

"Such a child." She quipped,

"Do I denote a tone of playfulness?"

Suddenly her tone changed. "Ford, there's something down here."

"Yes, I see it." He stopped Archimedes dead, the data showed a weave of tubes running along one of the walls. Each tube had off shoots which were thinner and ended abruptly. He angled the drone's lamps onto them and chanced a visual on the other screen, but could only make out shadows and more flares, "But I don't know what it is, some kind of piping?"

Greaves reply was thoughtful, "If it is, I'd say it's organic. It looks more like bramble."

Ford checked the data again; the visualisation confirmed something similar to what she described. If it was, then he couldn't explain why there would be organic growth in her location.

He asked, "This is still a corridor? I've not missed a door or something?"

"Yup, still a corridor." She said, "It looks like it's cutting in and out of the walls."

"Like a weed?"

"I guess so."

"Is it dead?"

"Yes, burned." She replied, "Like the rest of the ship."

"Well don't touch it. Don't want to get contaminated, or worse."

"I have a sample."

"Damn it Greaves. What did I just say?"

"It's safe."

"You don't know that."

"Yeah, yadda, yadda. I'm catching up on Archimedes."

Remembering he'd stopped the little fella, Ford tapped the command to continue his descent. Although he still wasn't impressed with his vid-feed, he was getting a good impression of the area through the data.

The 'bramble,' for lack of a better description, followed Greaves' descent, popping in and out of the walls and spiralling around the corridor. If it was a plant, it must have been growing unchecked for years. Trying to make sense of the madness, Ford could only imagine the crew being long since dead and this gargantuan weed slowly taking over the ship. Maybe it was one of those greenhouse crafts, preserving the plant life that was dying on earth. Perhaps even, the ship predated the Great War. That would make it nearly two thousand years old; they could be searching a historian's dream find. This could be worth a fortune.

"This is messed up." Greaves voice pulled him away from his thoughts,

"What?"

"This bramble, it's everywhere."

"And it's definitely dead?"

"It's as black as burned toast Ford, what more do you want me to say?"

All he knew was the situation was making him feel uneasy. His imagination was getting the better of him. An ancient, invisible ship, laced with dead bramble that somehow against all odds managed to find and smash into them. According to Archimedes the corridor had no other defining features aside from the bramble. Not a door or even a duct hatch. The architecture wasn't anything he recognised. It was too simple, too sparse to be human. *Stop it Ford, you're starting to sound like Bennie.* There should at least be a fire sensor or lamps, "How do you think they light this?" He said, almost absentmindedly

Greaves reply was distant, as though she was thinking about it, "I suppose there must be some form of lighting, probably flat against the ceiling under the soot."

"That's a lot of soot." He mused, not convinced.

Archimedes pinged; its sensors had reached the bottom of the shaft and revealed nothing but a flat bottom to the tube and the base of the plant, growing out the wall and a small portion of the floor next to it, "You're coming up on the bottom." He said, setting the drone to hover half a metre from the floor after moving it out of Greaves' path, "Anything new?" He glanced at the camera, ignored the flare and moved onto the data screen to follow her remaining drop.

"I have a door here." She said,

She wasn't quite at the bottom yet, so, Archimedes lamps must be showing her something his telemetry wasn't, "Can you open it?" Ford crossed his arms behind his head, leaned back in his chair and sucked air through his teeth. He wasn't sure if she should go any further, even if it were possible. His terminal beeped as her feet touched the bottom. He pressed the button and stopped the winch from spooling further.

At sixty metres he wasn't even half way through the cable, if she was going to go further, and the itch on the back of his neck told him she was, they'd have enough to lower her down another length of corridor.

Her next comms message shocked him but at the same time didn't surprise him, "There's still power." A pause, "I've disconnected the winch, pull it up and get out of the way."

"What? Why?" He knew what the answer was going to be already but still didn't like it.

"I'm going to open the door, if there's pressure inside it's going to knock the winch straight back up."

"Then tie it down, it's got a really strong magnet." He didn't like the idea of leaving her alone without the option of a quick exit.

"What if it snags on the top? You don't even know if the magnet will work."

Ford looked at the ventral camera, the jagged metal stretched across the opening from its left side to the right. The right side was bent over in the same direction, it wasn't big, but it left a smooth enough surface to rest the cable. "I'll be fine." He wasn't certain he would be, but it was still better than leaving her alone.

"I don't think so, Ford. This doesn't look like an air-lock; we don't know what's on the other side."

"All the more reason to leave you the winch, then."

"What good will the winch be if you smash into the side of the ship?"

Good point, he thought. "Look, can you please let me be macho, just this once?"

"Just pull the winch up Ford, that's an order. I'll secure Archimedes, if I need rescuing I'll hold on to him and you can pilot him out."

"He's not strong enough." As if weight had any bearing on their predicament.

"We don't have time for nonsense, just pull it up."

"Alright..." Ford submitted. He leaned forward and hit the retract command. As the winch rewound, he took control of Archimedes, placing its underside against the wall and engaging his magnet as the metre counter raced up to zero, "Winch up." He announced as per normal procedure, "And for the record the magnet would have worked." pulling back on his stick and moving Huey away from the tip of the Centurion. Not too far though, as he needed to be back in position should things go south, "I better not see you flying up. I don't think I could handle losing you." He said. Immediately realising his words must have sounded awful, "You know, so soon after finding you." He clenched his teeth, planting the glass of his face plate against his console and punching his leg.

"That..." She said, "Was sweet."

His fist remained clenched, holding fast against his thigh. Ford opened his eyes, not quite believing her response. He opened his mouth to reply, when he heard it. The blip was casual, just at the edge of Huey's passive scanners and he almost dismissed it as part of the debris. But the Seng's debris was scattering slowly from the epicentre of the crash. This had been on the peripheral, too far out to be one of the cargo pods. He switched to an invasive sweep of the area; the pods began blipping on the other side of the viewer.

"Ford?" Greaves called, "You still there, you receiving?" Had she called previously?

He pulled his tongue back in his mouth, "I'm here."

"What are you playing at?"

"I thought..." He stopped, if he mentioned the blip there was a good chance Greaves would be distracted from the task at hand, just as he'd been. So, as there was a chance of it being nothing, he changed his mind, "Nothing. I'm ready." Ford turned his attention to Archimedes' data screen. Whatever Greaves' was seeing, he couldn't.

"Okay, powers on at the door terminal. I'm popping it in three, two..."

Ford watched the uneventful tip of the spear. Sixty metres was a way to travel, but after a while the tell-tale signs of a breach were clear. Air came first, a freezing gale like the breaches on the Seng. Small debris next, particles he couldn't distinguish and then boxes, larger crates, various shapes and sizes raced out within a stream of glistening frozen vapour, all too fast for him to get a distinguishing item, "Bloody hell." Greaves' yelled.

"What?" He asked, reading Archimedes' information, "What's happening?"

"It's coming up."

"What's coming up?"

"Don't be near the top." The concern in her voice led Ford to move his hand on the control stick. He pulled back, furthering his distance from the tip. Sixty metres worth of moments sluggishly passed but the impact still caught him off guard. The corridor's mouth bulged in an instant and then popped as a huge crystallised mass of bramble and metal tore through the jagged opening. Trails of sparking shards sprayed out behind it, raining against Huey's hull as the mass continued into space,

"What the hell was that?"

"Big." She replied, "You okay?"

Ford continued to follow its course on his terminal in disbelief, "I think you just birthed a comet."

"I'll take that as a yes." She said, "I'm okay by the way."

"As you're riding my ass, I took that as a given." No more debris spat out the top of the firework, and Archimedes' screen confirmed it had ended. The air pressure inside the Centurion was spent, at least for the next compartment.

Greaves then announced, "It's clear, there's no gravity but I can get inside."

"Greaves?"

"Yeah?"

He disengaged Archimedes from the wall and directed him to stop in front of her helmet. Using his screen he looked at her face and tried to read her expression for any sign of fear but only found himself staring into her deep eyes, blackened by shadows but as alive as he'd ever seen them. Blinking, she smirked, "What?"

"Be careful in there."

***

They'd made good progress; Bennie got straight to work patching the pipe work, giving Natalie and Crudge the time to get him into a space suit. He put on a brave act, but the removal of the splint and having Nat check over his wounds had taken it out of him and they had to wait a couple of minutes before slipping the suit on. With all the morphine spent, getting dressed had been about as much fun as making love to a gorilla, and he'd cursed his way through every agonising moment of the procedure.

She'd heard him showing off his colourful vocabulary more times than they'd had breakfast. He was an engineer after all, and colourful language was nothing new or unusual. But this time was different. He didn't enjoy revealing his pain. Once the suit was on, she remade the splint and allowed him to get back to work, warning him, "Only until Ford gets back."

"Yeah, yeah," He replied, secretly hoping Ford took as long as he needed to fix the engines. From tunnel to funnel, he would fix this broken pipe and pump the coolant into the reactor core, and vent the excess plasma – even if it was the last thing he did.

From time to time, Crudge looked over to his daughter. She'd grown to be a strong and very capable woman, she'd made him a very proud father and he'd worn it on his sleeves. He was determined to fix the engine and thus be able to give her the chance of feeling the same pride with her own child, once that dick of a husband got his head out of his ass.

"Greaves is annoyed." Eddie shouted from the entrance, pulling everyone's attention to him.

"What now?" Natalie asked,

"Someone forgot to report in."

"Ed-Man!" Bennie yelled loud enough to almost pop Crudge's ear drum. The kid earned himself a fist bump to the crotch for that.

"I have ears you dumbass." Crudge said coldly,

"Sorry." He whimpered, his hand nursing his junk.

"Next time I'll rip it off." Bennie's face dropped and Crudge knew the kid believed his threat, "Get back to work, you'll have plenty of time to kiss your girlfriend when this is over." Crudge wrapped the bag of metal patches around the gangway's handrail.

"Where are you going, Chief?" Bennie asked.

"You're not the only one who needs to be working." Crudge replied as he moved down to meet Eddie, now deep in conversation with Natalie.

Eddie's first words to him were, "I knew it would take more than this to kill your stubborn ass."

"Good to see you too Eddie." He replied, giving him the middle finger at the same time.

"Natalie's been filling me in."

"Yeah, we've grazing and stress ruptures all over the place. Bennie's working on the auxiliary coolant pipe."

"And the cripple needs to see a doctor." Natalie added,

"All in good time, oh daughter of mine." Adding, "Ford gone back to the front?" hoping he had.

"No, Greaves wanted to check inside the UFO." Eddie explained,

"Glad to see curiosity is still a priority." Natalie countered.

Eddie grimaced, "Sarcasm doesn't become you."

Crudge added, "Bounette is wearing off on her." He was silently happy that Ford was delayed.

"Laugh all you want, I'm giving Ford a call. We've waited long enough."

"What's up?"

Natalie pointed at Crudge, "His legs are broken."

"Both of them?"

"How many do you think he has? He's not a tripod."

"Your mother would have disagreed."

While Eddie laughed, Natalie rolled her eyes, "That's disgusting."

"Would you have me any other way?"

"I'd have you in the infirmary."

"Dammit Natalie, you're like a broken record."

"Would you have me any other way?"

He'd not brought her up to be smug, so he blamed her husband for that trait, "No, I guess not."

"Okay, okay." Eddie cut in, "What do you want me to do?"

"Run a check on the phase converters, there was a spot fire right under them."

"Any blue brittle?" Eddie asked.

"If I knew that, I wouldn't be asking you to check."

"Yes, Sir." Eddie mockingly saluted Crudge and made his way to the duct network.

Natalie and Crudge watched him leave, "I better get back to it." He finally said.

"Make the most of it."

He pushed away, leaving her to her report and no doubt, call in the rescue team. When he arrived next to Bennie the man's face was one of disappointment, "Expecting someone else?"

"Errr, no, Sir." He cupped his nether region in protection as he spoke,

Crudge let the gesture fall flat, he was no longer in the mood, because they were all sat on a ticking bomb with too little time and he'd put himself at odds with the one person he couldn't afford to be without. In his best commanding voice he ordered, "Carry on up here; I'm going to run a diagnostic on the coolant terminal."

"You sure Chief? There's still a lot more to do here." Crudge could've reminded the kid that any one of these systems had further issues, and that he wasn't sure he could trust the one computer which was supposed to alert them of any faults. However, the truth was, he needed some time alone. Something he could fix, "You're a big boy, Bennie. I trust you, even if you are disgusting." He said, moving out of the way of a glob of Bennies floating oily spit.

Bennie produced the finger in his usual, casual manner, "Kettle black old man. Don't think I didn't notice your piss floating about up there." He pointed upwards, but Crudge didn't look. He wasn't going to justify his call of nature; he just produced his own finger as he glided down to the main deck, pushing floating debris out of the way before gripping hold of the desired computer terminal and starting to open the side panelling. No tools were necessary, it was a simple case of unclipping a few latches and the panel slid free. If only the rest of the job was going to be so easy. He pulled the diagnostic board and screen out from underneath. It was a standard ten inch QWERTY board with an eight colour monitor.

Each terminal like it aboard the ship contained the same emergency testing system. It basically worked like a safe boot up on personal computers. These secondary systems allowed you to run any number of programs such as diagnostics on the hardware and software without interrupting the critical services they provided. He unzipped his gloves and began asking the terminal some basic questions.

report on power distribution to board: one spike disruption to power.

report when spike occurred: spike occurred at 04:42 hours standard ship time.

The time corresponded with the time of the collision; if that was the only spike then he was off to a good start.

report on hard drive: hard drive corruption at 23%

That wasn't so good.

report on hard drive corruption: hard drive corruption 1% at 04:42 hours. hard drive corruption 2.6% at 04:45 hours. hard drive corruption 4% at 04:45 hours.

Crudge continued to follow the progress of the corruption until it reached 24%. The terminal had a partition of 25.7% for the core programming and would need at least 20% to compute its basic functions, maybe a couple more if it were dealing with user requests. Which meant it would become noticeably slower. Another half hour, give or take. After that the corruption would accelerate leaving them with a terminal about as useful as a papier-mâché exposure suit. He typed in his next question:

report on engine diagnostic accuracy: engine diagnostic accurate within .0009%

"That's something. Not a lot, but something." He glanced at the critical core warning, 50% and climbing. Even if they were able to make all their repairs, he wasn't convinced they'd be able to do it in time to reverse the damage.

He looked across to Natalie, still in conversation with Ford. She looked stressed, Ford couldn't be coming. He pushed off the floor plate toward the doorway, "Bennie?"

"Yeah?"

"You've got under half hour until I trust this terminal less than I do you."

Bennie's oil splashed head emerged from behind the pipes. His eyes were bold in contrast against the residue clinging to his skin. His reply made Crudge half smile, "Then get your fat arse over here and help me."

***

All the time he had been arguing with Natalie over the comm link, Ford had been aware of Huey's confined habitat. The heating must have been glitching too because he hadn't stopped sweating for the last half hour or so. His suit was sodden and the boots, sewn onto the legs had turned into paddling pools, every time he adjusted his seating they splashed against his ankles. He needed to get out of the horrid thing. However the chance of doing that in the foreseeable future was miniscule. The engine was up the creak without a paddle, Crudge, literally, didn't have legs to stand on, and Greaves was deep inside the space hulk that had brought this calamity upon them.

He'd done his best to multi-task, arguing his point with Natalie while piloting the drone so he was always a step ahead. Not knowing what they'd find inside, he'd rather lose the drone to some random event than watch it happen to Greaves. But as the argument intensified, Ford being a man, found it increasingly difficult to get his head around doing more than one thing at a time and Archimedes had fallen behind.

Greaves, being a woman didn't have the patience to wait, either. "I'll be there as soon as I can." He finally snapped. He knew he'd pay for it later, but the engine team had enough going on and Greaves only had Archimedes.

He switched channels immediately and scanned the immediate area. "What's happening?" He switched Archimedes into night vision. As is the case with all good science fiction stories he was presented with another basic corridor. So far they'd found little else. Slowly the Centurion had revealed itself to be more human than alien. Off the corridor were a few small rooms, laundry, a galley and a mess hall. But it was exactly as Greaves had described it, all burned, "Greaves, you better say something before I get an ulcer."

"I'm here. There's nothing going on, just more corridors."

"Well there's plenty going on up here. Natalie's lost the plot." He filled her in on the engine room dilemma.

"Natalie's just worried about her dad, it's not serious."

"I'm not so sure." Ford replied, "She took a chunk out of my side."

"That's how she is."

"No she's not." Not as far as he could remember, "Not with me."

"Ford, you've been away a long time. Trust me on this, if it was anything serious Crudge would have made the call."

"But he's dealing with a coolant failure."

"And he's got Bennie and Eddie working with him."

"Just saying." He didn't like the tone in her voice.

It took a while for her to reply again, when she did the agitation was replaced with a controlled calm, "I won't be long, just this last turn."

"Did you carry on or turn left?" He asked, noticing the intersection.

"Left, always left."

If there was some logic to this he couldn't see it, always going left would eventually take you in a circle. With that thought pondering in his grey matter he piloted Archimedes around the corner. The Centurion had suffered far worse than they had, scoring was rife and the mysterious plant was everywhere. Sparkling undergrowth climbed the walls, burned seed pods erupted from ventilation grilles and roots embedded themselves in the grilles along the floor and ceiling. It was a spooky atmosphere that was more akin to being in a cave on some distant alien world, and the silence wasn't helping, "Can you keep talking?"

"Awww, is baby feeling lonely?"

"Hardly." He motioned to wipe his brow, but hit his faceplate instead, "I'm up here in the dark, in more ways than one"

There was a moment's silence before she said, "I'm okay." This time he was sure she sounded sincere. "There's not much you could do up there if something went wrong anyway."

"Go team morale." He sounded deflated.

"I didn't mean..."

"I know what you meant." He lied, but he didn't want her repeating the fact that he wasn't in a position to save her should anything go wrong. Huey was too large to fit in the corridor, he'd have to abandon ship and climb out the roof hatch, drop the sixty meters to the bottom and search the ship based on the terrible second hand information Archimedes had given him.

"Ford, I'm coming up on another door."

He was still too far out; he couldn't see what she was referring to, "Can you stay where you are?"

"I have to manually open it anyway." She said, "There's no power."

"There a pump?"

"I can't see one."

"Then wait there."

"Okay already." The frustration in her voice was very clear.

"Don't get snappy." He said, knowing it was his anxiety fuelling it. Natalie had left him with a nasty chip on his shoulder and had left him further behind Greaves than he wanted to be, "Sorry."

"It's okay. You're right, I should have held back."

The small lamp from her torch became visible on the camera and he made an audible sigh of relief, "There you are."

She waved her torch up and down, "See, nothing to worry about."

Yeah, right, he thought. Nothing to worry about except losing you in this maze, "Don't ever leave me again."

"You flirting again little man?"

"Maybe." He grinned, "But seriously, don't do that ever again."

"Cross my heart." She made the cross across her chest with her hand as Archimedes approached. Not satisfied with the master shot, he went in for a close up, lighting her dark features with the drone's lamps and scrutinising her deep brown eyes, lavish eyebrows and pouting lips.

She blushed, smiling at the camera as he held it in position. He needed so badly to be with her in person. He didn't see enough of that smile, "Shall we continue?" He held Archimedes in place, remembering their one night on Asturas and how her lips felt against his, wanting her hands running up his back and into his scraggy red hair, "Ford?"

"Yes?" He asked, unable to recall anything she'd said.

"What's next?"

"Right." He said, thumbing the drone's stick back and spinning it around, "Maybe we should head back? We need to get to engineering, and this seems to be a bust."

"You may be right." She said to his delight, "Let's head back."

He took point, leading them up to the intersection where he'd lost her and made a right turn.

"Wait." She said,

Archimedes spun around; Greaves hovered at the junction looking to her left. Always left, "I thought we were going back?" He said, not wanting to press further into this nightmare.

She looked him in the lens and said, "Just a little further."

If he'd arms down there he would have dragged her all the way back to Huey, but all he could do was watch as she pulled herself along the wall in the opposite direction and then reluctantly follow her. There wasn't any power. The data didn't show any atmosphere. The ship was dead, this was pointless, "It's just going to be more of the same."

"There's another door." A moment past and Ford considered pulling in the big guns, all he had to do was flip the channel and tell his dad Crudge needed medical attention.

He wouldn't allow them wasting any more time in here, not when there were more pressing matters to attend to, "It's not powered." She said, her torch beam landing on the manual over-ride, "Bingo."

The comms channel lamp began flashing. He knew it was Natalie, wanting an update on their progress and to rip him a new one for cutting her off before.

"Let's leave it."

"We need to know what's in here."

"We really don't."

She shone her beam through the porthole in the door, "If you need to go back, go."

"Damn you're stubborn. You know we have to get Crudge to the infirmary." The lamp continued to blink, call waiting.

"I'm not stopping you."

But she was. He couldn't leave her, the thought of it tightened his stomach into knots, "Come on up, I promise to bring you back once we've sorted Crudge and the engine out. I'll even come down there with you."

"I like it you care." She said, melting his heart, "But I'm going through this door and you're heading back to get Crudge. You can pick me up on the way back."

The lamp continued blinking, a constant nagging to which he inevitably had to answer and once he did he knew he would have to do what he couldn't, "I can't leave."

"Don't be silly."

She was right. He was being silly – but only as silly as she was insane. She should be coming back with him. Who in their right mind would want to be left alone in this place?

The darkness surrounding them grew even darker, creeping toward their lights with a steady foreboding which turned his blood cold. If he left now, he couldn't be sure he'd see her again. His father could order her out. Ford didn't have that luxury as she outranked him. But on saying the former, she was stubborn enough to ignore his father anyway. He'd seen it, it was the first time he'd seen anyone do it. That was back when he was a teenager and when he first realised his crush, a crush that had grown into something far greater. In that moment, he realised something else. He cared for her more than he'd realised.

Confronted with that fact he recoiled, flipping the switch and granting the waiting caller an audience, "Where are you?"

"Hi Nat."

"Where are you Ford?"

"Still at the Centurion."

"Get the hell over here."

Ford charged the logic centres of his brain; he had to put the ship and the crew at large first. If he was honest with himself, he didn't know how to deal with the realisation of his feelings for Greaves or the extent of them. If he had, he would have never have said, "On my way."

"We'll meet you at the air-lock."

Where else! "Okay." He flipped her off the channel and found Greaves already pumping power to the door, "Greaves, I'm heading over to the engine. Do me a favour and lock Archimedes to your suit?" The drone's underside magnet fitted against the back of each exposure suit.

"No problem."

"I'll set him to idle." But after he gave the drone its commands, his stomach flipped once again, "You sure you're going to be okay?"

"Yes." She waved him off, her suit hiding all of her slender, enticing features.

"You're a pain in my ass Greaves."

"Stop dawdling."

Ford pulled back on the control stick, pitching Huey away from the Centurion and headed toward the Jian Seng's stern, he flipped the channel switch again, bringing the bridge into his conversation, "Captain?" then again when he didn't answer, "Dad?"

"I'm here."

He explained the situation as quickly as possible, glossing over the delay as best he could, knowing that was a conversation for later. One he intended to have while standing shoulder to shoulder with Greaves. With the Centurion behind him, his father thanked him for the update and added, "Bring Crudge home, I'll give Bounette the good news."

Ford grinned, it would be *good* news. The son-in-law fixing the father-in-law, both of whom loved to hate each other. If nothing else, the next couple of hours were going to be entertaining and something to distract them from his dawdling. They'd had a win, something they all desperately needed, "Dad?"

"Yeah."

"Any news on Jo?"

"None, but I'm sure we'll find her once power is restored."

He knew his father was lying, but at least he was lying with good intentions. Jo hadn't enough time to get out of the corridor before the Centurion smashed into them. Best guess was she was floating somewhere outside the ship amongst the rest of the debris. Not a good way to go, but not the scariest way. At least she wouldn't have lasted more than a couple of seconds before exposure took her. If she'd been wearing a suit when she was blown into space, she'd be spinning for hours waiting for her air to run out. That thought, despite the sweltering heat inside Huey, chilled Ford to the bone.

He was closing on section Eight's air-lock when Greaves' interrupted his thoughts, "Ford, we have a survivor."

"Seriously?"

"I've found three occupied stasis pods; one looks like he died from some disease. He's full of blisters and dried puss."

"Stop flirting with me Greaves, this is an open channel."

"Another's burned." She ignored his comment, "but the third has a young girl inside. Maybe ten? She looks fine, the tube has power. Readings are all green."

"Guess we've lost our salvage guys." Ford quipped without thinking,

"What?"

"Nothing... An old film."

"You're such a child."

"It keeps me young." He chewed over what Greaves had said, while parking Huey adjacent to the air-lock. The Centurion was decompressed, there was no way of getting her out of the tube without killing her, "Can you detach the tube?"

"Already on it."

"Good. Make sure she's ready for me to winch up on my way back." He said, watching the engine side air-lock opening. Two figures, both in exposure suits and holding on to each other slowly made their way across the five meters between Huey and the Jian Seng. The air-lock closed behind them.

"Thanks Ford." Natalie said,

"You coming along for the ride?"

"I'll need help holding on." Crudge replied for his daughter,

"If you're sure." She said,

"Please, the trip was harder than I thought."

Ford steered Huey away from the hull, "Hold on. We have another passenger to pick up along the way."

***

Crudge hooked his arm around Huey's handrail; leaving his legs floating free as the small craft hovered over Centurion. In all his years of space travel, he'd never seen anything like it. Not even a spec, or prototype at one of the many conferences he'd attended over the years. Well, that's not quite true, he reminded himself, marvelling at the sleek seamless hull. He'd seen it in movies and games, but those were things of fancy. Never had he seen something in real life like this monstrous construction that speared his beloved home.

Drawing down into the darkness of the torn tip of the Centurion was Huey's tensile hawser rope. They'd dropped it down to the bottom, over sixty meters Ford had said. But Crudge couldn't bring himself to believe the ship had survived the stress of lodging itself into the aft section and only breaking at this point. There would be, or should be skewing all the way down in complete contradiction to what the kid and Greaves had reported, and it all added to the ship's mystery.

He felt Natalie's hand on his back, "How you doing pops?"

He hated it when she called him that; made him sound like a child's breakfast cereal, "I'm good."

Confirmation was all she wanted it seemed, because there was no follow up. Both she and he were watching the hawser, waiting for the promise of the Centurion's survivor. To think they'd soon have a new member on board was a rarity. Only every five or six years would they'd have to back fill, crew wise due to attrition, most of the crew stayed on until retirement. However, when someone did retire they normally took one or more crew members with them due it being a family run ship.

With the length of time spent travelling between systems, there was no telling whether you'd see your parents again, and he hoped Natalie would leave with him, maybe after this run. It seemed like a good time to go, everyone had a finite amount of luck, or so his grandfather used to say. He looked over the damage to the Jian Seng and hoped his luck stream hadn't already run dry.

Before leaving engineering, Crudge had resolved himself to the fact that repairing the damage may not be possible. If Greaves was in there now, with Crudge and Natalie both, then there may have been a chance, but still only a slight one. It was Natalie with her impetuous resolve that had forced him to look at the bigger picture. Regardless of anything, he wasn't about to leave her in the aft section without knowing how long the core had left, so he'd insisted she came with him. Not that he told her the real reason. If he had, she would've stayed.

"Watch it dumbass." Greaves said over the comms,

"Tell me sweet-cheeks, how in the hell should I be doing that exactly?" Ford replied. Crudge smiled, the kid had his father's patience.

"Just go slower."

The argument continued until Crudge's limited patience drew thin, "You do know we can hear you?"

"Good." Ford said, "And don't think you can't make yourself useful when the stasis tube comes up."

"If it comes up." Greaves added.

"Greaves, you're killing me. You're literally going to be the death of me."

"You two should get a room." Crudge smirked,

"Never again." Ford snapped, "Wait? Are you laughing?"

Greaves was indeed, laughing, "I could have you anytime, anywhere little man."

"Can we please get a move on, this is worse than watching Space Dallas." Crudge said,

"Shut it grandpa, there's plenty of this to go around." Ford's tongue was getting a little too sharp for his liking,

"Grandpa?" Crudge asked, "Listen here you little..."

Natalie's hand rested on his shoulder, bringing him back from the edge, "You okay Ford? You seem a little tetchy."

"A *little*? I'm sweating my damned head off in here; I'm going to have to wring myself dry when I get out."

Crudge shook his head, the kid didn't know he'd been born, "I've broken both my legs but you don't hear me complaining."

"Yeah, I think I just did."

The conversation fell into silence, everyone was tired. By placing her hand on his shoulder, Natalie had reminded Crudge this wasn't everyone's usual behaviour. There was no point fuelling the fire by continuing the argument. He'd got one more sniper shot in before he'd realised that, but now in the silence he realised she'd thrown water on the whole thing. His old eyes drifted from the pit below to the serene blackness surrounding them, they were all at the end of their tethers while the universe continued, indifferent to their nightmare.

When and *if* they got out of this, he would definitely leave. Take his retirement fund and hit one of those luxury passenger liners to one of the border planets. As far away from the Church as he could get, something lake side with a garage so he could build something. Maybe a first generation hover car, nice and retro. Something to pass down to Natalie, or a grandchild, if she ever got round to it. If Jake ever got round to it.

Crudge knew Natalie would have had one by now but Jake had made himself abundantly clear he wasn't about to raise a child onboard. He hoped she wasn't staying just because of him, they'd mentioned leaving a number of times before Natasha passed. Not so much now.

"Almost there." Ford proclaimed,

Crudge pulled himself back from the darkness and looked down. At the tip of the Centurion the first shiny reflection of the tube's metal glinted under Huey's floods. It edged out of the hole, revealing inch by inch the smooth test tube. The glass and metal, if that's what it was, seemed as one, tinted with green. Not that green metal was unknown. The ore mines of Caliston IV produced it, but the device itself remained alien. He couldn't see any bolts or fixtures; even the control panel midway along its length appeared at first glance to be part of one solid structure. He'd give anything to explore the ship, tinker with its parts and see what made it tick. However, all of it was moot. Even if he had the use of his legs, there would be no more exploring of the Centurion. Eddie and Bennie were doing a knock up job with the repairs, but he could feel the inevitable calling and when the top of Greaves' helmet finally appeared, he'd made his decision.

Natalie moved around him, reaching down to the magnetic clamp and aligning the tube with Huey's underside. She pulled down the magnetic couplings one by one, securing the payload as Greaves emerged from the Centurion followed by the small camera drone. Crudge waited impatiently for her to kick up to him. When she grabbed the hand rail, Crudge wasted no time in bringing his Assistant Chief up to speed on the situation, ending with, "I've set her up for a twister."

"What?" Greaves asked. The twister wasn't a tested procedure. It wasn't even in the manual. The idea was to fire the surface thrusters and rotate the bow clockwise while moving forward; the stern would rotate anticlockwise and pullback. The spine, being made of connecting tunnel sections would theoretically tear apart; even the keel duct should separate easily. However, while the manoeuvre would save the front section from an exploding rear, it was irreparable. They'd lose all of their cargo but save their lives, using the bow as a life boat. Crudge had expected her reaction, he'd only before referred to the manoeuvre as an example of out of the box thinking and it was plain on her face that if Greaves had known the severity of the engine's damage, she would have never had given into her wanderlust in the bowels of the Centurion.

"It's the only thing left to do." He said,

"But the bow has been on emergency power since the crash." Greaves explained, and like luck, emergency power had a finite amount of time. They could preserve it, turn off non-essentials and put the crew in stasis. But without the engine there was no way of generating fresh power and eventually life support would fail, "We have to try and save the engine."

"She's right." Ford backed her up, "We'll be stranded otherwise"

Crudge ignored Natalie's gaze, knowing she'd probably realised by now his reason to bring her along and that his needing help in hanging onto Huey had been a lie.

"Worry about that when you have to, now, worry about critical mass and don't hang about if she reaches eighty-six." He explained, grabbing Greaves' wrist in the aim of letting her know not to ignore his warning.

At eighty-six the core would begin to buckle and the rate at which it expanded would grow exponentially. After that they'd only have a couple of minutes before the inner containment system failed and the fuel lines ignited throughout the aft section. With the current damage there was no way of telling where the weakest stress points on the lines would be, no way of telling which routes would be cut off, engulfed in flame.

"Eddie and Bennie are by-passing the coolant valves. If they succeed before it reaches eighty-six you should be able to stop it in its tracks, but you've only one shot at it. If it fails, activate the twister and get the hell out of there."

His words acted as an anchor on Greaves' jaw, with each syllable he spoke it slid further and further down until she was staring at him wide mouthed, a blank face of terror, "There is a chance." He said, "I just prepped for all eventualities." That was exactly what he had done, it was the first sequence he dumped into the engineering terminal after he'd realised the possibility of a core breach. He hadn't thought of himself; he'd only thought to save the front end's survivors, and Natalie.

"What about Natalie?" Greaves asked, finally coming to her senses.

He ignored Natalie's faceplate and answered, "We'll need her for life support." Before adding, coyly, "Besides, can you imagine Jake without her?" He regretted it as soon as he had said it. Up until that moment he'd only hinted at the fact that he was sending Greaves' into the engine room, knowing there was a good chance that she, like Eddie and Bennie, were not going to make it. He knew they'd try to the last to fix the engine, to give everyone else the best chance of survival - just as he would have done if he'd still been there. By saying those last words, he'd put his cards on the table and opened himself for Greaves' retort.

"Dad, I should go back. They need me." The remark was double edged, not in the telling, but in the receiving. On one hand he was filled with a bountiful amount of pride that his daughter was willing to sacrifice herself to help the crew. On the other, he couldn't bear losing her. He stared at her faceless helmet, the surface reflecting Huey's lamps into his eyes until he couldn't look any longer.

"We'll need you for life support. You'll know best how to preserve power." He said, knowing he was damning the aft team to failure, "You'll only be another pair of hands in engineering." It was a lie. Yes, she'd specialised in life-support, but she was also a very capable engineer in her own right.

"Can Eddie set it to twist now?" Ford asked,

It was a plan that had merit. They would sacrifice the engine early to save all of the crew. But in the long run, their life-support would run out, and with a callous calculation there was an argument that three less lungs to fill would give the rest a better chance of survival. These were hard choices, ones that many people easily criticised but repelled making themselves. Crudge had made that choice when he'd grabbed hold of Huey with Natalie by his side, and he would have re-iterated his order if Greaves had not stood up to the task. He looked at her posture, straightening with resolve and smiled when she said, "No. We need to give this our best shot."

He nodded at her, "Don't be there when it reaches eighty-six."

"Eighty-Six." She confirmed. She looked away and down to the approaching air-lock.

"I'll be back for you once I drop these two off." Ford said,

Greaves gave him a hope filled, "Thanks."

***

Greaves shut the outer door and pressurised the lock, the closing had a finality to it she didn't linger on. Better to focus on what she could control than worry about things she couldn't, what will be, will be. She had no intention of dying today and fixing this damned engine was going to be the way of preventing that so she pumped up the power to the inner door and opened it. Keeping her helmet on, she travelled through the garbled interior, weaving in and out between the floating wiring, noting how much the debris was going to slow a speedy escape.

It was possible, there was a chance, Crudge had said so and she trusted that. Both Eddie and Bennie knew what they were doing, and they were hopefully further along than the old man had suggested. If all else failed, they'd have time to escape. And she knew one fly boy who would be ready and waiting for them when they did.

She smiled, remembering when she'd met up with him on Asturas. It had been like meeting him for the first time. He'd jumped in years, she'd said goodbye to a teenager and hello to a man. An awkward charmer with a taste for imagination and an obscure humour that she'd found refreshing. She hadn't been the first to be seduced by the charms of someone off ship during shore leave. Still, she hadn't thought about him since that night, not as much as he'd clearly thought about her that was for sure. In truth, she had seen it for what it was: one night's fun off ship.

She hadn't considered it anything else, batting his flirtations back at him with ease until the Centurion. The crew all considered themselves family, and that bond was already strong but the concern he'd let slip in his voice...

She shelved the thoughts for later, hearing the raised voices as she reached the opening to the engine room. The short hand between the two reprobates was the best and worst on the ship, half the time no one knew what they were talking about. But somehow, it worked for them. Even when they were screaming at each other they both knew that the other was the most important person to them, "Guys." She called, pausing at the door to remove her helmet and locating the best place to drop it before interrupting the slew of insults again, "Guys!"

The argument stopped and then two heads appeared from separate sections of the room. Both covered in grease, both with shining white smiles at the sound of her voice, "That you Greaves?" Bennie yelled,

"It is I." She said, gliding into the room, "Someone speak to me."

"Where the hell have you been?" asked Eddie, pulling himself further out of his pit. He was completely out of his exposure suit, being useless for working in confined spaces it made sense. Greaves began unfastening hers too, but stopped when Crudge's voice echoed inside her head. Getting in and out of these suits was a time consuming chore. She needed more information before continuing.

"I'm here now." She said, looking around the room for some other form of information. With both of the guys up in the rafters they'd not have the up to date count anyway. She found it on the main terminal, her eyes focused on the glossy screen presenting a clear and present seventy-six percent toward critical mass. She only had ten percent to work with, "Still climbing?"

"We've re-routed the entire coolant system through the tertiary manifolds." Eddie said,

"What you mean, *we*?" Bennie shouted,

Greaves rubbed her thumb and fingers across her temples, closing her eyes and trying to think with the fresh argument ignited. The tertiary system was the backup, both systems one and two could be re-routed through it individually. It allowed repairs to be done on either one with no loss to power, at a push both systems could run through it but only for an hour. Any longer and the engine would need to be shut down for cold repairs. But to do that they'd first have to purge the plasma. That was clearly not an option or Crudge would have shut the core down as his first port of call. If they could get the coolant running for ten minutes...

"We need to start venting." She said abruptly,

"Working on it." Bennie said, waving a lose cable away from his face, "Where's Nat?"

"She's needed at the nose."

"Yeah..." Eddie said,

"Leaving us with the ass." Bennie added,

"Bitching won't help any more than praying will fix this engine."

"See that's where we've been going wrong Ed."

"That card game was probably a bad idea too." Eddie quipped.

"Where do you want me?" She asked, not wanting to be dragged into the banter.

They explained their positions, there wasn't much was left to do before they could run a stress test on the pipes. She glanced at the main terminal again; with nine percent left she decided to help Bennie as he had the most left to do, "Cut the chatter. I want us done in fifteen minutes." She said loud enough for both of them, "If not, suit up and get out. We're going for a twister, Ford's on his way back to pick us up."

"You're not serious?" Eddie asked,

"If we can't vent this plasma then we lose the whole ship."

Neither of them had anything to say after that. They took a moment to consider the ramifications, which undoubtedly had been part of their fears up to this point. She took it that without a senior officer to say so, it was never really something on the cards. By saying it, she'd made it real. They all took to their work in silence, but every now and again she would steal a glance at the main terminal's doomsday clock.

***

Ford uncoupled his helmet and breathed the recycled air of the Jian Seng through Huey's open lid, he took a moment to allow the artificial breeze to cool his sweat licked face but moved before it had a chance to turn cold. He set his helmet down on the console and climbed up onto the hull, jumping down to the bay's floor and hurried his passengers off the tug. Waving at Bounette and his father as they secured the Centurion's stasis tube onto an automated pump truck, while he helped Natalie lift Crudge onto a gurney, "How you feeling old man?" He asked,

"Save your pity." Came Crudge's callous, yet not entirely unexpected reply.

Ford smiled, twisting off Crudge's helmet, the man's face looked tired and worn. He'd been through a lot and had earned the right to be his cantankerous self for once. Natalie strapped her father's legs to the bed, "He'll lighten up once we get some morphine in him."

"Make sure you do." He grimaced, "I don't want to spend any quality time with your husband sober."

"Play nice." She replied, removing her own helmet. Crudge looked at Ford and rolled his eyes while snapping his thumb against his fingers in a yapping motion. Ford grinned; Natalie didn't find it anywhere near as funny, "Dad."

Crudge dropped his hand, rolling his eyes again, "Okay, I'm done." He gave Ford a wink as Natalie shunted his gurney forward.

"I'll get him to the infirmary." Natalie pushed the gurney into a roll, "You coming Jake?"

Jake Bounette wasn't paying any attention. Instead he, like Ford's father, was looking at their newest crew member. Natalie repeated her question, and Ford saw recognition flash behind those scrutinising eyes. The Frenchman arched his head around to his wife, his mouth open with nothing coming out. Eventually, after seeing Crudge waiting on the gurney, he said, "Yes, of course." He took one last glance at the tube before moving off.

Ford took his place at the foot of the alien tube. Its slim perfect construction was cold to his touch. The stasis bunk was silent. The only sign that it was operational were the flashing indicator lights on its control panel. That and the fact that it's occupant looked healthy. Greaves had been correct; the girl couldn't have been more than ten years of age. Her tiny frame was covered in an over-sized surgical gown. Long ringlets of ash blonde hair ran over her chest and made her pale skin look even whiter under the bay's glow lamps. She was so at peace right now, unaware of the tragedy that had befallen her ship. He couldn't imagine how scared and confused she'd be when they woke her.

"She's so young." His father said, running a hand over the tube's surface atop of her face.

For his whole life, Ford had been the youngest person on the ship. In his father's voice he heard the memories of his own childhood. Ford couldn't imagine anyone this young having to deal with what they were already fighting for, and said, "I think we should keep her in stasis. Until the worst is over."

John Dahl looked up from the girl and nodded, "Protocol dictates quarantine, there's a power hook-up for the tube.... if it fits our supply..."

The last remark seemed a little over the top to Ford, she was just a ten year old girl after all. But then he wasn't Captain, "Are you good to take her down, Captain?" Ford asked, "I need to get our wayward engineers."

"I'm good." He said looking at his son, "You're doing good work out there."

Ford nodded, knowing his father would retract those words when he discovered his delay at the Centurion, especially if the engine did indeed fail when Greaves' help may have prevented it. Now wasn't the time to discuss that however, he had to get back to the stern and gather his friends, "Thanks." He said, turning back to Huey.

"Ford."

He stopped, "Yes, dad?"

"Have you seen anything out there?" The question was surprising, odd even. It was space there was nothing to see but the Jian Seng and its floating debris. The Centurion he'd already reported on, albeit an abridged version. He thought on it a moment longer before remembering the sensor ghost, the faint blip at the edge of Huey's peripheral.

"What do you mean?" He asked,

His father shrugged, whatever the point he attempted to make was buried in the gesture, "I'm sure it's nothing. Just keep an eye out, we'll talk when you return."

Ford chewed his lip. There was something going on, that much was certain. He could stand there and discuss sensor ghosts and theories until the ship exploded but the engineers needed him, "I will." His father raised a hand and they shook, "Make sure you strap in, I'll see you on the flip side."

Ford climbed the side ladder to Huey's lid and dropped a leg in, taking one last look down at his father. He was hiding something, that something was unfamiliar in his eyes. Ford had only seen his father like this once before, when his mother had first fallen ill. He'd seen it in his father's face as he stood at her bedside, telling him she'd only fainted and there was nothing to worry about. Only to later discover it had been cancer.

***

Bounette took control of the gurney. From the Bay there was a short passage to the one and only elevator on the ship. Whereas other injuries would be taken to the infirmary via ramps and stairways an emergency from outside the ship had a direct route from the bay deck into the infirmary by means of the hydraulic cabin. They slid Crudge in, securing the gurney snug against the corner and pressed for the deck above them. He ran his eyes over

Crudge's splints, noting while they were hastily fastened and looked more like a braided ponytail than a splint, they had at least been done effectively.

He couldn't see the severity of the damage, not until he took off the exposure suit. So started compiling a mental list of the equipment he needed to perform the necessary surgery. He was three items down the mental list when he felt Natalie's hand on his, "Hey."

He smiled, looked into her sapphire eyes and said, "Tu m'as manqué." Telling her he'd missed her in French. She replied in French, "Et moi vous." and kissed him on the cheek. A breeze of serenity washed over him. He'd missed her so much. Worrying over stupid brush heads and cleaning duties when he should have been focusing on what was to come. The back of his head warmed, the old man's eyes were on them and when he looked down he found the old man staring back, his large eyebrows matching his hairline, "Hi." Said Crudge, with a false smile, the one he saved for Bounette.

The elevator stopped. Bounette waited for the doors to open, wheeled his Father-in-Law across the corridor and straight into the infirmary. It bounced, rolling over one of the many items he'd failed to pick up in his scramble to get the infirmary ready.

In this case it was a test-tube that had survived the crash but not Crudge's weight, shattering under the hardened foam wheel. The glass dug in, causing the front of the gurney to bank sharp to the left.

"Watch where you're going you idiot." Crudge yelled,

Bounette ignored him, stopping the gurney under the operating theatre lights and locked the wheels in place. He'd long since given up arguing with the old man. Only when he felt like winding him up would he lower himself to the ping-pong of insults. Instead he found it simpler to expel his own frustrations in French, which, despite spending several months in France with the rest of Bounette's family during the lead up to their wedding, Crudge had never found the inclination to learn. Within in the safety of Crudge's ignorance, Bounette informed Natalie to shut her father's mouth before he did.

"Hey." She said, informing him he'd overstepped the mark.

He gave her a brief frustrated smile followed by an accepting nod, "Get his suit off." He ordered, as he searched for his medical bag finding it stacked on top of his 'to sort later' pile of crap he'd not had time to organise. In fact, the infirmary was just a room made up of 'to sort later' piles. It was the best he could do to ensure the bio-samples and drugs weren't damaged, or that the blood reserves hadn't been ruined. The rest was nonessential and could wait until the ship was up and running. Who cared if the place was untidy, at least it was clean.

Natalie cut through her father's splint and suit with a laser scalpel, it wasn't a recommended use for the device but Bounette didn't care under the circumstances. Natalie had said she'd thought his legs were crushed, Bounette kept an open mind until the suit came away from Crudge's legs with a sickly tear, the congealed blood parting in thick strands. Natalie looked up but Bounette still paid her no attention. The air remained odourless until he lowered his nose to the wound, sweet almonds. Infection had set in.

He pulled his bio scanner from the small leather satchel; a device made of two parts. One part touch screen display, the second a detachable syringe gun which he snapped free and stabbed into Crudge's leg, "Ouch, you dumb fu-."

"Be quiet." Bounette replied, pressing the screen and activating the microscopic sensors in the old man's blood stream. Within seconds their findings were relayed to Bounette's display.

"You're enjoying this." Crudge said,

114

Bounette was tempted to agree, but the more he read the screen the less he felt the need to mock the old man. There was severe damage to Crudge's legs, his left had a shattered knee and fibula and the right was worse. He tugged on his nose in thought; if he had the artificial medical assistant, if his team was awake, or even if he had a nurse, just one nurse he could possibly do something. Sew up the nerves, fit braces along the broken bones... But whatever he did, Crudge could never walk again, not on those legs. The alternative he was left with... he hesitated.

"What's the prognosis?" John asked,

All eyes turned to the Captain as he dragged the stasis tube behind him. Bounette opened his mouth to answer but hesitated. He wasn't ready to make the decision in front of him, "You keeping her in stasis?"

"Best place for her." John replied,

"What about me?" Crudge asked,

Bounette looked at the old man's haggard face, pulled his nose tight and turned to Natalie. He spoke in French, "There's a case in the store room labelled surgery, can you grab me one of the bags inside it?" She nodded, eyes darting to the correct door. When she moved, he added, this time in English, "I'll need gloves and a mask too."

John had joined him overlooking Crudge, they clasped hands and shared nods as old compadres do. Bounette swallowed, mustering his courage while looking at his Captain and considering Crudge's outstanding question, but it was the engineer who spoke next, "No need for sugar Doc."

He'd known the man for near enough ten years and not once had he called him Doc, he couldn't help but smile, "I need to knock you out and cut off your legs."

"Try not to smile." Crudge winked, for all his torturous banter he at least knew Bounette's skills.

"Can I do anything?" John asked,

"Natalie's getting what I need. Let's get the tube into quarantine." He strode to the glass wall, entered the command and watched as half the triple glazing slide up into the ceiling before walking through. He waited as John rolled the stasis tube to the docking station against the wall and knelt to attach the cable, "It doesn't fit."

"I didn't think it would." John said, resting his hands on his hips.

Bounette scanned the control panel, "There's organic gel pack life... I don't know how long it will last."

"We should lock her in. Ford said we may have to twist the ship."

Bounette let the weight of his head fall forward and left it hanging, he'd not realised it was that bad. He clasped his hand on the back of his neck and rubbed, looking into the tube and the young girl. So young... she'd not even had a chance to live and now she was ignorant in that her short life may have already come to an end. She was so innocent, and didn't deserve this, "There's webbing in the stores." He said, having no intention of going himself. Bounette's mind had abandoned his body, finding refuge in the girl. Her all but flawless body was perfectly white. At first he'd thought it was the lights, the cold glow lamps of the bay – but here, under the quarantine lamps her skin held no secrets.

John dismissed himself, leaving Bounette staring at the girl's chapped lips and the crusted eyelids. Stasis did everything it could to halt every natural growth within the human body, but couldn't, not entirely. You still aged, if only at a fraction of what you would do normally. Had the girl's lips not been chapped, or the crusts around her eyes not looked overly ripe he would have walked away. Curiosity woke his hand and drew it to the control panel where he checked her vitals, finding to his disappointment that she was not as innocent as she looked.

"Here you go." John had returned, holding the orange webbing from the stores, "The room's a mess, you should be ashamed."

"Let's get this strapped in first." He said, ignoring John's remark and taking the webbing, fastening the stasis tube to the walls fittings. Once satisfied she wasn't going anywhere; he followed John out of the quarantine bay and punched the door release.

The glass wall slid down from the ceiling separating Q-Bay from the rest of the infirmary. He took one last look at the girl, knowing he'd have to corner John soon to let him know what he'd learned. It had been a mistake to bring her aboard. But for now, she was in the safest place for them all and there was nothing else he could do, except to attend to his grumbling father-in-law.

FOUR

Eddie hovered over Greaves' shoulders, "Look boss, I'm not one to rush an artist. But if you take much longer, there won't be a chance of slippers and cigars tonight."

"Give that a go." Greaves said, ignoring the remark and wiping the oil from her hands onto her chest.

Eddie looked up, nodding at Bennie who said, "Here goes nothing." and spun the valve open. Coolant rushed along the pipe, Greaves' ears gathered as much information as they could from the engine room. Searching for signs of a pressure build up or a leak, but thankfully there was nothing. The pipe held and yet, she couldn't allow herself the smile which both men eagerly met each other with. She'd left the biggest test until last. Looking at the main terminal was Schrödinger's Cat. The screen would tell her if they now had a casual stroll to Ford, patting each other on the back, or instead, run as fast as they could.

With a lungful of expectation and engine room fumes; she read the terminal. It was holding steady at eighty three percent. Relief trickled through her, relaxing her muscles; they'd done it. The crazy bastards had done it, "You should be an engineer." Eddie said, slapping Bennie on the back. Greaves tilted her head, closed her eyes and finally smiled, victorious. When she opened them again she took a long look at the devastation around her, hardly believing what the three of them had done, "Congratulations guys." She said as anxiety ebbed from her body and she felt the sweat on her back for the first time. Her whole body ached, eyes stinging from smoke, but she'd done it. All they had to do now was wait for the coolant to work its magic before they could start venting.

Eddie's arms wrapped around her, squeezing her so tight she had to battle free, both of them laughing. Bennie floated down, hands were slapped together, joyous yawps were announced and love was decreed, "Greaves, my beautiful angel." Bennie said, "Give us a kiss you gorgeous woman." He pressed his lips to hers and she felt her cheeks warm at his touch, but knew it was just banter.

"Hey." Eddie said,

"Sorry." Bennie shook his head, "I got caught up in the moment." He took Eddie's head in his hands and kissed him.

Greaves slipped out of their way, rubbing her nose and spreading a smear of oil over her nostrils. Leaving them to it, she glided over to the terminal. "Where are you going?" Eddie called, "There's enough love to go around."

"Rain-check, okay?" She grinned,

"She's dissing the love." Bennie shook his head, "I can't believe she's dissing the love."

"We are going to live." Eddie grinned, "I am raiding the galley tonight, and I don't care if the Captain wants us back in the tubes - I'm going in with a full stomach."

And thus the conversation continued in this vain without her. She left them basking in their own glory, after all they deserved it but she needed confirmation, solid confirmation all was well. Unblinking in her descent, the number remained steady on eighty three percent.

She reached the terminal and tapped the screen, "No..." She said, finding the terminal unresponsive. Her heart skipped, her first thoughts were to hope the screen was just freezing. The keyboard floated nearby, tied to the terminal's open podium by its cord. Greaves snatched it from the air, typed in her query and read the report. All was well; the touch screen had been disabled when the keyboard was activated. She breathed a massive sigh of relief, looked at the two friends, lovers, whatever they were, they were beautiful and alive. Her heart swelled, it was a perfect moment, the eye within the storm.

"What's next?" Bennie asked, looking down at her eagerly.

"Vent the plasma and re-establish main power to the bow section." She said, knowing the exact sequence of events required to survive, life support first. "Then we get more of the gang in here, fix everything else." With main power they could survive until the food ran out. They had a chance, "But first things first, we give everyone else the good news."

"Hell yes." Eddie shouted,

The comms terminal was a mess of wiring, someone had started what they couldn't finish, "One of you get down here and sort this terminal out." Then she remembered what Becca said, "Wait, belay that. There's a disruption somewhere along the spine. Finish putting out these fires, it's like a god damn sauna in here."

She looked for her helmet. With her suit, she'd be able to speak with Ford; he could relay the good news the magic number had reduced to eighty two percent.

Then, BANG! Coming fast as it did loud, pausing all words, breath and thought. Instinct kicked in and Greaves dropped her head down, arms waving above her head, between her and the source. The first valve had exploded way above her, somewhere above the ceiling grid. She couldn't see exactly where, the sound was so loud it bounced around the room, as did the valve wheel. The bang was quickly followed by a shower of coolant, thick oily rain jetting down into the room. She shielded her eyes with her arm just in time. However, the force of the jet knocked her against the floor, pounding against her arm and chest, pinning her. The downpour hit the floor around her and began to float upward, aimless and without purpose.

A hand gripped her ankle tight, dragging her free of the shower. Bennie hooked a shoulder under hers and moved her away, "Come on." He said and kicked away from the downpour. She looked upward to the shower's source, where she could just see Eddie's feet. She knew it was futile, even before she looked at the screen. The pipe was burst and it would end with the core hitting critical. The screen caught her eye, eighty four percent. They'd run out of time. "We need to evacuate." She yelled over the torrent, "Now."

Bennie nodded, pointing to his own helmet and gear, safely wrapped up near the exit. She nodded, leaving him to suit up, "Eddie, move your ass!" Greaves covered her mouth to breathe, wiping coolant from her face and blinking the searing blurriness from her eyes in time to see the terminal clocking up.

Eddie craned back, registering his compliance with a thumb of approval and Greaves returned to the podium. She held the keyboard with one hand, typing in the commands with the other.

"I thought we were leaving?" Eddie said, coming up behind her.

"We are. Get going, this won't take me a moment."

"Hell no, I'm not leaving you behind."

The terminal screen was at eighty six percent, "Get going, you won't have time to get to the airlock."

"Just hurry up and stop telling me to do something I'm not going to do."

"Boss, if you're staying. We're staying." Bennie yelled from somewhere behind her.

Outwardly, she furrowed her eyebrows and focused on the task, defeated. Internally, she was glad of the support. The key commands to setting the twister were simple. Theoretically, if you wanted to, you could instigate a twister if nothing was wrong with the ship. However, the whole damned concept was theoretical. Crudge had already laid the foundation. All she had to do was confirm the procedure with her user name as a prefix to enter the code.

"Greaves..." Eddie called, "Get a shake on."

"One minute." She said,

"We don't have another minute."

"Almost there." She said, "Go."

She typed the code as quickly as her fingers allowed: EM-TWIST-420 and hit the enter key. The cursor blinked twice and registered the command reply: EM-TWIST-ACTIVATED.

"Where did you leave your gear?" asked Eddie, his voice muffled. She turned around to see him fully suited.

"Under the chair." She pointed behind him to her helmet wedged between the floor and the seat, the gloves inside the helmet. Eddie nodded and went about collecting them as she fastened the rest of her suit up, eagerly accepting them as he returned, "Give Ford a shout." She said, removing her gloves and sliding them onto her hands.

"On-it." Bennie said, screwing on his own hat.

She dropped the helmet over her head, screwing it in place and silently cursed as the globule of coolant floated past her eye. Her suit's systems came on, and the heads-up display projected onto the inside of the face plate. The organic gel pack whirred to life on her back, the Heads up Display informed her pressure was good and the suit was sealed. Her communications system automatically found the nearest chatter, the conversation between Bennie and Ford.

"You handsome son of a bitch, where are you?" asked Bennie,

"Half way up the spine. You don't sound like you've good news." Ford's voice was as welcome as birds singing.

"None." She said, tapping Eddie on the arm and beginning their sprint, "The engine's going to blow, get to the air-lock we're on our way."

"I'll be there."

"Twister's going to kick in after a two minute delay." She said, clawing her way along the floor grilles.

"That enough time?" asked Bennie,

"It's going to have to be." She said, knowing that the time delay was spent sending power reserves to the manoeuvre thrusters so they could all fire at once. There was no way it was going off anytime sooner and if there wasn't enough power in the reserves it wasn't going to go off at all. She elected not to inform the rest of her group of that last 'little' detail. They were less than two metres along the corridor when she remembered the slow pace of working her way into the room, and her dislike for the unfavourable odds of escape. She'd also avoided looking at the main terminal before leaving, knowing its climbing percentage scale would only have fuelled her growing terror.

She moved as fast as she could, pulling herself along the floor grilles with her legs dangling out behind her. She weaved her way through thickets of floating tubes, bolts and cables. Looking back every so often to ensure the party was still together. Her heart pounded and breath fogged the inside of her face plate. But her wide eyes continued to pick out the obstacles and she adjusted her path accordingly. She had no intention of dying today.

"In position." Ford's voice was even sweeter sounding the second time around,

"Friend, I am going to do your laundry for a month." Eddie cried, pulling himself up alongside Greaves, "Nay, a year!"

Greaves stifled a laugh, but allowed a smile. Confidence in their survival growing with each metre they took. She glanced behind, Bennie steadily brought up the rear.

Time for the last push, she thought, as she grabbed a fist full of grille and propelled forward as the ship began to shake. Slow rumblings, the same type that Skiers learn to avoid. She pulled herself along faster, allowing another glance behind.

"Not far now." Eddie cried, cheering his buddy on.

Her arms ached from wrenching herself along the floor, and with tears building in her eyes she reminded herself the pain was temporary. Death was not. In an hour she'd be having a cold shower, and afterwards, joking about the death defying dash to freedom they'd made. She'd even give Ford, that despicable brat of a man, a big well deserved kiss for catching their collective asses from the airlock.

Her fingers slipped between the grate and took hold, she pulled hard moving at a personal best. She flew at least a metre and half before having to slip her left hand between the grilles again. They were still ten or so metres away from the next bulkhead, but things were going well. Her left hand grasped the next tile and the ship jolted. Greaves' armed straightened in a shot, popping her elbow free from her forearm; her teeth snapped shut, digging into her tongue. Iron filled her mouth as the ship shook violently around her.

"I think that was the G12." Bennie called out,

Great, Greaves thought, Bennie still knows what's going on. She spat, crimson spittle splashed against the inside of her face plate. Bennie was probably right; the G12 was the logical progression of the ship hitting critical mass. It also meant an acceleration of the process as the engine room would now be a fireball, one which would be racing toward them, "Then move faster you dumbass." Eddie yelled.

She turned to scold Eddie, but instead focused on the massing of gravity free flames washing around the corridor beneath them, "Move!" Greaves grabbed the grille with her right hand and pulled, death was no longer a nightmare. It was a tangible, fierce and resentful force calling for them all, "Saints save us."

"Saints help those who help themselves." Bennie yelled, pulling himself past Greaves and through an open bulk head, "Come on."

With both men ahead of her and through the bulkhead she tried something stupid, wincing as she stretched out her left hand. It was as good as dead, all the strain would now fall to her right and she feared she couldn't keep the pace and soon her thoughts began dwelling not on how much she wanted to live, but on how much she did not want to die.

"Watch your feet." Eddie said, pumping the manual dynamo and dropping the bulkhead in place as she finally sailed through. A couple of inches of steel wasn't enough to save them from the explosion, but it would slow the fire down. It would give them some time, until the pressure built up, or the engines gave in. Greaves took a moment, resting her burning lungs and left arm until Eddie's fist rapped against her helmet, "What you waiting for?"

Eddie was back lit by the orange lamps, giving him the shadowy aura of the Grim Reaper, she almost told him to move on without her. She fantasised about sitting it out, giving in to the throbbing and lightning shocks in her arm. It would be easy to sit it out and wait for the inevitable, "I think I've dislocated my elbow. I can't keep the pace." She admitted, stopping Bennie who was a couple of metres up,

"Hell you can't." Eddie said, slipping an arm under hers and hoisting her from the door. His face lighting up with yellows and whites as the flames splashed against the bulkhead's porthole. Death was closer than she cared it to be, and while Eddie said, "I'll carry you." She reflected on his words, snapping her from despair.

"I got it." She said, reaching for the grille and locking onto it. She pulled herself forward, forcing her eyes in the direction of salvation instead of behind her. She fell into a rhythm, ignoring the tension strain in her arm to the point where she believed she could make it.

"Just a little further." Eddie said with encouragement between his own heavy pants.

He, like her, and very likely Bennie too, were gulping their air a lungful at a time. However, she was unable to see the reserves on her faceplate's HUD because blood had settled there. She forced her breathing down, in through the nose, out through the mouth. Conserve it, she told herself. She'd need it for the trip back. She threw herself along the corridor, metre by metre as the ship began to shake again. She used only the tips of her fingers, straining them more than her arm it seemed with each pull, and then it happened.

Bennie was five or so metres ahead of them when a wheel valve span loose, firing like a bullet from the pipe and hit him square in the head. Both man and wheel hit the opposite wall and bounced off. Steam sprayed from the bust valve, while blood sprayed from Bennie's cracked helmet. He didn't move, just hung in the air, floating. He seemed impossibly distant, each pull along the grille did nothing to close the ground between them and all the time

Eddie screamed his friend's name, Greaves could find no words at all.

A distraught Eddie picked up the pace, leaving her behind to view the tragedy with a morbid callousness. They were almost there. She could see the air-lock just ahead of Bennie, who floated motionless, just another piece of debris in their way. She blinked tears from her eyes, they were almost there and she cursed again. She'd thought all of them were going to make it, but it was clear, long before she reached the men: this was no longer possible. Eddie held his friend in his arms, sobbing. The wheel had made short work of the helmet; Bennie's face was gnarled and ghoulish. Fragments of skull jutted out from a blow to the cheek which had caved in his entire face.

"Come on." Greaves yanked Eddie's arm. There wasn't time to mourn. There wasn't time to say goodbye, there was hardly time to survive. His eyes stared at her, unwilling to acknowledge the task she was asking of him, she'd lost one of them but she wasn't going to lose both, she slapped her hand against the side of his helmet, "Get your ass out of here." He blinked recognition and fractionally nodded toward her. His grip on his friend released, taking her arm instead.

He stayed with her, a mercy she'd never be able to fully repay. Of that, she was sure. A few more metres and they'd reached the air-lock, "Close it." She ordered, wishing she'd primed the doors up on the way in as she swam one armed through the air, landing against the exterior door. As glorious as a sun after a stormy night, Huey lay just outside. Ford was waiting for her, "He's there." She said, waving at him, not knowing whether or not he could see her.

"I said I was." Ford said,

"Thank the Trinity." Eddie muttered, pumping the dynamo while keeping an eye on the bulkhead further down the corridor, "Greaves, we're out of time."

She spun, keeping a hand on the door and saw instantly what prompted his comment. Down the corridor, the dropped bulkhead glowed a deep red, its steel whitening around the small porthole at its centre. Steel melts at two thousand six hundred and thirteen degrees and the transparent alloy the window was made of would melt just below that. They were out of time; the fire ball would race up toward them and cook them before the inner lock had time to close. She ran the calculation in her head; if she popped the outer door without depressurising first they'd have twenty plus metres of corridor pressure wanting out of the ship as badly as they did.

Without consultation she turned around and began pumping the dynamo. Acid burned through her muscles with each rotation and the counter increased at a meagre rate, "Eddie, leave it. I need you on this door."

"What's happening?" Ford asked,

"We're out of time." She said, as Eddie floated up beside her and took over the pump, "We're popping the outer door."

"Are you insane? You haven't decompressed, you'll be shot like bullets..."

"I hope not." Greaves replied, her eyes widening at the blistering bulkhead, glowing bright as a star. In her mind the door collapsed, blasting slag and fire toward them. She turned from the image; the door's power counter was still only midway, "I'm not one to hurry an artist."

Eddie laughed nervously, ploughing all of his strength into the dynamo.

She tried to think of something other than their impending doom, looking out of the porthole at Ford sitting patiently in the calmness beyond the ship, "Ford?"

"Yes?"

"I'll take you up on that drink."

There was a pause, hopefully the shock had knocked him off his chair, "I knew you'd see the light sooner or later."

"Oh you did, did you?" She grimaced, clinging to the hope of having that drink.

"Of course, no woman can resist my charms for long."

"You're an idiot."

"I know."

"That's it." Eddie proclaimed, "You ready?"

"As ever!" She replied,

"Good luck." Eddie punched the release button.

Nothing, "Crap." Eddie screamed.

Greaves looked back; the bulkhead was now completely white. A funnel of flame raced up from the porthole, "Again."

Eddie clenched his fist and pounded the button, once, twice and nothing, "What's wrong with this thing?" Greaves scanned the control panel and found the reason the same time Eddie did, "Inner door is open. I need to authorise the emergency release."

"This isn't the time for school boy errors." Ford jested, his voice laced with concern.

Eddie made the necessary command instruction and hit the release button for a fourth time. The sound of the door's inner mechanics vibrated through their suits and the emergency lamps began flashing. Both of them cheered at the same time, but it was too late. Down the corridor; the bulkhead burst, flames washed toward them and Greaves did something she'd never done before, she prayed.

The outer door opened, not the slow and lumbering manner it had when she entered but refreshingly fast and both her and Eddie were launched out of the open door chased by the torrent of fire.

She spiralled uncontrollably, nausea racing up her throat as the universe tumbled around her. Huey was far to her right and came up too fast. The lights of the tug's engines flashed through her face plate, followed by the blackness of space and then the fire ball racing toward her before Huey was once again dead centre, and then the blackness. Her back connected with the tug-ship's hand rail, cracking her vertebrae. She screamed over the snapping bones as her head and legs doubled backward. Huey's roof slipped between her fingers, "Sharon!" Ford's voice bounced around her helmet but she already knew it was futile.

***

"Greaves..." His voice faltered as Greaves collided against Huey, "Sharon!" The viewer sizzled from her impact, only to return as Greaves slid over the roof. She rolled, toppling into the void, becoming smaller and smaller. He pulled against his control stick as the viewer flashed a brilliant searing white and Ford's seat belt strangled his chest as Huey was flung away from the fireball. Ford tumbled over and over, his hands braced against the inside wall, pushing back against the inertia, allowing him to steal a breath before succumbing to his belt once more.

Thump, "F...Ford..." Eddie.... Thump, thump. He was clinging to the rail, "Do some...something. Before... I... throw up."

"You and me both." Ford swallowed his bile, pressing a hand against the roof, forcing him into the chair and took another breath. He yanked his control stick left to right until it finally bit, "That's my baby." He slowed the spinning, but there was no stopping her.

The explosion had done something to Huey; he just couldn't tell what, and didn't have the time to find out. With every second they were moving further and further away from the Seng. If he couldn't get Huey's engines to respond, then he'd have to think of another way. But the tug had nothing but the engine ring, ejection seat and a magnetic clamp. He smiled, the clamp was attached to a coiled winch.

"Ford?" Eddie's helmet tapped the viewer on Ford's right.

"Hang on, Eddie."

"Not much else I can do."

The Seng flashed passed Ford's view screen: once, he readied the firing mechanism. Twice, Ford took aim. The front of the ship was too far away and the target reticle flashed red. On his next pass he'd try closer, somewhere along the spine. The inertia, combined with the anchor, would still sling shot Huey toward the front of the ship – but with both ends of the ship corkscrewing away from each other, the manoeuvre wasn't going to be pretty, "You really want to be holding on."

"What?"

On three, the reticle flashed green and Ford paused. Huey's spinning would coil the winch around the tug. He punched his rage against the roof above him, watching as the Seng flashed passed again and again. He had to get the engines working. Ford closed his eyes, recalling his training. Under his left foot, next to his oxygen tanks was another compartment, he swivelled his chair around and opened it. If all else fails, manual reboot. Ford reached down, catching flashes in the corner of his eyes, and then they were gone. Replaced by the void and Eddie's hysterics, "Ford..."

Inside the compartment was a three barrelled cylinder with a handle on the top. He grabbed it, twisted it clockwise, pitching the cabin into darkness. He counted silently to ten as Eddie screamed obscenities, and twisted anti-clockwise. The lights flickered on; reboot notifications flashed up on all of the screens. Above them, strobed by Huey's spin, the engine section flashed a white and yellow fire, extinguishing in the vacuum. Hull fragments collided with each other as they raced away from the explosion's epicentre.

Ford took hold of the control stick and found it slack. He was trapped inside a spherical coffin, impotent except to watch the Seng's destruction as it flashed in and out of view. The resulting shock wave, while invisible to his eyes, was inevitably coming for him, "Eddie, I'm sorry." He mustered, "I think this is it."

Eddie didn't reply, or if he did Ford didn't hear it. All he could hear was his own heartbeat thumping loudly in his ears. Distracted and drowning in defeat he nearly missed the reboot messages being replaced by the operational dashboard. Ford pulled back on the control stick once more, he felt the engines bite and he fought to gain control of the spin, "Hell yes." He yelled, lips pulling back over his teeth in one massive grin.

He directed Huey, slowing the spin. A number of bumps against the outside alerted him that Eddie was still there, followed by a, "Woo Hoo." Ford continued to snake the control stick. He didn't have time to stop it, not entirely; the shock wave had to be only seconds away. He aimed the reticule until it flashed green and this time, Ford fired.

The magnetic harpoon took flight, as the Jian Seng's opposite ends tore away from each other in magnesium bright flashes. The harpoon would hit or not, it was in the Universe's hands now. He thought of Greaves, spinning into oblivion and in the corner of his eye he saw the engine give one last almighty effort in destroying him. A ball of fire so bright it forced his eyes shut. Space flashed white and the disintegrating Seng black, the image in negative burned against his retinas. Ford opened his eyes, finding the explosion gone, extinguished by the void, leaving dispersing chunks of hull.

"Saints..." Declared Eddie,

"Damn your Saints." The first explosion Ford now realised hadn't been the engine core. He planted his feet firmly against the floor, stretching his arms out to press his palms against the hull and closed his eyes a moment before the shockwave hit.

Huey lurched, Ford's hands slipped but held against the inner hull. His chair spun as his feet skidded over the floor. His scream met Eddie's as the Huey hurtled away from the blast, riding its wave. Ford opened his eyes, dropping his hands to the control ring and pulled against the spin. His body slowed, but his stomach continued, churning the vomit lashing up his throat. But the hawser was taught and bringing them in hard toward the collapsing spine, "Hell yes." Huey arched from the explosion, racing toward the Seng's bow, "Wow... wow..." He muttered, counting the collision bar reduction. He was coming in way too fast for comfort. He cut the tether, pulling on his stick and steadying their course as best he could.

Huey's beams did little to brighten the darkness, only momentarily catching the dislodged cargo pods and debris as they spun past. It wasn't over, not by a long shot. He was in effect, piloting a thrown hammer. He couldn't slow his approach enough and had no way to dodge the massive obstacles. He'd traded them the same slow death as Greaves for a quicker, crushing experience. Ford fought the controls, enough to stabilise Huey and at least see what was going to hit them.

His eyes trailed from the viewer to the sensors where he could track the blips better. Then found himself looking to his right, settling on the emergency eject button. Housed inside a plastic release cover and surrounded by yellow and black warning stripes. It was an option. His chair would fire up and was built with manoeuvre thrusters. It would be a stretch to land the chair but it was doable. However the decision came with one major flaw. Eddie would remain clinging to the side of Huey, "You still there Ed?"

"Just about."

"Stay with me, I'll get us out of this." He said confidently, without knowing how. Not yet. They were passing the mid-section of the ship, which from his vantage point was no longer part of either end. Thankfully, the explosion had propelled the middle on the same vector as the front. They were headed the right way.

"Ford?"

"Yeah man?"

"Nice knowing you."

"Don't give up." *Just don't,* there had to be a way, "Not yet."

A gargantuan cylinder idly spun into their path, along its side was printed, 'Cargo Pod Twelve.' It was moving too slowly to pass by, and they were moving too fast to swerve. Ford gritted his teeth, "Twice in one day..." his words were bookended by thumps against the hull. Eddie must have seen it, he was hanging on the starboard side which was about to smash into it. Ford turned Huey on its axis, "Move around to the other side."

"No way."

Ford flipped up the cover on the eject button, "What??"

"I'm not floating around here waiting to die."

They were too close to the pod to argue, if Ford waited any longer he'd be crushed inside the tug, "I'll come get you."

"Go to hell Ford."

Ford reached to the roof, spinning locks open as the one thousand metric tons of steel grew closer. He tore his eyes from it, looking up, not even half of the locks were open. He couldn't release the hatch in time, not with enough spare to allow Eddie to grab hold of him.

"What you waiting for?" Eddie screamed,

"I'm trying to save your ungrateful ass." What little time he had left slowed to increments. Joanne, Benjamin, Greaves, and now Eddie. Ford flipped up the plastic cover as Pod Twelve filled his view port.

"Eject. For Saints sake, eject." Yelled Eddie.

Ford slammed the button, ceiling bolts fired up along with the hatch. The pressure inside escaped, glinting metal flashed in front of him. Ford's dog tags were blown out the exit, he reached but they were long gone. A moment later Ford's chair launched into space, looking between his legs he watched Huey crash into the pod. He thought he could hear Eddie's final scream over the sounds of his suit being crushed. Huey pancaked against the pod's surface and then, silence.

There wasn't enough light to see much of anything. He had to rely on his Heads up Display and flickering lights from the Jian Seng to make out the black shapes moving around him. He was at the centre of a maze of lethal obstacles. Slowly, Ford recognised his own breathing, short gasps of panic which he fought to slow. There was enough reality ready to kill him without letting fear get in first.

Ford steered his seat as best he could through the debris field. If he said the controls were clunky, he would have been kind. He may as well have been steering a drunken three legged giraffe. The Jian Seng's nose was sailing away, its own mediocre thrusters pushing it further from the blast to maximise its own survival, completely ignorant to Ford's pleas. That would have been bad enough without the added threat of jagged hull fragments spinning out in all directions.

"Mayday, mayday." He said, "Hi Ford, what'cha up to?" He asked himself, "Oh nothing much, just playing a bit of blind pinball. Except I am the pinball and anything I hit is going to... woah!" The antenna dish blindsided him until the last second, thumbing the controls he span the seat and held his breath, willing it not to hit. The concaved disc rushed past with mere centimetres of grace; thank the 'verse. He continued to corkscrew a descent toward the bow.

Inside his helmet an alarm signalled the seat was running out of juice. He'd already used up the majority of the tank dodging and weaving. His current trajectory was parallel with the Seng, not good if he intended to land. He couldn't adjust to a direct line toward it because there was a cargo pod intent on crossing that path. If he went over it there was a chance he'd pass through a cloud of whatever was pouring out of a nearby pod. There was already torn sections of the spinal corridor below it, but it would have moved out of the way by the time he got there. It all depended on what was behind it, "Get it together Ford." He said aloud. There wasn't time to deliberate, "Think dickhead, think!" He forced a decision, "Over it is."

He fired the seat's thrusters again, the course took him away from the Jian Seng, but another correction once he cleared the pod's path and he'd be good to go. Providing nothing else was there, "Is there anybody out there?" He reminded himself that only crazy people talked to themselves, "Only if they answer back." The cargo pod past beneath him, "That's my boy." He corrected his course, pointing himself at the Seng. Now that he was closer to the second pod, he could see what was spewing from its innards. A white line, sparkling against his seat's meagre lamp, was being drawn in space as the pod moved out to oblivion. It was grain, from the terraforming hold.

Ford couldn't be sure of the speed of which he moved, or how safe it would be to pass through thousands of frozen grain and so avoided it, containing his curious urge to lower his fingers into it as he skimmed over the millions of still born seeds. Once past, he had empty space between him and the Seng, but only enough power for one last course correction, "Just one break, is that too much to ask?" a direct shot at home. The alarm gave a final, ear piercing bleep before dying with the last of the chair's fuel.

As the Seng got closer, it became more apparent on how fast his approach actually was, and it was too fast. His feet would hit the hull first, then his face and hands with the chair moving up through his ass and out his mouth. That was if he was lucky, "That's not going to happen." Ford unbuckled his belt, the Seng racing toward him. He fumbled his way out of the seat as best he could, with no gravity to help him he slipped his way to a crouch facing the wrong way around and pulled himself over the back of it as the chair began to spin. He succeeded in placing the chair between him and home, but only with seconds to spare.

The chair hit and bounced off the hull, Ford let go of the saddle and scrambled for something to grab hold of as he slid across the riveted surface. He found one of the plate bolts and pulled against it, he was still moving too fast. His fingers strained against the bolt until it tore free from his grasp. His arms and legs flailed for something to grab onto when he remembered his boots. Using the control panel on his wrist, he lit up the magnetics. A satisfying electrical hum filled his suit and both soles of his feet locked to the hull while his body continued on. He arched backward, the invisible force still pulling him along his original route. Ford yelled as his legs and feet attempted to separate from one another.

There he waited, listening to his breathing inside the suit until the pain faded. Outside, space looked just as peaceful as it had before the ordeal had started. Straightening up, he began to see the destruction behind the Seng. Like a cloud of bubbles, the rear parts of the ship danced. He couldn't count how many parts and didn't like to think on it longer than needed. How he'd managed to survive was beyond him.

"Greaves?" He asked the void, "Sharon, can you hear me?" She was still out there. Her air tank wouldn't have died yet. He knew she'd be too small to see from where he stood, so imagined she was one of the specs on the peripheral of the blast radius. The thought of her alone out there without hope sickened him, "Sharon?" He continued to call her name, searching the cosmos for the impossible. It didn't matter if he couldn't hear her, what mattered was there could be a chance, no matter how small, that she could hear him.

"Sharon, I'm here for you." He continued, "I got us that drink, Schnapps. The blue kind you had in Jefferson's Memorial." The bar on Asturas, "It's been quite a day..."

He didn't know how long he'd been standing there, talking and watching the debris field move further out. But eventually his air tank signalled its ten minute warning; a large red exclamation mark filled his visor, bringing him back inside his own suit. Not long now, he guessed if not already. He doubted she'd be breathing normal, calm breaths. But hopefully at the end, she'd found peace.

***

Bounette strapped the leg at the thigh, pulling the leather taught and then picked up the saw. He would have preferred to do it properly, but without an assistant there was no option other than to turn to dark age medical practices. He counted down from three, activating the rotary blade on two. It spun silently, jaws blurring into a transparent line at the edge of the metal wheel. Despite all the training and experience he'd gained over the years the apprehension before making the cut still caught in his throat.

The counting down helped focus him, when he reached one he touched the blur against his father-in-law's leg. The flesh sprung away from the cut, revealing muscle and spraying blood up along Bounette's green sanitised glove and white overalls. Drops splashed his face guard and then, just as the ship shook, the ripping vibration of bone invaded his ears.

He immediately withdrew his attack on the limb, switching off the blade as the ceiling lamps flickered. Bounette breathed in deeply, *what now?*

"Bounette?" John's voice spoke from the wall speakers,

"Here." The room shook again and a moment later it didn't stop shaking, a slow vibration causing everything around him to rattle.

"They've started separation."

"So have I..." He muttered,

"What?"

"Nothing." Bounette rolled his eyes, dropping a gloved hand to the side of the gurney and stabilising his own tremors. When on Earth, back at the academy he'd learned of the military class ships having gimbals supporting operating theatres; so that even in battle it was almost impossible for the exterior forces to impede the surgeons work, "And I have your worthless piece of crap." He told his unconscious Father in Law, "You do make it difficult." Then, a little louder, "Some notice would have been good."

"Deal with it." John returned sharply,

Bounette clipped the saw's handle to the side of the gurney. Grabbed a hand full of clips and weaved his fingers around the sinew until he found the femoral artery. There was a tie further up the leg, as well as Nanos clotting the flow. However, the thick dark viscous blood persisted. He intended on fastening the clip a couple of centimetres up from the severed end, "Tu es con." Bounette screamed as the artery slipped from his fingers and retracted back into the leg.

"Did you say something Jake?"

His previously stacked crates at the end of the room rattled, vibrations running up his leg, "I'm good John." He replied, fishing for the artery. The muscles slopped apart as he dug his fingers in deeper until he felt the pulsing tube. He squeezed tight, pulling slowly until he saw it and braced it with the clip, letting the jaws fasten around the artery, "Mords moi."

A violent crash hit the room. Bounette's back slammed into the ceiling before he realised what was happening or before he'd let go of the clip. The teeth pulled the artery out of the leg. It drew taught before tearing the tip clean, spewing out arterial blood. Bounette hit the floor a second later. The room spun, his vision blurred and his nose numbed, "Putain..." he cursed, bringing his hand to his face, touching his tender and swelling nose.

With the room still vibrating, he climbed to his feet. He couldn't be sure if the room was shaking more than before or if it was due to the bump to his head, but he forced himself to stagger to the workstation, finding it empty. The room was once again in disarray. He stumbled through the vibrations, falling to his knee. The shock shot up his thigh and tore out his throat in a horse scream. His eyes focused in an instant, cursing, he forced himself back to his feet. Swaying with the room he crashed into the wall, rolling along the cupboards until he grabbed a handle. He yanked it open, the dishevelled interior was expected but the electrocauter was right there on the top. Still holding onto to the door for support, he snatched hold of it.

Eyes wide, his mouth forming a maniacal grin, he laughed, luck was on his side now. All he needed to do was get back to the gurney...

Bounette's jaw dropped sharply. Inside the quarantine bay; the webbing that held the stasis tube in place had torn and the tube was wriggling free. It wouldn't be long before it was sliding back and forth around the room or slamming into a wall, and if that happened... The transparent steel wall segregating quarantine from the rest of the medical bay was strong. It would hold, he reminded himself. There was no chance of contaminating the rest of the ship.

His arm tightened, the room was now tilting at an obscene angle and he watched in dismay as Crudge's gurney slid on its locked wheels. Pocketing his new tool, he chased after it, bounding over the shifting terrain and caught the gurney with his crotch. His front landed on the old man's chest, but the comatose face didn't flinch. He wiped blood from his face and slid into position, retrieving the electrocauter and primed it. Locking himself onto the gurney with his elbow and knee, he delved his fingers into the man's leg once more.

The cloth under the leg was no longer white, but a deep dark red. Even with his pulse slowed and the Nanobots working, Crudge may have lost too much blood. Bounette took hold of the pulsating artery and pulled the rubbery worm free. He pressed the electrocauter against the artery's tip and sealed it. Then, another violent crash and this time, Bounette found himself mid-air and racing toward the quarantine bay.

***

Ford's knees slammed against the deck. His hands spun the helmet unlocking and releasing it with a deep gasp for air. The cold rushed around his clammy skin and he shivered right down to his paddling pool boots. His mind travelled through the ship, along its interwoven tunnels to his personal quarters and the bottle of Cockburn's waiting to be opened. He deserved it after what he'd been through.

Or at least, that's what he told himself. Bracing the helmet against the floor he used the leverage to stand.

He'd entered the tug bay from the port side personnel lock, the shortest possible route from where he'd marooned himself. He hadn't expected a fan fair on his return, knowing his companions were elsewhere and probably had more pressing issues to be attending to. Besides which, the last communication he had with the Seng was before the engine blew. They could think him dead, or the more appropriate fear was that he was the only living survivor.

The bay certainly gave that impression. What little of the emergency lighting worked, winked on and off every other second. It gave the huge hall a far too empty and haunting impression. He couldn't look at any one thing for long before it was snatched from him by the darkness. Familiar objects like the two remaining ducks or the alcove near the bilge pipes, where engineers went to sneak a rest, became no more than apparitions.

He bit into the Velcro strap on his right glove and tore it free, removing the second just as quickly before moving onto the sealed zip under his arm. The cool of the bay washed over his hot flesh, chilling his sweat and he stamped away the cold through his sodden socks, "This was a bad idea." He told himself, running across the bay to the engineer's room and leaving his discarded exposure suit on the ground.

He palmed the switch, which did nothing and the blinking emergency lamps continued to tease him, "Great." Next on his mental list, he pressed the comms button, "Hello, anyone there?" With no reply he carried on to his next objective. He knew the engineer lockers, lined neatly against the wall opposite, would have dry clothes. The only catch was that each had a thumb print lock. He rifled through the desk to his right, pulling drawers out glimpsing the contents before the lamps went off again, "I know you're in here somewhere."

Eventually he found them, Chief's master key. From there it was plain sailing. He inserted the cylindrical magnet into the hole of each locker. He found an orange jumpsuit that almost fitted and wasted no time in getting into it, pulling the collar around his neck as the locker door opened enough for the lamps to light the pictures stuck on the inside. Ford paused, unable to avoid staring at Bennie holding Eddie in a head lock, knuckling his friends' hair.

The picture had been taken on the Seng, Ford recognised the torn cushions of the rec-room sofa behind them, but he didn't recognise the time. It must have been before he'd returned to ship, they looked so happy he couldn't help but share the joy locked in that millisecond of time, if only for a moment. He wanted to say something. But a simple sorry wasn't going to cut it, he needed something with gravitas, but that something alluded him. Instead, he closed the locker door, wondering which one belonged to her. Sharon Greaves. The girl with the delicious eyebrows, who'd never share that promised drink. Ford shook the thoughts away, reminding himself that he had to keep moving and grabbed a pair of a boots. Next he moved to the engineer terminal and pressed the comms button, "Hello, anyone alive?"

The lights winked out again and he grabbed a flashlight from the charging station and headed back into the bay. The lamp's beam swept the floor, slashing through the shadows and leading him to the elevator. He pressed the call button, relieved to hear the mechanisms behind the door coming to life.

When it arrived, he entered the cabin and pressed the only option, the infirmary. He expected to find Bounette and Crudge, with maybe the girl's stasis tube in quarantine, but when the doors opened the first face he saw was Natalie's. Red faced and cursing, she was dragging his father through the door, "What happened?"

She threw him a scolding look, "Some Help..."

Ford rushed to his Father, shifting to a position under the old man's left armpit and helped Natalie drag him into the infirmary. John's nostrils and lips were charred black and turned Ford's blood to ice, "What happened?" He repeated his question.

"He was on the bridge-" She was unfocused, "Trying to put things back..."

"Nat."

"Jake..." She said, "Ford, I'm sorry." She lowered John to the ground,

Ford brushed John's hair line back, "Dad..."

John's eyes opened, tragically slow.

"There you are." Ford smiled, "I knew you'd be okay."

"I'm hurt." John mustered,

"Yes, you're in the infirmary. What happened?"

John coughed, giving up any intention of answering the question. Ford became impatient, looking behind him. Bounette stood on his own two feet, but he was groggy. His nose had bled, which was now crusted over his lips and he had the eyes of a mad man.

Bounette shoved Natalie away, whipping his arms about him as he staggered back against the wall. His shouts were articulate, yet French. But Ford got the meaning. He didn't want his wife or anyone else touching him. Ford tapped his dad on the shoulder, "I'll be right back."

He walked toward Bounette, "Calm down buddy, it's alright."

Bounette's crazed eyes looked through Ford as he barked more French.

"Stay out of it, Ford." Natalie spoke softly, her focus on her husband and she continued the conversation with her husband in French. Her tone and words were velvet, disarming Bounette's rage. The doctor's shoulders dropped, his arms appearing too heavy to hold up.

"Ford..." John called weakly to his son.

Ford took one last look at Doctor Bounette, who appeared to be submitting to his wife's soothing charms, "Yes?"

"I don't..." He coughed, rolling up on to his left side, "feel too great."

"No, you don't look great either." Ford sat on his haunches, "Jake will be back with us in a second or two, I think he got out of the wrong side of the bed."

John took one look at the doctor and nodded, "He never likes being woken."

"Welcome back." Ford shouted over to the Frenchman,

Bounette waved, "You okay, John?"

"Better than you."

Ford agreed with his dad's observation, Bounette's face was bruised black around his eyes. Caked blood stained his face, but he was becoming more attuned to his situation with each passing second, "Who's the doctor here?"

"I don't think there is one, unless you're counting that doctorate you crayoned."

"Why don't you walk over here and say that to my face." Bounette grinned back,

"Doc." Ford snapped, "Captain needs you."

Jake Bounette blinked, "Of course," and scurried over to John, "when did you turn up?"

"Natalie brought him in." Ford said, "Actually, Nat how did you get him down here?"

"He collapsed off the ladder, it wasn't pretty." She said, "Is there anything I need to do with dad?"

Bounette said something in French to her as he crouched next to Ford, adding, "Antibiotics are in the drawers over there." pointing over John's head.

"How is he?" John asked,

"Nothing some blood and a nice cold nap won't sort out." Bounette said, "Now, what happened with you, John?"

"Electrical fire."

"You breathed it?"

John nodded, unable to keep his eyes open. Bounette slipped his hand under John's arm, "Help me get him on the chair."

Ford complied, trying not to let his father's laboured breathing worry him.

"I hope this looks worse than it is." Bounette thought aloud, "If this is any indication of how the lungs are..."

"Where's everyone else?" asked John,

"Crudge is knocked out on the gurney." Bounette deflected,

"Everyone else?" John repeated his question to Ford.

At first, Ford's words caught in his mouth. He took a breath and forced himself to focus, "They're gone."

"Ford, get my bag. Natalie will know where it is."

"I'm not your errant boy."

Bounette said nothing, pushing against Ford's stubbornness until he relented.

"Fine."

"Merci." Bounette unzipped the Captain's jumpsuit and Ford discovered to his horror John's tattoos were painted with the man's own blood.

"Quickly Ford." Bounette ordered.

Ford who was now in no doubt of the emergency of the situation left his Father in the Doctor's care, rushing to Natalie, "Nat, where does he keep his bag?"

"Second drawer on the left." Natalie answered and Ford reached for the drawer, "No, not that one, the big drawer. No, the other one. You got it."

Ford lifted the bag out when a glint of metal drew his attention; underneath the bag was a waiter's friend. He pocketed it, intending to use it on his port once this mess had been sorted, "Got it."

"Good. Bring it here." Bounette ordered "Now I need a foil blanket."

Ford dropped the bag at the doctor's feet, "Where would I find one of those?" Natalie showed him.

By the time he returned, Bounette had cleaned and stapled the wound in John's gut, and proceeded to wrap him up in the blanket like a taco. He then jabbed him with microbes, and surveyed the internal damage.

Ford grimaced, "How is he?"

"Not good. I can inject some repair-crobes..." Bounette addressed John directly, "But I have to put you on ice, Captain. I can't fix you with what I have."

"No way." Ford folded his arms, "We can't do that."

"It's the only thing I can do."

"What are we going to do without him, he's the Captain?"

"I'm sorry Ford, I've done what I can."

Ford's veins protruded from his temples, his hands found the back of his head before he turned around, kicking at the floor.

"It's okay." John said, "Swap me out with Mason."

"Mason's not half the man you are." Ford snapped,

"Wrong, son. He's more." John coughed, "At least at the moment."

"This isn't happening." Ford stared at his feet, unable to process the information, "There has to be another way."

John went to say something, but lurched forward as a bout of violent coughs racked his body and black mucus dribbled over his lips.

Natalie grabbed Ford by his shoulders, "Ford, get a hold of yourself."

"What, you're my mother now?"

"Back off..." Bounette stood between them, "Now."

Ford laughed, he couldn't help himself. Bounette couldn't fight his way out of a ration bag, "Fix him."

"How many more times do you need me to say it?" Bounette puffed out his chest, "I can't, and delaying the matter only makes it worse."

Ford couldn't explain it, this need for his father's presence. He'd left ship to get away from him, but now he couldn't face losing him, "I can't process this."

"I'll be fine, son. Just get me on ice before I cough up the other lung." The lights went out as if to elaborate on John's sense of urgency. The ship was dying and now the only light came from the Ultra Violet strips inside the quarantine bay.

"Jake." Natalie called urgently to her husband. Everyone turned to see what she was pointing at. The young rescue now stood staring back at them. For the love of the Trinity, the girl was standing. Her stasis tube had broken free, the top end was smashed and whatever it was made of covered the floor. Bloody foot prints tracked over the shattered tube to the centre of the room. Her skin, other than around her right foot which was red, remained porcelain white. The surgical gown hung like ghostly rags on her slight frame but it was her expressionless face that haunted Ford.

Natalie stepped up to the inter-com and spoke into it, "Hey there."

The girl didn't respond, in fact she didn't move. Not even to breathe.

"My name's Natalie. You're on board our ship, we rescued you."

Still, there was no response. Ford felt his blood turning cold, and whatever negative vibe she gave off had infected Bounette also, "Natalie. Step away from her."

"What?"

"Step away from the wall, please." Bounette repeated, "She's just a little girl."

"Nat." He frowned, "Get the hell away from that wall."

She did, rejoining the group a metre away, "Why?"

"Because I'm scared!" Bounette's bruises were now in dark contrast with his clammy face; sweat gathered along his hairline, his were hands clenched and his knuckles white.

"What do you know..." Ford began asking when Natalie interrupted,

"How the hell do you think she feels? She's woken up with a bang, cut her foot and found herself on a strange ship."

"Look closer."

But Ford had already noticed the source of Bounette's concern.

"She's not breathing."

Natalie shook her head, "That's absurd."

"What's wrong with her?" Ford asked,

"I don't know." Admitted Bounette, "But you've all got bigger things to worry about right now."

"Bigger things than little miss zombie?" said Ford,

"He's right." Natalie said, "We need to re-establish power. I can already feel the temperature dropping." Now it had been said, Ford noticed the chill in the air. If the heating and lights had both stopped, then it meant the life support systems were shutting down. He could still hear the fans in the air-flow ducts above them so they were still breathing the freshest air the Jian Seng could offer, but it was only a matter of time before that too, shut down. The dead girl standing would have to wait. If he was honest with himself, he hadn't the faintest idea how to deal with her anyway.

"I mean putting these old timers on ice." Bounette replied, but patting his arms warm all the same.

"Any ideas?" Ford asked, "For the power, we can work out the details on route to stasis."

"Yes." Natalie stated, "The ducks have independent power cores. I should be able to route one of them to life support, it won't give us a huge amount of time. But we can extend that by dropping some bulk heads around non-essentials and then turning off the rest of the ship."

"You're the smart one." John said,

"The smartest." Bounette added, touching her shoulder.

"We should see if we still have access to cargo pod six." Said John,

"Huh?" Ford,

"Terra-forming gear."

"Worth a shot." Natalie said, "There'll be suits, possibly generators."

Bounette knew John was wrong, "Pod six is filled with cosmetics and prosthetics."

"You sure?" John raised an eyebrow, "When did you start taking an interest in carg..." He failed to finish his sentence in favour of another bout of coughing. He'd run out of time, John had to get into stasis now.

"There's some new tech from the spring catalogue, I asked Jo to show me when we left Saturn 3."

"Oh." Both of John's eyebrows reached for his receding hairline, "Then we'll check the manifest and see which one it is."

"*We* will." Bounette said, "*You*, you're going on ice."

John opened his mouth but thought better of it, simply nodding in agreement.

"Good." Bounette said, "We don't have another gurney, so we're going to have to wheel him on the chair. We won't be able to get him up to deck one, so he's going to have to slum it in the emergency tubes."

"I'll wheel dad." Natalie said, "Then we should strip down one of the ducks, we'll have time to search the pods once the power is back up."

Bounette nodded, he saw that Ford did too, "While you're doing that, I'll be keeping an eye on our guest."

"You're sure?" Natalie asked

"It sounds a waste of time to me." Ford added,

"Yeah, once the power is back I'll have access to Q-Bay's analysis systems. We should know what we're dealing with." Bounette appeared to have a work avoidance issue.

"You're okay with being alone with her? You were pretty scared of her breaking out."

"I didn't want her breaking her skull against it." Bounette said, tonguing his loose teeth, "Besides, I need to set my nose."

Natalie stepped up to him, kissing him on the cheek, "Don't do anything stupid."

"Too late for that." He replied, "I married you."

FIVE

It had been a short painful trip, pushing the gurney from the infirmary. More than a couple of times, Ford had lost control and nearly tipped his father onto the floor. Natalie at least, seemed more proficient in steering. At least, Ford reminded himself, they didn't have to climb any ladders. By the time they arrived at the emergency stasis bay, John was in and out of consciousness. This was probably a good thing as Ford didn't know what to say anyway. Natalie wasn't in a talking mood either and after discussing the power situation further, had gone ahead with Crudge's gurney, returning to help Ford for the last leg. *No pun intended.*

On entering the room, Ford noted Crudge's gurney waiting for them. They rolled John up to the closest tube and Natalie opened it as Ford got ready to heave his dad's dead weight into what could well be his final resting place. Of course, if they were rescued then he'd probably survive his injuries. But with everything going on, Ford couldn't help but feel like it was. One by one, everyone he knew had died, or a good chance of being dead sooner or later; him included. Like a broken record, all he could hear was his greatest failings as a person and as a son. He hadn't been there for his Mother, he'd not been there for the engineering team and had yet again he'd failed to be there for his Father.

"While we're here, we should wake up Becca and Mason." Ford suggested,

"I..." Natalie gritted her teeth and dropped her eyes from Ford's gaze, "don't think we can. We don't have any power, the more lungs we have the less time we get. Depending on how much power we get from the duck..." She looked up, "Ford, I can't see us waking anyone. Not unless we put you, me or Bounette to sleep." She'd spoken from a defeated heart and Ford couldn't question it. Their backs were firmly against the wall.

He shook his head, "We're in the crapper, aren't we?"

"Yes, yes we are." She grimaced, stepping up beside him, "Ready?"

He nodded and slipped his hands under his father's arms while she took his legs. They counted to three and lifted him onto the bed. John mumbled something, mucus foaming at his lips. Natalie looked to Ford with an expression asking him whether or not he wanted some time, his initial thought was, 'for what?' His father was non-responsive. He shrugged, she raised an eyebrow and he gave in, "Okay." He leaned over the tube's side, resting his arms on the lip and spoke into John's ear, "Dad?" He didn't respond, all Ford could hear was the laboured wheezing of his father's chest. He looked to Natalie, but she'd already moved on, leaning over her own father.

Ford ran his eyes over the tube's control panel; it was already receiving information from its occupant and displaying the medical concerns. Most of it he couldn't understand, but the long list of faults was enough. He looked at his dad, peaceful and at rest. He didn't want to disturb him, but this could be the last time they ever spoke, "Dad?" a little louder. This time his father's eyes blinked, but they didn't stay open, even the dim lighting of the emergencies seemed too bright for him. After a slight cough, he opened his mouth and spoke.

"Ford."

The smile grew, unintentional and unrestrained on Ford's face, "Dad." He repeated, still having no idea what to say, "You're in the stasis bunk, you're going get through this." It was the second promise of its kind he'd made. But now; under the shadow of disaster, he feared his promises were empty.

John's head rolled toward his son's voice, "Be." He said and then coughed so violently his upper torso leapt up from the bed. Ford reached to support his father's back as he emptied his lungs over this chin and chest. The fluid was sickly and black, a mixture of congealed blood and burned tissue.

Fear whispered in his ear to run, run and hide from this. It would have been easy, but for his sister's scolding over not being there when his mother had finally past. He hadn't realised until that moment, not truly, what both Becca and his father had gone through without him. His mother had died a slow, miserable death. Now here, witnessing his father's demise he understood the resentment she'd showed him. He'd needed to be there, not just for his mother but for them. Just as he now needed her to hold his arm and tell him it was going to be okay.

The coughing continued, echoing in the small chamber and enough for Natalie to crane her head around to check if everything was okay. Ford nodded, letting her know to go back and make peace with her own father. When the coughing subsided, John was fully aware of his surroundings. Ford lowered him back onto the bed, where he made shallow breaths to avoid another fit. He licked his lips, preparing himself to speak.

However, it was Ford who did so first, "I'm sorry, dad. I'm sorry I wasn't here for you. I was stupid, so stupid. I wanted to make a change, to stand up to you and instead I ran away." John just smiled. He reached out and tapped the back of Ford's fingers, now curled around the edge of the bed, His son continued, "I should have been here for you, for mum."

"She knew." John murmured, "You loved her..." He coughed, "As she did... you."

Ford breathed sharply, his father's words cutting him deeply as he felt tears run down his cheeks, "I should have been here."

John smiled, tears building in his own eyes as he shook his head in the contrary, "Your... life..." was all he managed before another coughing fit consumed him. Ford now found it ironic that the time he actually wanted to speak with his father was the time his father couldn't properly return the conversation. Ford wanted now, more than anything else, to tell him everything. He'd not done so on his return or at any time since and the regret pooled in his stomach like the oily mucus that slewed from his father's lips. But this was not the time for a confessional, his father needed to be put on ice. This conversation had to end and his regrets left unsaid.

He laid John down again once the latest coughing bout had finished, using his sleeve to wipe the fresh mucus from his father's mouth and chin, "Don't speak." Ford said, "We'll pick this up on the flip side." He grimaced, knowing his words to be hollow. John cleared his throat, but Ford raised a hand, "No, I'm closing the lid." On the tube and the conversation, "The next time we speak, we'll be in a real hospital, one with all the whistles and bells."

"Wait." John whispered, waving his son closer.

Against his better judgement, Ford obeyed his father one last time and leaned in closer to hear what he had to say.

"Go to... bridge." John said, almost inaudible; with gaps long enough to make Ford turn his head believing his father had finished, "Beware... Albacore..."

Ford lingered, waiting for a continuation, which did not come. He finally raised his head and saw his father had passed out, his chest raising and falling peacefully once again. *What did he mean? 'Beware Albacore?' What the hell was an Albacore?* He looked across the room and found Natalie leaning against the next stasis tube. She was looking back at him but also at her sleeping father. Ford stood upright, typed in the commands and lowered the lid of his father's tube, waiting until it closed before stepping away. He made his way around the bed, to Crudge's gurney and got in position to lift him.

When Natalie arrived at her father's feet, she finally gave in to her curiosity, "What did he say?"

"I don't know." Ford answered honestly, "Yet."

***

Ford wasn't an engineer, but knew the basics from what Crudge taught him. Along with that, he'd taken many mandatory courses so when Natalie handed him one end of the cable from Dewey and told him to take it as far as he could to the bridge, he knew, not only that it was not going to be long enough, but he was going to have to daisy chain it across the Tug Bay to the electrical riser cupboard. But as long as there wasn't a break in the power conduit, a simple hook up would have power running up and down all decks.

"The bridge is fried, so you're going to have to lump a couple of cables up there and run a line direct from the top riser." She smiled,

"Anything else?"

"I think that's enough for now, don't you?"

"We could wake Mason... a couple of others and make short work of this?" He pleaded, "They can go back on ice once we've finished?"

"We're running on reserves." She dismissed him, "Once we get the auxiliary up and running, we'll free up some power, run some maths to see how many we can wake. But Ford, you have to realise that without the engines this is just a waiting game now." She stressed, "The more people we have awake, the less time we give ourselves."

He nodded in compliance, "Never argue with maths. Do we have enough cable?"

Natalie pointed across the bay. Behind Dewey was a floor to ceiling cage, "We should have reels of it in there."

After checking the power conduit in the riser non-functional he considered re-suggesting waking the crew. The thought of lugging cables up ladders for the rest of the day had him planning an escape to his room and the Cockburns waiting for him. But getting drunk was just as bad idea as approaching Natalie with the same plan she'd shot down twice already. Resigned to the task at hand he entered the crew cage.

The cables were ten metres long with a hermaphrodite socket on both ends and heavy as hell. It took him close to half an hour to string them all together, taking one end as far as it reached before trekking back to collect another and then drag its heavy ass until he reached the end of the previous one, and so on and so forth until he reached the Bridge. On the third return to the bay, he noticed a trolley parked in the corner. Thankfully, Natalie had long since disappeared.

It sped things up, at least on the bay deck but he still had to work the ladders and the command deck by himself. Given its thickness the cable didn't like being spooled as tight as it needed to fit on the trolley either and it slipped off more than once, but he felt like he was saving time.

The bridge was in a worse mess than Ford had last seen it. Whatever his father had attempted to do up here, the twister had destroyed it. The one chair that still stood was the Captain's, remaining stoic in the face of disaster. Ford gritted his teeth, ploughed into the mess, carving out a route to the power inlet.

After connecting the cable to the power inlet, he sat in his Father's chair as the systems rebooted and the lights came on. Joanne. Benjamin. Edward. Sharon. He made a promise sitting there in the Captain's chair that he'd be the one to tell how their deaths meant the survival of the rest of Jian Seng's crew. A moment later, he remembered his father's warning, 'Get to bridge, beware Albacore'. He looked around the, wondering what his father had meant. None of the bridge systems were online, most had been smashed when the ceiling grid collapsed and everything was covered in fire suppression dust.

He pressed the comms channel on the chair's armrest, "Guys?" Both remaining crew members acknowledged him, "Power's on at the bridge."

"Good work." Natalie said, "Take five, I'm just about done checking the stasis chambers and we can take a look what's for grabs in the storage pods once I get to operations."

"Is everyone okay?" He asked,

"So far so good, I've another section to check. Becca is fine."

"Copy that." He said, allowing the relief to ebb through his veins, "Hey, either of you know what, or who an Albacore is?" He looked over the bridge again, but nothing stood out to him.

"Albacore? What you talking about? Sorry, Ford, I've no idea." Natalie said. Bounette agreed.

Dissatisfied, Ford left the chair and wandered the bridge. His earlier observations repeated themselves; while not all of the terminals were smashed they were all out of operation. Ford chewed his lower lip, slowly rotating on his heels while taking in a feel for the room. Part of the ceiling had fallen onto the right hand side of the deck. He rubbed the top of his head, remembering the bump from the vent grille. The fire suppression dust covered what had fallen, so the fire had started after it collapsed. In fact the only place the dust didn't cover was the Captain's chair. His father had been supremely lucky in not being hit.

He knew his father had been sat there, the dust told him that and knowing his father he would have remained on the Bridge as the ship went down. Therefore, whatever John Dahl wanted him to see would have to be accessible from that position. Ford returned to the chair, looking at both left and right arm controls. On the right arm was a button for internal comms with an all hands symbol underneath, which Ford had just used. Just under that, was an external comms button, on, off, mute and a frequency finder.

He thought about this for a while and slowly came to realise that Albacore could be an external factor. He pressed the button and found nothing but static. He pondered on whether or not to call out and test his theory that the Albacore was out there. His finger hovered over the button. He teased the thought further and would have pressed it if the second part of his father's message hadn't been a warning. He needed to know why first. He put himself inside his father's head, trying to work out what the old man wanted him to find. It had to be here, on the bridge. But the bridge was a demolition site. Yet it had to be here, it had to have survived...

A glint in Ford's eye brightened as the answer formed in his mind, "Nice one dad." He stood and started climbing over the fallen ceiling grid to the wall on the other side. Grilles shifted under foot but held his weight. As he crested the top of the heap he lost his footing. Metal sheets groaned under his weight, sliding under foot and sending him toward the bottom. With an impromptu obscenity, Ford raised his hands to balance himself and hit one of the air-conditioning pipes above him. He grabbed it with both hands as the heap collapsed below him. He felt it's chill in an instant, but it was a small price to pay to avoid being crushed. Once steady, he moved his foot to the terminal poking its head out of the mess. From there he jumped to the floor. The ship's black box was accessible from two areas of the ship, one was the main computer. The other was behind the panel which he now stood in front of.

He pried open the panel and undid the black box form it's resting place. Now standing, with his back against wall he looked at the mess before him and wondered what his chances were of making it back across carrying the added weight. There was only one thing to do, so with all his might he threw the black box across the debris. The recording device was built with disaster in mind and the throw across the room didn't do any harm. Following it, Ford treaded carefully and ensured a safe landing on the other side.

"Ford?" Natalie's voice called from the speakers, just in time for him to reply.

"Still on the bridge Nat, I'm going to need a couple more minutes."

"What are you doing?"

"I'm about to listen to the black box."

"Ford." She sounded pissed, "We've got more important things to deal with."

He couldn't believe he was going to say this but, "Dad told me to. That's what he whispered to me before we put him on ice."

160

"And, what's that going to help with, Ford?"

"I don't know. But it's got something to do with Albacore, whatever that is? You still in Ops?"

"Yeah."

"I'll meet you there."

***

"Did he give any indication of what's on it?" Natalie asked,

Ford shrugged, the box lay on the Ops table and he was busy feeding a data line from one of the sockets along its metal frame, "Nothing other than go to the bridge and beware Albacore."

Natalie hopped her ass onto the table, leaning over the box to examine it, "That's not ominous... at all"

Ford snapped the plug into the socket, "All yours."

"Have you ever seen one of these before?" She asked, pressing her hand flat against the glass top and activating its touch screen.

Ford recalled his part of a search and rescue, waiting on board the hopper while his team searched the wreckage of a downed bird. It had been three months or so into his tour, they'd found no survivors but they had retrieved the bird's black box, it was far smaller than the one he'd hauled from the bridge but both were bright red with yellow fonts announcing what it was to whoever read them, "Yeah." He said.

"Oh?" Natalie probed as she keyed in her request. Ford ignored her, watching as a virtual link presented itself on the table's surface. A green throbbing light surrounded the black box, with a line drawing itself to a list of commands which were also outlined in green. "What's on it?" He asked,

"See for yourself." She said,

Ford craned his head toward the list for a better look. The box recorded sections of conversation from the bridge, each was time coded at the beginning of the conversation and ended thirty seconds after the last word was spoken. Knowing the time line of events, he extrapolated five conversations from the black box. The first would have been when he was also there. The second would have been Mason recording the Buoy's transmission. The other three would have been his father. "Play the last three?" He suggested,

"You're the boss." She said,

He tapped the third recording from the bottom and heard his father's voice. A typical back and forth exchange between him and Bounette. Both Ford and Natalie looked at each other and grinned as Bounette moaned and groaned over having to clean the infirmary by himself. However, the smiles didn't last long. Ford's own voice now joined the conversation, updating his father on their progress and how he'd sent some of the crew onto the engines while he and Greaves were going to investigate the Centurion. He lost track of the conversation from there, his mind wandering to his last moments with Greaves and how she'd died, floating all alone out there. He picked up on his father's abrupt ending to the conversation; at the time he'd was overjoyed not to get a grilling.

The voice of an unfamiliar third party interrupted, while static interfered with the message it was clear it had been from another ship. Another ship called, Albacore. Ford found Natalie staring at him, so he raised an eyebrow but there was nothing on the message that raised any alarms. Not yet, but it did remind Ford of how his father was acting when he dropped Crudge off with him at the hanger bay.

He'd wanted to know if he'd seen anything out there. At the time, he'd said no. But of course he had and that was when the alarm erupted in his head. The conversation, albeit a one sided one ended and his father continued to bicker with Bounette for a while before the recording ended. Only then did either of them speak, "It's a ship then." Natalie stated,

"Sounds like." Ford said, eagerly anticipating the next recording, "Shall I?"

"Knock yourself out."

He pressed the second from last recording, this time it was his own voice which came on first. It was his second progress report to his father. Nothing new, nothing of importance other than the guilt of those he'd left behind. He felt Natalie's hand on his shoulder; he looked her in the eye and smiled, "I'm okay." He stared at the last time stamp, he wasn't sure but he'd bet his worth on it being just prior to the twister and that stayed his hand. As much as he wanted to hear what John needed him to, he didn't revel in the idea of hearing the bridge collapsing on top of his dad.

Natalie must have sensed what Ford was feeling as she reached across him, "Here, let me." and pressed her finger on the time stamp.

John's voice said, "Bounette."

"Here."

"They've started separation."

"So have I..."

"What?"

"Nothing."

After a moment's pause, the sound of a belt being pulled from its spool ran through the speakers, "Where are you Nat?" John's voice continued. *Click*, his belt was secure.

Natalie's own voice was heard to say, "I'm in Ops. I'm not going to make it back in time." This was followed by the Captain ordering to get strapped in where she was because they were starting the twister.

Both Ford and Natalie leaned in closer to the speaker. Ford became very aware of her breath breaking against his neck. The next sounds they heard were those of chaos. Explosions, alarms and a lot of cursing. Conversation had stopped, at least for the majority of the group. John continued to call their names, his concern for his crew overshadowing any fear in his voice. Natalie's hand squeezed Ford's and he saw the terror in her eyes as vivid as the sounds that surrounded them. These were real sounds, triggering memories of the ship tearing itself apart. He placed his free hand on top of hers as the Albacore returned to the party.

John's voice sounded almost desperate, "...Albacore. Do you copy? Over." They'd returned at their bleakest hour, with a fleeting hope of rescue. A rescue which Ford knew now hadn't come.

"Albacore." His father's voice, "This is the Jian Seng, we hear you. Over." His voice was accompanied by a torrent of violence, so much so Ford wasn't sure whether he'd have understood him unless he'd known his father's voice enough to pull it free from all the noise.

Then, "This is the UES Albacore. Do you copy? Over."

"Albacore, this is the Jian Seng. We Copy. Over." John repeated,

"This is the UES Albacore. Do you copy? Over."

John's final word was an expletive; a loud vibration was quickly followed by an ear piercing bang. The speakers screamed and failed. After that it was dead silence, leaving Natalie and Ford leaning close together. Ford considered the messages, which he was convinced was not a two way conversation. If it had been, the dialogue tone would have changed. The other ship would have reacted to what his father was saying. Natalie slipped away from him, sliding off the table and stopping a couple of steps away. "It sounds like a recording." She'd noticed the same thing.

"Yes, I got that too." He slid off the table, but continued to rest his ass on it for support and crossed one leg over the other, "If it is a recording, then it could be anything."

"A deep-space comms ghost?" Natalie asked,

Ford shrugged, a deep-space comms ghost from the Albacore to another ship; a long time ago, in a system far, far away. The message could have been travelling for hundreds, thousands of years and they had no way of determining if it had. Other options began to filter into his mind, "Maybe they couldn't hear us. That would explain why they didn't react to Dad's reply."

"That's true, he did keep trying, we have to presume he was changing frequencies." Natalie added,

"And we don't know the extent of the damage to the comms system. I mean, *we* could barely talk to each other, let alone anyone else." Neither of those theories would have given his father reason to warn him of the Albacore. His eyes met with Natalie's and he knew she was on the same page.

"They could be baiting us." Her words gave his thoughts a cold unsatisfying cohesion.

"If we're going to consider this, then I need to say something first." Ford waited for her to nod, "When I was up in Huey, I thought I saw something on the scanners. It was far off, right at the end of Huey's reach. But for a second, I could have sworn I saw a blip and then it was gone. Then after I dropped you off, dad asked me if I'd seen anything strange. I said no, it could have been anything. I knew something was up with him. He wanted to discuss it later." He jabbed his fingers against the table between them, "He wanted to have this conversation."

Natalie folded her arms across her chest and looked past Ford in thought, "If they are flying the Jolly Roger, why are they waiting?" She asked,

"I don't know." He said, "Maybe they're waiting until it's safe to come aboard. They don't know how many of us have survived. They may think this section is up for exploding next. Hell they may know something we don't."

She tilted her head, "They could be collecting the pods. There's a whole lot of booty just floating around out there."

He grimaced at her use of the word booty, "If they are out there there's a good chance they've destroyed our buoy, which means no legitimate rescue. Regardless, I think we need to treat this as a clear and present threat."

She uncrossed her arms, her face serious, "What good will it do?"

"I'm not following."

"What good will it do us, knowing this? We don't have any weapons. We can't put up a fight."

"We could set traps."

She shook her head, "Traps?"

"We've chemicals in the launch bay. We could set tripwires, make some explosives."

"We're on a pressurised spaceship; we can't go blowing things up willy nilly."

"I'm not talking blow a hole in the hull bang, I'm talking blow your legs off bang." He saw the look on her face, "Sorry, didn't mean that."

"It's okay." She said, avoiding his eyes, "It's a good plan. Of course, it doesn't help us in the long run; we're still stranded, even if we do fend them off."

"What are you on about? You think they're flying around with jet packs?"

"No." She said, then smirking as she caught up, "You really think your daft idea will work?"

"It has to. But it depends on how long they're prepared to give us before boarding, it's going to take some time to set up the traps and we still have get the life support back up and running."

"I started to look at the inventory while I was waiting for you." She said, walking back to the table and bringing up ship plans. The entire ship fizzled to life above the table: The bow outlined in the usual yellowish green he was accustomed to. Most of the spine and stern was outlined in red, indicating parts now unreachable by the crew.

"Do we have any spare OGP's?" If they had Organic Gel Power Packs then they'd have power. At least for as long as they all had charge, every gel pack used in space flight or terraforming had universal hook-ups, so as long as you had those, you had power, "Or generators, something like that?"

"They were the first thing I looked for and were on Pod Nine." She pointed at the red lines, indicating no OGPs, "If that doesn't brighten your day you should check out Pod Fourteen, this one is the real kicker." She pressed the red pod, bringing up its listing. Most of it was small arms but it also carried personal shield generators and other auxiliary military items.

"What in the hell?" Ford asked, insulted by the many years of hearing the 'I will never resort to transporting weapons' speech, "Why would we be carrying those?"

"I didn't know we were." Natalie said, "Doesn't matter anyway, we can't get at them." She closed the pod listing down, "Let's concentrate on what we do have."

Ford understood and agreed Natalie's point, but John had always been against violence. He'd all but castrated Ford when he'd told his father he'd be staying to fight on Otzu. His eyes focused on Natalie's snapping fingers before she gestured across the table top. The majority of the ship disappeared, leaving them with the four remaining cargo pods and the bow's inventory stores. Gone were the plans, replaced with manifest listings. The remaining pods were one, two, four and five. Natalie took the first two, Ford started reading Pod Four.

It was soon apparent it wasn't going to be of any good to them, what he was reading was no more than a collection of heavy metals, prefabricated sections of a terraforming hub. But there was no way to build them, and no way to fill them with atmosphere if they could. If they were lucky he could find some tools of use, but the further he got down the list the less likely that became.

Pod Five had medical supplies, pharmaceuticals, cybernetics and the like. There were some really useful items for survival in there, but nothing to combat the threat of a boarding party. Ford suggested sending the list to Bounette in the infirmary. Maybe he could say if anything would be of use. Other than that, Ford couldn't fight the feeling he was wasting time. That was until Natalie announced, "We've mining lasers in Pod Two?"

Ford stepped closer to her, looking over at her list. Mining lasers they could use. They were short range, but they'd cut through the hull easy enough. You wouldn't want to be on the business end of one if it were charging at you at full burn, "At last..." He tapped his middle finger against his thumb before realising he'd removed his glove, "Damn."

"Here." Natalie removed hers, dropped it on the table, "I'll put a list together for you." She began typing on the table as Ford reached down.

"Thanks." He slipped the smart glove on and it tightened around his hand, "If it's just Pod Two, I may as well get started." He re-tapped his middle finger against his thumb and brought up the glove's menu, cycling through the options before placing his hand flat against the table and copying Natalie's list.

"Other than the medical supplies no." Natalie reminded him, "I'll speak to Jake first and come meet you."

Ford nodded, still reading the inventory, "There are exposure suits." These were specifically designed for off world mining and they'd used the same model on Otzu. The fabric was made of a molecule thick woven metal and the fronts had extra armour sewn in around the chest, abdomen and thighs. Ford checked the list and smiled, the complete set was there. Helmets, boots and gloves: all armoured. The helmets also had a HUD built into its visor. All in all they were very similar to their own spacesuits, but wouldn't last half as long in the vacuum of space. They came with a two hour air supply with a fully replaceable canister, "It says here, there are one hundred suits. Plus, four hundred air tanks. We've another thousand hours of air."

"That won't last long."

"It will do in a jam." He continued reading, "And that's not all. We've a bunch of CO_2 scrubbers in there too."

"Now those we can use." Now she was smiling, in fact she looked so happy that Ford forgot their troubles and simply stared at her.

"What?"

He shook sense back into his head, "Oh, err, sorry, nothing."

"That doesn't look like nothing." She said,

"It's just that I haven't seen anyone smile like that for a while."

Madam Bounette smiled, but her arms came across her chest and Ford got the feeling that she wasn't used to anyone getting this close to her other than her husband.

"We could just get through this." She changed the topic, rapping her knuckles on the table top and stood back, "If we divert controls down here, we can cut the power to the bridge, leave on the infirmary, rec-room, stasis...

"Keep the showers on this floor, we can grab what we need from our quarters and bunk together here. Then all we need to keep running are the essentials in the data centre." By shutting down the non-essentials, they'd not only stop wasting power to the computers around the ship, and the servers in the data centre that ran them, but they'd also lower the set temperature of the room which meant less drain on power for heating.

"Then all we do is drop bulkheads to the parts of the ship we're not using and turn off life support." She spoke fast, faster with each word uttered. When she'd finished, she held her hand up and Ford gave her a well-deserved high-five. However, in the silence of their verbal victory, both of them also returned to the exterior threat, "It could still be a comms ghost." Her top lip quivered,

"Could be," Ford agreed, "But we can't afford to think like that, better to prepare for the worst than get caught with our pants round our ankles." He couldn't ignore the disappointment in her eyes, "Hey. We can still do this. We wake up two more from stasis. There must be someone who knows how to hold their own."

Natalie pondered on this a moment. Aside from Ford, the only people who had seen military service were her father and Bounette, neither had seen the front line. There was always Mason. Officer School covered combat and tactics in basic training. Gail Faraday was Martian, everyone knew they were always ready to fight, but as far as either of them knew she'd not had any training. Daichi had a boxing championship belt but was in his sixties. No matter whose name they suggested, it always came back to Ford.

And that was when it hit him, "Balls..."

"What?"

"I just realised, that's why dad didn't put me on ice. He must have considered this right from the start. Anyone could have piloted Huey, it had to be this." After all it was one of the first things John had said to Ford after waking up; what were the chances of two ships colliding out here? It could have been a trap; this whole thing could have been a set up. Smash one derelict into a transport, swoop in and grab the loot.

"Guys?" Doctor Bounette's voice echoed through the static of the damaged speaker, "Can you come down here?"

In all the excitement, Ford had almost forgotten about the good doctor working alone downstairs with their guest, "What is it Jake?"

"It's best you come down here." There was a pause, the void filled with static, "I really don't have the time to explain it over the comms."

Ford forgave his arrogance, if only to save himself from having to listen to jargon over a broken speaker, "We'll be with you in five."

"Don't dawdle." With that the link went dead.

Ford leaned forward and stretched his back out before clearing the table, taking a moment to look around for anything he needed to take with him and pocketed the printed shopping list. Natalie looked as though she was deep in thought. "Nat?"

She started at the sound of Ford's question and ran her hands through her hair, moving the blonde out of her face, "Ford, when we're down there. Promise me something?"

"Of course." He said, intrigued.

"Don't tell Jake about the message."

It was an absurd request, "Why?"

"He doesn't need the distraction. He's already got the girl to worry about."

As Ford listened he remembered Mason's warning about Bounette. The warning about his mental instability and that it was Natalie's job to keep him on an even keel. He couldn't help but wonder if that was exactly what she was alluding to. The concern on her face painted the perfect horror of rape and murder for Ford, something he himself didn't want to linger on. It was conceivable that given

Bounette's love for Natalie, his tenuous grip on reality would snap if given the same image, "My lips are sealed."

***

When they arrived at the infirmary, Bounette was sat on a stool in front of the transparent wall of the Q-Bay. The stool appeared to be the full extent of the Doctor's attempts in clearing up. While Ford and Nat had been busting their balls, Jake Bounette had clearly been doing nothing but playing with his new toy.

The girl had turned one hundred eighty degrees since Ford had last seen her and was now facing Q-Bay's back wall. She stood with her body swaying eerily from side to side, so slight were her movements that Ford didn't notice them until he reached Natalie's lazy husband.

On the right hand side from where Bounette was sitting, was a projected touch screen interface. On it were layered diagrams of the girl displaying the information from Q-Bay's medical scanners. Ford paid no attention to this knowing that other than the pictures, he'd understand next to nothing of what Bounette was reading. So while Natalie and Jake reacquainted themselves, Ford stepped up close to the screen and peered through.

She'd dragged her feet, or at least dragged the injured one leaving a smeared blood trail on the floor. But other than that and her mental patient demeanour, Ford was couldn't offer anything new. Except... Ford pressed his hand against the glass and shielded his eyes from the ceiling lamps. It was more guess work than anything else, as he could only the back of her head, but she appeared to be looking at the small air vent near the ceiling of the back wall.

"She moved when the power came back on." Bounette answering Natalie's question, Ford had missed the beginning of the conversation, "I didn't see it, was grabbing the stool."

"She looks..." Natalie began,

"Touched?" Ford finished,

"She's not breathing." Jake ignored Ford's crude observation, "At least not breathing in the conventional way." He pointed to one of his virtual screens, but to Ford it was no more than gibberish.

"She has gills?" Ford asked,

Bounette smiled, "Of a sorts, yes." He pointed to the oxygen levels inside the bay, "The O_2 has been rising steadily since the room's systems have been recording."

"What's that mean?" Ford asked,

Natalie grabbed Bounette's shoulder, "She's exhaling oxygen?"

Her husband nodded, "Essentially, yes." Jake turned his head away from the data for the first time since they'd entered the room.

Ford continued to watch the girl sway from side to side. He couldn't see any indication of her breathing, no shoulder or chest movement other than the sway. But he still didn't believe what he heard, "That can't be right."

"It is. She's not breathing in the conventional way through her nose or mouth. There's mucus sealing those, as well as her ears shut. Perhaps she's using her eyes or just passing it through her skin like some kind of osmosis. C'est un bon puzzle."

"Is she..." Ford hesitated, not wanting to sound stupid, but he couldn't think of anything else other than zombie, "Dead?"

"I don't know." Bounette pressed a hand against the wall, "This isn't science, its science fiction."

"What *do* you know?" Natalie asked,

"Not much. The data makes no sense."

"I could have told you that." Ford agreed, looking back at Bounette's virtual screen.

"I understand it, Ford." Bounette craned his head around to look at him, "It just doesn't fit," He pointed at another screen which again Ford didn't understand. Bounette continued, "She has a heartbeat, but it's so slow it may as well still be in stasis.

"She's not though, is she?" Ford argued,

"You know what I mean."

If the Doc was confused then Ford was oblivious, "You don't know whether she's alive, or dead. You say she has a heartbeat but isn't breathing, can I ask why you brought us down here?"

Bounette sneered, "Because she moved. And, let's not forget who brought this gem on board without the proper checks. God help us if she turns out to be dangerous."

"She was in stasis when I brought her in Doc. I didn't think she'd be moving around. And she moved, what, an hour ago?"

"Don't make me play mother." Natalie snapped her fingers, "A little less testosterone, please."

Ford nodded, patted Bounette on the back and took a couple of steps away from the group. He couldn't argue with either of them, they were both right. He had brought her on board without the proper checks and it all came back to him allowing Greaves to waste time on the Centurion. He needed a way to remedy it and quick. They had a couple of months at best. Therefore, they didn't need this science experiment on board taking up Bounette's time and hanging over them all. He stopped in his tracks, finding himself a good ten paces from the group when the idea came to him, "Can we eject the bay?"

Bounette shook his head, "I'm sure the military frigates you flew had that option, but this ship is older than our ages combined. She's not going anywhere unless we open that door."

"Well that's a pretty crap design flaw." Ford admitted,

"It's not the only one." Natalie added, "You'd think someone would have erected stairs between each deck instead of ladders."

Ford couldn't argue against that either, although he knew that they had ladders over stairs because the Seng didn't have artificial gravity when it was built, but that or the quarantine bay still didn't get them anywhere, "So what do we do?"

"Did Greaves see anything?" Bounette swirled around on his stool, "When she was on the other ship. Anything out of the ordinary?"

"Yes." Ford answered, "There was something that appeared to be organic, Bramble... coming out of the walls. It was all burned up, but it was everywhere. She took a sample to bring back but..."

Bounette pulled on his nose, pursing his lips together and stared at the floor while Ford and Natalie shared an uncomfortable glance. When he looked up, both of them expected him to say something, but he instead turned around and tapped his fingers on the virtual keyboard. An image of the girl's face appeared, larger than all of the other pictures. He tapped again, zooming into her eyes and again so only one eye took up the picture. Through the pupil, wisps of white tendrils waved in a similar motion to her body, "What - are - they?" Ford asked, digesting the image.

The image zoomed in closer again, the white wisps thickened revealing hook like thorns along their lengths, "I think." Bounette said, "She's infected with some kind of plant life."

"The same plant life from the ship?" Natalie asked,

"Possibly, they do share a commonality in that they appear bramble-esque."

"But the bramble on the ship was as thick as cables." Ford corrected, "Thicker even."

"You asked me what I thought. This is it. She's scrubbing CO_2 from the room, expelling oxygen. While I can't see how she's doing it, it is common within most plant life to do this."

"Don't plants need sunlight to do that?" Natalie said,

Bounette shrugged, "Plants grow in worse conditions."

Ford couldn't take his eyes from the tendrils, like a nest of vipers writhing inside her eyeball. Nevertheless, disgusted as he was at the image he couldn't connect her with the description Greaves had given or what he'd seen through Archimedes poor images, "So earlier, when you said you didn't know anything, you were keeping this from us?"

"Don't be pathetic, Ford. I'm telling you now, I'm not keeping anything from you."

"But you called us down here to tell us she'd moved."

Natalie stood between them, "Leave it Ford. Jake gets wrapped up in the details he forgets the rest of us need to be caught up."

"Oh come on Nat. What sort of rubbish is that? I asked him a direct question. He gave us a nonsense answer and then dropped this on us."

"After he processed it, Ford."

"I can speak for myself." Bounette interjected,

Ford looked at the ceiling and took a deep breath, Bounette was getting to him. Natalie knew her husband better and Ford trusted her enough to take her word for it, but he didn't like it. They could argue here some more or work out a solution to their problem. Ford had no experience of this kind of thing and he felt it was happening because they'd been given a reprieve. It was hard to believe the only thing they had to worry about ten minutes ago was the possibility the Albacore was a ship full of ravenous pirates. He clenched his fist and tapped the wall to his side. Fate had to give them a break at some point and with a raised eyebrow he figured this girl could be it, "Can we use her oxygen?"

Bounette shook his head dismissively, "I thought of that, but she's not giving off enough to sustain us. I wouldn't want to introduce that into our atmosphere anyway, not without further tests and filtration."

"She contagious? She's looking right at the damned vent."

"The vent is part of a sealed system and I turned it off when I realised she wasn't breathing. As for her being contagious, well, she is human. However, whatever is inside her is not. Other than getting in there and taking a biopsy I don't want to say anything, except it's too much of a risk at the moment. Give me more time to study her and who knows."

Natalie who had been listening carefully to this exchange, chipped in with, "If she's dangerous we should flood the room with O_2 and ignite it."

"That's definitely an option." Ford agreed,

Bounette, disagreed, "I wouldn't want to do that until I can assess, given our current circumstances, whether or not using her oxygen will be of any harm."

"You know, Jake." Ford pointed at him, "You just said her oxygen wouldn't be enough to sustain us? If she's a threat we should eliminate it. We don't have the luxury of playing scientists."

"Ford, if I agreed with any of your points, believe me I would say so." Bounette argued, "But what we have here is something that has never been documented and we've colonised more than four hundred moons and planets. This is alien life, proof we're not alone in the universe."

"I think the *Trinity* would beg to differ." Ford snapped,

"Excuse me, but last time I checked you were a heathen and past on the chance to call for their help?"

"What's that got to do with anything?"

Natalie again shook her head, "There you go again with the testosterone!" She looked at her husband, "Jake, do you think she can help us survive?"

"There is a possibility."

"How much of a possibility?"

"More importantly how much of a risk is she?" Ford asked,

"She's locked up tight. As long as she remains secure there's no risk to the ship."

"You're wrong." Ford snapped, "We don't know anything about the other ship, or why it crashed into us."

Bounette crossed his arms, "I think it's safe to say the plant didn't drive it into us."

"Then what about the vent?" Ford said, pointing up to it, "Can she use it to escape? She's been staring at it since we got here."

"As I said, it's a sealed system. Besides, we'll need that to fill the room with O_2 should we decide to burn her out."

"We should burn her now." Ford shook his head, "Natalie, we have generators and CO_2 scrubbers in Pod Two, we don't need her."

"Yeah that's true, but we don't know how long we're going to be out here. If she's no risk inside Q-Bay, then I say we let Jake continue his research while we unload the pods."

"Fine... I'll head to Pod Two." Ford said, taking one last glance at the zoomed image of the girl's enormous eye and its writhing snakes.

***

Ford brought up the holographic inventory list from his glove. Everything he needed was in Pod Two, but each pod was the size of a warehouse and he didn't have the luxury of a jet back get around. The task would have been a hell of a lot easier if they were in dock. He'd have removed the pod, sectioned it off and driven a loader into collect the loot. But oh no, not up here, not on the Seng. He scanned the hand list, everything had the prefix A. Good he thought, everything was in Section A.

He clenched his hand, eliminating the list and stepped onto the gangway. Where once he could stand and look down the wide tunnel, now he could only see as far as the dropped bulkhead door at the third collar. There was another, open bulkhead exactly where he stood, and if the breach had occurred in this section it would have dropped instead. He reached for the illuminated hand rail, running his palm over the warm amber light. His path should have taken him down the centre of a spinning corridor, running the length of the spine. But it now lay dormant. Without the spin, the pods wouldn't have their centrifugal gravity. *At least the crates would be weightless.*

Each collar had three doors, each leading to a pod. The collars could be stopped independently from the rest of the spine, allowing staff to enter or exit and avoid jumping through a moving door. Once inside you could start the spin again and restore gravity, but not without power.

Ford paused at the first collar. Pod Two's door had stopped essentially at a ninety degree angle to his right. Pod One was just above his head while lucky door number three, leading to outer space, was under his left foot. Maybe his luck was changing after all. He stared at the door, only big enough to fit two abreast through. Normally there was never any cause to remove anything from a pod, because they were designed to detach. One of the ducks would lock on at the opposite end and transport it to a carrier craft. Therefore, these doors were just for administration checks, what Joanne had been doing when all this had started. He shook the thought from his head.

The doors worked in similar respect to an airlock. Thankfully, Ford knew a way around this. He removed the control panel housing to the left of the door and began rewiring the unit as he'd been shown so many years before by Mason. As teenagers and if there was a spare pod on a flight they'd pump water into the first section of the tank and use it as a diving pool. They were reckless; they didn't stop the collar's rotation. They'd just take turns jumping from the gangway as the pods rotated. Ford grinned, remembering the lurch in his stomach as he would passed the gravity shift from corridor to pod before plunging into the water, only to climb back up to go again. They'd joked and planned on filling it with jelly or syrup, but they'd always used water. Water was what the Jian Seng had in abundance and could be recycled without raising an eyebrow. *Those were the days.*

He bypassed the necessary circuit and reset the power, both doors opened simultaneously, "And that's how it's done." Now he could bring the crates straight out. He'd worry about getting them to Ops later.

He stepped off the gangway, bringing his foot up high on the curved wall and grabbed the lower section of the door. Gripping the cold metal, he pulled himself up and crawled into the airlock. He shivered as he stood, hairs straightened all over his body. The pods were cold by default but without any power, it was as colder than a meat locker. Frost crisped over the walls, obscuring the emergency lamps so that they only provided the slightest of dull orange light. The second doorway led into a black filled chasm. Ford brushed the frost off of the panel to his right, keyed in the override and hit the switch. One by one, frost laden lamps flickered on in a meagre attempt at illuminating the warehouse. This was going to take him longer than he hoped...

He stepped further in, preparing himself for the lurch. Two more steps and he left the Seng's artificial gravity field. His stomach jumped first. Then his limbs began to feel lighter. He kicked off into the air, floating through the second door and into the cylindrical warehouse. Shelves upon shelves; between them was a network of gangways and ladders, all clinging to the walls right down to the 'floor', on which was another circular door leading to Section B.

Ford opened his arms. He'd always found it easy to relax when floating in Zero-G. He turned slowly as he passed the first web fronted shelves. Their weightless contents strapped into position. It was peaceful and immense and if it wasn't for the cold he would have hung there indefinitely. Ford's breath fogged in front of his face, he rubbed his hands against his arms, scaring off the cold a little longer while catching his bearings. Everything he needed was in this section. He brought up the holographic list, reading the items and their locations. Five exposure suits... he stopped and smiled, knowing Natalie intended to wake up at least two more crew. Next on the list were five extra oxygen tanks, twelve CO_2 scrubbers, five handheld mining lasers and one portable heater.

"Shopping time."

✦✦✦

"This is everything." Ford proclaimed upon entering Operations. He dropped the last crate on top of the first and stretched his arms over his head.

Natalie pointed to the make-shift serving counter. A stainless steel table pulled from the mess with a portable cooker and percolator set up on it, "Coffee's ready."

"I thought you'd forgotten about me." Ford said, making his way to the coffee station.

She didn't laugh, "Have you cooled off?"

He could have started back at her, continued the argument for another three rounds but it wouldn't have gotten them anywhere. Instead, Ford took it on the chin, "All chilled."

"Good, because I have something I need to talk to you about."

"Oh?" Ford poured his coffee, hoping it would be the only thing bitter in this conversation. Natalie rolled her head around her neck, rubbing the top of her back. She looked like she'd been sat in the same position for a while, "You need a rub?"

She smiled, "I'm good. Listen, what happened to you on Otzu..."

Ford sucked his next breath in through his teeth, "Isn't a topic I enjoy..."

"I don't need to know details, I just want to know if you saw combat."

"Why?" He asked,

"Because of what could be out there." She said, "I'm not being nosy Ford, I just want to know what our chances are... I want to know if, I mean, can I..."

"Spit it out Nat."

"I was thinking of sending a prayer."

"No way." He raised both hands in objection,

"Hear me out. We're in worse shape now than when your dad made the decision and while I may be ranking officer, this is your ship. It's a viable option, one that could save our necks."

"Listen to me Nat, we're not devout. They may not answer the prayer."

"May not." She mimicked,

He ignored her jibe, "And if they do, they'll want nothing less than us all to be baptised or whatever ritualistic shit they do." Ford thought it funny that given the choice he chose exactly the same way his dad had, "You don't know the Church like I do. I've seen them in action. They are not benevolent, they are cruel and ruthless."

Natalie nodded; in fact she backed off the argument so quickly that it gave Ford pause. Natalie had lived on this ship longer than he had. Crudge and his father were the best of friends and both of them were heathens. Ford couldn't believe she had even suggested calling the Church, anymore than he would believe his father doing so, "What's the real issue?"

She stopped dead, staring him in the eye, "Do you think I can kill someone?"

"That's what's this is about?"

She nodded, Mrs. Natalie Bounette. Life Support engineer, model builder, *closet killer*, "Sure." He said, "Why not?"

"I'm serious."

"So am I." He said, "You'll know when the time comes. That's the best I can offer."

"You're not much help."

"No point worrying about something until you know it's worth worrying about." He winked at her and blew the steam from his coffee before drinking. By the 'verse it was good to drink something hot.

She folded her arms in front of her chest, "Talk to me."

"I thought I was."

"You know what I mean."

"Fine." He relented, "But you're not going to like it."

"Tell me."

"Well, for starters. You're asking me whether or not I think you can kill someone. Which, to me, makes me think you don't believe you can?"

"I want to believe it." She said, "I want to believe that if it comes down to it, given the choice my life or theirs then I'd make the right one."

"Most people do. They never think they will, but adrenaline is worth every credit they charge for it." He said, "But," he paused a few seconds, "I won't tell you I think you can kill someone, because you may think I'm right and thinking I'm right while not believing it yourself are two different things. You could put yourself in a situation because you think I'm right and unintentionally prove me wrong. That's on me and my ledger is already full."

"Jake will be a liability."

"He already is." Ford's face creased as the words left his stupid mouth,

"I know what you think of him Ford, but he's a good man."

He was tempted to let it drop, but he'd also started something he couldn't stop, "I'm sure he is, but he's not helping us."

"He's doing what he needs to do."

"Yes, he is Nat. That's exactly my point. He's doing what he needs to do. Nothing more, nothing less. He can't deal with all this, can he? So he's sticking his head in the sand and dealing with what he can deal with. This, just so happens, is what he wants to do. I'm not saying he's not a good man, he's the best doctor I've seen but he's selfish, unstable and not pitching in."

"Then what? Put him on ice?"

"Yeah." It was a good an idea as any, "Swap him for one of his staff if you think you must, but I say we swap him out for a gear head like yourself. We need engineers, even if that means swapping me. I'm a pilot with a ship that has no engine. There's no need for me either." He couldn't believe he was saying it, but the more he talked the more truth he heard, "You're better off with Becca, we should have someone working on the communications systems. Not tomorrow, not in the next hour, now."

When he stopped, he found her staring at him. When she didn't say anything, he wondered himself where he could go from there, so instead he found refuge in his coffee mug.

"You running Ford?"

He placed his mug down and thought about her question, "Running?"

"It's easier isn't it? To jump into bed and wait until this all blows over. I've thought about it. I'm sure Jake has too, though he'd never admit it. You, I didn't think so. But now I see it. We've all been putting out one fire before running to the next, but you were close quarters to their deaths, weren't you?"

Ford remained silent, knuckles whitening around the table's edge.

She continued, "You say Jake is burying his head in the sand, it's an easy observation to make of someone else but I wonder if you've noticed you've been doing it too. And not just with this, I know you've avoided your dad and Becca since you returned to ship. But you've done great things Ford, you steered us away from the Centurion, enough to give us a chance. You saved me and my father..."

"I taxied you back," He cut her off, "That's all."

"You saved us." She repeated. While he knew she meant well all he felt was failure, "You're your father's son, Ford. As much as you want to be apart from him, you are. I've known both of you my entire life and you are cut from the same cloth, so I know you'll make the right decisions when the time comes. You just have to have that confidence too, because right now you're the liability.

You stormed out of the infirmary when things got heated, we hadn't finished. I was wrong. We should be waking more heads. I was going to suggest swapping Jake out myself when you..."

He turned to face her, knowing she was telling the truth in the first second his eyes landed on hers, "And you let me rattle on?"

"You needed to get something off your chest." She smiled,

"Yeah." He agreed, rapping his knuckles against the table, "I killed them." He admitted, surprising himself and again when he continued to tell her everything. Every decision and distraction. Everything he believed he had done to cause the deaths of Joanne, Bennie, Eddie and Greaves and the injuries to Crudge and his father. At the end, he felt better. Not healed, but the weight he'd carried had certainly been shared. Natalie had remained quiet for most of it, asking questions along the way to keep him on track. But she gave no judgement; she only offered an empathetic face.

"Survivor's guilt." She said, "That's what you have hun. People die. Yes it's hard. Yes we feel the need to lay blame, but each of us did our best with what we had to prevent it. Those of us who are left have it worst, I'm surprised it's hit you as hard as it has though, you having been in a war zone."

"I didn't fight." He admitted, "Not all that much. I saw one battle, the rest of the time I flew rescue hoppers, picking up the wounded... and the dead."

"One battle is more than the rest of us, even Jake wasn't on the front lines."

"One is enough." Ford rubbed his hands against his thighs, "I saw one, did I tell you? A Saint."

"No shit?"

"I can't tell you if it wore a suit or if it was all machine. But the stories are real. It had to have been ten feet tall, armour of silver and gold. If it wasn't so terrifying it would have been a piece of art."

"And yet you've been dissin' the Trinity more than your Father since you got back."

"Not because I disbelieve they exist." Ford explained, "For what they, it, did. Its armour, had etchings. Scripture I think. There was nothing remarkable about it other than the workmanship, until it got outnumbered. We launched everything we had at it. Then the Saint glowed white, it took me a moment but I saw it was the scripture glowing. Then this song, like angels singing. We just stopped dead in our tracks. I felt this overwhelming urge of penitence and found myself, like everyone around me, on both sides... just drop to my knees. It was all I could do to hold my head up, but after I saw what it did next I couldn't bear to watch."

"What?"

"It cut them down. I don't know if it chose who to spare or random. It just walked from man to man, cutting our numbers in half with a giant flaming sword. We couldn't do anything. We were on our knees, but the Saint showed no mercy, just murderous callousness. Nothing of what the Trinity preaches." Ford hadn't spoken of the events since that day, not even to his sister or his father.

Her hand took his, "It's okay."

"I was powerless, frozen, but for whatever reason I was spared, with less than half of my battalion. It just jumped off to the next battle while the Church Militant surrounded us. An unconditional surrender was ordered less than an hour later."

"That was then, this is now."

"Get that from a cookie?" He smirked,

She laughed briefly, "Ford, none of us would have had a chance if you hadn't been at the pilot station."

"Yeah, but..."

"No buts. That's the truth."

"Yeah."

"And if we're going to get out of this, you have to pull yourself together. You can't be carrying all this baggage."

This, at least, he agreed with, "You're right."

"And when I'm right, I'm right." She smirked, standing from her chair, "Want a hug?"

"Hey, you're a married woman." He matched her arm span, bringing her in close.

"Then don't grab my ass."

"I can't promise anything, it's a good ass."

"It's better than good, but taken none the less."

As they stood there in the cooling room, he sucked in the cherry scent from her hair. Her warm cheek against his, damn it if he didn't miss Greaves.

"Okay fly boy, that's enough." She said, breaking apart.

"I need to crash anyway." He admitted, "I'm exhausted."

"Don't get too comfy, I need you to head down to the Data Core and shut down any redundant servers. Once you get that done, you've earned your cat nap."

She sounded like his sister, "Yeah, but something else may go wrong before I get another chance."

She smirked, "Nice try. I'm going to head down to the infirmary and make sure Jake's okay, I'll program the life support unit from there..." Her voice trailed off, head turning back to the console. A constant pinging was coming from the communications terminal.

"Is that?" Ford asked, not knowing whether or not the system was booting up or if she'd done that as a priority.

"Someone's calling us."

SIX

Neither Ford or Natalie answered the call at first. He wanted to, but couldn't bring himself to accept it. It could be a rescue team or the devil himself and the likelihood veered to the latter. Their chat over the last couple of hours had been a welcome distraction. It had even been fun in parts. "Shall I?" He finally asked, ending their moment.

She shrugged, "What else we going to do?"

"You do it." He said,

"It could be a rescue ship."

"Then you definitely do it, you're luckier than me."

She rolled her eyes, tapped the button and the man's voice came through loud and clear, "Commercial Transport Jian Seng. This is the United Earth Ship Albacore. Do you copy? Over."

Natalie opened her mouth to reply but instead of saying anything her eyes widened and looked to Ford. Resolved to the task, he leaned over the microphone and answered, "UES Albacore, this is the Jian Seng. Over."

"Jian Seng, this is first officer Dante. Good to hear your voice. Over."

"Good to hear yours." Ford looked at Natalie as to whether he should give his name. In a surprising act of random telepathy she shook her head to the negative.

"We weren't expecting anyone to be alive." The voice, Ford realised, was not the one from the message his father had heard earlier. Perhaps it was desperation, but Ford thought this man sounded smoother, friendlier somehow. But no matter how smooth he sounded Ford couldn't ignore his father's warning, "You guys are in beat up shape."

That line was telling. The Albacore would have to have superb scanners to see the debris field if they were far away, "How close are you?"

"A couple of hours out." Dante replied, "You should be able to see us on long range."

Ford bit into his tongue, they had no long range sensors to check. If they were close enough, they'd know that. It was all too convenient.

"How many of you are there?" Dante asked, disrupting the pause.

He looked to Natalie but found her mirroring his own dumfounded expression. She raised her hands up dejectedly. Should he tell them they were three plus more in stasis, or should he lie and tell them all thirty were awake. If they were a rescue ship they would need to prep accordingly. There was no way to tell, they couldn't ping the Albacore to confirm its registration code. Neither did they have long range comms to confirm the registration with the nearest outpost. Even if they did it would take days to send and receive.

"Jian Seng, are you still there?"

"Still here." Ford replied, "Can you repeat your question?"

"How many survivors?"

"Twenty plus." Technically, he was telling the truth. It had the added bonus they'd be able to put up a fight should the worst occur. Ford chewed this over, making note that it was now Dante who wasn't saying anything.

"Well sit tight." He then said, "The cavalry is on its way. Over and out."

"Over and out." Ford repeated and terminated the transmission.

"Two way conversation." Natalie stated the obvious, "What do you think?"

"I don't know. He asked a lot of questions."

"Isn't that normal? I mean, they'd need to know what they're getting into."

"Yes." Ford knocked his knuckles on the frame of the table, "But I still don't like it."

Natalie tapped the table and brought the computer's menu floating to the surface, "Let's see if the sensors are up and running."

"They're not."

"Let's just see, anyway."

"The damage is outside, Nat. The dish took a hit from one of the dislodged pods."

"You sure?" She asked, repeating her question to the computer.

"I met it outside, we shared a moment."

"No need for sarcasm."

When the computer finally confirmed Ford's assessment, she slapped both palms against the table's surface and cursed, "Isn't there a chance they're not flying the Jolly Roger?"

"Yeah, there's always a chance. But the odds aren't good"

She swung her head around to face him, her pony tail whipping out to her side, "Do you think your dad's warning has us paranoid?"

"We're not being paranoid." At least, he didn't think they are, "We're being cautious, besides, what's that saying? Even if you're paranoid, it doesn't mean no one is out to get you?"

"Then convince me, because he sounded genuine."

"We can't presume they're here to help us Nat." He took her hands in his, "Why is there no record of any other ships being in the area. Also, if they were as far out as he says, he shouldn't be able to tell what shape we're in. So they either have really good scanners, or they're lying about their position. Dad may have been paranoid, but I also saw something on Huey's..." He followed that thought a moment longer before continuing, "Sensors... Something was out there, which means, they could have been around to see the engine blow. We've already had this discussion Nat, we need to focus on confirming who or where they are, until I can prove otherwise, I have to consider them a threat."

"Now you really sound like your dad."

Ford smiled, he did a bit. "So for now, let's say they are flying the Jolly Roger." He looked around Operations for the crate, "We should suit up with the armoured exposure suits and carry a mining laser each."

"You still need to show me how to use one."

"No time like the present." He said, approaching the crate and lifting its lid. Inside were the remains of Pod Two's first expedition. Natalie lifted the first mining laser from the box, "It looks like a rifle."

Ford picked up the second one and agreed, there was an OGP housing at its end which doubled as a stock. From that, the particle generator made up the receiver. There was a trigger and guard, a rear and front sight. He disengaged the safety and thumbed the power on at the same time, a yellow indicator light confirmed its activation. Along the stock he found the main differences to the rifles he was used to, a small three buttoned control panel with a small display. He found the menu, "You control the length and thickness of the beam here." He showed her, she copied. Setting it to its minimum safe length of point one metre, he aimed across the length of the table and pulled the trigger. A sharp white light emitted from the muzzle and the laser began to thrum in his hand. The gel pack also began to warm against his shoulder. He waved the laser back and forth, the beam swinging around in a tight arc, to the left and then to the right. When he released the trigger the beam disappeared and the gel pack instantly felt cooler through his overalls, "Not bad. Be careful not to leave it run for long, the gel pack warms up quick. You don't want to blow your shoulder off."

"Noted." Natalie said, firing hers up, the same length but far wider. It fanned out from the muzzle at a ten degree angle on either side and was completely flat. The controls would allow you to adjust it further, making the beam do all the work without having to tilt or reposition the laser itself, "Cool." She said, dismissing the beam, "It will cut through the hull?"

"Yes. Please don't try that." He said, "Okay. I'm going to take Dewey up, use its sensors to see if they're out there."

Natalie's eyes rounded, "Seriously? You want to take Dewey? Out there?"

"I can't think of a better way to find them, can you?"

She shook her head, pulling her hands free of his, "As scary as that sounds, I think you have the better end of the deal."

"How so?"

"I have to tell Jake."

***

"Are you alive even?" Bounette was aware of Natalie's voice, but only as a thread weaving through an elaborated tapestry. He was too deep in his work, examining peptides and DNA strands all pulled from the air filters in the quarantine bay. The girl was magnificent and he was only scratching the surface. All he wanted was to get inside, grab a biopsy and see exactly what was happening with her, "Hey asshole."

Bounette's thoughts dispersed and he reluctantly tore himself away. Natalie leaned against his workstation. She was wearing an armoured suit, coloured a dull khaki with black plates on the front. His first instinct was to ask her about the suit, where had she found it and why she was wearing it. However, the look in her eyes as she crossed her arms had him considering a far safer option, "I'm sorry."

"Doesn't begin to cut it." She said,

Guilt pressed its hands on his back and pushed him forward into her arms, "Encore une fois, je suis vraiment désolé."

"Well you should be, I'm getting jealous of your new friend."

"Her?" He tugged gently on her pony-tail, "There's no need, she's not exactly one for conversation."

"And you are?"

"I can be." He pressed his lips to hers, but she pulled back, "What is it?" He asked, failing to read her face.

"We've had contact."

"A rescue?" He smiled, it would soon be over.

"We don't know. Ford's taking Dewey out to take a look, it's a ship. The Albacore." She stopped, as a flash of recognition crossed his face, "You know it?"

"I..." He'd forgotten, it seemed so long ago, "I overheard John speaking with it earlier."

"And you didn't say anything?"

"I forgot."

"You forgot?" She mimicked him, her eyes orbing as her rage spilled out of her, "You didn't think it was important enough to remember when Ford asked us about it?"

"It was..." He tried to remember, "Back before the engine blew. Before we had your father back, I got side tracked."

"Bloody hell Jake!" Her brows met in the middle, "Side tracked, they could be pirates. We could have done with this information a little sooner."

He didn't have anywhere to run, "I thought John would've said something. He took the call."

She almost laughed at him, "It wasn't me, it was John? Are you seven?"

"I'm sorry."

"Stop saying that."

"I really am."

"Whatever, we need to get back to Operations and suit you up."

"What?"

She tapped the plate on her chest, "Armour, just in case."

His world imploded, he'd been so focused on the girl he'd not considered any other factor. His teeth began to chatter, heart pounding in his ears. He needed to sit down, "Chair." He said,

"Oh no you don't! You can have a panic attack in Ops. We're moving." She grabbed him by his arm and yanked him into a march. They were out of the infirmary and heading toward the junction ladder before he could react. He tried to focus on the walk, taking each step as it came to him but his chest had turned to lead. All he could think of were pirates, boarding parties and Natalie being raped in front of him: visceral fantasies of screaming and blood, gallons and gallons of blood.

"Can't... breathe." He mustered, clinging to the ladder's rung unable to pull himself up.

He felt her hands on his back, urging him to move, "Tell me about the girl, Jake. Focus on her"

The girl, he couldn't think about the girl. Not when he had an image of a scarred brute forcing himself on Natalie and knowing in that instance he would also be fighting for breath and powerless to help. How useless he now felt, no more than a flaccid whelp. He couldn't protect her, couldn't be the man she needed him to be.

"Tell me about the girl." She repeated, sounding both stern and soft at the same time.

He knew what she was trying to do, get his mind off of the terror that consumed him, "She's... contagious. Her skin is human. Its pigmentation has been altered, but it's definitely human. There's still elasticity in it, so she's still alive.

As for the foreign agent, the computer can't give me a proper scan without the biopsy. But it's apparent that whatever it is, is changing her." When he'd finished, he found he'd climbed two decks.

"You had me at contagious." She bumped his ass with her fist, urging him off the ladder.

He smiled, "I love you."

"What's not to love?"

"You want to make out in the storage room?" He grabbed her as she stepped off the ladder.

"As tempting as that sounds, we have to get you into some clothes instead of out of them."

"Now who's dedicated to their work?"

"I wouldn't start making light of it just yet." She pulled away from him, tracing his jaw line with her finger.

He grabbed her hips and pulled her close, "How long will it take?"

She raised her eyebrows and pointed down the corridor, "Move."

"Okay, okay." He followed her direction, keeping the demons at bay long enough to reach Operations. When he got there and saw all the equipment he realised how much he'd missed, "Wow."

Natalie ignored his reaction, grabbed a suit from the crate and threw it at him, "Put it on."

He complied, focusing on the small task while maintaining the wall inside his mind. By making everything about the suit, he wouldn't stray. Straying would be bad, that would bring the demons to his door. He had to concentrate on putting his feet into the suit. It was heavier than he expected, even without the armoured plating the fabric itself had a dense weight about it. He pulled it up his body, fastening it around his torso. As well as being heavy, it was uncomfortable, nothing like his lab coat.

Natalie threw down the boots next to his feet, "Okay, quick version of events so far." She said, handing him his gloves, "Try not to freak out."

"That doesn't help."

"Well, this could be it, so you need to deal with it."

He didn't want to, 'deal with it.' Instead he focused on putting his boots on. Thick treads, magnetic fastening clamps midway up his shins. Armoured like his chest. *Where did you find these?* Being able to wonder that, Bounette realised Natalie wasn't speaking, "Why have you stopped?"

"I'm waiting for your full attention."

He wasn't sure he could give it, because he knew that as soon as she started giving him the details his protective wall would breach and the demons would come flooding in, "Just go for it." He said, fastening his left glove into place with the magnetic cuff.

She told him, in bullet points how they weren't sure if they were pirates or a rescue party. She was careful not to use the exact word pirate, instead dropping Jolly Roger and bad guys in as a substitute. It really didn't help. She ran over the operative functions of the mining laser, but stopped half way when it was obvious he'd stopped listening. He was on the third rendition of her rape when she punched him in the arm, "Pay attention."

"Pardon."

She continued, adjusting the controls on the stock for making something larger. She tried to sugar coat it, telling him that there was still a chance it was a rescue party but he knew that she wouldn't be teaching him how to use weapons if they really thought the Albacore was to be their white knight. If they believed that, they'd be on the bridge inviting rescuers in, talking to them, basking in the good news. Operations was defendable with two solid doors, but what good would it do but slow the inevitable. If they could get through the hull, they'd be able to get through the bulkheads. Deck by deck, they'd take what they wanted and smash everything else until they reached them, living dolls to toy with. If they were lucky they'd be killed outright. If not, they were certain to face physical and mental torture. He'd heard rumours of entire crews being skinned alive and killed, then arranged together as some sadistic art piece.

They'd rape her for sure and would make him watch. He couldn't be sure which they'd enjoy the most, having her or the entertainment of him wailing over the act. Or rape them both while skinning them. Cutting their limbs off and using all their holes as they saw fit, because how the hell would they be able to fight back with no arms or legs."Jake!" Natalie said, "Focus."

"Focus, focus, focus." He began his mantra, knowing it was futile with each repetition. Sooner or later he would be consumed by the terror. He'd be a cowering shadow of the man he needed to be. On his tenth 'focus' he found

Natalie staring at him, fear in her eyes. Not for herself, but for him. She knew as well as he did that he wasn't going to be able to help. He stopped talking, taking pause to gather his horrid thoughts and said the only thing he could, "I'm sorry."

She smiled the sad smile of someone who was on the brink of giving up, "You'll be okay." Nice words, but he didn't believe her, and there was nothing she could say to change that.

But there was something he could do, "There are always anti-anxiety patches..."

"No way Jake" She cut him off, "I'm not spending the last moments of my life with you if you're high."

"I won't be. It's just to take the edge off."

"You may think that, but all I get is an apathetic jerk to talk to. You'll be no good to me, or yourself... or anyone else."

"Like I'm going to be any good as I am." The fear curled its arms around his chest and squeezed, "Besides, there's more than enough for the both of us."

"Please, please don't ask me again."

His breath left him and the room began to spin. He staggered forward, grabbing the main table for support but it was too late. His legs gave up and he collapsed to the floor. She rushed to him, lifting him up onto her thighs, running her gloved hands over his head, "Jake, baby listen to me. You're not you when you take those things. You are strong. You just need to focus, don't think about what's going to happen or more importantly what might happen. Concentrate only on what is happening. Concentrate on the immediate here and now. When you rely on the drugs, you're not giving yourself the chance to beat this thing."

But Bounette had stopped listening, he was too busy drowning in his own terrifying delusions to understand what she was saying. They shouldn't have left Earth. He should have insisted she live with him and his family. Be damned her father and be damned the Jian Seng. Let them all die out here, but let him travel back in time to that moment and have her live with him in peace, waking up to the sound of the lake each morning, having breakfast on the terrace. Fresh croissants and squeezed Clementine juice, "Jake, I love you."

He stared at her, hearing the words and knowing he should reply in the like. But he didn't, she didn't deserve his tainted love. Hell, he wasn't even sure if he did love her. Because if he did, he'd throw himself between her and harm. *Wouldn't I?* Bounette leaned his head away from her and began to sob uncontrollably. Natalie left him there while she stood up. *It was better this way*, he thought, lying under the table. Just leave him there. They may take pity on him, or not even find him at all.

Then, filled with guilt he acknowledged his stupidity. He didn't move however, instead he lay there a couple more moments, gathering what little of his strength he had before sitting up. He raised a hand to the table's edge and finally pulled himself to his feet.

He couldn't look at her, he knew he'd not only scared the life out of her, but also hurt her. He'd acted like a complete fool and there was no denying it. He listened to his breathing, calmer now that he had the full use of his lungs back. Natalie had moved across to the other side of the table and distance, it seemed, made the heart grow fonder. He followed her, not allowing his guilt ridden eyes the glory of her face but continued to track her movements until she stopped and began working the table top computer interface, "Ford's already outside," She said.

Bounette nodded, keeping her hands in view at all times, "Any news?"

She didn't answer. The silence continued and he managed to hold his breathing steady with the utmost control. That was until Ford's voice broke out from the table's speakers, "Topside's clear." Bounette felt an even bigger fool. This was great news, surely. There was nothing out there. Natalie had said something earlier about the ship being far away if it was really a rescue. They were going to be saved! He looked up to find her face stern, staring down at the table and oblivious to everything else in the room, including him.

***

Ford had suited up, apart from the protective plates sewn into the chest, abdomen, crotch, thighs and shoulders; it didn't feel that much different from the suits he was used to. On reaching the tug bay, he'd found Louie still being siphoned for power so it left him with Dewey. The duck he'd spent the least amount of time in. Not that it made a difference they were all the same model. Each one had their little quirks though and he was just accustomed to Huey. Thankfully the heating systems were working and he wasn't going to be sitting in a sweat box for the next half hour.

Unfortunately, the tug came with the trinkets of primary pilot, Emily Green. The seductive smile and bulging muscles of a naked Dominic Travis interstellar superstar looked back at Ford. Lead artist from the band 'Huck Rivals' and fantasy favourite of Emily, who'd placed the double paged magazine poster of the man in a very conspicuous position, "That's not real." He reassured himself.

He'd already checked above the ship, finding nothing and was now heading down to the underside. Once past the hull he was greeted with much of the same as he'd seen on top. Just debris and space. This time however, he found himself pausing before pressing the button. This time would be the last time. This time would reveal whether they had bigger problems than little Miss Zombie and a dead spaceship. His finger hovered in the air, unwilling to move. He stared at his shaking hand not wanting to find out. *Leave them out there if that's where they want to be, they're not doing us any harm now.* If he pressed it, they'd come running and if the stories were right they'd beat him, rape him and kill him and once they were finished, they'd wear his skin as this season's fashion trend... not knowing was what held his finger in place. His mind was filling in the blanks with the worst tales possible. But that's all that they were, tales. There was no knowing exactly what was going to happen. Iron swelled in his mouth, teeth sinking into his tongue. Not knowing was the biggest fear. He'd dealt with each catastrophe as it had happened and he was still here, alive and kicking. If they were out there, then he'd deal with them too.

"The hell with it." He pressed the button. The diameter pulse erupted from the centre of the screen and rippled out from the holographic exterior. One kilometre... nothing... two kilometres... three... nothing. Four... his eyes wide, his heart racing, nothing. Five kilometres... nothing. He laughed, punching the air he wanted to sing, something, anything.

There was nothing out there. Boy had he let his father get to him. He was still shaking, joyous but shaking, he pressed a button, opening communications with the Jian Seng. No need to keep them waiting. The sensor bleeped.

Just before the five k marker an engine had fired, "Shit."

"Ford?"

He swung his chair to the direction of the engine burn, searching the starfield for the ship. It was too far away for him to make a good visual but he could make out the exhaust trail, streaking toward them. His Father had been right all along. They'd been waiting. With the engines off the sensor sweep had passed over them like another piece of debris. Perhaps it was because of the sweep, or perhaps they always intended to wait until now, Ford didn't much care, because for whatever reason they'd decided to act.

"Ford?" Natalie's voice called again, sounding more urgent.

"They're here." He replied as the sensor bleeped again, a new blip moving toward him. Faster, much faster than that of the ship's approach. He yanked back on the stick, reversing Dewey as quickly as the duck would allow but he already knew how it was going to end. Dewey's manoeuvring thrusters were just that. They weren't meant for speed, and the new blip on his scanner could only be a torpedo. It was already past the three k marker and racing toward the two k, he didn't have enough time to get to safety. The ducks had no defensive capabilities, but the Seng did, "Natalie, countermeasures, now!"

Magnesium flares launched out from the Seng in all directions, a fireworks display in the heavens. Ford piloted Dewey away from the torpedo as best he could, hoping the flares would confuse its targeting system enough for him to get away.

The proximity alarm kicked off, filling the cabin with its screaming klaxon. The torpedo had now gone past one k marker, it was going to hit and hit soon. Ford rolled Dewey's top to face the Seng at a forty-five degree angle, watching the blip closing in on him and hit the eject button.

***

Jake Bounette rubbed his hands over each other repeatedly in a futile attempt to stop them from shaking. He'd retreated to the floor soon after Ford had told them they were here and barely registered the call for countermeasures. The last thing he'd paid attention to was Natalie's expression as she'd called Ford's name over and over again once she had launched the defences. Nat continued in her attempts.

His constant blinking was annoying him, but he was too involved in managing his breathing to contemplate a war on another front. His vision flashed a dull red every other second or so, leaving the room in a constant state of blurriness. He had no idea Natalie had approached him until he felt her hands on his knees and the smell of her cherry hair near his face, "Jake..." She may have finished the sentence. But if she did he didn't hear it. He already knew what she was saying, 'Ford is gone'. And he felt nothing except the gripping fear clinging to his heart and lungs.

The speaker belched static, turning both his and Natalie's head to the table. As Natalie raced into position Jake remained on the floor, running his hands up and down his arms. He was cold, far colder than he should have been wearing an exposure suit on top his overalls, "Jian Seng." An unfamiliar voice caught his attention, "This is the Albacore, prepare to be boarded." And that was that, he thought. The end of everything he knew.

"Jake."

He turned his head, slowly but as fast as he could muster. She was stood over him, for how long he hadn't the faintest idea. Her eyes were wide, brows dipped in the centre. With her hands on her hips and feet standing apart from one another, he could tell he was about to get a telling off.

"Get up."

He sucked his lips into his mouth and bit on them, furrowing his own brow while the shaking moved into his legs, she knew as well as he did; he wasn't moving. She repeated herself, reaching down and grabbing him by the arms and like a spoilt brat he pulled against her until she finally gave up and stepped back.

"We have to go."

"There isn't anywhere to go." He said flatly,

"So this is it? You want to sit here until they turn up?"

He shrugged. It was as good a plan as any. She breathed sharply, taking a step back. She wasn't impressed. She argued her point of moving on. Running the maze they knew and the boarding party didn't. They had mining lasers and they could make a stand, but now it seemed it was all for nothing. They'd both end up dead and they would have the added 'luxury' of enraging the pirates for their efforts on catching them. Jake even told her so, she was not impressed. He could tell she was thinking of leaving him there. But she didn't and he never thanked her for staying. That was something he'd later come to regret. However, right then he couldn't think outside his own selfish pain.

"Fine," She sighed, "I'm going to shut all the bulkheads, make them work for their bounty."

"Knock yourself out." The look she gave him left him in no doubt that was exactly what she wanted to do to him if he didn't get his act together. Only then did he roll out of his position and pull himself up to the table. Feeling ashamed he looked at what she was doing, "How long do you think it will take them?"

She shrugged; and when she didn't reply, he filled the gap himself, "I'm not okay."

"I know."

"I..." He wanted to tell her how crippled by fear he was, how paralysed... More than at any point in his life, but she'd never fully understood. She couldn't get her head around it. Just pick yourself up was her resolution. And on the whole it had worked. Throughout their life together he'd suffered only three attacks such as this one and normally her logical fix it attitude had resolved the problem. But not this time, because he knew no matter what she said to convince him otherwise there was no denying they would both end up dead.

"What?" She was looking at him, somewhere between 'I...' and 'What?' all the exits had been sealed and whatever else she'd been doing at the table was completed because she now stood arms folded.

"I can't..." Do this. Reality took a side step to the left. Everything looked the same. The control table remained the centre of the room. Its metal rim was still cool to the touch, hard and rigid as it was supposed to be. But something was off, something he couldn't put his finger on. A whispering rage pumped through his veins, the need to stop time overwhelmed him. He told himself that there had to be a way he could help. The laughter and applause was distant but all too close for comfort.

"Every time it gets tough, it's the same thing with you Jake. Headaches, backaches, exhaustion, you name it you get it until you can get a damned fix."

"I'm not an addict."

"No?"

He wasn't. Sure he'd used stimulants during the war, all of the medical staff had. There hadn't been enough medics and too many casualties, but he'd kicked it once he'd ended his tour. This was *Post Traumatic Stress Disorder*. He'd been validated by Doctor Witherspoon. She'd prescribed... He turned his head to the laughing only to find an empty corner. "I'm not an addict." He repeated, gulping the dry from his mouth.

"Jake, for a very smart man, you're not very self-aware." She moved around the table, closing the gap between them, "You don't fight. Not for anything, not even if you feel strongly about it. All you do is break down and beg for something to take the edge off and you, one of the best doctors I know, let those quacks tell you it's okay to do so."

He looked down, surprised not to find the stab wounds he'd felt as she'd been talking. He needed her and all she could do was pull him down, fear swirled within him, churning into hate. *What a bitch!* All she had to do was tell him what she wanted and he would do it, she didn't have to cut him the way she had. Bounette stretched his arms, pumping the hate into his muscles and breathed. She called his name, but it was muted under the sound of his heart. Snarling, he gripped the stool's seat and heaved. And heaved until both he and his arms screamed.

"What are you doing?"

Blinking, spitting and still shaking, Bounette released the stool, remembering it was bolted to the deck. He couldn't even do that right, "I don't know."

"That's the first time you've been honest with me for a while."

"I want to smash something."

She held her hand over her mouth, but he could see the tormenting smile creasing her face, "Okay." The sound of bodiless laughter taunted him once again; the room was empty save the two of them.

"It's not okay. They're boarding and there is nothing we can do. I don't know how many of them there are, I can't fight them. I can't even throw a stool across the room."

Natalie dropped her hand, her smile gone. Her eyes shone as bright as the day they'd met, tears welling up, "I can't, I won't do it."

"Do what?" He asked, confused by her statement. He didn't remember asking her anything.

"Baby, I can't save you." The tears smudged her face and he blinked them away, "I can't stop them." He lifted his hand toward her but when she stepped forward he recoiled, "All I can do is make it that they can't hurt you." Her sincerity was clean and as sharp as if it had come right off a whetstone. It punctured his thoughts as well as his heart. How dare she, he was the man. He was meant to protect her and here she was telling him she would be the one protecting, "But for that to happen I have to hurt you. *Yeah baby, you hurt me so good*, "Jake, I'm so sorry."

"Don't." He snarled, "Get the hell away from me."

"Jake?"

"I mean it, don't come near me." He beat his fist on the nearest stool, wishing it were her head. The act of doing so scared him to the bone, "I'm losing it."

"Jake, honey." Her tone was soothing, but all he heard was condescending babble. She was scared and needed him to calm down.

He stood there screaming out a barrage of incoherent words. His face grew purple, the veins in his neck and temples engorged. When he yelled, he threw all of his fear and malice at her, spraying spit as carelessly as his love, "I hate you. You brought us here, you couldn't leave your dad alone and dragged us into this steel coffin and now where's it gotten us? We're going to die. They are going to tear down that door, split you open and rape you while holding me down to watch and it's all on you baby." He waved his finger at her, glimpsing the pain he'd caused.

Jake spun around shielding his face from her. Erratic and embarrassed, he supported his retreat by running a hand idly against the table's edge until he reached the end. There were no more places to run. He caught his demented expression looking back at him in the round clear surface of the coffee machine and sighed deeply, "Where does one go, when there are no more places to hide?" He dropped to his hands and knees, breathing the cool air.

"Are you done?" Her question disregarded his and everything else he'd blurted out without thought.

"No." He spat his reply to the floor and studied the bubbles as they popped into nothingness.

"Then get up and finish it."

He did no such thing, but he was far from done. He would smash Natalie's head against the bulkhead to save himself the sight of them torturing her long before he surrendered and before he did that, she would know who was to blame. His shoulders and back rose and sunk with his breaths, deep and powerful, charging his rage for the next bout.

"Get up, you coward." She yelled.

Jake reached for the table, pulling himself to his feet. Standing and breathing heavily while still staring at his deformed face in the coffee machine, his true face, the face of a monster. A monster that only looked after himself and no matter how much he tried to deny it, that part of him was the stronger. Today, he realised was the day the monster would win. "I want to hurt you."

"You can try."

***

Ford clung to the rivet; clenching his teeth he pulled against the force which yanked his body straight. His deep panic filled lungs fogged his visor, a panic he had no control over. His life, short as it was, had flashed before his eyes. The torpedo had slammed into Dewey, leaving nothing but particles. One silent explosion and it was over. His chair spiralled out of control on a head on collision with the hull he'd so carefully aimed his ejection toward. It forced him to act only on instinct, uncoupling his belt just in time and as he now held himself in place he acknowledged he was dangerously tempting fate with these close calls. This close call however, was far from over.

His laboured breathing and the buzz from the gel pack powered lungs on his back were the only sounds he had and there was no telling how long he would have before the Albacore rounded the front of the ship to confirm their kill. He counted the seconds as the g-force ebbed away before moving his arm as soon as he was able.

He clambered across the hull as quickly as the suit allowed, kicking against the rivets along the plate section. Without magnetic boots the travel was slow and deliberate. *No mistakes in space.* He paused, arching his back up, gathering as much information he could. All around him seemed to be the same blank plating.

But wait, far up on his left...

If he squinted he could just about make out the shape of an air-lock. However, with the pirates moments away, it was too far. He needed something else. Something the smooth plating couldn't provide. He needed shelter. He carried forward, pushing himself in the direction of the airlock, despite knowing he couldn't make it. By hell or low air he would. In desperation he glanced around. Coming up on his right was a red blinking light, beautiful and beckoning. It was the port lamp on a small raised blister, not much bigger than himself, *but big enough?* It sat on the outer casing of a manoeuvring thruster nacelle. It may just work. He dropped his head, pushing himself as fast as he dared.

He counted the rivets as he past them, glimpsing up to the lamp and slowing when he came parallel with his goal. From below, the distance had looked achievable, but now holding onto the hull and staring across the expanse, doubt and fear set in. The nacelle was big enough, but there was no way he could make the jump. The exhaust funnel was tight so the jump would have to be precise. Ford closed his eyes, he was so damned close. He turned his head, searching for the airlock. Not close enough. He needed to be off the hull...

Out of the corner of his eye, coming around the front of the Jian Seng was the Albacore. Its search beams stretching out over the Seng's hull, looking for him. He sucked a lungful of oxygen, pivoting on the rivet and locked his head forward. He was out of time. He kicked off stronger and fast. With no rivets to guide him he glided, un-tethered toward the nacelle. The space between him and the ship grew, his course remained forward but he was also floating away.

Ford controlled his breathing, fighting back the urge to panic. Seconds went by slowly; the exhaust funnel grew larger, bringing hope with each encroaching foot. The search beams stroked the hull above and below him, scissoring toward his position. A metre out and he knew he wasn't going to hit home, but he was going to be close. He reached out, preparing his hands to grab the fringe, "Come on." Ford grabbed the lip, fingers dropping like bars on the inside. His body continued past, shutting his eyes he braced for and accepted the pain. Sharp needles in his knuckles as his legs dragged along the nacelle's outer surface until his elbows snapped into position. With the Albacore's lamps closing on him, he pulled himself over the lip and reached inside the smooth tube for the service grip. With one hand secure he dragged himself the rest of the way in as the flood lights met at the nacelle's mouth.

Squeezed into the hole, Ford could barely see out. His view was obscured by his own limbs folded around him. All he could make out were the white, dazzling searchlights. They'd moved across the ship looking for him and now held position as if sensing their prey was near. Ford clenched a fist, banging against the thruster's exhaust diaphragm. Nothing. There was nowhere to go and so he waited. Tightly coiled up his breathing was laboured, his throat dry, his visor blanketed with the fog of his breath. Seconds became minutes without motion from him or the enemy.

Then darkness! The lamps where shut off. The temptation to move tickled his confined limbs, but the fear of being caught overrode the urge to move. Ford waited, counting the time by his depleting air supply, its unavoidable blinking on the lower right of his HUD.

When the lights returned, they were dimmer. They'd moved away and out of view, allowing him to breathe easier. He waited, still unwilling to give temptation a second footing. All the time watching his air supply diminishing. Fifteen minutes wasted in the hole and still he refused to move. The lights were now as low as dusk, warming the red tint of the Seng. Ford recorded the timer click over to nineteen minutes. A sharp jolt shook his hovel, followed in quick succession by another three. Ford's hands pressed against the sides, he was sliding out. Teeth gritted, his boot jammed against the wall and then it was over. Just as quick as it had started it was over and the Albacore's lights dimmed into darkness.

When he finally moved, another five minutes had passed. He shifted his hands against the inside of the tunnel, pushing himself around with his feet. He corkscrewed round so his head came out first. Weightless he clasped the mouth of the nacelle thruster and just hung there mouth agape at the sight before him.

The Jian Seng's port side airlock was on an umbilical tunnel that reached up to the front of the Albacore, which had a rounded head with bulbous view ports, sitting on a wide shoulder section reaching down to a far thinner tail. The whole thing was at least fifty metres in length, he surmised. Long thin legs clamped on the Seng's hull and Ford attributed these to the four tremors he'd felt inside the nacelle. It looked less of a ship more a monstrous robotic insect, *a mosquito*. All it was missing were wings. Instead of superfluous extremities it was laden with military hardware. Judging by its size and the amount of weapons it had to be a gunship, which meant the crew compliment was no more than twenty if they wanted space for cargo.

His hand came around the back of his helmet, casually rubbing the rear while his mind drifted from the spaceship's design to the very real danger. He'd spent enough time in his hole for the pirates to board the Seng.

Natalie and Bounette would be waiting for him, inside. No, that was wrong. They'd think him already dead. He'd not been in contact with them since Dewey got blown out of the sky and there'd be no way of Natalie finding out if he'd survived. Ford needed to get inside but had no clear idea of how to do it without being spotted, or what he was going to be able to do once he was inside. He looked up to the top of the ship, the nearest available airlock was on the top side.

"Let's hope no one stayed home to look out the window." He muttered, starting his climb.

***

Bounette rested on the floor, his back against the wall, looking at the bulkhead. The voices were so distant and muffled that Bounette first thought them in his own head. It wasn't until the pounding against the bulkhead came, that time, he realised, was up. Between the dull thuds came raised but muffled voices, familiar expletive words spoken in anger through the nine centimetres of alloy between them.

The fear in Bounette's face was palatable but despite the wrong he had done her, Natalie remained there for him. She touched his arm, "Do you remember the cottage?" He did. It was a wonderful two bedroom house just outside Perpignan in the South of France. It was untouched by the plagues and the wars. His cousin owned it and had been renting it out for years. Too small for his own family to use, but he was unwilling to sell outside of the family. He was holding it for Bounette like a carrot, beckoning him to return home. Or rather as a plea for him not to leave Earth. For it was well documented, you age at a different pace when working the trade routes. That's why the ships became home and the crew family, "We should buy it." She said, in a perfect French dialect.

He smiled, "We're not getting out of this."

"Don't be like that, it's a good idea and I won't let you poo all over it." Her elbow nudged his arm, narrow and sharp it caught his elbow causing him to flinch, "And don't think you can be all depressed around the kids." They'd wanted children but he'd stopped them exploring that particular reality. He couldn't get his head around having children on a spaceship, it just wasn't sanitary enough. There were too many safety issues. So they'd agreed that when Crudge retired, they'd leave the ship together and head back to earth to start a family. Age wasn't really an issue anymore, medical centres extended life to an average of one hundred and forty seven and women frequently had children in their sixties and even seventies.

"Stop it." He said, nursing his elbow, "I know what you're doing."

"Do you want to waste what could be our last moments together?" She brushed his hair back, kissing his cheek.

"I..." He didn't know what to say, lost in the soft touch of her lips, the scent of cherry in her hair. Of course he didn't want to waste their last moments, but he also didn't want to pretend nothing was happening, "I don't know."

"They still may be a rescue team." She reminded him, as she lovingly twisted his wedding band around his finger. He liked the way she played with it. It was something she hadn't done in years. It would be nice, he thought, if she were right. It wasn't fair, that even now at the end she needed to be the strong one. He wanted that to be him. He'd breathed in deeply; convincing himself there was nothing to fear. Sadly, the pounding of the bulkhead would always bring the fear clawing back into his throat. It prevented him from saying anything nice, anything sweet. All he wanted was for her to be as terrified as he was and so he'd say nothing, "Hey." She said, punching his arm, "We're a team remember?"

"Yes we are." He grimaced. She was amazing. She put him to shame every which way. How he'd managed to win her never ceased to amaze him. She'd told him it was because he was sweet, funny and handsome. But he'd never believed her. Not really. He always expected her to turn around, point and laugh like so many others had done. But she never did, not even now at the end. Natalie would always find a way to pick him up when he succumbed to the darkness, protecting him when he couldn't stop the weight of the 'verse crushing in.

Even in her death she would protect him, just like she'd done earlier. How stupid he'd been. How thoughtless and irresponsible and yet somehow she'd seen through it all and accepted his apology. She was in every molecule of her being, perfect. And as the small, diamond bright glare from a cutting laser formed at the top of the bulkhead he couldn't help wonder how she'd be able to continue being there for him. Because as sure as the amber slag now cascading down the bulkhead meant the laser would fell that door, he knew whatever came through would be the most unpleasant thing they'd ever encountered.

He squeezed her hand, the white light was moving slow but steady, leaving a glowing red wake behind it as it trailed down the bulkhead and turned inward at the bottom, "I'm going to call him Hadley." He said, referring to their unborn Boxer pup he'd wanted since he could remember.

"Hadley's nice." She said, "But I'd like a Retriever too, I can't be dealing with just one ugly dog."

"Boxer's are not ugly."

"They drool everywhere."

"That's..." He couldn't deny it, "true." She leaned in, her warm breath on his neck had never felt so enticing. Her soft lips kissed his jaw and he turned toward it sharing in the kiss. He closed his eyes, tasting her in his mouth and caressing her face, oblivious to the light's progress on the bulkhead. They were alone, for this one last time they were alone.

The cut out piece of bulkhead slammed to the floor with a mighty clang and for a long, agonising moment it remained a gaping wound. Smoke bellowed into the room, clinging to the floor like dry ice bringing with it the stench of burned alloy. Bounette brought his hand to his nose, squinting through the darkness wishing for time to catch up with itself. When it did, he changed his mind. The first of them appeared, back lit from another's shoulder lamp. From Bounette's position on the floor, they appeared like giants. Six in total, all wearing patchwork armour, consisting of, a thigh casing from an Earth Alliance uniform, a battered chest piece - maybe Church Militant, modified with spot welded spikes. All of them were daubed with war paint, all armed with a plethora of torturous weapons. His doom had finally arrived.

No sooner as his dread came to terms with the six, the group split into two columns of three and fanned out. A seventh then entered, wearing teal and crimson armour. Black netting hung in patches, a cobalt helmet painted with a white skull and a deep red plume feather springing from its top, displayed like demonic peacock. His rifle was ridden low against his hip, and on his bandolier was strapped a series of grenades and ammo pouches. He stopped mid column, raised his hand and snapped open his helmet, pulling it free. His face was covered in glowing tattoos, a dragon branding his cheek. His left eye shone a beautiful yellow, the other a deep foreboding red. He smiled with a full set of broken teeth. Bounette's grip on Natalie's cold stiffening hand tightened and the peacock asked, "Any heroes?" His tone was raspy and mocking.

A moment of silence echoed in Bounette's ears, his voice long gone, "I'll take that as a no." The pirate master leaned to his left, clicking his fingers and ordered, "Scratch, split them up."

Scratch revealed himself, stepping out of line and unscrewing his own faceless helmet. Bounette squinted, unable to comprehend the hideous caricature. His head and face were hairless; his skin was black as oil and shimmered just as. Like his master, he too was daubed in tattoos, but his glowed neon blue, matching his maniacal eyes and wicked grin, "Pleasure boss." His voice was as oily as his skin. He stepped toward Bounette, eyes dazzling like two stars flicking between Natalie and Bounette, "No need, Boss. Just one."

Bounette's brow furrowed at the remark as reality rapped its fist against his skull. He slowly turned his head towards his wife. His mouth became dry, his chest heavy, refusing to breathe as he choked on the truth. Her beautiful face was stale and gaunt. Memories of violence raged within him, her jaw hung flaccid from her head. Her skin was burned, her eye sockets scorched black while Bounette's were filled with tears. He'd screamed her name in passion and she screamed his in terror. He took her chin in his hand, pulling her dead face to his and kissed her; still unable to comprehend the heinous events leading to her death. One by one, the pirates, hyenas all, began to laugh.

With teeth clenched, Bounette, staggered toward the leader, screaming at the top of his voice. The sharp, hard blow came to his kidney, dropping him to his knees. His attacker stood over him and removed his red helmet. This character was cleaner than the others, perhaps less ugly. However, he had the cold black eyes of a shark.

But, it wasn't the Shark's eyes that disturbed him the most. Low on the man's waistline was a far more malevolent trinket, a prized trophy no doubt. A band of weaved gold, gnarled and twisted where it had been torn from the owner's head, a Saint's Halo. *Saints save us.* The Shark must be a considerable foe if he'd bested one of the Trinity's unstoppable warriors. He gazed on it, staring at its intricate design made up of hair thin strands of gold woven into a plait. Glinting off the low, blue stale lighting of the room and then, it was gone. The Pirate leader stepped between them; he crouched on his haunches, "Hi."

His breath swam with the fishes and Bounette hardly heard him. It was happening all too fast. Bounette's breathing was as heavy as swine on a hot day; he rested on his knees, hugged his kidney and shielded his nose from the stench. The Pirate leader tapped his shoulder, "Name's Garret." Somehow, Bounette removed his stare from the floor to the leader's face, "Do you speak English?"

Bounette wasn't surprised he chose to answer the man in French, "Va au diable."

"Super, jé deteste le francais." But he was surprised when the man replied in kind. Bounette looked at the other pirates, all of whom had now removed their helmets. Most of them had tattoos, a couple of them were women, all of them were as ugly as they were menacing. Their leader spoke again, "How many of you are there?" Bounette continued breathing heavily. Natalie, the only person he cared about protecting was dead, killed by his own hands. He could tell them what they wanted, make a deal for his life, but he wasn't thinking logically. He wanted every single one of them as dead as Natalie, "Are there any other survivors?" Garret demanded as he unsheathed a serrated blade that was at least nine inches long.

The knife flashed across Bounette's eye line. The shark had moved around behind him and held his head steady. There were no more questions, not for as long as it took to saw through the cartilage of his right ear. Bounette's screams of agony triggered another roar of cheers and laughter amongst the pirates and then as his own severed ear waved in front of Bounette's face, Garret said in a tone that was made more menacing by the quiet way he spoke, "I won't ask again."

Scratch crouched over Natalie's body and flipped her over, revealing her once red, now scorched hair. A charred hole no bigger than a fist, sat at the top of her head. Scratch held her skull in his hands and rotated it, peering inside with a child-like interest of the blackened hollow where her brain once rested. Bounette's own ear waved in front of his face again. His world spun uncontrollably, he couldn't fathom hurting her and yet she was dead. He swallowed, but it was dry and it hurt. He tried to breathe, but his chest was tight and would not yield. *By the Trinity, what did I do?*

"Stay with me." The Pirate called Garret said, slapping Bounette's cheek but Bounette only stared through his dismembered ear, unwilling to give the man any further satisfaction.

Garret turned his head to the rest of his crew, "You waiting for an invitation?"

The largest of the group slung his rifle over his shoulder, "We should be out there with the pods."

"Just do your job Harvest." Shark said,

"This place's a death trap." Harvest produced a large middle finger in the Shark's direction, "It's a waste of time Dante, even the damned pussy is stale."

"Like that's ever stopped you." Garret replied, then rolling his eyes, "Dante, get back to the Albacore and run some more scans, just to be sure. We won't move until Harvest has finished with her."

Bounette flinched, glancing at Garret and knew by the man's smile that he'd caught the terror in Jake's eyes.

"You speak English." Garret grinned, rubbing a gloved hand over the wound where Bounette's ear had previously resided. The fabric of the glove was coarse, tearing against his flaps of skin. Bounette closed his eyes, trying desperately not to think of that necrophiliac monster Harvest with his wife, "You killed her," Garret mused, licking his lips while rubbing Bounette's warm blood across his nose, "You thought to spare her... this? Because she was scared?"

Scratch giggled, "Scared, yeah."

"Or was it to spare you?" Garret asked, grinning.

Bounette avoided looking at the man's gnarled smile, ignoring the suffocating remorse and focused on the seared 'P' scarred on the centre of the pirate's forehead, "You're wrong Harvest." Garret stated, "Her quim is as fresh as home-world air." Garret's hand grabbed Bounette's cheeks and squeezed, forcing his mouth open, "Put a show for the man." Jake shook his shoulders, but Garret's grip was too strong for him to pull away.

Harvest, chuckled. The beast actually chuckled as he unfastened his waistline bandolier and strode past. Bounette yelled his rage from his chest. It was almost animalistic as he was unable to form any coherent words with his jaw locked into place by Garret's hand. Bounette's large eyes followed Harvest as best he could, not noticing Garret closing in until he heard him hocking back and by then it was too late. Not that he could have done anything. Garret spat into his mouth.

Thick strands of phlegm hit the roof of Bounette's mouth, dropping the taste of rotting teeth onto his tongue and as the sickly liquid ran to the back of his throat, an idea... If they wanted fresh pussy, he'd give it to them, "Survivant." Garret's grip released and Bounette leaned forward, coughing the vile spittle from his mouth.

"Quelle?" Garret asked, tilting his head sideways.

"There's another survivor." Bounette blurted, continuing to spit out the vile taste, suddenly aware of the warm blood sliding along his jaw-line, "A girl."

Garret grinned, "Where?"

Bounette brought his head up, meeting the man's yellow and red eyes, "Infirmary."

"She hurt?" The question came as a shock to him and Bounette couldn't quite work out how to answer it, thankfully Garret had a follow up question, "Is she fresher than your beloved?" One that Bounette knew exactly how to answer,

"Ten."

Garret stood up, tapping his legs and laughed, "Hoorraah." He said in an elongated accent and false excitement. Bounette dropped to the floor exhausted, rolling his head to see Natalie, crumpled against the wall with Harvest standing over her, "Leave her be."

The beast looked almost upset; standing with his dropped shoulders and unfastened armour. It was only when Harvest grinned, giving him a good look at his fire damaged face and a knowing wink, that Bounette knew he was playing and maybe had been all along. It didn't matter, they thought they'd found his lynch pin. But his plan was safe... for now. He hid his smile behind the throbbing pain of his ear, hid his intentions in his pathetic doll like pose. If he was right, they would all regret stepping on board the Jian Seng.

***

The pirates had sat Bounette against the wall next to Natalie's body, while they set up a forward station in

Operations. The Doc's wrists were bound together in electrical tape. Around him the pirates made short work of fitting their portable computers to the Seng. Most of the time they worked in silence or with some benign banter. They all had jobs and all knew precisely what they were doing. Some of them had now left, replaced by others who came and went, always taking something with them, always bringing something new. Only Garret and Scratch remained there all the time. Scratch doing all the work, while Garret reaped the information from his underling's efforts. *Benefits of being Captain*, Bounette thought to himself, remaining quiet. He continued to watch them without moving, only occasionally flinching when the memory of his deeds resurfaced.

He didn't understand most of what they were doing. There seemed to be a lot of hand held computer tech brought onboard, which Scratch would play with and then hand to Garret. This would be followed by chatter between the two until one of the other pirates returned with some more things or information. *Interesting*, Bounette mused, *they don't like using the internal comms system, but have no issue speaking in front of me.* He'd taken note of some more names and possible positions. Garret was clearly Captain, everyone reported to him and he was the one who spent the most time antagonising him. Probing him for details about the ship and its crew, asking if there were any traps set out for them.

Bounette answered honestly, he didn't know. Harvest had beaten him once to try to get more details, but after it was clear Bounette's story wasn't changing, Garret stopped the violence and allowed Bounette time to sit in silence.

Dante, the shark who'd gone back to their ship was possibly the next in command. However, it was evident to Bounette that at least three of the crew didn't like him. Harvest, the hulking necrophiliac was one of them. A man with serious burn scars on his face, called Jonah was another and one of the women, Bounette thought she was named Xian, but couldn't be sure, was the last.

They'd only addressed her by name once and it was too quick for him to grasp. They tended to call her 'babes' or 'bitch' to which the common response was equally affectionate. She chain smoked slim cigars and revelled in tapping the ash onto Bounette whenever she sauntered past.

"He's honest." Scratch said in a giddy voice, repeatedly tapping his wrist-strapped screen, "There's a youngen in the infirmawee."

Bounette ignored the comment, better to leave it play out than push the matter. It was only a matter of time before they went investigating.

"Manifest?" Garret asked, taking the pad from the neoned fool.

"No, Doc's notes."

Bounette stared at the floor. Trying to remember what he'd written and what he'd saved. Were they looking at his submission document, or the investigative report? Garret read the pad and passed it back to Scratch with anger and disgust, "I asked for the manifest, I want to know the name of the bastard who escaped the tug."

With that snippet of information Bounette breathed a little easier, avoiding an obvious show of the elation he felt over the knowledge Ford may still be alive. Then came the counter point, like the sunny morning after a storm revealing the extent of the damage from the previous night, he thought on how he could possibly explain himself to the kid. He'd never understand or forgive Bounette for killing Natalie, he'd see him as the murderous charlatan he was, 'then don't tell him,' the voice in his head said, using Natalie's tone.

Jake turned to face her; everything was as it was moments before. Except there was no longer any sound, everything was playing out like a silent film. Faces looked at each other, mouths opened and closed, but nothing was said. He shivered, feeling her cold hands around his neck. Her thumbs pushing up into his hairline and fingers caressing his throat, 'tell him they killed me, Ford won't need more than your word'. He nodded, she was right. She was dead, but she was right. Her icy lips pressed against his cheek and when he turned to look, he found nothing.

"You okay there Doc?"

Jake Bounette looked up, finding Garret staring at him. The Doc dropped his eyes and stared at the floor without uttering a syllable as Natalie's lie took form in his mind. His neural pathways fired, purging his memory and making a new one. Redirecting the guilt he felt against himself toward his wife's true killers, because without them he would never have done it. Like an artist's brush, his subconscious whitewashed his pain and began painting a new one. With each stroke his guilt was buried and a new reality born. One where Harvest, the man-beast took her as his love doll and discarded her as such when he was satisfied, 'Avenge me, my love.'

"I will." He mouthed,

"I didn't hear you." Garret said and when there was no reply forthcoming, "Okay, be like that." And moved his attention to Scratch, "You done yet?"

"Give Scwatch a moment." Scratch replied, continuing to search.

Garret sat at the table, "Can you get this piece of shit to work?"

"One thing at a time, boss."

Bounette noted Garret's impatience and considered it to be an advantage.

"Captain." Dante returned to the room, "There's a whole bunch of them on ice."

"Well well." Garret said, drumming his fingers on the table, "Pussy down the well."

Bounette could feel him staring, but refrained from looking up.

"Want to extrapolate Doc?" Garret said, the beating of his fingers underlining his impatience.

"Not really."

"You sure Doc? I could, let's say, incentivise you, if you'd prefer."

Natalie's charred face flashed in front of Bounette's eyes, "Feel free to jump out the airlock."

Garret's fingers halted and Bounette looked up to see him smiling back at him, "I'm glad you found your balls Doc. I was getting worried."

"I'm touched."

"I'm serious." Garret stood up, walked over and crouched down, "I don't agree with throwing away useful things and you were looking to be quite the disappointment."

"You're wasting your time, boss." Dante said from the doorway,

Garret grabbed Jake's face, pulling his chops toward his, "There are three options for you Doctor Bounette. You can die." Garret held up one finger, "We can sell you with the rest of your crew." A second finger joined the first, "Or, if you're feeling particularly wild this morning, you can join us." He extended his third finger and pressed their tips against Bounette's forehead, pushing his head back, "Chew it over, but don't be as quick to dismiss us as you did your beloved."

Bounette looked blankly for a moment, not understanding his meaning. Neither, did he care for the quizzical expression Dante was giving him. *Don't bite, Jake.*

"Manifest, Boss." Scratch announced, handing the pad back to his Captain.

Garret stood, grinning as he read down the list, "You weren't lying when you said a whole bunch, this is quite the payload."

Bounette recited the names of his extended family in his head. All of them to be sold to the highest bidder and he could be one of them. He'd not expected a choice, but there was only one name he cared about and the pirates had... *Natalie...*

Garret clicked his fingers, waving his hand toward Dante, "Grab Shodan, tell him he, Xian and Banks are on Popsicle duty."

"Aye." Dante said, moving out of the way, as Harvest walked past carrying a utility box, which he set down on the table and then took a seat.

"Then come back here." Garret past the pad back to Scratch, "Find me something else to salvage."

"Yes, Boss."

Then the room fell into silence, but Garret, to Bounette's surprise, remained stood in front of him. When he looked up, the red and yellow eyes were staring at him, "Hi." He said, crouching again, "There are no children on the manifest."

Bounette looked blankly at him, but noticed Harvest's ears pick up at the word 'children'.

"Who's the girl?"

"We rescued her from the ship, the one that hit us."

Garret returned his blank stare, "The ship that caused all this?"

Bounette nodded, not wanting to go into any more detail, but knowing he had to give him something, "She was in stasis."

The Doc's words brought Garret's attention back, "Injured?"

"She's in the infirmary." Bounette forced a smile, "What do you think?"

"I'm liking you more and more." Garret patted Bounette's shoulder, "You really should consider joining us."

The thought of fixing their wounds and breaking bread with them sickened him, "I'll chew it over."

"Good man." Garret said, standing again, "Scratch?"

"Yes, Boss."

"Anything new?"

"Erm... there's tewwafoaming pwe-fabs. Med-sups and dwugs and seeds in the pods. The ship's got a JCN nine thousand puter core. Looks like it was fitted wecently." He flashed his neon teeth, "Food in the stores and more med-sups in the infirmawee..."

"We'll be visiting your little friend then." Garret said, winking his yellow eye at Bounette, "Harvest, you're with us."

"About time!" The hulk announced, removing himself from the chair and grabbing Bounette by the back of his suit, lifting him easily to his feet. His breath stank of rotten meat, "I've been itching to get some action." Bounette said nothing, what was there to say...

SEVEN

Ford wasted no time once he'd made it back through the airlock in removing his cumbersome suit. In his mind it would slow him down and its heavy boots would be loud and draw too much attention. It had armour, but it would have little use if it brought the entire pirate crew down on him. Better to be agile and attempt to pick them off one at a time. The top deck was simply the airlock, a lobby and an observation lounge. It was a dead end, one he did not intend on being caught in. The only place he intended to risk time in was the wall locker next to the inner airlock door. Every deck had them and he was sure the pirates were aware of them and their contents. However, he gambled the risk of being caught was at its lowest here on the top deck.

Inside were emergency supplies: A haversack, wrist-lamp, medical box, a small toolbox and oxygen mask, with a fitted air tank and an hour of supply. He filled the haversack with the goodies and sealed it before dropping to the next deck. He'd had plenty of time to consider the possibilities while climbing the side of the ship. Once on the second deck he travelled to the aft ladder, taking him down to the bridge deck and giving him more options. In his mind, the pirates would move slow and methodically in their exploration of the ship. That was his edge. His knowledge of the Jian Seng was absolute, every corner, every duct, every damned circuit breaker. The ship was both his best defence and attack.

The pirates only knew the basics. At best they would be arrogant and careless; at worst cautious and vigilant. Ford didn't have the luxury to believe in the former without fearing the latter. What he did have was a deep knowledge of the ship and all its nooks and crannies. He would have preferred not to have grown as much as he had however. Being able to crawl through the smaller ducts and slipping behind the pipes that ran horizontally along the walls would have been a great advantage. But you work with what you've got and he'd been given knowledge. This was his sandpit and no bastard was making castles but him.

With the damaged bridge not being a viable option, the only other places to spy on the pirates would be Operations or the data core. While he felt an obligation in returning to Natalie and Bounette, the path would put him on the pirates' boarding deck. The temptation of seeing the pirates up close was palpable. Knowing how they were dressed, what weapons they carried and how they interacted with each other was premium information. But, Natalie had dropped a number of bulk heads which would make the journey difficult. *Too many bottlenecks and dead ends.* The risk of him being seen, or worse still being caught had him believing his true direction was to the data core and it's security bastion, which contained the servers that ran all of the ship's internal cameras. Using its terminal he could find out their numbers, positions and extrapolate their search patterns. The drawback to the plan was the room's tactical disadvantage. It only had one door in and out.

Listen, move, stop and repeat. Ford's routine was slow but necessary. He listened over the ladder drop, cautious of the silence. He was fairly certain the invaders were still on deck eight and the entrance to the core was on deck eleven. Hopefully, they'd found something of interest to slow their expedition. From the bridge deck, he chose to use the starboard side ladder. It was further to reach, but it was on the opposite side of the pirate ship and the safest option.

He crouched at the ladder pit a few seconds, ears twitching at the creaking of the hull. With the temperature continuing to drop the metal cooling was only going to increase. The Jian Seng was slowly dying of hypothermia and the aching hull signified her final death throes.

When satisfied there was no one beneath him, he stepped onto the ladder and began climbing down. He stopped mid way, his foot hanging millimetres from a rung. His ears strained through the silence, the quiet echoing back. He was sure he'd heard something. What exactly, he couldn't be sure of. But it was something and it wasn't the creaking hull. Ahead the corridor stretched out dark and quiet, tormenting his senses. The blackness swirled, vents breathing. But there was nothing there. *There is nothing there, get a grip, man.*

He sucked the cold air up his nose, "Come on." He whispered, dropping his foot to the next rung and stopping as the sound returned. It was a low base driven laugh, short and curt with a hint of mocking. He stepped back up, backing away from the pit and crouched low. The voices grew steadily louder and words once fogged by distance became tangible. Two voices in conversation, two sets of boots clacking on the grilles beneath their feet. More laughing, "...but do you trust him?"

"I trust his abilities." The other replied to Laughing Boy, "What's your beef with him, really? You afraid he's going to piss on your boots? I know It's not the share of the bitches you're worried about, he's not blinked at the opportunity."

"That is the problem, I can't trust a man who doesn't stick it somewhere, even an animal would be better than nothing." Laughing Boy grunted at his own warped humour.

Ford edged over the pit, looking down as the voices past underneath. One shoulder, dark red hanging nets and it was gone before he could see any more.

"I don't know what to say." The other said, ahead of Ford. The owner of the dark red shoulder, "What do you think Doc? Should we trust him?"

Ford's heart skipped beat, *Doc?*

"Hey, Captain's speaking to you." Laughing Boy said as Bounette's scraggy head and deflated body trundled passed the ladder. A large hand pushed against his back, "Answer him."

"You know Doc, you're really testing my patience." The Captain said, "You're hot one moment, cold the next..."

"Want me to cut the other one off, boss? It's not like he's listening."

"Let's wait until we see if he's lying first."

With all three gone passed and their voices ebbing away, Ford brought himself back onto his haunches. They'd reached Operations faster than he'd hoped and had split up. He rubbed his cold fingers against his face, cooling his forehead. *Damn it.* He focused his attention on the conversation. They'd been talking about a man; *someone close to them, maybe a part of their crew?* A possible ally, someone whom Ford needed to discover the identity of. Bounette was still alive and didn't appear too badly off. How long that lasted was probably up to him, in so much as how long he was useful to them.

Bounette was heading forward, in the direction of the infirmary. Medical supplies, the girl... Ford's heart skipped again, he wouldn't? *Would he?* His blood chilled at the thought, then went even colder when his mind jumped to Natalie. Alone with the rest of the pirate crew.

He dropped another level after ensuring enough distance was between him and the tourists.

If Bounette was taking them to the Infirmary it clearly wasn't by choice, which had to mean they had Natalie. Therefore, he couldn't possibly try anything which would put her life at risk. Resigning to his original plan, he continued down to the Data Core's entry level.

He moved down the rest of the decks unhindered, but as he neared the core's entrance his confidence began to wane. The entrance was the only way in or out of the core. A perfect place to end up trapped. He slowed his approach, wishing he still had the mining laser. The door was shut but the indicator light was on. Propping himself against its side, he tapped the release button. The door slid open with a soft hiss, expelling the stale recycled air from inside. Ford covered his nose at the acrid smell. He knew the stink all too well, burned circuit boards - lots of them. But he'd made it; this was the last piece of cover before reaching his destination. Counting silently to three, he peered around the corner.

The Core was a black silent hell. Ford pealed the haversack from his shoulder and opened it, grabbing what he needed and returning it back over his shoulder. Taking a deep breath, he slipped on the wrist-lamp and switched it on. He scanned the aisles of server banks. Rows and rows of non-functioning circuitry, if he had come down here earlier to switch everything off he'd have felt better. But now, with everything seemingly down without his helping hand, his future became bleaker with each step. It wasn't until he reached the stairs that hope called out to him.

There was the faint whirring of server fans, coming from below. If he was lucky, something would have tripped and knocked the remaining servers off. Each floor was on a different circuit. The floor below him was still running. The security bastion was on the lowest.

Ford swung the beam down, through the gangway and squinted to see the bottom. More banks of servers, all dead, and there was no way of telling which ones were which without getting close enough to read the labels and then he wouldn't know if they were burned without powering them up.

If the last deck was without power he'd need to disconnect all the servers and then power up the security bastion along with its server stack individually. If they didn't trip, he could go right into it. If they did trip he didn't have the skills to remedy the problem. He raised his wrist-lamp to the top deck noting his breath fogging through the beam, noticing the cold more than ever. Emergency power was designed to keep all of these computers running cold. Therefore, it was cool in here on a normal day, but now with only a handful of them working... He dropped the light beam ahead of him and walked to the deck plan, located just along the gangway.

He shone the light on the large plan. It stood at six feet tall and three feet wide, depicting all five levels. He already knew the location of the security bastion. He just needed to confirm the locations of the power distribution nodes. He pressed his finger against the red line, all he needed to do was reroute the power from the deck's buzz bar so it supplied the security servers instead of life support. With any luck, he'd have the security terminal up and running within half an hour and then he could get himself the intelligence he needed.

***

Harvest must enjoy pushing me, Bounette thought as the massive hand nudged him forward yet again. He wasn't moving any slower than the other two, but the brute continued to prompt him to keep up, "Hey." Bounette objected, but Harvest and Garret only laughed it off. He could hear the sound of the portable generator running in the infirmary. He rubbed his hands together, warming his palms in anticipation. It was good to know how little they thought of him.

"Captain?" The Shark's voice, Dante, came through a comms unit.

Garret leaned to his left, rolling his eyes at Harvest, "Speak my friend."

"We're losing life support. Scratch thinks there's a problem in the Data Core, so I've sent Logan down to investigate."

"Sabotage?" Garret's unwavering glare focused solely on Bounette.

"Possibly," Dante replied, "One of the crew is military."

"Dead or in stasis? And how long we got before life support fails completely?" Garret asked, eyebrow arching.

Knowing neither of them were paying attention, Bounette allowed a painful smile. He knew exactly who Dante was referring too.

"Not in stasis, name's Clifford Dahl, spent a couple of years with the militia fighting over mining rights on Otzu. As for life support, we're still checking."

This was great, thought Bounette, they'd now waste time looking for or preparing for an attack. Either way, their attention was split, 'Don't get too confident hun'. Natalie's voice reminded him.

"Wasn't the Captain a Dahl?" Harvest asked,

"Yeah, it's his son. There's a sister too, she's on ice."

"Keep her separated from the rest, just in case." Garret ordered, "Good work."

234

"Scratch thinks he could hook into the security systems if we get power to the servers. Should make it a bit easier for us."

"Logan's down there, isn't he? Is it worth sending Scratch down?"

"He's still working some kinks out up here. I'll have him down to assist Logan when he's done."

"Tell Logan not to touch anything, I don't want his ham fists smashing anything up before we get the chance to use them. Garret, out." Garret turned to Bounette, "Well?"

A moment later, Bounette felt Harvest's over-sized paw push against his shoulder, "Captain asked you a question."

Bounette halted, as much fun as this was, they were right next to the infirmary and he wanted to get it over with. He looked Garret in his eyes and shrugged.

Garret caressed the hilt of his serrated knife.

Bounette contemplated losing his other ear. But his eyes were gradually drawn to Garret's fingers, which continued to caress the hilt of his knife, "You know Doc, Eunuchs go for a good price on Udachy, more so without their teeth."

"I don't know." He answered, shrugging again, "It's been a bad day. But if he's alive I guarantee he's pissed, I'd watch your back."

Garret flashed his broken teeth, "See Harvest, I told you he'd warm to us."

Harvest grunted and shoved Bounette's shoulder again.

Bounette stepped back unsteadily from the force but kept his balance. It wasn't elegant, but it made them laugh. As long as they continued to laugh, to underestimate him, he would have a chance. He turned and headed to the end of the corridor, took a left, seeing the glass wall and the infirmary inside, "We're here." He announced, stopping at the doorway until Harvest pushed him inside.

The force was more than he'd been accustomed to and he found himself jogging into the middle of the room. The lights were off again and the portables he'd set up only lit the areas where Bounette had been working, leaving much of the infirmary in shadow and all the adjoining rooms were black. Jake paid them but a glance. His focus was set on the contents of Q-Bay at the back of the room, behind the vision wall, which had gone into screensaver mode. Instead of the Bay were slow rotating pictures of Yosemite, 'We should go back', Natalie whispered.

"Get the lights." Garret ordered,

"There are artificial organs and augments through the door." Bounette pointed to the black room to his right.

"You carry augments?" Garret asked, snapping his fingers at Harvest who promptly followed Bounette's directions.

"We're contracted with Asuka to provide Medical..." Bounette trailed off as Garret began snickering, "You don't give a damn do you?"

"Na." Garret waved a hand, "Just breaking you in Doc, I've a feeling you're going to say yes."

Bounette grimaced, backing up toward his workstation as the pirates split up, "How so?"

"You're a survivor." Garret said, his eyes following the blood trail on the floor, "Maybe not before today, but not killing yourself after killing your own wife, that takes a rare breed of stones. You'll see sense."

While Bounette listened to Natalie's soothing voice, telling him to ignore the Pirate Captain's vicious lies, Garret looked around the room. His attention was far away from the Doctor.

'Now', she said. Bounette obeyed, half turning and grabbing his laser scalpel from the workstation. He slid it up his sleeve as the Pirate grabbed one of the portable lamps and aimed it at the blood trail. He followed it to where the gurney Bounette had used during surgery, "Who's injured?"

"Do you care?"

Garret twisted the lamp stand so the beam hit Bounette's face, "Only if it's the Captain's son."

"Then forget about it."

Garret swung the lamp's beam away from Bounette's face, "Keep it up Doc."

"Garret." Harvest called from the dark room, he now carried a flashlight and was grinning, "There's some grade 'A' shit in here."

"Then start packing it up." Garret ordered, waiting until Harvest returned to the store room before turning to the Doc, "He's not too bright."

Bounette smiled, wanting to stab his scalpel into the bastard's yellow eye.

"The girl?" Garret demanded, looking around the room with the lamp, stopping as the light shone on the quarantine bay wall and the image of Yosemite standing tall amongst a desolated forest. Bounette marched over, tapping the window with his palm and removing his medical scan with a quick flick of his wrist. The image stuttered and died, showcasing the bare sterile room beyond with its sole occupant. To Jake's relief, other than the blood around her feet that had finally congealed into a dark crust, she hadn't moved or altered. She stood in the same spot, swaying side to side while staring up at the dead ventilation grille, "I thought you said she was in stasis?"

Jake answered without moving, "I didn't lie. She *was* in stasis."

"She's not now."

"No." Bounette conceded, "When the engine blew, it damaged her pod and the safety protocols opened it."

"What's wrong with her?" Garret was standing shoulder to shoulder with him now, peering through the screen with scrutinising eyes, "Why is she all... wobbly?"

Jake had expected that particular question ever since Garret spat in his mouth, so he answered without hesitation, "Shock."

Garret stood the lamp, pressing his hands up to the glass. With his back turned, the doctor looked toward the storeroom and saw Harvest obediently following his orders, stacking crates outside of the storeroom door. Bounette didn't know exactly what was going to happen, but he intended to place enough distance between him and everyone else when it did. He stepped away from the vision wall, nearing the wheeled trolley where he'd left his face mask.

"Where you going Doc?" Garret asked, looking over his shoulder.

"The screen controls are just here."

Garret nodded, turning his attention back to the girl, "Poor girl."

From the corner of his eye, Bounette could see Harvest taking an interest. He'd clearly heard Garret mention the girl, 'don't let him interfere', advised Natalie, but Jake didn't need any tutoring. He was at the precipice, ready to execute his plan and by the Trinity's will, the two pirates would be held accountable for Natalie's death. If Harvest was too close, he'd get into the mix of things quicker and there was no telling how fast this was going to play out once he pressed the button.

"How long has she been like this?" Garret continued with the incessant questioning,

"Since she came out of stasis." Bounette said, adding the lie, "It looked promising she'd talk, but you came aboard and I had to leave her."

Garret smiled his broken teeth at Bounette, "She just needs the right motivation."

Bounette wondered how things would have transpired if there was nothing wrong with the girl? How far would he have gone to defend her? Would Natalie still be here, or would they have all killed themselves together? All the horrid *what-ifs* vanished, when Jake unconsciously pressed the release button and the quarantine bay wall lifted, *Have your fun.*

Garret stepped between Bounette and the girl, "Hey there little thing." The pirate said in a surprisingly sincere and soft manner, one that made Bounette feel sick to the stomach when he realised he'd probably used that voice and very line before. He eagerly watched as the pirate stepped over the Quarantine's threshold, "Daddy will make it better."

With Garret no longer blocking Bounette's view, it allowed him to see her tiny frame. She still swayed, ignorant of the pirate's advance. *Disappointing,* the scans had shown some radical changes to her biology, ones he couldn't understand but which were very similar to some fungus on Earth. Of course, that fungus had never been recorded to invade such an entity as a mammal, but was well documented in insects and crabs. If he was right, he shouldn't have to wait long.

A loud bang from Bounette's left alerted him to Harvest, dropping a crate on the floor. Inquisitive, the beast had now stepped away from the storage cupboard and was almost stomping all over Bounette's plan with his Sasquatch feet.

Bounette tore his eyes off the approaching man and back to Garret, who was back stepping back out of Quarantine. "What was that?" Garret demanded in a scathing tone, "You'll scare the girl."

The lamps flickered and the *girl* moved, her bones and muscles cracking as she shifted inhumanly fast toward the pirate. Bounette glanced at Harvest, who thankfully was more concerned with his Captain than of him. Taking advantage of the situation Bounette grabbed the facemask and strapped it on, while Garret turned to the girl. The pirate unsheathed his serrated knife, which glinted under the nearby portable lamplight.

The girl pounced, as fast and as powerful as a lioness. She landed her hands and feet on Garret's chest, knocking him to the floor. The knife slid and clattered between Bounette's boots, but Jake paid no attention. To him there was nothing in the universe except the girl. Garret punched and flailed, but even his strength would not move her. She was amazing, a beautiful and perfect predator. She took every punch he threw with only the smallest of reactions. Her hands and feet sprouted white tendrils that raced into the gaps in Garret's armour, rooting her to him.

Bounette, absorbed by the events stepped forward. A line in the middle of the girl's face, running from her scalp to her chin separated, tearing open while Garret screamed a torrent of obscenities in a futile effort to stave the writhing tendrils and the white fluid that sprayed over him. Bounette clasped his hands in front of his face and grinned, she exceeded anything he'd imagined. Only the pounding of Harvest's footfalls managed to distract him.

Harvest ran to his Captain's aid, oblivious to Bounette who slid the scalpel from his sleeve as the man closed. He ignited the scalpel's laser tip and dropped to his haunches, swinging the blade across the back of Harvest's calf as he past and severed the beast's tendons. Harvest fell, losing his own sidearm in the process and slid up against Garret. He yelled obscenities but Bounette only smirked as he stood, transfixed on the abomination.

The girl's body tore itself apart, as seething thorny tendrils lashed out, slapping around her like wet leather whips. They curled around Garret's limbs and held him still. Jake stepped back, watching as a fleshy pulsating sack worked its way up the girl's torn oesophagus. He stopped,

'Time to go Jake' Natalie warned. But he couldn't, not yet. He needed to see it. He needed to see Garret die.

Harvest called out, "I'm going to gut you." Jake stepped back further, slipping on Garret's discarded knife. His ass hit the floor with a hard thump and his coccyx took the brunt. Harvest continued to snake toward him, his eyes and face red and full of rage. Jake scrambled backward, leaving behind his scalpel. Then, Doctor Bounette saw what he'd been waiting for. In a glorious and sickly belch, the fleshy sack opened, expelling thousands of minute spores over its prey and fogging the room.

Harvest snapped his head around to see what had widened Bounette's eyes, the source of the sickly wet explosive sound; which gave the Doctor the impetuous he needed, 'run'. Jake rolled around, clambering to his feet and bolted through the door, oblivious to the continuing horror inside the infirmary.

***

The screens lit up one by one, loading up the internal cameras. Two of them instantly revealed perfect images, the rec-room and launch bay. Both empty. The other pictures showed the message 'Vision Sensor Not Available.' Ford expected this, as they were ones set up in the bridge, spinal corridor and the engine room. From the menu tab, he made some changes and brought up the infirmary. The camera showed an image, but one filled with what looked like a white cloud. He checked the alternative sensor aimed at the Quarantine Bay and found it the same, dismissing it as a fault with the camera he cycled through the list until he found Operations.

Ops was lit with blues and yellows. Standing lamps had been set up to compensate for the low power. Computers and crates filled the main table's surface and a black creature, daubed in neon sat hunched in front of the blue glow from a monitor. Panning the camera he found one of the bulkheads lying flat on the deck. This was obviously the pirates' base of operations on the Seng. But, there was only one of them present. Communications officer, he surmised, if they had such titles. However, there was enough alien equipment in the room to back up his theory.

With nothing else of interest, he looked to the next screen and began cycling through options. Then, from the corner of his scrutinising eye he caught a glimpse of a pair of boots and legs. The colour of the overalls was unmistakable. It had to be her. He switched back to the original monitor and panned the camera further, edging up the waist and torso until he caught sight of her face. Repelled by the sight, he raised his hand to protect himself from the image. His fingers separated, hand lowering as her scorched eye sockets looked straight at him. The top of her skull was wide open. The bastards had killed her.

The proof was laid in front of him and yet, he still couldn't believe it. A fire ignited in the pit of his stomach, boiling his rage and closing his hand into a fist. His knuckles tightened, ramming into the screen. In the quiet that followed he was left alone with the pain throbbing in his hand and the anger which still burned within him. If he could have reached through the screen, he would have happily wrapped his hands around the neon freak's neck and squeezed until those lightning blue eyes popped.

Ford's ears pricked up. He switched off his wrist-lamp, looking toward the whistling above him. Someone with him, entering the Data Core. He snapped the buttons, extinguishing the monitors and pitching him into darkness. Ford ducked away, moving as quietly as possible as he worked out exactly where the whistling was coming from. In his blindness, he reached a hand out to his right, using the server aisles as guides. He arched his head up, squinting at what little he could see of the grilles by the only light source in the room, the open main door. That light wasn't going to help him much, so instead, he favoured his hearing. Listening to the whistle, and smiling as he noticed the first of the heavy footfalls walking on the grilles above. He breathed as quietly as possible, while putting as much distance between him and the security bastion as possible.

With no way to confirm whether the newcomer had heard him, in retrospect, he'd wished he'd been a little more conservative in his reactions. The sound of him thumping the screen could easily have tipped the newcomer off. But that was in hind sight and it was too late to cry over spilt milk. If he had heard him, he wasn't making it obvious he had. He was still whistling, which was a good sign.

Ford followed the sounds until both the whistling and the sound of feet came to an abrupt stop. He was still on the middle level, probably checking the status of the core. The core had received an overhaul at their last stop at Mars' Shipyards and had been fitted with updated navigation charts and trade routes. Ford realised it would serve the pirates well if they took it, if they could get it all on board their ship that was. *Damn.* The newcomer was now stood almost on top of him. He could have been looking right at him.

"Logan..."

"Tell Dante to keep his pants on, Scratch." Logan replied,

"Not that, we just lost contact with Harvest and the Captain."

"The doctor?" Logan asked, "You kidding me?"

Ford's premature smile faded as the doctor's plan formed in his mind. Like Logan, Ford could not believe Bounette had the ability to take two of them out, not without help...

"Dante's checking." Scratch said, "Is there any sign of our guest?"

Ford gritted his teeth in the agonising seconds that followed, and while he couldn't see the pirate standing above him, the growing anxiety in his chest told him that Logan knew he was there.

"Nothing yet." Logan finally said,

Ford didn't breathe; fear perched on his shoulder and whispered in his ear, telling him it was a ploy. A trap to make him feel a sweet false sense of security before the hammer fell.

"Do you want someone down there with you?"

Logan's feet shuffled above Ford, giving the impression he was looking around and providing more incentive for Ford to get the hell out of there.

"Where's Dante, I'll meet up with him."

"Dwake's checking on the Captain. Dante wants you there, we need the life suppowt wunning and I want the camawas up."

"What do you want first?"

A pause, but not long enough for Ford to think.

"Camawas." The voice answered,

"Then tell me where the security terminal is?"

"The lowest level. Gwid... Five. And Logan," Scratch said, "watch your back."

With the conversation ended, Logan moved directly to the ladder that led down to Ford's level. Directly being the appropriate word. He didn't pause or feel about in the darkness, which solidified Ford's theory this Logan fella could see in the dark. Logan had asked to leave and meet Dante, which to Ford meant the pirate hadn't discovered him, yet. With that front and centre in his mind, Ford slid from the central aisle. He had no intention of being caught.

He timed his steps along the aisle with the clink clunk of boot falls on the ladder's rungs, crouching when Logan walked toward the security terminal and just listening as he passed the end of the aisle. *So far, so good.* Logan wouldn't take long to 'fix' the terminal as Ford had only just switched it off. It all came down to whether Logan was intent on hanging around to see what was happening on the screens or move onto the life support, back on the middle floor.

Logan began whistling again, the same tune which Ford was not familiar with, but damned if it wasn't catchy. He listened to the melody until the screens flickered to life, illuminating the end of the aisle. Crawling on all fours, Ford took his time. Surprise was his only ally, he knew nothing about Logan except his name, an educated guess the man could see in the dark and the ability to work a switch.

At the aisle's edge, he peered out. The pirate had his back to him, silhouetted by the glare of the screens. He was taller than Ford. However, his physique was hidden by the bulk of his armour. Armour which posed a problem in as much Ford had no weapon to pierce it.

Ford looked the other way. The ladder was within distance. If he could reach the next level before Logan noticed him he'd have a good chance of getting away. But Logan had a comms unit and could soon summon assistance. They'd be actively searching for him around the ship, and they'd have the internal vision sensors to help them. He had no choice; he had to take Logan out and without him announcing Ford to the rest of his team. He brought his haversack around him and slowly opened it, keeping an eye on the pirate as he slid his hand into the bag. He fingered the mask, then found the spare oxygen canister. It had some weight to it and could knock Logan out, if he got a good swing in. If not, he'd have to hope Logan wasn't much of a scrapper.

Keeping low, Ford moved into the main aisle. Logan was crouched, in front of the screens, curiously switching between cameras and searching the ship. Ford closed the gap between him and the pirate without noise, each step painstakingly slow. Luckily, Logan appeared to be engrossed. They'd lost contact with their Captain and that was obviously a problem.

Ford was close now, less than eight feet. Tremors of hope danced at the back of his neck; holding his breath, he slowly raised the canister over his head as he positioned himself behind his target. Ford glanced at the cameras and saw himself on the lowest left screen about to make the blow. He paused, hope slipped from his grasp as suspicion of Logan's trap crept in. But the pirate did not move. Out of eight screens Ford was only on one. It was possible the pirate's attention was elsewhere, searching for his Captain. But with each passing second, Ford's chances of surprise dropped considerably. He drew his breath and swung the canister fast and hard.

He'd expected Logan to move, but nowhere near as fast as he did. The man swerved to his right, Ford's swing glanced off the man's shoulder and crashed into the desk's edge sending vibrations up his arm and denting the canister. Logan's jab crashed into Ford's side, a hammer into his ribs sending Ford stumbling away.

Ford steadied himself, ignoring the throbbing in his side, looking toward the pirate. Cast in the blue light of the screens, Logan looked cold as ice. His eyes were like dark elongated shadows, his devilish smile cutting his face in half, "Hello worm." He said, raising an ancient six shot Revolver style pistol. It looked over a thousand years old and absolutely terrifying. Logan's other hand was reaching up to his chest, where Ford could see the personal comms unit nested in his armour.

Ford was less than three feet and only a couple of seconds away from being announced to the rest of the pirate crew. He brought the canister up hard and fast, clipping the Revolver's muzzle, knocking it free from Logan's hand as quickly as he knocked the grin from his face.

Abandoning his radio plan, Logan stepped back and brought his fists up in a boxer's stance. Ford dropped the canister to the floor and balled up his fists, mimicking the pirate, telling himself that the harder they are, the harder they fall, "Bring it."

Logan smirked, but didn't fall for the bait. They danced about for a time, testing each other's reactions. Ford had the feeling Logan was faster than him, his foot work indicating he'd spent some time in the ring, or maybe the streets. However, his armour was heavy and slowing him down. He also favoured his right for jabbing, keeping his left back, maybe for a good old fashioned hay-maker? Or with any luck, it was because he wasn't any good with it. This was something Ford had no desire or intention of finding out. He needed to end this thing fast, the longer it dragged out the more likely he was to lose.

Ford ducked another jab, bringing his own right in quick for a counter. This time his fist connected with Logan's cheek and it was like punching the hull. He hollered in pain, shaking his fist certain that his knuckles were broken. Logan gave him no reprieve, he grabbed Ford's throat and thrust him against a server bank, "What is wrong with you man?" Ford screamed at his attacker,

Logan smirked, "Sub-Dermal armour."

"Damn that hurt." Ford struggled in Logan's grip, it was firm but not life threatening. Logan wanted him alive and Ford intended to keep it that way, "And... not... fair..."

Logan laughed, "And sneaking up behind me with a club is?"

"Fair point." Ford grimaced back, noticing the dented canister behind the pirate. Slipping his hand into his pocket, he thumbed out the corkscrew on his waiter's friend and made a fist around the handle. He planted his feet against the server and kicked hard, forcing Logan to step back onto the canister and lose his footing. The man fell, pulling Ford over him as he jabbed the corkscrew hard into Logan's neck. Ford hit the deck with his back, rolling his arm out and slapping the floor with his throbbing hand. Ignoring the glaring pain, he scrambled away into the darkness in search of the other dropped weapon.

Logan stood up, staggering on his feet and reaching to the corkscrew still lodged in his neck, "You're a sneaky runt, I'll give you that." He pulled the offending item from his neck and threw it across the room in anger. He stepped into the darkness, unsheathing a demonic shaped machete from a leg strap, "But too much trouble to bring in alive."

Ford moved, searching the floor with his hands for the lost pistol, knowing he had to buy time, "You sure your boss would approve?"

"I'm sure he'll enjoy the story of how I castrated you."

Ford's fingers scraped the tip of a metal tube, "I don't think you need to castrate me."

Logan gave a little snort of derision, "I like that you think you're in a position to decide what happens next, it's cute."

The pistol's grip now in his palm, Ford rolled over onto his back, finger on the trigger he aimed and fired. Logan stared at him a moment, definitely surprised this time, blood leaking from his left eye and neck. His machete dropped before he did, but didn't make as much noise. The floor grilles shook at the impact, his armour must have weighed a ton.

Ford climbed to his feet, the weight of the pistol in his hand felt good, felt right. It had been too long since he'd held a firearm, even if this one was older than the Jian Seng. He knelt next to Logan's corpse, laid the pistol at his side and ran his hands over the armour, unfastening clips and removing segments. If the rest of the pirates were dressed the same, he needed to up his chances. It wasn't a full set, Ford soon realised. It was painted as if it was, but he recognised the shoulder guards as Earth Alliance. He couldn't be sure of the chest piece but if it does the job... Around Logan's neck, he found the dog tags. *Not always a pirate*, snapping the chain from the dead man's neck and holding it into the light, he read, 'Logan Chesterfield, Private First Class'. Ford removed his own gillet and fastened the armour around his jumpsuit. Not as heavy as he'd first thought, but hard and durable.

He'd never considered them having lives before piracy, when discussed they were always portrayed as bogeymen, never as people. What had happened to cause Private Chesterfield to pursue the life of an outlaw was a question for another time. For now, he had to move on, but before he did, Ford surprised himself by saying, "Sorry brother." Maybe it was because both of them had served, or maybe on some level he respected the man's combat prowess. He still needed to move fast so he left the chest piece, taking the forearm guards, shins and the weapons.

When he stood he felt better, a little unsure of his footing but definitely better. Looking at his fresh kill, he hoped Logan had been one of their best. He'd gotten lucky, that much was clear. If they were all as good as him he'd have a tough battle ahead. But now at least, he had a machete and a pistol. Holstering the latter he crouched back down, searching the corpse one last time for any spare ammo and found a small bandolier pouch with three speed loaders. Ford added it to his collection.

He was about to pull the plug on the security screens when Logan's comms unit burst into life, "Xian, meet Dwake and Dante at the infirmawee." It was the same voice as before, Scratch.

"Where's the infirmary?" Came a female reply, which made Ford raise an eyebrow in slight surprise. Like not thinking about them having lives before piracy, it had never crossed his mind about any of them being women.

And while Scratch gave directions, Ford unclipped the comms unit from Logan's chest piece, and almost turned it off. Instead, thinking it may come of use he clipped it to his belt, dialling the sound down low while looking over the screens. He cycled the cameras until he found what he was looking for, Jake Bounette running along deck two toward domestics, "Mother of..." He exclaimed, remembering what Mason had told him about the Doctor and what he kept under his bed. His quarters had the only firearm on the ship. He unplugged the security terminal and left.

***

"What is that?" Dante pressed his hands on the glass wall, looking into the infirmary with morbid fascination. Lamps flickered, arguably not giving him the best view, even with his enhanced eyes. He recognised legs, as small as they were, kneeling in the middle of the room with shreds of bone and bleached human tissue surrounding them. It was a hellish mess, he thought he could make out an arm, but it could have been another leg, that would make it three. Never had he seen such a brutal destruction of human form.

From the base of the human debris grew a mass of throbbing pustules and horned bramble that were snaking out from mass, reaching toward all corners of the room.

An abomination, that's what it was and worse than he could have imagined.

"That's... unpleasant." Drake said, sounding as revolted as Dante felt.

Dante followed the tendrils with his eyes locating several patches of blood. The long pale brambles wriggled through the pools. There had been a struggle that much was evident. There was arterial spray across the floor; the bramble was working its way to that too. Whatever 'it' was, it was carnivorous. Garret's knife and Harvest's pistol were both present, but where were they? Hopefully, they'd gotten away. If not, well maybe it had eaten them somehow. Maybe the cloud of spores hanging in the air was all that was left of them.

They'd not run into them in the corridor, so they must have gone the other way. But without any blood trails to follow he'd have to wait for Xian and her scanner, "This must have come from the other ship." He mused, not expecting a response from Drake.

She answered regardless, "The Doc said so."

"How so?" His interest peaked, gritting his teeth as his mind formulated the answer before Drake spoke.

"Doc said the girl was from the other ship." She shrugged, "He say anything else?"

"No. But then he wouldn't have had Garret and Harvest running down here as quick as they did, would he?"

Dante nodded, clenching his fists as he agreed with her assessment of the Doctor's subterfuge. He should have seen this coming, anticipated it. They'd been tracking the other ship, the Centurion. Garret was too impulsive. Dante knew this as much as he knew he shouldn't have abandoned Operations. Now he was left with this, this thing he couldn't understand or know how to control. If it were in the quarantine bay he'd have felt better. That room at least could have been sealed, was designed to keep things inside. But this poor excuse for an infirmary had no hope of containing the creature should it decide to want out.

Drake was over a foot and half shorter then Dante, who stood just over six. Drake was a product of her breeding. Due to its heavy gravity, all who grew up on the mining colonies of Rabbas IV were stout little creatures. Heavy set and strong, they looked strange and were commonly mocked by most as they didn't consider them a threat. Dante however, respected them. He knew their meagre traits were exaggerated and they encouraged that perception. The heavy gravity gave them superior strength in the faked earth gravity fields generated in ships and on most colonies.

All the Rabbations Dante had met were also keen observers and held good reason. So it came to no surprise that she, like him was intrigued by the creature. Whatever it was, it made him feel uneasy. It wasn't running at them, or outright attacking them, but it had come from what he'd presumed to be human. The quicker they found Garret the better.

The creature's tendrils were growing as they writhed, edging their way up the walls to the air vents. Somehow it knew where the grilles were and would reach them eventually. Soon, given that he could see it growing in front of his eyes. He had no doubt they could out run it, but if left unattended this thing could well engulf the ship. At least the door to the infirmary was closed; Drake had shut it before Dante had arrived.

"Can it get out?" She asked,

Dante smiled at her question. She'd been smart enough to close the door; most of the crew would have walked straight in for a better look. She was also smart enough to doubt the room as he did, "I hope not."

He pushed back from the transparent shield, rubbing his tired black eyes. They'd been agitating him since they were installed and he promised himself a service on the next shore leave, provided of course they chose somewhere that would service outlawed cybernetics. But even with all their enhancements, being able to see a person's heart rate, heat signatures and even see through walls, he found himself missing the wondrous colours only biological eyes could decipher.

He lowered his fingers and looked at the creature again. It didn't register any heat. He could pick up its spores floating around the room, though. They hung in the air, circling the mass. But despite their defiance of gravity, Dante's more nagging question was what the spores needed to seed? The legs under the pulsating mass gave him a dark and twisted theory as to why they had not found Captain Garret, Harvest, or the Doctor. The only thing they currently had going for them was the creature appeared rooted, but Dante couldn't ignore the remaining spores, he raised his wrist and pressed the button on the side of the radio, "Scratch."

"Yeah, Boss."

"Is there any air circulating on board?"

"Na." Relief washed over Dante like a cool shower on a hot day, "I got Logan fixing the camawas first, you want them up and wunning? I can-"

"Please don't." Dante was sure that course of action would end badly. Stepping further away from the shield, he noticed Drake was pressing her face against it, "That's not a good idea. You don't want to antagonise it." She tilted her head to him, raising her right eyebrow at him before returning to the freak show, Dante said, "Scratch, can you seal off the Infirmary, I don't want a microbe getting out." He looked again at the circling spores, "There any air flowing in the infirmary?"

"No. Nowhere on board." He repeated, "Is there a pwoblem there boss?"

"Yes." Dante wondered how much to tell him, "Take a look once Logan has the cameras up and running." It was better for him to see it himself and Dante's theory needed more evidence, spores included.

"I think Logan's having pwoblems. They were up, then down. Then up and now down again. Wegular Yo-Yo, boss."

"Have you called him?"

"No, boss."

Dante hid his disdain, inwardly snarling as he flipped the channel on his radio, "Logan?"

He looked at Drake, still too absorbed in the other side of the glass to be paying attention to his conversation.

When Logan didn't reply he repeated himself, idly thumbing the golden halo at his waist before flipping the channel back, "Scratch, I can't reach Logan."

"I spoke with him five minutes ago."

"Keep trying him, I'll send Drake to check on him when Xian turns up."

"Yes, Bo-"

Dante cut the channel before Scratch could finish. *First the Doctor, Garret and Harvest, now Logan,* "By the Trin..." He stopped himself, an old habit still unwilling to die. He glanced at Drake, but thankfully, she was still engrossed in the infirmary's alien. From the schematics he'd read, the Data Core was a long way off from where he now stood, "I think Clifford Dahl may have survived the tug we toasted."

Drake turned to face him, folding her arms in front of her chest, "I don't miss my targets."

"You didn't." Dante said, not caring for her tone, "You hit the damned tug, I think he ejected."

"We searched all around the ship."

"That just means we didn't find him."

Dante did not like fighting blind. He had too much going on and not enough information. *This damned job is cursed.* He unsheathed his pistol. If this was the work of that Clifford Dahl guy, he needed to end the problem quick. He unclipped the magazine, checked its power supply and set it back in place before returning it to its bed. Satisfied, Dante touched his comms again, "Xian?"

"Not far." She replied.

"Be vigilant, but hurry up at the same time." He really needed her scanner and needed Drake to check on Logan. If it got any worse they'd have to walk around in threes, which meant only two groups, which also meant they would remain on this ship for far longer than he wanted. He decided then, that they would locate the missing team members and cut their losses.

"Dante..." Drake said in a surprisingly timid voice. Her face, against his earlier warning was pressed up to the screen. Her breath was misting around her gaping mouth.

"What?"

"Can you see the far console?" She pointed into the room.

On the back wall, a series of computer terminals were up and running, flicking through pictures. Faces of people he did not know, guessing it was the crew, he didn't think it was worthy of his attention. They already had a full crew manifest, which already had copies of their medical histories. Then it clicked. He wouldn't bet on it, but he couldn't remember seeing those terminals on when he'd looked earlier, not that it was a priority with the monstrous creature shouting, 'look at me! look at me!', "Yeah, so?" He asked, already fearing what she was about to say.

"I think it just turned them on."

She was right, the bramble had reached the far wall and its tendrils were feeding into the terminal. Weaved themselves under the plating, and gotten into the circuitry.

This creature... plant he corrected himself was moving too fast to have been here the whole time it must have been dormant, possibly in stasis.

Only now it was acting, reaching for the vents and now somehow turning the computers on. The Doctor had lured the Captain and Harvest to it, this was his trap and now it was trying to find a way out.

He flipped his comms channel to general, "Everyone." He began, "Bring me the Doctor's balls."

EIGHT

Ford ducked into the Bounettes' love nest only to find it empty. He closed the door behind him and remained for a time in darkened silence wondering if he'd already missed his chance to reunite with the Doctor. "Doc?" He whispered, half expecting an answer, but not surprised when he didn't receive one. He palmed the lamps and the ceiling flickered on, illuminating the room. Flipping on his flashlight he searched underneath the bed frame. His hand instantly hit upon a wooden gunstock. Ford flattened himself on the ground, reached under the bed and grabbed the shotgun.

Except that it wasn't a shotgun. The barrel was long and narrow, it had a silver receiver and a steel loop Ford could slip his hand through while placing a finger on the trigger. Whatever, it was old and dusty. Whether it was older than the pistol he'd taken from Logan he couldn't tell. It had to be a thousand years at least. He pondered a moment on why anyone would keep such antiques, but was soon taken in by the beauty of craftsmanship in the rifle.

He wiped the barrel until it shone under the warm lamps. Even the walnut stock still held a polish once the dust had been removed, "Doc looks after you, doesn't he?" Pulling on the loop revealed the loading mechanism. Empty, unless the Doctor kept his bullets elsewhere in the room. Placing the empty weapon on the bed, Ford began opening draws and cupboards. He had a purpose and that was the only thing on his mind, there was no concern of riffling through someone else's belongings until he found Natalie's lingerie draw. He quickly dropped the delicates and closed the drawer defeated.

"Where are you?" He asked the room. The door hissed open. Startled, Ford fumbled for his pistol while dropping to his knee and aiming at the intruder. With his eye trained down the sight he saw Bounette's panic stricken face staring back at him.

"Don't shoot." He said, holding his hands up in front of him.

Ford lowered the pistol, "Bounette!" He returned the weapon to his holster.

"I thought you were dead." Bounette exclaimed. He was panting and clearly out of shape.

"Running much?"

"I think I'm going to have a heart attack." Bounette stepped into his room, closing the door behind him.

"You took your time."

"What?" He found the edge of the bed and flopped down.

"I saw you on the internal vision scanners. Thought you'd been and gone."

The doctor took his time, bringing his breathing back under control, "Nearly ran into them, had to double back. Nat dropped so many bulk heads, there's no direct route. Wait... How'd you know I was coming here?"

Ford opened his mouth to tell him, but noticed Bounette's bloody face, "What happened to your ear? And what happened to Nat?"

Bounette raised a hand to his missing appendage, looked Ford in the eye and said, "Pirates."

Ford took the word as an answer to both his questions and didn't pursue either. He holstered his sidearm and watched as Bounette searched one of his drawers to find some ointment, "Don't worry about me, I'm sure they'll do worse to you if they catch us."

Ford wasn't so sure, given the recent conversations he'd been listening to.

"So..." Bounette continued, "How did you know how to find me?"

"Your Shotgun... I mean rifle" Ford nodded to the prize,

Bounette's lip curled at the inaccuracy, "Winchester, model 94. It won't help, it's deactivated. I only keep it because it's a family heirloom."

"That explains why I can't find any ammo."

"You've been searching?"

The question sounded more of an accusation to Ford. Quickly changing the subject, he said, "Only a little. Why did you come back, if not for this?"

Bounette sat upright, rubbing the back of his neck and closed his eyes, "Habit?" the doctor was clearly lying. Smiling, Bounette lay back on the bed, moving the Winchester out of his way and stretched out, moaning in satisfaction. When he was finally done, he rolled onto his side and looked Ford up and down, his eyes twinkling with interest over the younger man's get up, "What happened to you?"

"They blew me up and then beat me up." He said and was about to reflect Bounette's question back to him when he remembered the photo and the security camera. In that same moment, Bounette's eyes glistened in the light, giving him away. Bounette blinked, looking to the ceiling and anywhere except at Ford.

"We're the lucky ones." After his telling words, Bounette's relaxed stance shrivelled into a tight knitted contortion. Pain and loss ebbed from him like warmth off a fire. Ford felt as though the rug had been pulled from under him. He had no place to look other than at the man who had no intention of explaining the sorry look in his eyes. He could only hope Nat's death had been quick, but something told Ford it hadn't. Whatever had happened, he was sure Bounette saw it all.

The Doctor moved and for a second, Ford thought he was going to say something more. Instead he just slid off the bed and walked towards the photograph Ford picked up earlier. Lifting it up from the counter top, he held it close, tracing the outlines of Natalie's features with his finger, "I nearly broke my leg after this photo was taken." He said, "Have you been to Mount Tholus?"

Ford shook his head.

"It's gorgeous. So still, serene. I've never before or after found a place like it, it was like we were the only two in the universe. You know?" He didn't look up, so Ford allowed him to continue, "The thing about Mars is that you can't tell how deep the soft stuff is. The sand, one minute you're moving across it quickly and the next you end up neck deep. My right foot went in, luckily, my imbalance threw me over and I rolled over and over again. I was a mess." Tears welled in his eyes, "But she, she was strong. She was always strong. She slid down right behind me and was there to pick me up." He wiped his face, "Look at me." He placed the photograph flat on the counter and headed into the en-suite.

Ford waited outside as he listened to the taps running, then through the closed door called, "You have a plan?"

The tap stopped and Bounette returned, wiping his face dry with a towel. His eyes lingering to his left, long enough for Ford to question it and take interest in what he was looking at, but all he could see was the cabinets he'd infiltrated earlier, "What?"

"Huh?" Bounette asked, bewildered.

"You were looking at something."

"I was?" He dropped the towel, picked up the photograph and removed the picture from the frame, "What did you say?"

Ford rubbed the back of his neck, "I asked if you had a plan."

"You don't have one?"

Ford shook his head, "Not really, I've been making it up as go."

Bounette looked him up and down, "You seem to be adapting."

Ford checked himself over, noting Logan's armour and weapons, "I got lucky." Something about Bounette made him think he wasn't fully paying attention. Something, but he couldn't make out. He put a pin in it for later and pushed him for more information, "I heard you took two of them down?"

Bounette stared at his photo for a moment, almost to the point that Ford was about to repeat the question. Then when the doctor's mouth opened to talk, Ford held his tongue waiting, but Bounette stalled, he looked Ford in the eye before saying, "Yeah, about that..." He opened up, much to Ford's surprise, detailing every event from how the Pirate Captain, Garret had spat into his mouth and put the idea of infection into his mind. Each step including how many pirates there were, how they had lost one to the trip mines, the journey to the infirmary and the gruelling deaths of Garret and Harvest. Ford didn't utter a word, not even to question, making mental notes with the intention to return once the man had finished. It was the longest Bounette had ever spoken to him.

When he'd finished, Bounette slid himself up his bed and rested against the headboard and waited for a reaction. It was then Ford realised that Bounette had known she was infectious. He wondered if he had been keeping anything else from him? The camera in the infirmary had been white washed, there hadn't been any malfunction or error messages and so it must have been because of the spore eruption. "What will happen to them, doc? Tell me everything you know about this monster."

Bounette raised his right eyebrow, "I didn't have much time to study it."

"Let's not do ten rounds, I only asked what you know. You were down there a good couple of hours while Natalie and I set up the generators, you must have found out something or you wouldn't have known she was infectious. Let it out, theory or otherwise."

"You heard of Cordyceps?" Ford's blank expression answered the question before he opened his mouth, "It's a fungus that infects insects and such."

"We're not insects?"

"And this isn't Cordyceps. Do you want to know or not?"

"Sorry." Ford snapped back, "Please, continue."

"Okay, this thing, creature or plant. It acts in a similar way. I was trying to shortcut the explanation."

"It didn't work."

"Clearly. Okay. Now, this thing inside the girl was feeding on her biological make-up. It was either re-writing her DNA or growing a separate entity inside her. Whatever it is, it controlled her motor functions. Motor functions only. It didn't control her personality or replace it, that's why she was…"

"…all little miss zombie."

Bounette rolled his eyes, "Yes. So the thing, the fungus isn't smart enough to mimic a real person, but it is smart enough to control the girl... or the host for its own purpose. And that is the same primordial purpose shared by all living things, it wants to survive. When the door opened, the girl attacked Garret right away. There was no thought, she didn't eye up the rest of the room, she went for the closest thing to her. The host becomes a vessel to pass on its spores. You following?"

"Please don't tell me that's why she was looking at the vent..."

"Exactly, and this is where it gets scary. I think it knew the vent was shut. If it were on, I believe she would have expelled her spores into the air supply."

"I thought you said it wasn't smart?"

"I said it wasn't smart enough to create a new personality or control the personality of its host. However, it was using all of her motor functions and probably all of her sensory functions too. It waited Ford, that's the scariest part about this thing. It waited, looking at the vent which was the best possible way to survive until the screen rose. Then, given the sure opportunity to infect someone else, it took it."

"So Garret and..."

"Harvest."

"So these spores are now wandering the halls looking for someone to infect?"

Bounette avoided the judgement in Ford's eyes by setting his own to the floor, "That's the theory."

"A pretty ugly theory." Ford said, feeling the thirst, "You have anything to drink in here? Aside from tap water."

"There's some whiskey and vodka in the cabinet." Bounette pointed to a featureless wall.

"Where?"

"The cabinet." Bounette repeated, "Don't you have one?"

"No."

"You got to press it."

"The wall?"

Bounette muttered something in French, climbed off the bed and walked to the wall. He pushed his hand firm against it until it pushed back and slid open. Behind it was a glass-shelved cabinet with a mirrored wall. Miniature lights dazzled the room, glinting from the drinking glasses and two bottles of expensive spirits, "Sweet." Ford said in appreciation, "All my years here and still this old shit-kicker surprises me."

Ford poured himself a glass of whisky, Bounette declined the offer. Ford took a sip while thinking of how to use the information Jake Bounette had just passed onto him. On the fourth sip he realised that he already had a plan, the one that he and Natalie had discussed in Operations, "What's the range of these spores?"

"I don't know." Bounette replied,

"How many of them will it take to infect someone?"

Bounette shrugged, "Again, I don't know."

"Anything you can tell me that will help us?"

"Don't get close." Ford didn't fully appreciate the glib response. But what else did he expect from Bounette, at least he was beginning to appear more like his old self, who then said, "I don't think bullets will work. The entity isn't reliant on the host's organs to survive. She wasn't breathing, so I'd take a stab and say her heart wasn't beating. You could have riddled her with holes and I think she'd keep on coming."

"What about a bullet to the head?" It always worked in the movies,

"Again Ford, they aren't zombies." Bounette followed the sentence with a slew of French, but the follow up didn't appear to be aimed at Ford. He wasn't looking at him. But when he did look at Ford he added, "Her head opened up like a rose bud, if it's using any of her brain it's the most

264

basic parts. Maybe, if you hit the brain stem... I don't know."

"Then how do we kill it?"

"You said Greaves saw the plant burned on the other ship. I'm inclined to suggest fire, but Ford..."

Ford guessed what he was about to say, and jumped in with, "You don't know if it will work."

Jake, rolled his eyes and sighed, "This is unprecedented, no one has come up against this before or there would be records. We need something to give us help."

"I know what unprecedented means doc, besides which. You're wrong. The Centurion came up against this. It's just that no one survived to tell the tale."

"That's comforting."

"Yeah." Ford admitted, "It sounded better in my head." However, his original plan of stealing the Albacore could still work. "We'll use it to our advantage. It will be distracting the Pirates, they've already lost two of their men and they'll have less of an idea of how it's working. Hopefully, they'll be dumb enough to try and save the infected. You said they've been moving our crew onto their ship?"

"They may have finished moving all the stasis pods by now."

"Then we'll have a full crew and new ship. We leave these assholes with the plant to die."

"We won't have a full crew." Bounette corrected, bringing Ford back to those names they'd both lost.

"No, we won't have everyone. But we can save those who are left, and ourselves."

"Vivre sans aimer nest pas procurement vivre." Bounette said, his eyes returning sadly to the photo in his hands.

"I don't speak French, Jake." Ford was aware it was the first time he'd called the doctor by his first name, but Jake Bounette didn't show any acknowledgement of it.

"It means..." The man paused, "You'll forgive me, English doesn't quite capture it, but it's along the lines of, 'to live without loving is not to really live.' I've lived my life Ford, I came here to die."

Ford watched Bounette over the rim of his glass while sinking its contents. The Doctor's truth, such as it was, did not help him, and Ford didn't like the idea of leaving him behind when the task ahead was already going to be next to impossible, "Don't talk like that, Jake."

"But I did, I let that thing out to get away. They weren't sure you were alive. All I wanted to do was get back here and see her face before I died. Be my guest to use that thing to your own advantage. I've accomplished everything I set out to do. I'm sorry Ford, but I've condemned us both to death."

Ford placed the glass on the counter top, "You're going to let them get away with it? Killing Natalie in front of you, I mean?"

The Doctor paused, eyes diverting to his left again, "Harvest did it and I fed him to that thing."

"Jake, I can't begin to think-"

"You're right, you can't. So don't waste your time trying."

The words were cold and definite, "Okay." Ford lifted his hands, "I was wrong to go there. But Jake, you're not the only one to have lost someone; my mother, to cancer." He raised a finger, "My father is waiting to die in stasis." Another finger and another... "Jo, Sharon, Ben, Eddie. They are all our friends, all our family. But we also have those who are asleep and don't have any idea what's going on right now. My sister is one of them. Your staff, you must like at least some of them. All of them are going to be shipped off to be sold as slaves and we have a chance to stop it, so I need you to get your head out of your ass and help me."

Bounette's eyes boiled with a rage Ford had never before witnessed. The man's veins were out and looked primed to pop. Ford suddenly found that he was afraid he may have gone too far and that Jake Bounette would somehow fly from the bed like some howling banshee and take him down. He waited, feet slightly apart for the attack and as the seconds continued to tick by with nothing said and no action taken it appeared there would be no retort, verbal or otherwise. Jake's recent and obsessive tick returned. His eyes looked to his left again before returning to Ford, "You're sounding more like your dad every day."

Ford was reminded of an earlier conversation, in which Natalie had said something similar.

***

"See anything strange?" Dante asked over the comms,

"Nothing like the infirmary." Drake answered, squatting over Logan's corpse, "He's been picked clean." She ran her hand over the open chest piece.

"Logan never loses." Dante muttered,

"Ain't that the truth" she said, as her fingers trailed along his neck line, "His dog tags are gone." This was bad, really bad. Her touch found its way to Logan's placid face, his muscles hardening with rigor mortis. There was a dark bloody hole between his eyes. Drake stood up, found the security terminal and switched it on. One by one, the screens flared into life. Logan's demise danced at the outskirts of her mind. The images presented on the screens were of the data core. She stared at the image of Logan's corpse on the small screen; icy fingers ran up her spine, "This captain's son could be a problem."

"He's not the only one, Xian's tracked Garret and Harvest to the ladder system. One of them went up it, the other..." She stopped listening to Dante's report when the gangway above her creaked, as if the very metal were in pain. She held her breath, staring into the light shafts above. The light beams shifted, the creaking returning, she had company, "Come back to..." Dante continued. She raised her hand over the comms unit on her chest plate, muffling the rest of the order, "Operations, Molotov is in the last run of stasis beds. We'll regroup and plan the next move."

She half listened to the muffled voice, more focused on the sounds above: thump, growing closer, slide. She extinguished her flashlight and stood up, backing slowly way from Logan's body, while keeping her eyes up.

She couldn't see who had joined her, and the room had fallen back into silence. She hoped it was the fool responsible for Logan. Knowing she'd never been that lucky, Drake switched off the safety on her assault rifle before stepping backward. Slow as slugs and always watching the gangway. She reached a hand out behind her, grasping for the ladder. She stepped up as quietly as her armour allowed, pausing as her head levelled off with the gangway. Dead ahead of her, stood in silhouette were the new arrivals. Large and heavy set they were an easy target. She climbed up, shouldering her rifle at the target, "Hey there."

Drake tightened her grip on the rifle, waiting for the response to her taunt, "Drake..." Dante called to her over the comms, loud and clear now her hands were elsewhere. She continued to aim at the interloper, who still remained still, "Drake... do you read me? Don't do this to me. Talk to me."

Keeping her finger on the trigger, "I'm here."

"What's going on?" asked Dante, "Scratch - cameras - now."

For a moment, she didn't know how to answer? She knew she had, 'something.' But didn't know how else to explain it. As much as the 'guest' was in her way, it seemed to be ignoring her. She took a breath, trained an eye down her gun sights and scanned the silhouette.

It was all too familiar. The outline of the body was smooth with disjointed pieces of armour. Armour she recognised. The stance was all wrong though. The body leaned on its right leg, the left foot was angled outward. Then as the sights hovered around the mid-section she recognised, "Harvest?" She asked, anxiety coiling tight in her belly, waiting to spring, "That you buddy?" It had to be, she'd know those rodeo thighs anywhere.

Dante called again, "Drake, I have eyes, but it's too dark in there."

Drake tapped the rifle's muzzle against the switch on her wrist, activating the strapped flashlight and illuminating her target. It *was* Harvest, and he'd seen better days. His skin was grey as stone, blisters rising and falling across his face. His expression locked in a look of anguish; eyes as white as salt, jaw hanging slack and his tongue rolling out over his bottom lip like some rabid dog. He twitched as the light crossed his eyes, Drake startled. She stepped back, her left heel dipping over the side of the ladder fall. She stopped, catching her composure and managed, if barely, to keep her rifle trained on her target, "Dante." She said, "I have a problem."

"Are you in immediate danger?"

"I don't know." Harvest remained in the doorway, his exposed skin wriggling under the light, "I've found Harvest." Her eyes scanned the room to her right before focusing back on her target, then to her left, searching for another way out. There wasn't one.

"Is he?"

"I think so..." She stepped forward, her rifle and eyes trained on the thing in her way, "He's not moving."

"Do not engage."

"He's in my way." She licked her dry lips, resisting the urge to blink, "I can't see another way out." She stepped forward. With each step, finding something new and disgusting about her old friend - a swollen wound on his right hand, twitching head. His left eye bulged from its socket, the pinhole pupil staring right at her.

"Help's coming." Dante's voice was a calming influence, but she didn't believe him. There hadn't been anyone near her position when Harvest had arrived, they'd be too late. The only chance she had was to escape. She stepped forward. Harvest's neck began to swell like a water-balloon filled with baby snakes. The man, dead or alive had at least six stone on her and a far greater reach. She'd be seriously handicapped in any form of close combat.

"Dante..." She stilled her trembling jaw,

"Keep the hell away from him."

"Is there another way out of the core?"

"We're checking."

"Check faster." This was not a position to be in. She felt helpless, like a kitten in a tied sack, plummeting off a bridge. Panic whispered in her ear to run, run as fast as her legs could carry her. She swallowed, moving her aim from the target, searching for a way out. *What are you doing?* Her lamp and aim snapped back to Harvest and thankful for the small pitiful mercy that he hadn't moved. Drake swallowed, pushing her jaw forward and grating her teeth against her top lip, "Dante..."

"One second."

"You've had five already." What was taking so long and why wasn't Harvest moving? He'd dragged his sorry ass all the way from the infirmary and for what. To take up residence in a doorway like some Halloween special Concierge? 'You're coat ma'am.' Sweat beads ran from her scalp, distracting her for a split second before forcing her attention back to the monster in the doorway, "For Saint's sake Dante."

"One second."

The only way out of this was for her to do it herself, "Harvest?" She took a tentative step forward, "Harvest, baby. It's Drake." She mumbled, giving into the terror, "Don't make me shoot."

"Don't shoot unless you can kill him." Dante advised, "You don't want to piss him off."

Her sight was dead in line with his face, "I have a head shot." She advised, fully aware that despite her ability she may not be able to take the shot. His face was of warped stone but recognisable all the same. She'd lived and killed alongside him for more than nine years and with that thought her hand began to shake, "Dante, where are they?"

"Too far, but we think we have something for you."

She held her stance, arms wavering under stress, part of her willing her old friend to move, at least it would be an end to this impossible fear crushing her lungs, "How?"

"Are you on the main level, facing the door?"

"Yes, just at the ladder. Door-side."

"Okay, there's a cable riser to your right. It won't have a ladder, but it should be big enough for you. You can use the cables for support. I want you to slide down, four levels. You'll end up in the launch bay."

"Should be?" Her eyes travelled slowly to her right, trying to penetrate the blackness, "That's the best way?"

"You could climb the cables, but going down is faster. Drake, it's the only way."

She breathed the room's stale burned air, bringing her eyes back to the lifeless statue in the doorway. She couldn't see the riser and as much as she wanted to believe Dante she preferred a plan she could visualise. Even with Harvest in her way, she could see another possibility: charge while firing, maximising the advantage of his handicap and slipping out of the door. Easy as pie, "I'm going to make a break for the door."

"Drake, think about it. Think about the infirmary."

It was all she could think about. That grey mass of writhing obscenity, part mammal, part plant. A creature so hideous and repugnant the image had branded itself into her memory and it was now inside her friend. "I have this." She stepped forward, but so did Harvest. She stopped instantly and so did Harvest. Drake's eyes widened, he'd broken the pattern. Now, there was no doubt he was aware of her and her escape plan seemed a little less tempting, "Okay, scrub that idea. I'm going to go for the riser."

"Good choice. Now, if you can wait another second..."

He didn't need to explain why, because before he'd finished speaking the main lights flickered to life. Server cabinets, gangways and terminals all became visible and so did Harvest's grotesque form. His slack jaw trembled, mouth gaping. His nose widened, ripping in two as his face fell in shreds. She didn't wait a moment longer, only heard the tearing of flesh and cracking of bones from behind her has she sprinted in the direction of the riser. Hope swelled in her heart, for at the end of her run was a plain metal door, nothing special other than the promise of survival.

The ground shook beneath her but she kept running. Not looking back, her eyes trained on the door, *eyes on the prize*. The floor shook again. To her left she saw something large and white, inhuman and moving as fast as a freight train along the parallel gangway. It was him, the creeping horror was not only running, he'd passed her. Heading toward the riser and would get there before her. Drake skidded to a halt, turned on her heels and bolted back toward the ladder, while Dante told her to remain calm. She flew around the corner, the floor bouncing under her feet. Her foot came down, missing the step. Her boot twisted, falling outward on the grille, heel bending inward.

Daggers of pain shot up her ankle but she just managed to grab the rail, narrowly missing the ladder pit and continued to run as best she could.

From the corner of her eye, she saw him coming up the corridor like a charging bull, tendrils whipping around him. She screamed. Each step with her right foot rang like a bell of agony, but with each ringing shot of pain the doorway got closer, "Drake, what's happening?" Dante asked, his voice was lost under her breathing and beating heart. Making it to the exit was everything, and she was going to do it.

"Get ready to close the door." She only needed to reach the door, looming before her like the pearly gates of Valhalla. "Come on." She told herself, timing her footfalls with the gangway. The shaking grew more violent, Harvest was gaining on her and she was slowing down, she held her rifle back behind her and fired.

Drake circled her arm in a frantic and desperate motion, spraying bullets all over the room. Ricochets pinged off metal, then an unholy belch of anger signalled at least one shot struck her target. The floor banged, her foot fell flat against it and she was thrown forward. Instinct kicked in, her rifle slung and hands rising up in front of her to brace her impact toward the oncoming gangway.

She hit it and rolled, the door was in reach, but the monster was closing. Drake rushed to her feet, pulling her rifle up, aimed as best she could and fired. The bullets drilled into his approaching torso, cutting through fatty tissue and his swelling body, puncturing his chest, peppering up his throat and smashing into his skull. Her erstwhile comrade's head snapped back, just as her magazine clicked empty. But he (it) was unfazed, its head swung behind its shoulders as it stomped toward her. Harvest's body ripped apart, convulsing in violent spasms as redundant flesh sloughed off. His arms swung around his body like dead weights, urging him on faster.

Drake dropped her rifle and ran. The gun clacked against the armour on her leg as she fought the pain in her ankle, and prayed to reach the door before him, "Run Drake, run!" Dante screamed. As soon as she breached the doorway, a tendril caught her ankle, feeding itself through a soft spot of armour and punctured her skin. She plummeted forward. Her unguarded face smashing into the grille. The sound of her nose snapping echoed between her ears as she got dragged back into the room.

She scrambled to try and escape, clawing at the grille and holding her place, but only for a moment. Her legs shook as the tendrils lashed around them, finding their way inside her armour, piercing skin like hot needles. She hurled every obscenity she'd learnt over the course of her pirate career and beyond. Her legs lifted, body followed, fingers clinging to the last of her hope until she dangled, upended in front of the monster. His chest was open, organs squirming with ominous threads of slime-lathered brambles. A white washed horror; raw egg whites, bleached lungs and a pulsating sack pushing to the forefront.

She freed her pistol from its holster and emptied it into the fleshy horror. Organs splashed open, translucent gunk sprayed back at her. Tendrils snapped forward, wrapping around her pistol arm and holding her splayed, crucified and helpless. She screamed, calling Dante's name while the sack pumped faster and faster before finally, it erupted. A cloud of razor sharp spores engulfed the air, littering her skin. In a frenzy she brushed her free arm across her face in attempt to remove them. Blood ran as their hooks tore her cheeks. More spores found her eyes, blindness. With deep panicked breaths she pulled more up her nose, packing her mouth and choking her as they filled her throat.

***

"Drake?" Dante called again, "Drake?" He stepped back, kicking a wheeled chair past Scratch, "Can no one on this crew take a simple order?"

Scratch raised his hand, "Scwatch can boss."

Dante stared at the simpleton, knowing one of his best was now probably dead. It also meant Harvest and Garret were definitely dead, or whatever that damned creature did to you. Dammit, why didn't Garret mention the girl before going to investigate? *Because he didn't trust you.*

Newest member of the crew and all, but it was more than that. The crew had a pecking order and while Dante had solidified his position as a person of respect, he was still at the bottom. It wasn't so much that Garret didn't trust him, it was more that he wanted first dibs on the prize. Greedy ignorant fucking pirates, "Stop Xian." He snarled, "I don't want anyone going near that thing."

Scratch lowered his hand and hit the comms, relaying Dante's order.

Xian immediately replied, "I'm nearly there."

"Ask her if..." Dante began, but the awkward features displayed on Scratch's face made him re-consider. He switched on his own personal comms, "Xian, drop it. Drake's infected with whatever had Harvest and Garret."

"Let me check."

"Negative, we can't afford the infection to spread any further. Did you store all the Seng's crew?"

"I lcft Molo and Jonah with the last train."

"Go help them finish." He thought the scenario through, three of his crew infected, maybe the doctor too, and whoever took out Logan, "Seal the Albacore when you're done and head back here. Scratch will run a biological purge, just in case one of the infected is on board."

"How long will that take?" She asked, stress evident in her voice.

Dante looked over to Scratch, who was rubbing the back of his head in thought, "Six hours?"

"Six hours?" Xian's stress levels were peaking,

"It's better than jumping ship and finding our boat just as infected as this one."

"I say we run, and to hell with this place."

They could run, cutting their losses and meet everyone back at their ship, but he didn't like leaving without knowing where Garret was. Or Clifford Dahl for that matter. Either of them could be waiting on the Albacore, "No, it's too risky. We have to make sure our escape route is clear and Xian, when you're on the Albacore don't head deeper into the ship, stick to the cargo hold. Once they're all strapped in, don't mess around."

"Understood."

"One more thing," this was the important one, "kill anything you're not sure of, if it doesn't drop straight away high tail it."

"Aye, aye."

"Have Shodan and Banks get their asses back here too." He ordered, walking to the table and leaning into it, "You been able to find anything out from the infirmary computer?"

"Scwatch been playing opewator boss."

Dante stood upright, craning his head back at the man.

"Will get back on it now, boss."

"Good." Dante had no intention of hanging around longer than they needed to once it was done. If he couldn't get what he needed from the infirmary, then he'd get it the old fashioned way. They would have enough time to get that done, as long as they sealed off the hazardous areas of the ship. *Unless the creature could open doors*, the thought chilled and mocked him at the same time. He'd already seen, or at least thought he'd seen it switch a terminal on.

He raised his fist, bringing it down hard onto the table and cracking the glass surface.

Scratched shot him a wide eyed look, "You good boss?"

Dante swung around, "Yes Scratch, Boss is good."

Scratch grinned, nodded and returned to his work. Good Scratch, Dante thought to himself and pressed his palm against the table's surface. Beneath the spider-webbed glass, the computer flickered unresponsively. In his rage, he'd rendered it useless. Bad Dante, he also thought, "Is there another terminal?"

Scratch didn't look up, he just pointed to the far side of the room near the crates. It didn't take Dante long to find it, it was one of theirs. Set up at the edge of the table and had been used to circumvent the security protocols on the table. It was hardwired into the ship's systems and already done its duty, but from there Dante was able to bring up the communications terminal.

He searched through the system and selected the data cores visual scanner recordings and pressed play. The sound of his own voice blasted through the speakers and so he was quick to press pause, finding Scratch looking directly at him with an expression suggesting, 'I'm working here'. Dante didn't apologise, "Ear plugs?"

"Didn't bwing any." Scratch said,

"This going to bother you then?"

"Quieter please, boss."

Dante lowered the volume by seventy-five percent and pressed play again, this time his voice came through lower than conversational level, but high enough for him to hear it. He also switched off the various speakers around the room, so only the one at his end of the table was emitting. Scratch lowered his head back to his work, so Dante let the recording play out.

He wasn't sure what he was watching, but he had to at least try to understand what had happened to Drake. He owed her that much. When the recording was over, he was none the wiser. The visual sensor had caught her running to the door and he remembered the horror he felt when he'd first seen what was chasing her and how he'd called for her run faster. The next sensor was outside the room, facing the door and only showed her being dragged, screaming back through it. He reversed the time, back to when Harvest stood in the doorway, in the dark. There was a block of time where Harvest, or what used to be Harvest, hadn't moved. He wondered why that was and whether or not the lights coming on had triggered his attack.

None of it made sense to him, or to Drake, judging from her comments. If she had thought of something, she hadn't voiced them. When the lights came on, Drake had run and so had Harvest. Maybe, it was her running that had triggered him. There wasn't much dialogue from there on in, just thumping and screams and the sound of her assault rifle followed by an unearthly cry. She'd had to have hit it and it had to have felt it to have reacted in the way it had. Bullets, must do some damage, he was now certain of that. If they could hurt it, then they could kill it. But how to kill it, was something he couldn't work out. Not yet.

"Boss." Scratch said,

"What is it?"

"Come have look."

Dante pressed pause on the recording and met Scratch at his station, "What?"

Scratch pointed to numerous graphs on the right hand side of his screen, "Power's on."

"So?" There was already power, they'd even located the generators.

"All over ship." Scratch identified, "Life support, secuwity, even wall sockets."

"When did this happen?"

"Just now?"

"Can you see where it's coming from?"

"No." Scratch typed on his board, the rat-a-tat of the keys becoming irritating to Dante with nothing else to hear, "Main 'puter is up. Someone's in the core, checking ship's systems."

"A diagnostic?"

"Seems so."

"Dahl?"

Scratch shrugged.

"No log on then?"

"Don't know."

"What do you know?"

"The ship's power is on. Summon's in the core, and they'we checking the ship's systems."

Dante finished Scratch's sentence with him and moved away, taking a breath and a moment to think. If Dahl was back in the Core, then Harvest must have left. Moved on, looking for more of his crew to infect. But he couldn't think of any reason for Dahl to return to the core, he'd moved on once Logan had found him. Drake would have seen him, unless he was hiding, but he thought that unlikely given his ability to take out the former pirate. Dante forwarded the visual sensors to real time, cycling through the data cores list until he stopped at his answer.

"Scratch..." He said, wanting to un-see what was evident on his screen.

"Take a look at this."

The dark skin left his perch and joined Dante, "You found Harvest."

Scratch was to the point, if nothing else, Dante had indeed found Harvest. Or what was left of him, knelt at the base of the data core. Like the infirmary, Harvest's upper torso was nothing but shreds and his lower body nothing but a pot for the plant to grow from. Bramble and tendrils ran, pulsating across the floor and into the surrounding server banks. If he wasn't looking right at it, Dante would have found it incredibly difficult to believe. Even staring at the grotesque evidence before his very eyes, he didn't want to believe. First the infirmary and now this. The creature had the ability to control not only the host bodies of his companions, but also the computers.

***

Bounette called to Ford "Wait a second."

"What is it?"

Jake raised a hand, "Quiet. Is that the air con?"

Ford listened. Very faintly he could hear the fans up in the ducts, "Yeah?"

A look of panic crossed Bounette's face, "We have to get off the ship... now."

"That's the plan." Ford dismissed Jake's statement; silently cursing he'd only stopped to be told to move again. If they had time, perhaps he'd have been more inclined to discuss the imperative of running.

Then, in the direction they were heading the corridor lit up, flashing bright white against the dull orange lamps. This was accompanied by the sound of automatic firearms being discharged.

At that point all the lamps in the corridor flickered, quickly turning the tunnel into an erratic light show. Defeated, Ford rolled his eyes, "You get the feeling this isn't our day?"

Another muzzle flash from the end of the corridor and they were joined by one of the pirate crew. A woman back peddling, aiming fire down the adjacent corridor. Whatever she was firing at was out of sight, but Ford had an educated guess. He pressed himself against the side of the corridor, training the revolver's aim on the pirate as she backed off further. She was walking backwards, completely oblivious to him, "Keep out of sight." He whispered between the shots, "They'll go right by us."

Bounette nestled up behind him without a word. He didn't need to say anything. His breathing was loud enough to give away their position, "Quiet." Ford whispered. But the breathing continued growing progressively louder and harder. He was hyperventilating, "Jake, stay with me." Turning, he could see Bounette's bone white knuckles as he clutched the support beam, which now doubled as their hideaway. The man's eyes were wide, pupils enveloping his irises, "Jake." He repeated, but the man was no longer with Ford.

The gunfire tore his attention off his paralytic companion. The sound was closer, the pirate had turned down their corridor. Her back was still to them, still walking backward. At the corner Ford finally saw what she was firing at. Chunks of grey flesh blew from its body, exposing sinewy strands and macabre brambled tentacles that slapped around its stout form, "Hell is that." Ford mouthed. He startled as Bounette's hand gripped his shoulder and squeezed.

"We need breathers." Bounette gasped, "Suits. Full exposure suits."

The pirate continued toward them. She fired every other step, popping flesh off her target. But, with grave persistence it lumbered toward her, "What?"

"We need suits." Bounette repeated,

"That's the plan. We're heading to the pods." He tried to balance the conversation with judging the best place to run, "Remember?" The creature's arms and legs were in shreds, muscles hanging loose off the bone, interlaced by the writhing tendrils controlling its body. Tendrils used the heating pipes above it, helping to move along as redundant legs dragged across the floor.

"We need them now. Life support is on, we can't get infected." Bounette pointed to the suspended fog surrounding the creature, "Those are spores, they can't touch us."

"Then it's time to go." Ford said, grabbing Bounette's arm and yanking him up.

The pirate must have heard something, for she turned around just at that moment and for a second, her eyes met with Ford's. Anger took over her face, her nose wrinkling as she spun around taking chase. All three of them bounded down the corridor, thought overcome by fear to the point Ford didn't know exactly where he was leading them. A fact at that point he didn't care about. He needed to put as much distance between them and the creature as possible. At the first opportunity, he left the corridor, turning left, finding Bounette not only next to him but passing him.

The pirate fired. Sparks flew off the wall to Ford's right, forcing his arm up to shield his face. He paused, long enough to check his six. The pirate was gaining on him, a wicked grin on her face and the creature was still lumbering behind. When he turned back, he caught a glimpse of Bounette ducking into a door on his right, "Jake!" He shouted, but the doctor didn't return. Ford took chase; hands flat, cutting through the air ahead of him as he bolted as fast as he could. The door raced to meet him, reaching out he grasped the frame and swung through.

With a hand still on the frame, he came around, facing the wall and slapped the door control. Stepping back, hands lowering to his knees he watched the barrier drop, but not quick enough. The pirate woman dived through, rolling past him as the door sealed behind her. His hand jumped to the pistol, swinging around to face her as her boot came up fast, knocking the weapon free of his hand. They now stood facing each other. Silent, save for the panting he met his adversary eye to eye. Shorter than him, hair matted into dreadlocks and tied from her face. A sinister tattoo of stitched flesh extended her grin. She lifted her rifle, "On your knees."

Ford glanced around the rest of the room, searching for Bounette. Bare pews ran up the middle of the room, leading to the Divinity's Triple Moon statue. Dust covered everything. The church was empty; one of the doors at the back was open, the other... closing. Bounette had abandoned him. It was a room as hollow as the pirate's eyes, a place of worship devoid of hope.

"On your knees." She repeated.

Nodding, Ford obliged. Bending his knees, watching her muzzle as it lowered with him. Then he sprung, reaching out with the aim of knocking it clear, but he was too slow. She pulled the trigger, expelling one bullet before the rifle clicked repeatedly. The bullet clipped Ford's neck as he hurtled toward her. Surprise washed over her face as Ford barrelled forward. They dropped to the floor rolling, kicking and punching and snarling. Her teeth gnashed together, chomping toward his ear. He brought his knee up hard between her thighs, leaving her clutching her crotch as he rolled away to catch his breath.

He knelt, clutching the pew and used it to help him climb to his feet. His pistol was but a few steps away. It felt good to have control again; the weight of the sidearm reassured his convictions. Calm flowed through him as the pirate flapped about the floor, squealing like a pig. He raised the weapon at her, "How many of you are left?"

The squealing subsided. The pirate opened her mouth to say something, just as the church lamps flickered, followed by a ferocious crash from behind as the front door indented. Both of them instantly turned their heads to the metal slab, now a little weaker. On the second hit, Ford watched the metal buckle inward. But not the pirate, her leg swept, catching his ankles and throwing him backwards. His back hit the deck, head followed and his vision blurred.

She leapt on top of him, fist hammering down on his balls. Retribution flared as white fire, burning his loins. Her second punch suckered him in the gut, air expelling from his lungs. She continued to pummel him with her fists, screaming and snarling like a rabid animal. It took all of his uncoordinated strength to swing the pistol. It crashed into her face, knocking her off balance. Ford kicked himself free and scrambled to his feet. The big bad still banged on the door, *let me in, let me in*'. His exit was clear; there was only one door open. The other shut by the coward Bounette.

The room slanted as the pirate's shoulder ploughed into him, Ford crashed into the end pew and rolled over it. His shoulders caught the back of the next row. Quickly, he aimed the pistol between his legs, right at the Pirate bitch. He yanked on the trigger, firing the gun. Her hair puffed up as the bullet tore through it. He tried to move his head, but couldn't, he was jammed between the seats. The pounding on the door ever-present.

He wriggled, lowering his pistol to the floor and wormed his way down to the ground between the pews. There on his knees, he reclaimed the weapon and raised his head slowly. Cresting over the back of the seats, he caught her running through the last open door. He stood, knowing it was going to be close even if she didn't... The door slid shut. Ford's heart quickened and he spun around to see the front door buckling even more. The nightmare was seconds away from entering. Holstering the pistol, he took chase on Bounette, deciding it was better to follow someone who would incidentally get him killed than someone who actually wanted him dead.

He ran so fast his body slammed into the door, hand slapping against the release, but the door was locked. Ford keyed in the command and stepped back, waiting, hoping then repeating. The door refused to budge. He slapped the pistol's butt against the door, calling Bounette's name. The thumping behind him continued. The door was beaten, thinning and cracking with each strike. Ford's knees trembled, not from fear but from the vibrations of the creature's force as it threw its weight at the buckling door.

Ford thumbed the pistol's ammo wheel. Four bullets, not that they gave him any confidence, with each barbarous thump came the slow realisation that this was the end.

No.

He ran to the second door, hitting its release. It had to work, but it didn't.

No.

Fear bubbled to the surface, a distorted scream of anguish and contempt, "Bounette!" Veins pulsated in his temples, cheeks flaring cherry. The front door belched, splitting open and with no time wasted the bramble whips snaked through the gap. They reached in, curling back on the door like fingers and pulled apart. Metal screamed, warped and crumpled under the monster's strength. Ford raised the pistol and fired; the monster howled but showed no sign of slowing. He fired again, until all four rounds had been spent.

From his haversack he claimed the quick loader, refuelled his weapon. He knew it was futile, he could no more kill the beast than shoot through the hull. The pirate had unloaded far more bullets than he had left. The only thing his bullets were good for were... at the bottom of the sack, *hell yes!* He took the box, unclasping the side and opened it. Inside a panel release tool, cable clamps and cutters. He licked his lips into a grin, rushing to the door panel.

With trembling hands, Ford pushed the abomination's wailing to the furthest reaches of his mind. Metal screeched, battered and tore behind him. Chunks of door fell, slamming against the church floor. The beast was inside the room. Its brambles grew ever closer and its malformed gaping maw howled louder, calling to Ford.

The panel finally released, his fingers reach inside. "Come on." He whispered, but it was too late. At the corner of his eyes, a shadow moved. *This is it*, he thought, the last page of his story. He gritted his teeth; he wasn't going out on his knees. He would face it. He turned on his heel, exchanging his release tool for his pistol. Brambles curled over the pews and the beast hauled itself forward, dragging its human corpse behind. It had no body, just a collection of throbbing organs from the previous host. It was a sickening, wretched and violent weed. Ford swallowed, steadying his aim, he popped off all six shots in quick succession. Each shot hit, but did nothing to impede the beast.

It lumbered toward him, slow enough for him to reach down to the sack between his feet and grab the last quick loader. He discarded the spent shells with a flick of his wrist and fed in the fresh, raising his pistol and fired into the devilish mass. The encroaching spore cloud spread across the room, a contagious haze he had no intention of breathing. Ford backed off, finding the rear wall. The monument to The Immortal Three cast him in shadow, blocking a clear view of the beast and it of him. Ford slid down to his haunches, checking his ammo count. There wasn't any version of this story where he would allow that creature to infest him. His count was true, one last bullet.

In the shadow, he blinked, lowering his head to the upturned pistol and resting the muzzle between his eyes. Thoughts swam in anger, aimed at Bounette. Then on to fear and loss for those who had departed before him.

Finally, to his sister Becca, "Sorry." He said, "I'm so sorry." His thumb curled around the trigger as a hiss from his left tempted attention.

"Ford." Bounette called, frantically waving at him from the now open door, and snapping Ford from his sorrow. Bramble whipped around the monument, flashing in front of his escape.

Ford's feet kicked up, launching him into a run. The bramble struck, but too high. It rushed overhead striking the wall. The door came up fast, Bounette slid to the side, waving him through and so he did. Rushing, breathing hard and hitting the corridor wall hard. Behind him, the door slid down, metal smacked metal and Ford breathed a little easier. It was over. He couldn't believe it but it was over. If Bounette hadn't had come back... the man had saved his life, but Ford couldn't pull that free from the fact that he had first put his life in jeopardy. His cowardice had trapped him, "I'm sorry." The doctor said, stepping toward him.

The gun was between them before Ford had chance to think, "Stand back." He said, mind rushing through events.

"I'm sorry Ford, I am. I really am."

Ford waved the gun at him, "I said get back."

Bounette did so, raising his hands up like a no good hoodlum caught by the cops. He was pathetic, too pathetic, maybe. A liability... Ford's finger slid into the trigger guard, hovering over the piece of metal that would decide Bounette's fate. Jake Bounette remained silent, eyes tearing up. His legs were shaking, unable to hold him in place. That is when Ford saw it, just off the back of Bounette's boot. Long, thin and white.

Hooked barbs along its snake like length, part of the bramble, cut off when the door had closed. Ford had been luckier than he first thought, and yet that wasn't the thought that held his attention. The bramble wriggled, its sloppy broken end flapping up and down, missing the rest of its length. It curled around the grilled floor tile and pulled itself forward, reaching for Bounette, "Doc..." Ford hesitated,

"Do it."

"No, Doc. Move. Forward." Ford said, "Now."

The door buckled toward them with a horrendous knock. Bounette leapt into the air, screaming in French. He landed, facing the door and screamed again on seeing the bramble curling toward him.

Against all reason, Ford took the doctor by the shoulder and led him down the corridor.

NINE

Pipe-work creaked all around as the life support brought warmth to every corner of the ship; expanding the metal in the walls, joists and fittings. With each creak, Ford thought he heard the creature's approach. He tried to tell himself they'd lost it, had run as far as they needed to. But he'd heard the beast knocking at the door, its unholy thumping against the metal would have surely broken through as it had the previous one. It was just a plant, the human element dead. Like a discarded puppet. He couldn't perceive the monster being able to track them, but then again, he also couldn't see how the monster existed in the first place.

Jake Bounette muttered to himself constantly. There were brief moments of clarity when Ford directed conversation his way, but other than that, the man was in a world of his own and all Ford could think about was the warning he'd received from Mason. More than once Bounette's voice became loud enough to catch Ford off guard. He glanced back, catching Bounette nursing his jaw, "I'm going to need a dentist." He complained,

"We'll both need an undertaker if you don't keep quiet." Ford snapped, unwilling to listen to his complaining any longer.

Bounette's eyes seemed to latch onto his thoughts, a knowing realisation washing over him, "You could have left me."

Ford had to admit the idea had crossed his mind, "Like you left me?"

Bounette looked away, "I got spooked."

"Yeah."

"It was reflex, I came right back when I realised what I'd done."

"You want me to thank you?"

"No, I just need you to understand."

"That you're a coward?"

"I'm not... on top form." Bounette rubbed the sweat from his hands onto his trouser legs, "I need my medication."

"That sounds like a great idea." Ford grimaced, checking the corner was clear before continuing along their path, "Listen, we have to stick together. Have each other's backs, what happened at the Church. That was a one-time deal."

"Do you think it's following us?"

"I think you better agree with me before changing the subject." Ford countered,

"Yes. Yes of course, you're right. I'm sorry."

"And stop apologising."

"Yes, sor..." Bounette stopped, "It's just when I opened the door... You were."

"I'm not talking about that." Ford didn't even want to think about it.

Bounette grabbed Ford's shoulder, "I feel that same way. You understand me now."

"Understand what?" Ford halted in his steps, facing the doctor, "That I had no escape?"

"There is no escape. Not from this."

In the moments before the door had opened, Ford had not been sad, he'd been filled with hatred and regret. He had hatred for Bounette. Despite the doctor's sincerity, Ford couldn't understand how being trapped was to know what it was like inside Bounette's head. The man clearly had issues and more than one person had attested to that fact. Bounette was sick, borderline psychosis, anxious, whatever. But to Ford, Bounette was nothing more than a coward, "I'm not ending up a grow bag." Bounette's eyes welled with tears and Ford put his hand on the Doctor's shoulder, completing the loop, "And neither are you. You came back Jake and that gives me hope that you're still in there somewhere."

Jake Bounette looked at Ford, blinking away tears and nodding, "Thank you."

Ford released his grip, allowing Bounette a moment to compose himself, "Are you good?"

"I'm good."

"Then let's keep going." Ford took a step away,

"Do you think its following?"

"I hope not."

They continued in relative silence, Bounette's whisperings acting as a slow boil to Ford's patience. When he checked around the corner, finding their final destination he breathed a sigh of relief and whispered, "Okay, it's clear." Ford was now looking down towards the remaining storage pods. Just as he'd left them, except the spinal corridor was spinning, "It doesn't make sense," he muttered. Whichever way you cut it, running this part of the ship was a colossal waste of power. Whatever plans the pirates had, he couldn't make head or tail of it, "You coming?" He asked, noticing Bounette hadn't moved from the previous corridor.

"I was thinking I could wait here."

Ford imagined Bounette running away as soon as he entered the pod, "And keep look out?"

"Yeah, why not?"

Ford didn't intend on making it easy for him, "Okay, what's the plan?"

"I'll wait here and shout if something happens."

"And then what?"

Nothing but a blank, gawping face looking back at him.

"You shout, run off and leave me in a cargo hold with a doorway leading straight into whatever you've run away from? I thought we'd covered all this? *You* are coming with me. At least this way you won't tip them off where I am by warning me."

Bounette took a deep breath, the situation clearly had some hold over him, but Ford didn't have the time to nurse him. Reluctantly, the Doctor left the safety of his shadows and entered the brightly lit corridor. He took one look down the tube and said, "Why in hell have they turned it on?"

"My thoughts exactly."

They past the first bulkhead and stepped onto the gangway. Standing still while the corridor spun anti-clock wise normally didn't faze Ford, but today something about it grabbed onto his stomach and dragged it around for a spin. He shook off the nausea, "Let's get this done." The doors to Pod Two were still open, as he'd left them.

"I should stay out here." Bounette said as Pod Two revolved under the gangway,

"You can wait in the lock, you don't want to be standing out here with your dick in your hand, if anyone comes around that corner." Ford glanced back the way they'd come, suddenly very aware of how precarious their position was. He couldn't leave Bounette guarding the rear with nothing, so he handed him the revolver.

Bounette stared at the pistol, "I don't think so."

"Don't tell me you're going to pull the pacifist card now, especially after releasing Audrey Two?" Ford pushed the pistol into Bounette's hands, "Shoot first, save the Q and A for once we're off this boat." He looked through the door, his heart sinking at what he saw. Water, tons of water, "How in the hell?"

Bounette peered through, "Typical." He went on to surmise, "One of the supply tanks could have ruptured when the gravity spin kicked in?" He shrugged his shoulders as he watched the door pass overhead and down to his right.

"Something must have caught fire." Ford argued, "But the water should have run dry by now."

"Is this going to be one of those times where you explain something you know nothing about?"

"When have I ever done that?"

"How about your ridiculous answer about how far we've drifted off course."

"That was an educated guess"

"And this is?"

Ford took one more look at that water, "I have no idea. There's lot of it though, at least a third of the first hold."

"Going to let a little water stop you?"

"The gear is under it smart arse." He said, following the door as it continued to rotate. The centrifuge gravity held the water at the end of the pod, "But it is the first section," he thought out loud, "If I swim to the bottom I can open the next bay, the gravity will pull it through."

"Like pulling a bath plug?"

"Essentially, yeah." He began counting, silently in his head. As a child he'd done it a million times, but age is funny thing and he couldn't help but hear his mortality telling him it was a bad idea. He considered the ladder, the safe and responsible way into the pod.

"Well?" Bounette asked, arms wide in wait for something spectacular, no doubt.

The door moved under the gangway, in a couple of seconds it would be a clear shot. Ford counted down and then, just as he readied to jump, the lamps flickered. He paused, remembering the church and the corridor before it. Then as his breath escaped him, at the corner of his eye he caught glimpse of it. Grey skinned, crawling tendrils, its tattered skin and whipping brambles unmistakable as the creature he'd previously encountered. In a split second he wondered why in hell it hadn't chosen to chase after the pirate bitch, "Shit. Pass me the gun."

"What? Why?" Bounette turned around, "Merde."

"Get into the pod." Ford said, snatching the pistol.

"It's a dead end." Bounette turned, eyes crazy wide, "And flooded!"

"Climb in, stay near the door." Ford said, realising the plan as he spoke, "Hold onto the racking, just make sure you're away from the main corridor."

"What?"

"Just trust me."

Bounette, very reluctantly climbed into the doorway on its next rotation, making short work of the ladder and reached out to the racking shelves before disappearing, leaving Ford in the corridor alone, rooted in place as the grotesque creeper approached.

The monster was in no hurry. Somehow it knew there was no escape for them. Ford raised the Revolver, remembering its futility back at the church. The human parts were only remains, he reminded himself. He closed an eye and looked down the sights, taking the shot a moment later. The hammer fell, the bullet flew and a puff of white matter exploded from soft pulsating centre of the

294

thicket. It stopped, staggered momentarily, before continuing it's slow but inevitable journey forward. That was it, his last round. Not enough to kill it, but to ensure he had its attention.

"Is it dead?" Bounette's childlike optimism brought a much needed smile to Ford's face.

"Nope." He said, holstering the pistol. Taking note of the pod door's position and began counting.

"Good plan."

Ford ignored the comment and continued his count. Four, three, the door swung underneath him, two, the door rolled up in front of him, one. He jumped, clearing the first lock as it continued to rise. His stomach lurched, riding the hump bridge at speed. He left the gravity of the corridor, entering the gravity of the pod. Shelving and gangways blurred past. He raised his arms in front, piercing the surface.

Ice-cold jets rushed up his sleeves, water smacking his face with an electrifying. He brought his knees up to his chest, wrapped his arms around them and slowed his descent. Not slamming into the bottom was a huge step forward and the added bonus of the lamps flickering on was an unforeseen pleasure. Somewhere, above the water a Frenchman of whom he had little regard for, was looking out for him and for that he was grateful. Pale lamps illuminated his path through the water. He kicked out and swam to the bulkhead; taking grip of the side rail he typed the authorisation code on the control panel.

The tell-tale sign of flashing amber lights announced the door's opening and not too soon. Above him the star like form crashed into the water. Like an encroaching ink drop, it spread its tendrils in all directions as it sunk toward him. It was time to move. From the door stretched ladder rungs in four directions, dividing the circular floor into quarters. Each ladder ran to the side hull and back up to the top of the pod. Ford reached for the nearest one, pulling himself away from the door and the approaching monster. A second later the current began, pulling against his progress as the water spilled through the opening door. He didn't look back, knowing it would only slow his escape and entice capture from the horror which, with any luck was being pulled into the next chamber.

Ford fought the increasing current, each arm stretch more laboured than the previous. Fixing his foot into the rung against the torrent and using his legs to propel him forward when his arms became too tired to continue. His lungs burned from lack of fresh oxygen. He reached the edge of the floor, and began his ascent. Only then did he allow himself a quick glance behind.

The creature was nowhere to be seen. In its place a maelstrom of white foaming water pulling everything it could with it through the door. Ford propelled his arm through the force, grabbing the next rung and kicked up with all his might. The angle was too slight and his foot slid free, yanking his body against his left arm. He felt his shoulder pop and expelled too much of his already feeble air supply. Panic struck, he swallowed a mouthful of water before he could stop himself.

Ford locked his foot back against the rung. He kicked again, this time with a secure foothold and raised himself from the floor, beginning his climb with the water trying its damnedest to pry him free. He fought every movement, every rung; focusing on the next until eventually the water level dropped. The drag of the water diminished and finally his hand broke the surface. His head broke soon after, coughing the lungful of water out he hooked his right arm through the rung and waited, breathing the air and watching the remaining water whirling down the bath plug.

***

With the last of the water expelled to the second section of the pod, Ford sped down the ladder. His left shoulder screamed each time it moved his arm above or below his head, in fact, it hurt like hell the entire time. So much so, with eight rungs left, he estimated the fall to the ground would hurt severely less than the current method of descent. He stepped off the ladder, hitting the floor with the flats of his boots and rolled forward.

"Where are you?" Bounette called from somewhere above,

He wanted to shout back, but he hadn't the strength to breathe, let alone shout. So he just lay there, staring up at the shelf which in mockery of his efforts, dripped water against his forehead.

"Ford?"

"I'm okay." He laboured, rolling to his right and coming up onto his knees. There was no time.

"I'm almost there." Bounette hollered, but Ford was intent on closing the door. He couldn't see the creature. It must have been dragged into the next chamber. If it had gone to the bother of hunting them all the way from the church, the thing wasn't going to let a bit of water get in its way. He stopped at the edge of the doorway, peering down at the new pool below. His reflection; portrayed in silhouette from the backlight of his compartment glistened in the wobbling surface.

Ford crouched down for a better look when he saw kelp breach the surface. Fine strands floated to the top of the water and weaved together. Pulsing buds, bobbed then burst, releasing more shoots and slowly formed a cap of tendrils on the surface. With the creature's bulk and the host's armour there was no way it could possibly swim. It must have planted itself at the bottom of the compartment, reaching up. The premise was as intriguing as it was horrifying, if it adapted to new environments this fast, he didn't want to ponder long on what else it could do. As the floating mass thickened, he hit the door's control panel, wincing at the ache in his shoulder and was rewarded with the loud and satisfying sound of the mechanism within the floor whirring up. This wasn't some interior door like at the church. It was inches thick, capable of withstanding vacuum.

"It took the bait." Bounette called over, stepping off the ladder.

Ford looked over to him, "Yeah..." and then to the closed door at his feet. His mind registered a warning, "Spores..." He looked up again to see nothing but clear skies. But the spores could have been released into the water.

"What are you doing?" Bounette asked,

Panic had Ford by the throat. He had to fight to breathe, but his focus was on his clothes. He couldn't take them off fast enough. If just one spore managed to find its way into him it was all over, "We can't go back to the infirmary."

"It got you?"

"I don't know." He offered, wincing as he pulled his sopping jumpsuit drop off his shoulder allowing it to drop before stepping out of it. "Check me over."

He peeled his shorts and socks off, standing naked in front of Bounette. It wasn't the first time, he'd taken the mandatory medical check when rejoining the crew, but the water had been unforgivably cold. The doctor remained professional throughout; in fact Ford thought the distraction did him some good. Bounette slipped into his old self and his new found ticks took a back seat.

Ford winced as Bounette's hands moved from his neck to his shoulders. The doctor raised an eyebrow, "You've dislocated your shoulder."

"Great."

"I'll come back to it. Open wide." Bounette said, not waiting for Ford's jaw to fully lower before throwing his finger in, holding his tongue down as he peered in. The doctor's thumbs pulled on Ford's eyebrows and cheeks next, taking a good look at his eyes before ducking down and looking up his nose.

"Anything?" Ford asked,

Bounette didn't reply, not until he'd checked his ears, ran his hands through the ginger scalp and unceremoniously parted Ford's ass cheeks. Ford closed his eyes, feeling the warmth in his face as laughter echoed around the warehouse. He looked behind him, "Hey..." but realised it wasn't Bounette who was laughing. Ford searched all around him, ending with his head tilting back and seeing two tiny faces staring down at him from the airlock in the roof, complete with tiny smirks, "Are we interrupting?" One of them said, the other doubled over, howling.

"Shit." Bounette, King of the understatement.

"You think?"

"How do we get out of this?"

"I'm working on it." But there was no way out, not without going through the pirates.

One of them shouted down, "Why don't you boys finish what you're doing and come on up."

"Don't worry, we'll be right here," the other added, "waiting, for you."

"Those guys sound like child molesters." Ford said without thought,

"They're worse." Bounette commented, "You're good." He gave him a reassuring tap on his back, "I'd prefer to run a deep scan on your internals but I can't see any evidence on your skin or orifices."

"That's comforting." Ford regarded, waiting for the two of them to disappear, "You seem... better."

"Yeah." Bounette replied, placing his hands on his hips and leaning backward until he faced the roof, "Didn't seem such a climb when I was coming down."

"It never does." Ford agreed, it would be a long climb and his arm hurt like hell. They had one pistol with zero rounds, the mining lasers on the shelves were too short range and too large to conceal, "I don't have a plan." He said, looking around the chamber, "No sarcastic remark?"

"What good would it do? Besides, I'm still dying; just it'll be here instead of my room."

"We're not going to die. If they wanted us dead they would have fired a couple of shots down here instead of shooting off their mouths." He paused, *they must want us alive.*

"They made me an offer." Bounette said, rubbing the back of his head.

"What kind of offer?"

"To join their crew."

"I think that offer may have expired." Ford said, splashing his bare foot through the cold puddle on the door.

"I think so too."

"Pop my shoulder back in?" Bounette nodded, placing a hand flat against his front and reaching behind with the other, "It's probably best we don't speak of this again."

"Who would we tell?" Bounette's tone was so flat, Ford wondered whether he was attempting some gallows humour or if he was simply stating fact. The distraction helped with the sharp pain as Bounette punched with the flat of his hand, popping Ford's shoulder into its socket. Ford took a sharp breath between clenched teeth and counted until the urge to scream passed. He wasn't about to give the pirates anymore reasons to laugh.

"Shall we get what we came for at least?" Bounette asked, stepping away.

"Why not."

The both changed into fresh exposure suits, with Ford grabbing a helmet when the pirates decided to heckle them, "You won't need those."

But they did need them. Without the full suit they wouldn't have protection from the spores or get outside to steal the Albacore. Ford looked down at his hand, wondering what would happen if he ignored the suggestion. He had the feeling it would have something to do with the rifle aimed loosely in their direction, "I disagree."

"Disagree all you like." came the reply, "You bring em, you get a bullet in your head."

Unable to rebuke, he dropped the helmet to the ground, "You good?" He asked Bounette.

"As I can be, I guess. Let's get this over with."

Ford followed him to the ladder and despite his burning shoulder, climbed it without complaint. They were three quarters up when he first heard it, a deep resonating thud, calling to him from below. The sound announcing the beast had grown tired of its watery dungeon, "Move faster."

"I know." Bounette said, racing up the ladder.

The reverberation from the next thud travelled up pod, shaking the very rungs Ford grasped.

"It sounds big." Bounette commented, "And really pissed." Even the pirates had returned to the roof portal for a better look.

"What's that?" One said,

Before they had chance to answer, the other followed with, "Hey, answer the damned question."

The third thud echoed through the chamber, a war drum calling out and then silence. Curiosity getting the better of him, Ford leaned back on the ladder, looking down to the floor and the unscathed door at its centre, "It can't get through." He smirked, "The bastard can't get through, it's too thick."

"That's great." Bounette called back, not slowing.

The door's amber lamps began flashing and its mechanisms whirred to life, "No way." No sooner as Ford mouthed the words did the door begin cycling open, thick white kelp feeding through the gap. "I said move." He yelled at top of his voice. Bounette was already off the ladder, running the gangway to the exit. The rungs flew between Ford's reaches, feet propelling him faster up the last of his climb and he was more than grateful when his boots landed on the gangway. His lungs a furnace, arms like noodles he caught his breath and jogged the platform to its centre and the lowered rifles of the pirates, blasting downward.

The monster pulled itself up through the hole by its brambled roots, clinging to the storage shelves. Gone was any similarity to the human it had once inhabited. In its place was a massive unholy terror which stopped Ford in his tracks. Bullets struck, perforating the stems, clipping buds and puffing out white flakes but nothing slowed the beast's advances, "I'm coming up." Ford yelled over the hailing bullets.

One rifle slid back, replaced by a crazed face with one ravenous eye. "Move" It rasped, "Or I'm locking ya in."

Ford nodded, stepping up and jumped into the lock's gravity shift, "Close the door."

"It opens doors..." One eye replied, returning to his rifle and opening fire.

Ford stepped back, watching the beast climb the shelves, "Bullets are useless." But the door would at least slow it down. He hit the button, forcing the pirates back into the entry neck while the inner door slid shut.

One Eye rolled onto his back and aimed his rifle at Ford's head, "Get away from the controls, slow like."

Ford raised his hands, backing up as far as the inner door, saying as he did so, "We have to get far away from that thing." He'd just remembered something about the pods he wished had come back to him sooner, "Shoot the panel, lock the door down." He snapped, turning to see

Bounette waiting in the corridor as the pod collar travelled over him. Ford jumped, dropping to the gangway. The door cycled around, passing his left.

"I have an idea." Bounette said, standing at the pod control podium.

Guessing what Bounette had in mind, Ford said, "Hurry."

Bounette tapped furiously, the door cycling under the gangway. The metal lurched, folding Ford's knees and bringing his hands flat against the surface. The beast had reached the inner door, "Take your time, Jake, no rush." He said, with more than a hint of sarcasm. Both pirates looked up at him through the second door as it cycled up to his right, "Out of time." He commented as the pirates jumped into the corridor. They rolled to their knees, too quick to their weapons. Another thunderous collision against the inner door and the pod collar stalled its rotation.

Once more, One Eye indicated with his rifle for them to back away. Ford raised his hands, stealing a glance into the stalled pod as the beast punctured the inner door. Tendrils flashed around, pulling the metal back. Ignoring the pirate's orders Ford jumped to the control panel and closed the outer door just as the bramble shot forward. The door shut, snapping the attack off in a burst of thick white gloop. One Eye screamed, firing at the door.

Ford leaped, dropping into a ball as the bullets ricochted down the tunnel. There followed a moment of pause, then another loud, violent crash. The beast wanted out. Ford stood, marvelling that no one appeared to have been hit. One Eye kept his beady on the door while his friend, now ghastly pale had flight in his eyes. The pirate screamed and shoulder barged past Ford, knocking him against the railing.

One Eye kicked the leathery bramble off the gangway as the corridor flashed bright orange. Bounette had done it,

Ford wanted to kiss him. He had bloody done it, the pod was being jettisoned. The monster beat against the outer door, denting it. One Eye was distracted and Bounette launched himself at the pirate. A farce of punches and knees had them both on the ground rolling around as the next hit bent the door in even further.

Ford stepped back, considering the retreating pirate's plan as the best option. He snapped forward, grabbing Bounette's shoulder and yanked him away from One Eye. They had to make it out of the corridor before the monster had chance to breach the door.

His feet hammered against the gangway, legs propelling him forward. The next attack brought the sound of wrenching metal, the door punctured. All up and down the spinal corridor, lamps flashed red. Pod 2 was disengaging and with its outer door open a hull breach was imminent. His thighs burned, chest pounding, both compelled him to stop but the bulkhead ahead was already closing. Behind them, One Eye screamed, the monster had him. Its tendrils wrapping tight, holding him in place as it crawled on top, the engorged sack purging its contents.

As if fuelled by the horrific sight, Bounette sped past Ford. At that same second, air whistled past them, the pod had disengaged. The door breached and the bulkhead shutter sunk lower. Ford was a metre out when he jumped headfirst, rolling over the threshold as the shutter slammed shut, they were safe. Even if the beast could survive the vacuum there was no opening that door, not when there was a breach on the other side. It would have to find another way, and that at least gave them time if nothing else.

"Let's..." Bounette coughed up his words, "Not *do that* again."

Ford laughed, fighting the urge to cough himself, unaware of the returning figure until it was too late. The first pirate, the one with the smarts to run had come back. Complete with cracked teeth, a 'P' seared into his cheek and a necklace of nose bones hanging around his neck. He announced himself by the click of the safety latch of his rifle being disengaged, and saying, "Wassap Doc."

***

"Molotov, right?" Bounette asked from the floor.

Tonguing his cheek, the pirate refused to confirm his name. He waved his rifle, which Ford not so secretively coveted. He and Bounette outnumbered him after all. However, Molotov had the upper hand for now, standing and in possession of a fully automatic weapon. But things change, especially today. Ford didn't delay; he stood as quick as his body allowed, "Ford." He announced,

The pirate kept his eyes and weapon aimed at Ford, while saying, "Move it Doc. We dunts have all day." Bounette wasn't dawdling, but the events were clearly taking their toll. The man was clearly out of breath and needed some rest. Ford offered his hand, which Jake took, allowing Ford to pull him to his feet, "Ain't this sweet." Molotov said, "You two tight, right?"

Ford pulled his shoulders back, squaring off at the pirate, "We're crew."

The pirate grinned, his tongue sticking through his cracked gnashers, "Maybe I'm thinking you not worth the trouble." He waved his rifle muzzle between the both of them, "Maybe... I kill you instead."

"Instead of what?" Ford asked,

Molotov made a loud, gurgling sniff and smirked.

Bounette tugged Ford's arm, "I need to catch my breath."

The pirate's face was contorted with rage, focused on Bounette. "He no in charge no more." From the side of his rifle's muzzle a bayonet shot out, locking into place as he pointed it at Jake. Who reverted instantly to the man he'd been in the shadows earlier, his eyes dropped to the floor, sporadic shaking taking control of his limbs as he succumbed to the fear.

"Wow." Ford said, "Let's calm down."

The bayonet blade pressed against Bounette's throat and Molotov's crazy wide eyes flicked to Ford, "Calm you self, streaker." The bayonet swung from the doctor, pressing against Ford's own neck instead, the pirate saying "As I just said, you no in charge no more." With cold steel pressed against his jugular, Ford agreed with the statement, carefully nodding. Ford couldn't see any advantage in aggravating him further, "Pass pistol."

For the smallest of moments, Ford considered questioning the pistol's existence, but as crazy as Molotov appeared, he'd not given them any indication he was stupid. Ford moved his hand behind his back, uncoupled the holster clasp and removed the Revolver. The bayonet pressed harder into his throat, not enough to break the skin, but enough to dissuade him from using it, not that he could. Ford brought the pistol around, turning it in his hand, offering the pirate its hilt.

"Good boy." The edge of the bayonet fell away a millimetre, Molotov stuffed the pistol into his belt line, "You two, take point." He said, stepping out of the way.

"Where are we going?" asked Ford,

"Operations."

It was a lot of area to cover, but the silver-lining was that they only had to worry about the monsters lurking around the ship. The pirates had revealed their hand and they wanted them alive. To what end, Ford didn't know. All that mattered was how Molotov would react when they came into contact with one or more of the creatures, "Okay." Ford said, taking lead.

"No." Molotov said, "Doc first. Want you close."

Ford glanced at Jake, nodding as he passed him.

"And no looky at each other." The bayonet glinted under the corridor's lamps and Ford became acutely aware of the blade once he'd turned his back on it.

Bounette led the way through the ship. Molotov didn't like it when they moved at anything faster than a snail pace. He was clearly on edge and wasn't familiar to the sound of the Seng's creaks and groans. Ford empathised with him on that one. The pirate kept them close, only allowing one of them to climb to the next deck at a time. If they came up against a closed door, it was Ford's task to open it and Bounette's to walk through it first.

As they reached a junction, the two compatriots started in a particular direction, "Not that way." Molotov said agitated,

Bounette and Ford were turning right, the corridor led past the computer core and to a junction ladder, "You want Operations right? Then this is the quickest way." The doctor said,

"Another way."

"He's right." Ford confirmed, "It's the most direct route." instantly regretting it as the point of the bayonet pressed into his back.

"Find another way." Molotov wasn't one for committees.

Bounette stood in thought a moment, Ford took the time to work his own directions, "If we go left, we'll need to drop a deck and head through B-Section, then we can climb again?" It didn't give them much wriggle room to adjust if things went south; B-Section was nicknamed the bastard-section because of the conditions, unbearably hot with no room to manoeuvre. One tight corridor running from port to starboard, ladders at each end.

"The only other option is, we could double back," Bounette continued, "Climb one deck, head through the mess hall and then drop back down to this deck."

"Yeah, cut across the avenue and straight up to Ops." Ford finished the route, it was the longer of the two options but the one he would have suggested.

"Take first route." Molotov said, "You first, Doc."

"It will be harder to defend if we get into trouble." Ford offered.

"Don't care, much." Molotov sneered. His lips curled away from his broken teeth, "Got distractions, if gets into trouble." Ford nodded in acknowledgement; the pirate had more cards on the table and so, kept his further objections to himself.

"Move." Molotov ordered. They turned left, as planned and Ford tried to settle his mind. They'd be fine as long as there wasn't anything waiting in Bastard Section for them and their retreat didn't get cut off. As tight as that section was, if one exit remained clear they'd still have the option to run.

They made it to the ladder, pausing around the portal to the next level and waited instruction, "You're up Doc." Molotov said, training his rifle on Ford.

Bounette took hold of the ladder and climbed down, winking at Ford as he descended from sight, "Your turn Sweets." The bayonet yanked toward the ladder and Ford wordlessly followed the instruction. When he exited the ladder and turned around, Bounette was tapping a valve switch. All became clear; the clever bastard had remembered the steam valves.

The corridor was littered with them, they could let one loose as they passed, dowsing Molotov with a face full of scalding steam.

"Step away." The pirate called from above, Ford did so, giving Bounette a knowing wink as he did so.

The three of them made their way along the corridor, single file. You couldn't do it any other way, not without someone braising their arm on the pipes. Stuffy, was too charming a word to describe the damp heat. Ford couldn't believe he was about to make it a whole lot steamier. Every metre he passed a switch and glanced to see how far Molotov was. Too far, if he hit the switch the steam would break out between them, it needed to hit him. He slowed, closing the gap but was reminded to move forward with a sharp point pressing into his back.

They were almost at the end before Molotov became more concerned with what lay behind him than in front. It was easy to see why. In front of him he had his distractions, as well as the ladder of escape. Behind them, the tunnel faded into darkness. The creaks and hisses trailed back further than sight, calling out to them and Ford was reminded in why he wanted to avoid this place in the first place.

Ford slowed as he reached the next valve, the bayonet touched Ford directly between the shoulder blades. He jerked forward, reaching for the switch. A nasty violent hiss spewed from the pipe. Molotov screamed, a cloud of boiling air bursting into his face. Ford hit the valve again, silencing the steam. He knocked the rifle muzzle aside and thrust his fist into Molotov's face. The Pirate staggered back, dazed but still clinging to his rifle and fired. The bullet ruptured the pipe to Ford's left bursting a fresh jet of steam into the corridor behind him.

Ford yanked on the rifle, expecting it to come away from Molotov's grip, but instead he jerked the pirate along with it. Without time to raise a punch they butted heads. Molotov's nose smashed against Ford's forehead. Warm blood ejaculated from the pirate's nostrils, spraying over Ford's face as he grabbed the man's throat and spun them around, pitting Molotov's injuries into the steam. He pulled on the rifle, which this time came free. Spinning it around, he slammed the butt into Molotov's neckline, knocking him to the floor before barrelling through the steam.

Bounette was waiting to greet him, frozen in place with a pistol pressed against his temple. Behind him, was the familiar scowling face of the pirate Ford had tussled within the Church, "Nice try." She said, looking at the rifle, "But you can put that down."

Ford held his arms and the weapon in the air.

"I said put it down." She repeated her order, pressing the pistol harder against Bounette's face causing him to wince.

"Okay." Ford obeyed, dropping the rifle as Molotov stumbled through the steam, blood gushing from his nose.

"You good Molly?" She asked, her eyes never leaving Ford's.

"Cretin broke me nose."

Ford smirked, his eyes never leaving hers.

"Jonah?" She enquired,

"Dead."

"Plant thing, or these guys?"

"Bit of both... You alone?"

"Yeah, creature feature got Banks and Shodan." Her eyes remained on Ford, "On the subject of the creature, it's behind me, we need to turn around."

Ford did just that and was greeted with a fist to the face. He staggered as the woman laughed. Ford checked his nose. It wasn't broken, small victory, "Glad to see you made it." He said, glancing back at the cackling hyena.

"No thanks to you." She huffed,

"I didn't realise we were on the same side." Ford replied as he spat a glob of red stained spit to the floor.

Molotov looked puzzled, "You know each other?"

"I ran into these two idiots earlier while being chased by one of the creatures."

"There's more than one then..." Ford said,

The woman smiled at him, but continued her conversation with Molotov, "Think it may have been Drake. Well, used to be, maybe... the Doc here didn't disappoint, he left this one in his dust and dropped a door between them. I'm surprised to see them together."

Ford kept his gaze on the woman, "Name's Ford."

She eyed him at length, "I know what your name is. You're the one who killed Logan."

"That was..." Ford chose his words carefully, "self-defence."

"Stop flirting Xian and let's get moving" Molotov ordered

She smirked, pushing Bounette into Ford, "Get jogging."

***

They doubled back, taking the route Ford had first wanted to use. The pirates kept to the back, with Ford, leading the group. The only change in order came when they climbed to the upper deck, Molotov went first and waited, rifle ready as Ford and Bounette joined him with Xian pulling up the rear. There was never a chance of escape or diversion. A gun was always pointed in their direction.

Ford spent the down time working out how many pirates he thought were still on the ship. He'd killed Logan, Bounette had turned two of them and they'd kicked Jonah off the ship. Xian had said the two she had been with were now dead, which probably meant turned. That meant, at least by his reason, seven pirates were now dead. That was a hefty number as Bounette had counted less than ten. Ford was sure their ship couldn't take more than twenty, probably less, hopefully less.

Bounette sunk back into muttering. If that was distracting to Ford, it outright annoyed both of the pirates. Jake received the business end of Molotov's bayonet on more than one occasion. He'd curse; fall into silence and the pirates would settle down. But eventually he would start again and the whole process would repeat.

Ford was hoping for an opportunity within that cycle to present itself; when he turned a corner and stopped dead in his tracks. He stopped so suddenly that Bounette bumped into him, "What's the problem?" asked Xian, moving around the group to join Ford at the front. Down at the end of the corridor, the lamps were flicking off and on, "Get moving, it's just the lights."

Ford disagreed, "No, it's more than lights. Each time that thing has turned up, the lights have gone crazy."

Molotov sneered from the back, "You're talking crap."

"I'm not sure he is." Xian stepped out ahead of the group.

"What? You're buying his lies?"

"The lamps flickered in the church." She stepped aside, "Molo, take the doc and check what's what."

"Hell no."

"Just do it." She snarled, "And keep *him* on a short leash."

Molotov rolled his eyes, "Doc, you're with me."

Bounette jumped forward. He looked scared to death. The bayonet flashed into Ford's eyes, "Up against the wall handsome." Xian aimed her weapon in his direction.

"You know, we could be working together."

Xian smirked, "I bet that sounded more believable inside your head."

"I'm right."

"You're talking too much." She glanced along the corridor. Molotov had pushed Bounette ahead, toward the flickering lamps at the next junction.

Time slowed to a trickle, each step Bounette took became a lifetime of anticipation. The lamps continued to wink off and on. Each time the lamps went out, Ford expected to see the monster on them when the light returned. Thankfully, each time he only saw the two of them, edging to the junction. Then, at the corridor's end, Bounette stopped. He looked right, then left and jumped back. His scream reached Ford a split second later, just as the man's hands came up and pointed at something out of Ford's sight. Molotov stepped up, took a quick look and turned to face Xian. The lamps went out. Bounette screamed again, louder this time, more urgent and afraid.

Molotov shouted, "Shut up will ya?" Bounette squealed. The lamps returned, revealing Bounette steadying himself with one hand, the other clutching his chest. Molotov was shaking, laughing at the doc, "I didn't hit you too hard, did I?"

"Come on." Xian said, grabbing Ford's collar and pushing him ahead of her. His feet were like lead, but the gun aimed at his back meant there was only going forward, for now. Bounette and Molotov waited at the corridor's end. As they closed in on them Molotov took his eyes off the doctor to speak with Xian.

"You have to see this."

To their left and obstructing their route was a body. Crouched, facing the wall. Its upper torso, hung in shreds while pulsing veins poured into the wall. No, Ford corrected himself, not the wall. It was the electrical riser, the bow's vertical power conduit which fed every deck. It was one of the main power arteries. If the conduit was live and it was touching any one of those cables it should have been a blackened husk.

"Hell, it's Banks." Xian said, bringing Molotov to the front of the line.

Tendrils spread out from his corpse, weaving in and out of the floor grate with the occasional deformed flower or pustule. It was a web of sickening matter, much like the kelp formation Ford had seen in the Pod, but in this instance, it looked as though this host had completed its task. It wasn't moving, wasn't aware of their presence or at least it wasn't reacting to it. It was rooted into the floor and wall; Ford guessed it would take some time to tear itself free. Unless, it was baiting them, "I think we should find another way." Ford said.

"Head back? Again? It's a weed. We should be smoking it." Molotov said, exasperated.

"I think so too." Xian agreed, pulling on her respirator and indicating to Molotov to the do same.

"Want one of these?" Molotov grinned, noticing Ford's eye line.

"Only if you've one going spare, wouldn't want to be a burden."

Molotov's chuckle muffled as he hooked the respirator over his mouth, "Too bad."

Ford turned in the other direction realising they could still get to the mess, they just had to pass the crew quarters to do so. The mess hall had four exits, three from the hall and one leading into the galley, which had its own back door. Once they got there they'd have options, but until then, this was the last route.

Banks was a puzzle to Ford. The other creature had pursued them. It had made every effort to spread its spores into new hosts. That was its purpose or so Bounette had described. Sticking its head into the power conduit was an oddity. But then again, the monster had opened the pod door, "How are you guys powering the ship?" Ford asked. He got no answer, "Did you bring a generator on board? Or did you hook up your own ship's power?"

"They're not the ones powering the ship." Bounette said in a low tone,

Ford closed his eyes; it was the very thing he didn't want to hear, "The plant?"

"Think about, it's like the tropics in here."

"But still. It's a plant?"

"What are the chances of two ships colliding out here?" It was the question Ford had started the day with, and now

Bounette was using it as evidence that his plant was not only able to infest the biological, but also the mechanical and electrical. Jake raised an eyebrow, "Just saying."

"Shut it." Molotov growled, "Or I'll put a bullet in your foot."

Ahead of them, where the corridor should have continued another ten metres, completely blocking their route was a sealed emergency bulkhead.

"Can we cut through it?" Xian suggested,

"Do you really want to try?" Bounette asked, Ford agreed.

"I'll put your head through it if you carry on." Xian said, "Let's head back, find another route."

"There isn't one." Ford admitted, or was there?

Ford looked around the corridor, casting his mind back to playing hide and seek with the other kids. His eyes landed on their way through. It would be tight but doable. He opened his mouth to suggest it but Jake Bounette beat him to the punch.

"We can use the ceiling ducts."

Everyone turned to look at Bounette, it was Ford who looked the most surprised.

"I don't like it." Molotov said, "I say we head back to Banks and feed it Doc, maybe it'll let us pass." When he grabbed Bounette's arm, Ford was sure he saw a smile pass the doctor's lips.

"Molly." Xian shut him down, slapping her assault rifle against his arm and freeing Bounette.

"He wants it!" Molotov snapped, "Look at him, Doc's got a hard-on for it."

"I don't give a Saint's prayer." She said, starting to say "Dante..."

Ford clenched his fist, eagerly anticipating the opportunity.

"Screw Dante, he's sat way up there in the ivory tower."

Xian aimed her rifle at Molotov. "Then take the order from me."

"Where then? I ain't going in no damned ducts. Not with all this going on."

"See this." Bounette said, banging on the wall, "The mess hall is on the other side, we just need to pop up and over. Four metres tops."

Molotov turned to Xian, "They could have just put a door in." He commented.

Bounette stopped directly under the duct entrance. A small square hatch, looking more of a suicide note than their way into the mess, "I think I'm with Molotov." Ford stated,

"Who you trying to make friends with?" was Molotov's reply.

"Open it up." Xian ordered,

Bounette raised his hands, taking a moment to stretch and clasp the hatch release. With a slight hiss, it fell open. On the inside was a small chain ladder, which he quickly unfastened. Their route was now open but not one of them motioned toward it.

"You're all feeling it." Molotov snickered,

Xian looked at him with a sneer on her face, "And you're going up first."

"What? No way, get the Doc up there."

"I need you in the mess first, to cover these idiots."

"Yeah right, you go." They stared at each other for as long as it took Ford to step into position, he could grab Molotov's pistol from his belt and shoot Xian in the face before anyone reacted. That was if Bounette on the same page, which, from the cursory glance they shared, he seemed to be.

"Okay." Xian said, shouldering her rifle.

Molotov stepped back, smiling as he noted Ford's position. He was clearly pleased with himself and fingered his pistol while checking both ends of the corridor, "Better hurry." Xian took hold of the chains and climbed up into the duct, "You're up Doc," and so it went, Ford being the third up into the cramped space above the ceiling. As soon as he was up there, he envied Xian. At least she could see what was ahead of her. All he had was Bounette's heels and ass waving about in his face. If anything happened, they were all dead, of that there was no question.

The trip was short, stopping almost as quickly as it started. Ford crawled to the exit, dropping his head and shoulders, he lowered himself through and landed feet first on the floor. Feeling a pinch, he rotated his shoulder, trying to relieve the ache.

"My, my, you are a talented one." Xian commented as she perched on the edge of one of the mess hall tables. He avoided eye contact with her, feeling quite conscious of her stare and chose to wonder why Bounette appeared to be dallying around the empty mess, "Stay close." She added.

"I will, mum." Ford murmured, looking around at the damaged mess. *Mess is the apt word for it now.* Grease thickened the air, Ford's nostrils flared at the stench of burned oil. The mess had survived a collision and the engine explosion. The refuse bins had scattered their contents over the floor and there was a flickering light coming from the kitchen door.

"I'm going to grab something to eat." Bounette offered casually, sauntering toward the gallcy.

"That's not a bad idea." Molotov said, stepping off the chain ladder and taking control of his rifle, "Want me to grab you something, Xian?"

"Nah, I'm good, you knock yourself out."

Molotov raised a careless hand and strolled after Bounette.

Ford felt her eyes on him. It was actually hard to ignore her while he stood there doing nothing, so he busied himself, looking around the room for anything he could use as a weapon. There were knives in the kitchen, but the only thing he could see out here in the mess were tables and chairs. He could crack a chair over her head, take her rifle and make short work of Molotov as he stuffed his face with pastrami...

"Ford." Xian called to him,

"Yes?"

"You asked earlier, it's Xian."

"I know."

"What else do you know?" She asked, tapping the side of her rifle with her hand. Xian was as unwomanly as it was possible for a woman to be. From her armour to her posture, nothing gave Ford the inkling that she saw herself as a lady. She looked like she could bench press a ton without breaking a sweat. He imagined her on a gymnasium advert, 'if the bar ain't bending, you're just pretending'. With that in mind, he didn't care much she'd bested him in the Church. But when she followed his silence with, "What else do you want to know?" it took Ford by complete surprise. Then in an almost sultry voice she added, "Don't be scared."

He tried to laugh, "I'm not scared."

"Oh, you are." She said, sliding from her perch, "I can't figure out what you're scared of, yet. You're not scared of girls are you?" The question was clearly meant to be an insult, of that, Ford was certain, "Because if that's not your thing, I don't mind strapping up."

"Xian, why are you trying to seduce me?"

"I wouldn't expect any foreplay, if that's what you're asking." She crossed the space between them, allowing him a better look at her rounded face. She still had both of her eyes and that's where anything good finished. Much of her left face had been patched up with synthetic skin grafts and her right bore a lengthy scar running from her jaw, up to her hair line. She probably had a hell of story for each. She shrugged, "Dante's going to make you an offer. I'm getting in first."

Ford didn't move; he hoped she was trying to scare him. As for the offer, if this is what Dante was going to propose then he already knew his answer, "What sort of offer?"

"Protection what else? Your passage off this death trap."

Ford raised an eyebrow, said nothing more on the matter as her pungent breath assailed his nostrils, except, "Speaking of which. Shouldn't we get going?"

She stopped her advance, inches away from his face and smiled, "You're eager. I like that."

The whole situation was surreal; Ford gave her an enigmatic smile, "What are we waiting for?"

"I'm waiting for Molly to finish stuffing his face." She leaned in further, her black lips edging toward his. He noted her rifle was still at her side, her footing in a better position than his. If he moved, she could easily unbalance him, "I'm guessing you're waiting for an opportunity." When she kissed his lips, he felt the jagged point pressing into his inner thigh, "You won't have one." She said, pressing her knife into Ford's thigh just hard enough to cut the material.

"And I thought we had something."

"Just messing with you." She laughed, backing off. She raised her knife up in the air, she'd drawn blood and as it ran down the blade, Xian put it to her lips and licked it clean, "Had you going didn't I?"

"Always a comedian..." He smirked, trying to maintain an air of confidence while his insides ran for the nearest airlock.

"Maybe after we're clear of all this?" She backed off further, sheathing her knife and swinging around on the balls of her feet, "Let's see what those idiots are up to."

Ford took a moment and composed himself, Xian was a terrifying individual. If they got clear of this, the only thing she'd give him was nightmares. When she was a safe distance away, he probed the hole in the material on his thigh. He stepped away from the table and followed her to the kitchen. *Another suit ruined.*

There was a silver lining to all of this, he told himself. They were getting confident around them, comfortable even. That meant they were going to slip up soon and when they did, he'd be ready.

In the galley; Molotov and Jake Bounette chowed down on a ham. It was eerily cute, Molotov, clearly unwilling to allow Bounette near a sharp object cut slices and threw them to the doctor like an owner to his dog.

"Ain't this homey." Xian said, after making the same assessment.

Molotov lifted his blade at her, "You want some?"

"I'll take some meat." She joined them at the table, "Cut our boy Ford a slice."

Molotov smiled, "Taken a liking to your pet?"

Ford ignored Xian's remark, "Eat something." She waved the slice of ham in his face, "Come on, I can't tell you when you'll next have a chance to eat something, but I can promise you that the ship will still be falling apart around us when we head out."

He couldn't disagree with her logic, "Thanks." He took the ham, raising it to his mouth.

"Manners." She smiled, watching him chew his food hungrily. She raised her own slice to her lips and tore some off with her teeth, all the time watching him. Ford scratched his head in an attempt to appear nonchalant, but as he did the lamps faded and died.

"We should go." Molotov spoke with a full mouth, "Shouldn't we?"

The lamps flickered on, and then off again, "Yeah, I think you're right." Xian said, readying herself.

"Which way?" Molotov stood now, his face wracked with panic, "Where is it?"

Ford caught movement behind Molotov, at the galley's rear door, an egregious shadow. It had found them. It shuffled its swollen weight on two engorged stumps which had once been legs. Armour hung in pieces off the enormous carcass, its red and yellow eyes glared at Ford with the same evil hunger that Xian had. It groaned, a wet, mucous laden sound as if it were drowning.

"Saints save us, it's Garret." Xian said, un-slinging her rifle.

"Not anymore" Molotov launched into action, firing his rifle indiscriminately at the approaching beast. The bullets struck, sinking into the mass of fleshy thicket encasing its torso.

"This way." Ford shouted, backing into the mess hall, elated that all four doors were clear.

The pirates continued to fire into the creature, which in turn continued unfazed by their assault, pausing only as it began its turn down the aisle toward them. It hovered there a moment, before changing its mind, taking the next aisle along. Bounette clambered over the table-top, joining Ford, "Come on man." But the doctor's words were muted; Ford was mesmerised with the creature's ability to make decisions. It had chosen another path and the only difference between the two were electrical conduits throwing out sparks. Ford remembered Natalie's suggestion, back when they all stood in the medical bay. When this thing was just a little girl, and then also Bounette's offering in his quarters.

"Shake it." Xian shouted over the gunfire and backed away from tendrils whipping around the creature as it approached. Molotov followed suit and once he did, Xian didn't wait. She bolted past, grabbing Ford's collar and wrenched him along with her.

Bounette moved fast. He turned and grabbed the knife off the table before Ford realised what was happening. The Doctor looked demented. He was drooling at the mouth, eyes burning wide as he stumbled toward Ford, the knife swinging left to right. For a moment, Ford thought he was coming for him and instinctively raised his arm in front of his face. However, much to his relief, Bounette turned at the last second. Molotov didn't have a chance. Bounette must have been studying their armour very carefully over the last hour. He sank the blade between the plates in the pirate's side. Blood sprayed up to the ceiling as Molotov collapsed onto the floor, yelling obscenities. The second stabbing motion ended with the knife hilt pressing deep into Molotov's neck. The man's eyes rolled back white, as he coughed blood over his scarred lips.

Bounette bolted, passing Ford and screaming incoherently all the way out the galley. Ford was aghast, partly over Bounette's actions, but also at the monster as it dropped on top of Molotov. Ford kicked against the floor, scrambling back to the mess unable to turn away from the horror. Garret's weight pinned poor Molly, its tendrils feeding through the man's armour. The red and yellow eyes separating as its remaining human features split into several petals, revealing its engorged spore sack, promptly bursting over Molotov's dying face.

"Ford." Xian shouted, but he couldn't hear. He was locked in Medusa's gaze, frozen in place, watching Molotov being force fed alien spores, the same spores which spread out like an evening mist across the galley. "Ford..." Xian yelled again, finally catching his attention, "...last time."

He nodded, taking his first step as the Garret creature finally ended its torture of Molotov. It roared; bubbling viscous from its empty sack as it now careened toward

Ford. From the side of the flaccid tissue a second spore sack worked its way forward. Ford ran, kicking a heavy canister out of his way. *An organic gel canister*, "Wait." He shouted, calling Xian to stop.

She laughed, shaking her head, "No way shit for brains."

He picked the gas canister up, "Humour me." He turned, and rolled the canister through the galley door.

Xian watched the canister skid, nodding at Ford as he ran past her. She shouldered her weapon as the Garret-Beast staggered into sight. She dipped the muzzle and fired. The monster balked, shuffling forward as the canister exploded right beside it. Flaming gel splashed up its side, popping buds and lighting the spraying mucus. Screaming, the beast stumbled, bramble striking out in all directions, fire burning through its foliage. Xian fired again, full automatic, knocking it backward into the fire-slicked air. A second canister blew; setting off another, the explosions cascaded through the red containers. The galley erupted, pseudo-napalm engulfing the beast. Its scream, half human half demon, charged across the room.

Charred flesh and vine stomped forward, flaming tendrils whipping across the mess.

"It's not dead." Xian said, skipping backward.

"No shit." Ford replied, noticing that she'd turned and was running for the door, "Good idea."

TEN

They didn't speak much the rest of the way. Bounette was especially quiet. He had the posture and gait of a man riddled with guilt. If Xian picked up on it she didn't comment, other than to bark orders when needed. Her efforts to connect appeared to have died with Molotov. Not that she bothered asking how he'd died; Ford guessed she hadn't seen Bounette stick the knife in. If she had, Bounette would most likely be dead. Luckily for him she hadn't waited around. She'd left her friend to his fate and fate hadn't been as forgiving to him as it had to her.

She kept them moving, staying back far enough to avoid any trouble they may give her. Ford did not intend to make trouble. He needed the pirates now. For better or worse, he needed entry to operations. He spent most of his time replaying the scene in the galley, how the spores avoided the sparks and how quick the monster burned. Fire didn't just hurt it, it ravished it. The speed in which the flames burned the monster was incredible.

Xian didn't believe the fire had killed it, but none of them had stuck around long enough to find out. Part of Ford wished he had. Knowing for certain was key to defeating it but at the time, running seemed to be the best option.

When they arrived at Operations, Ford was surprised at the number of the remaining pirates. With Xian behind him, there were only two more. One wore dull red armour and doll black eyes, the bags underlining them were red sore. The owner looked as strung out as Ford felt. The other looked as if he'd been dipped in tar and painted with glitter. They had wrecked Ops, uprooting tables and stools. Crates were stacked all over the place and they had fitted their own computer terminal at the top of the table. Xian herded her prisoners into the centre of the room. It was only then Ford noticed the table top and its splintered glass splaying out like spider-webbing from a fist sized indent near its middle.

"I can't say it's nice to see you again, Doctor." Doll Eyes said, clicking his fingers. The door they'd just come through slid shut, "And I presume you're Clifford Dahl?" Ford remained silent, to which the man only nodded.

"You're Dante. I assume." Ford said, noting the surprised glint in the man's black eyes, "And this must be the ivory tower..."

Dante's head tilted slightly, eyeing Xian over the comment and letting Ford know that not all things were tight within the remaining pirate circle, "Anyone else?" He asked,

"Just us." Her voice was filled with venom. Bounette's plan had worked, the pirates were decimated.

"Then seal the door." Dante ordered, working his way around the table to Bounette. Dante punched him in the gut, dropping Bounette to his knees, winded, "You're due a lot more, Doctor."

"I..." Bounette struggled to talk, "I didn't... start this."

"But you tried to finish it." Dante was enraged, "Did you have any idea what you let out of the infirmary?"

Bounette smiled, "A little."

"Did you know it's infecting the ship?"

Ford's ears twitched at the question, looking to Bounette before asking Dante, "What do you mean?"

"This plant, this thing, can manipulate the ship's computer systems." He raised his hands in the air, leading Ford's attention to the lighting, full and bright, "It's why the power is on."

"That's horse crap." Xian said, hopping onto the side of the control table.

"Scratch?"

The oily one looked up, "Plant is powawing ship, Boss."

"You could have a point," Ford interjected. "We came across one. It was growing into a power conduit."

Dante pointed at him, pontificating on Ford's words with a dancing finger, "See, this is an open mind, willing to comprehend the unexplainable." He paused, glancing across at Xian, "Clifford, is it?"

"Ford."

"Well Ford, your friend here let out an alien species."

"That's blasphemy." Xian snapped, bringing on the fury of Dante's eyes.

"She's right." Bounette interjected, "There could be any number of reasons why it's here. We could have made it in a lab somewhere."

"You see Doctor; this is where I disagree with the devout." Dante's black orbs locked onto Bounette, "You and Xian here believe it blasphemy that somewhere in this great universe another life form has evolved. Yet you equally believe that we can create it... we are no more gods than the Trinity." He glanced at Xian, "I say that it's blasphemy to create such a monster, something that not only can make hosts of us, but the ship itself. Scratch, tell them what you found."

"Harvest set up shop in Data Cor." Scratch began, "Then powa start up, that deck first, then deck above and below. More systems com on line, Life support, sensors and terminals lit up. Scwatch saw all this on own screen, no power source. Guess some exchange happening inside cweature, make power. Secuwity systems com on, creature block Scwatch at first, but Scwatch smart. If not working against cweature, Scwatch piggy back systems. Look, no touch. Navigation 'puter accessed. Find location, scan nearby. Engine contwols accessed."

"The engine is gone." Ford blurted,

Dante grimaced, "It didn't know that."

"It tried to take over the ship?"

"It already has."

Ignoring the remark, Ford put his knowledge to what they were telling him. Everything he'd noticed supported Dante's theory, but he still had a hard time believing it. The monster didn't appear to have the intelligence to accomplish what was being explained. He'd seen it jump from Pod Two onto One Eye, there was no intellect at work there or it would have left the pirate to save itself.

"What you're saying is impossible." Bounette interrupted, "It's biological, it can't infect the ship."

"We're biological and we can control the ship. It just does things... differently." Dante explained.

"And this is what you've been doing all this time?" Xian asked, "We've been dying out there and you've been working on this theory?"

"*We* have been working on an escape plan." Dante snarled.

"It's smart." Ford finally agreed, telling them how it adapted to the water in the pod and how it had tracked them there in the first place, "There's some level of intelligence, I'm not sure if I'm ready to believe it can pilot a ship, but what you say makes some level of sense. The Centurion came straight at us, if it can pilot then it would explain why it crashed into us. It was looking for another ship."

Dante pointed his finger at Ford, "I was thinking the same thing. Ford, you weren't here when we boarded, so it's only fair you get the same offer your friend got. Well, not quite the same, you're not worth the trouble to keep around until sold, so you can either join us or die." Dante's black eyes bored through him, "Don't feel like you need to answer right away, but I do hope you decide to join us."

"A pirate's life for me..." Ford muttered,

"Don't dismiss it." Dante raised his favoured finger once again, "It's true, you've no reason to trust me, we lied about our position instead of helping you, and I fully intend to sell off your crew. But consider this. We haven't actually killed anyone... yet."

Ford looked at Bounette, who just stared back at him, "Natalie?" Jake's eyes dropped to the floor, muttering under his breath, "What happened to his wife?" He rephrased, turning his attention to Dante.

"Her?" Dante pointed to the exposed feet under the bed sheets on the far corner of the room, "She was dead when we boarded."

Dante's words blew over him like abrasive sand in a windswept desert. As Ford's mind worked through the evidence, Natalie's body, the ease at which Dante flaunted his claim they'd not killed her, thoughts of Bounette's erratic behaviour whipped the wind in his mind, creating a storm. Blinded by the white sands of emotion he was completely unaware he was now staring down at Bounette or that his brow had crumpled into a pitted 'v'. He couldn't believe what Dante implied. If Natalie had died before they arrived... Something must have happened. Something tragic that had broken Bounette. Jake couldn't hold Ford's gaze, he was content to stare as his own hands. Hands that were now red with guilt, "What happened, Jake?" Bounette jerked at his name but didn't reply. Ford repeated the question, ignorant of Scratch's sniggering and the mocking jeering from Xian, but still nothing, "Answer me, man." He snarled, "What did you do?"

"I..." Bounette stammered, "watched." He looked up with tear rivulets staining his grimy face, "I watched." He shuddered, eyes twitching, "No... they... I... can't." His head flopped down into his hands, his sobbing drowning out Xian's delight.

"She killed herself." Dante offered,

"No." Bounette snarled, "That's not what happened, she would never. That beast, Harvest. He killed her."

"The hell you talking about whackjob?" Xian asked,

"You murdered her." Bounette barked in return,

"Right back atcha..." Xian grinned, clicking her tongue.

Dante snapped his fingers, sending Scratch to the bed sheets. Taking grip of the corner, he lifted it off for all to see. Bounette was the only one who refused to look. She still clutched the mining laser, Ford gulped. The same laser Ford had shown her how to use. Her head hung back on the shoulders, soft tissue under her chin scorched. Her eye sockets black and empty.

"She couldn't face us." Dante surmised, "Or judging by our good doctor here, she knew he couldn't face us."

"Womantic." Scratch offered,

"Is that what happened Doctor?" Dante asked, "Did she kill herself to spare you the anguish of us hurting her?"

"You killed her." Bounette repeated, spraying phlegm in anger. His hands balled into fists, knuckles pounding his thighs, "You did this. Not her, she would never..."

"Calm down Doctor."

"Bounette, Jake, speak to me" Ford pleaded,

But the doctor wasn't home. His fists battering his thighs were just the start. Eyes widened, foam lathered his lips, "You killed her. You, you bastards..." He raised his fists, baring his teeth and punched his own head. His face snapped to the left, but he didn't give himself time to recover before hitting himself again. Ford stepped in, grabbing Bounette's hand and used all of his strength to hold back the doctor's attacks as the man spewed a string of obscenities.

Xian whistled, distracting Ford's attention and allowing Bounette's to hit Ford in the face, a source of amusement to Xian who already had her rifle aimed their way, "Leave him be." She said, "If he wants to beat himself up, I can use the entertainment."

Ford nursed his jaw. Natalie had been the lynchpin to Bounette's psychosis. All the muttering, all the acts of violence and cowardice, everything came back to this room and the lies the doctor had told himself. Still, he couldn't allow his friend, his family to do this. He stared at Dante, willing him to share his opinion. But the shark showed no sign of empathy and the self flagellation continued without sign of stopping, "Please." Ford asked,

Dante chewed on the inside of his lip, "Restrain him." he ordered.

"Thank you." Ford said,

"I'm not doing it for you." Dante snapped. It was Xian who stepped out of line and manhandled Bounette into submission, binding his hands behind his back. He struggled, revealing the strength he'd shown in the kitchen and spinal corridor, but failed to prevent the inevitable. Bounette snapped his teeth together, attempting to bite Xian as she finished up.

"You want a muzzle too?" She snapped back, glancing Ford's way.

Resigned that he may never know for sure what happened to Natalie, Ford was inclined to believe Dante's former statement, 'they found her dead.' And whatever fantasies Bounette clung to were now tearing him apart. But whatever Bounette was and had done, he was still family and that was something Dante could not claim, "You waited on the side line as the ship destroyed itself." Ford said, his eyes still on Jake.

"Only partly true, your ship was destroying itself. We couldn't board before it was safe. Do you have any idea how hard it is to get rescued out here?" Xian scoffed.

A callous logic, but perhaps it was needed to survive the life they chose. Self preservation was after all the oldest instinct. Was Ford supposed to ignore the fact that this pirate crew just hung back while his friends died, while Sharon died and Jake lost his mind? And now Dante wanted Ford to accept his proposal to join him along with his plans to sell off his family.

"Time is wasting." Dante said, as if reading Ford's mind, "I can see you don't like to make snap decisions, so how about I sweeten the deal?"

Ford took the bait, "How?"

Smiling, Dante nodded to Scratch. The painted man tapped some instruction into his console before turning his screen around for everyone to see. The image showed a corridor with small text at the bottom. Despite his knowledge of the Seng, the corridor could have been anywhere on the ship and Ford couldn't make out the text. Dante hadn't revealed the reason for showing them the footage, but was acutely aware that Xian has stepped in closer for a better look. Another command from Scratch and the image came to life and the recording played.

Flashes of light, blinding the camera, two figures falling back, pirates both, one of them new. A man, carrying a very large weapon with a huge muzzle flares. Another stood just behind, shorter but stockier. Ford blinked, resolution was poor in the lighting but he knew that second figure. Xian recognised herself too and she shifted uncomfortably on her feet.

The characters on the screen continued back peddling, firing their weapon off screen, "Dante..." Xian exclaimed as she watched, "I can explain..."

"Shut up." Dante cut her off, allowing the film to continue. The characters backed off screen, with all too familiar whips of bramble chasing after them, crashing into the sensor and shorting it out. Scratch made some adjustments and another view appeared before Xian had chance to object. The monster was momentarily obscured by the backs of the pirates, but as they continued to retreat it took centre screen. Ford's heart stopped. His pupils dilated as he recognised the beast which had chased him into the church and into Pod Two. This had happened moments before he'd run into Xian, "Dante, I can explain." Xian repeated,

"I said shut up." He didn't yell, his voice was calm but deliberate in its intention.

In the room; Xian shouldered her rifle.

On screen; Xian tripped and fell, losing her rifle as she clambered to regain her footing.

"Don't do this." The Xian in the room pleaded, to which Bounette rattled off a fiery laugh.

Scratch now stood, arms outstretched toward Xian with two long barrelled pistols in his hands, "Rifle, down."

On screen; Xian kicked the back of her friend's knees, dropping him down. She whipped the back of his head with something, a pistol maybe and grabbed her rifle from the floor as she sped away. The monster reached him, pulling him closer and spewed spores over its dazed prey.

Dante stepped between the stand-off. He looked at Xian with a mixture of hatred and pity, "I could understand if

Banks were injured or hindering your escape, but he was neither."

"I..." Xian began to stutter a reply. The look in her eyes said she knew what was coming and Ford connected the name Banks to the poor plant pot they'd found in front of the power conduit.

Then a flash of red; Dante's arm was held outstretched, his hand open. A concealed dagger flew through the air and stuck deep into Xian's left eye. Blood and juice poured down her cheek. Bounette cackled, arching his back and thumping his knees with his fists in applause. Xian trembled; lowering her rifle as her body slowly came to terms with death, until finally she dropped. Ford stared at the corpse in disbelief as it continued to twitch.

Dante reclaimed his blade, yanking the dagger from the skull and cleaning it on her sleeve before returning it to its sheath. Next to it was a ring of braided gold. Ford's recognition brought palpitations to his heart. The object brought back memories; the snowy killing fields of Otzu. This trophy was different, not a gleaming ring of gold but a smaller, mangled, shadow of its former glory. Yet, he couldn't have mistaken it for anything else. It was a Saint's Halo.

Sweat beaded and rolled down Ford's face, this was a man capable of besting a Saint. He couldn't see how it would be possible to beat him now. Especially considering the speed in which he had thrown the dagger. He had to be augmented in some way. Robotic limbs or juiced up muscles. If he once was, Dante was no longer human in terms of natural law. With the dagger secured, Dante's hand tapped the halo and winked, "I'll tell you about it someday. Should you decide to join me."

Dante's attention fell to Bounette, who still cackled away and rocked uncontrollably. Dante raised his hand high, but with no sign of the madness ending, he brought it down fast, slapping Bounette across the face, silencing the cackles. The doctor cowered against the wall, holding his arms up in defence of further attacks while spitting blood from his mouth.

"That was sweetening the deal?" Ford asked, keeping up the bravado against Dante's unholy eyes.

Dante explained, "Xian showed her true colours in that moment and I cannot abide cowardice." His words were filled with venom. Ford couldn't help remembering how he'd aimed that last bullet at Bounette after escaping the church, "I could have waited for a more opportune moment, perhaps feed her to the plant to allow our escape but I felt it more important to show you that I don't care about past affiliations."

Dante sat on his haunches, his dark soulless orbs staring right into Ford's mind, "I know you killed Logan, and knowing Logan, he probably didn't give you much of an option. But you wasted no time in stripping him of anything useful. You're a survivor, Ford and I need survivors. You need off this hulk as much as we do. If you say no, then so be it. You'll just be another soul lost to the black. However, I'd rather have your help. As you may have surmised, I'm running low on numbers thanks to the doctor's science experiment."

Bounette growled and swore in French, which was silenced by a swift back hand to the face.

"You had your chance Doc and you chose to turn a simple business transaction into a massacre."

Ford asked the obvious, "What's the catch?"

Dante's gloved hand ran through Ford's auburn hair, reaching around the back where he tightened his grip. He yanked back on Ford's head, "Nothing you won't step up to." He said, smiling. Dante then released his grip and stood, towering over Ford, "As I said, you're a survivor."

Dante uncoupled his holster, pulling a long barrelled pistol clear. It had no visible moving parts aside from its trigger and looked fake; as if it were whittled down from a block of titanium. Yet, something about it reminded Ford of the Centurion.

Bounette coughed and said, "You talk an awful lot of shit."

Dante smiled, "That's ironic."

Very calmly Ford said, "It's a flat no if you kill him." It was the calmest he'd felt since meeting the pirate. Ford had leverage now. He wasn't sure on how much, but it was apparent by the conversation that Dante's interest in him was real. He needed him.

Scratch giggled, or gurgled, Ford couldn't really tell.

"Funny," Dante said, "I was going to offer a similar agreement." With those words it all fell into place for Ford. Dante's true nature revealed, a stern, grinning sadist. He held the pistol high, hilt toward Ford, "Kill the Doctor and reserve a seat on the Albacore, the last and only way off this hell hole."

Scratch clapped his hands together excitedly, definitely giggling this time. Ford's eyes were transfixed to the hilt of the pistol. He couldn't even look at Bounette. This was his choice. He hadn't even decided yet what involvement Bounette had in Natalie's death. Dante may have just planted the ideas in his head, knowing Jake's ramblings would only persuade Ford to take Dante's position. Jake's head lolled to one side and Scratch's smirk was just as unhelpful. Jake Bounette wanted death. He'd killed the Pirate Captain and had then returned to his cabin to die. *It was me who had changed his mind, dragging him along only to end up here.*

"Take it." Dante ordered, thrusting the pistol into Ford's hand.

Mindfully, he took the weapon from Dante, feeling its feather light weight. He could kill the pirate now. He just had to pull the trigger. Fire a round into his face, Scratch would fall next. The only reason he didn't was the thought the pistol may have been empty. It was light, too light for him to regard it as real. He'd not seen or used such a weapon before. Hell it could have been a toy and this could all be some sick game to see if he'd pull the trigger. All it would take was one false click in Dante's direction for Scratch to unload the strange weapons he still held high. Ford turned the weapon in his hand, looking along the gleaming barrel. He couldn't recognise a safety catch, or a way to eject the magazine.

"An absolute betrayal of a friend and crew member? Or an opportunity." Dante said, "Your choice, but don't imagine for one second he's worth dying for."

"I left you behind." Bounette said, the madness in his voice banished.

"Well, well." Dante said, "See Scratch, young Ford has the same decision I had to make."

Now Ford knew Dante was playing with him, this was his entertainment. He'd lost his crew and now he wanted to vent his frustrations by having his prisoners kill each other. Ford let the pistol's weight drop his hand to his side, "You messing with me?"

Instead of answering, Dante raised a hand, signalling to Scratch, who for the first time left his workstation. When he stood, he was surprisingly tall and he moved with dancer's gait. He unsheathed a serrated red blade from somewhere on his back. A short sword made of Talissian Steel, once reputed to have been carried by the Brothers of Karthull. The first and only devout to break from humanity's crusade into the stars. They had been led by Jameil the first heretic.

The brothers had been hunted and killed in the name of the Immortal Trinity and it was said their skulls now render the walls of the Chantry's Gardens, worn smooth by the visitors who rub them for luck. It saddened Ford to know such an iconic weapon had fallen into the hands of a despicable leach.

All thought of the blade's history disintegrated as it was pressed against the side of Bounette's neck, execution style. Ford knew the metal would not need much force to remove the man's head. The serrated side designed and tempered to cut through the armour of a Saint. Perhaps it had, it could explain the trophy worn on Dante's belt. Flesh and bone would prove no more resistance than a block of butter to an arc welder, "Is he really worth saving?" Dante asked, winking his deep black pit of an eye.

"Go to hell."

"Take you head out your ass, we're already here." That was true. This was Hell and the Devil had offered him an eternity of damnation or a staffing position, "Do it, all will be forgiven."

"Will it?" Ford asked,

"If not, it certainly will be forgotten." Dante crouched next to Bounette and pressed his cheek against the Doctor's, "If it helps, you can pretend you're aiming at me." The level of his arrogance stank out the room. How sure he was that Ford wouldn't aim the gun at him instead. And what of the plant? It could be doing anything, could be marching to them right now. Not that Dante seemed bothered; all these theatrics had to be performed. A cruel script forced into Ford's hand to play. Dante smirked "Take your time." Scratch began an insidious drum roll with his rasping lips.

Ford looked at the pistol, trembling in his hand. Shocked he was considering it. If he handed the pistol back, refused the offer, closed the book... Both he and Bounette would surely perish. But then there was the rest of the Seng's crew, all asleep and unaware of their peril. A terrifying possibility his sister had pointed out when she climbed into her stasis tube. Natalie was right. Ford had mocked her at the time, but she had been right all along. Everything always came down to mathematics and as much as the act disgusted him, this was nothing more than a simple equation.

"I lived." Bounette said, so profoundly that it even gave Dante pause,

"What?" The pirate asked, slapping Bounette with the flat of his palm, "What was that?"

Ford knew, recognising the words from a conversation a life time ago. Ford raised the pistol, steadying the barrel's sight on the centre of Bounette's head and pulled the trigger. There was no recoil, just a high pitched thrum as the mechanism inside the pistol launched its deadly payload with a white flash. It crossed the distance from muzzle to Bounette in an instant, hitting the man square between his accepting eyes. As they closed the veins and capillaries under his skin burned red, illuminating his face. His skull became a shadow as the smell of cooked flesh rose in wisps of smoke, filtering from the entry wound.

Shock.

Ford's arm remained locked in position. At his feet Jake Bounette lay dead, killed by his own finger. It didn't seem real, coerced into murdering someone. He may as well have been watching himself from across the room for all the emotion he felt. His mouth was dry; no level of spit could wet his lips.

Dante's took the pistol back. Ford's eyes remained on the shiny toy. Rumours of energy weapons were abundant, especially in the outer colonies. Always fertile grounds for fantasy and mysticism, where they still hoped to break free from Earth's control.

He had killed Bounette outright, but the damage continued. The hole, that at first was no bigger than a thumbnail, grew. Blackening the skin as though frostbitten, reducing its molecular structure to something that looked like burnt paper. It flaked off, reducing Bounette's head to nothing more than a pile of ash. Only at the collar did it stop, leaving glowing embers on the bones and charred flesh. Ford shivered, bringing his outstretched arm to rub the chill from his shoulder.

"Ford." Dante snapped him out of it, whilst holstering his pistol. He then slapped Ford on the back. There was no smugness on his face, not like Scratch who could no more restrain his elation than you could hide a black bear on a snowfield. Dante's face and eyes reflected the emptiness Ford held inside, and he questioned whether Dante had endured a similar torture. The thought evaporated as Dante said, "Welcome to the crew."

Scratch raised his red blade over his head, crying out something in Spanish before following it up with a belly driven whoop-whoop. All of it was far too distracting for Ford, who wanted nothing else than to be alone with his guilt. A guilt nurtured by the pirates' callousness over his actions and that solidified his intention to destroy them. He watched as Scratch sheathed his blade as he made his way to Dante. He then started searching his pockets for something, "I don't have it boss." He held small denominations of barter chips in his hands.

"I know you're good for it." Dante replied, waving him away, "Let's not waste any more time." Dante pointed to the blank images on Scratch's terminal, "We followed you up to the cargo pods, but after that the plant took control of the sensors. Scratch is doing his best to win them back, but he only manages to get a couple of seconds of use before it shuts us out again."

Ford sniffed. His right nostril had become blocked. He sniffed again, unable to dislodge it. Ford tracked Dante's hand as it waved in front of his face. The crimson gauntlet rose to his face and a cold finger extended to his forehead, "Ford?"

"Yes."

"Are you with us?"

Ford parted his lips and nodded.

"Did you hear what I said?"

"Yes."

"Well..."

A *pirate's life for me*, "The cameras." He said, recalling Dante's words.

Scratch butted in, "It shut the camewa power down. Scwatch wedirect contwols and power back up. Have woute on standby."

"We've also had problems with our own communication systems, which have nothing to do with your ship." Dante added,

As much as Ford despised the man, he respected the cold steel of his logic and welcomed the task of defeating a common foe, "It didn't think to save itself, when we detached the pod it focused on attacking the one-eyed guy over self preservation."

"Jonah." Dante said,

Ford shrugged, "We were able to escape the corridor before the bulkheads came down because of it." He went on; describing the evolution of the beast from host to what he thought was the final incarnation, a mass of weeds with no discernible body. "I've seen it open a bulkhead and I've seen it smash through a door." Scratch stole a glance at the two entrances, "We were clear of it until we got to see the plant pot, Banks?" Ford waited for another nod, "His top half was all plant. He was in the power conduit. That one didn't attack. I can't say why."

Dante looked to Scratch, "Ideas?"

He shrugged, "None, boss."

"Then you met Garret in the galley?"

"Yes." Ford went over the information provided earlier, explaining the gel canisters and the speed at which it burned, "It really doesn't like fire. That's for certain, when we boarded the Centurion, the insides were all charred. I think they tried to burn it out."

"Didn't do much good." Scratch said, tapping at his console.

"In the galley, before the explosion, it sacrificed a direct route to us to avoid an electrical fire."

"How quickly?" Dante asked,

"I don't follow."

"Was it reactive or did it consider options?" Dante's eyes continued to probe Ford as he tried to remember.

"It paused, a second or two maybe. But I couldn't tell you with any certainty if it made a calculation. The spores however, they avoided the fire."

"Avoided?"

"Yes, when I first saw them I thought they moved like seeds in the wind." Ford stopped when he realised he'd lost Scratch, "Seedlings, you know, just blowing about, hovering. But in the kitchen, they swarmed."

Scratch grinned but Ford still wasn't sure if he'd got his message across. "How many of you were there? How many of you came aboard."

"There's at least one more of those things walking about." Dante said, catching Ford's thread. He looked to Scratch, "Did we pack any flame throwers?"

Scratch rubbed the back of his neck, thinking before shaking his head in the negative. Ford prepared to lay out the plan he'd been thinking about since the mess hall, "I..."

"We incwease oxygen fwom life suppote." Scratch blurted.

It was surprising to Ford for two reasons, the first being that if any of them were to come up with an idea he would have guessed it to be Dante. He never considered the neon freak to be anything else than that and the second thing was that he'd stolen Ford's thunder, they'd had the same idea.

"No way, those spores will be all over the place." Dante shook his head,

"We sealed in here." Scratch protested, giving Ford his opportunity.

"He's right." Ford said, agreeing with the great big neon grin, "If we remain sealed, we can saturate the rest of the ship with oxygen."

"Zactly, then we burn it in a flash fire." Scratch added, lifting his hand to a high five which Ford left hanging.

"Can it work?" Dante asked,

It took Ford a couple of seconds before he realised the question was directed to him, "Should do, all depends on how much oxygen we have left."

"Enough." Scratch said,

Dante nodded to his twitchy companion, "Can this creature work out our plan?"

"Your guess is as good as mine, but..." Ford replied, remembering, "Bounette discovered it was expelling oxygen, it may not like the change in the atmosphere."

Dante thought on it, then turned to the last member of the group, "Scratch?"

"Same as he said."

"How do we start the fire?"

Scratch, ran his thumb across his jaw, staring into space. Ford shrugged and Dante got impatient, "Well that's half a plan."

Ford took a step toward Scratch's computer, "Can the terminal you're using control the doors?"

The Talissian blade crept toward Ford's stomach, its end waving him away from the computer, "Don't think so."

Ford backed off, hands in the air, "I thought I was part of the team."

Scratch's neon teeth spread into a luminescent crescent, "Pwowbation."

"What do you have in mind?" asked Dante,

"If we have control of the doors, then we can seal off the mess hall too. We fill the rest of the ship up with O_2 and open the doors once it's primed."

"What good will that do?"

"The gel fire should still be burning in the galley, at least for a couple of hours. We'll need to keep a couple of rooms open to it, so it doesn't starve of oxygen, but I think it will work."

An enthusiastic smile grew across Dante's unshaven chops, "Then I guess we have a plan." Dante turned to Scratch, "How long will it take?"

"Doors, not long. Oxygen, longar."

"I didn't ask for a poem Scratch."

"Sowy, Boss." Scratch sheathed his dagger, dropping his ass on his terminal chair, "Will check."

Dante shook his head, looking to Ford, suggesting he needed brighter acolytes, "Once we blow all the oxygen, I'm guessing we'll need to use personal air supplies to reach the Albacore?"

"Yes Boss." Scratch said, not looking up from his station,

"In that case we'll also need a direct route to the ship. I don't want to have to cut through any obstacles, dead or alive."

"Thwough launch bay." Scratch said, "Alweady thought of, locked bulkheads and blocked plant out."

"That's not direct." Ford said, knowing the twists and turns and ladders they'd have to overcome, "We'd be better climbing to the top deck. There's an airlock dead and centre, we can reach your ship from there."

"Had an escape plan all worked out?" Dante asked, "Don't be ashamed, I'm not surprised or disappointed."

"I'm glad." Ford forced the comment out.

"No matter." Scratch interrupted, beckoning him over with a finger, "Direct as can make it. Look."

Ford rounded the terminal screens and looked at the image on screen, his heart sank. The infirmary was lost, the scene was reminiscent of the Centurion. Bramble coursed through the walls and floor, pulsating sacks and flowers branching off in all directions. The Data Core and a number of other areas were fast becoming the same. Then the image snowed out. Ford hadn't realised how lucky he'd been when Molotov forced their route.

Scratch, thankfully had been proactive. He'd shut the doors, preventing the plant from accessing the route he'd penned for their escape. The speed at which that thing grew... "We can't wait." Ford said, "We have our escape route. We should run now, its avoided breaking down any of the doors up to now, but we know it can. It hasn't opened any of the bulkheads but it's only a matter of time and incentive, it's got access to the computer. It's turning things off and on, learning the ship's systems..." He stopped, realising fear had rung the words from his throat while everyone watched.

"You want to take a moment and..." Dante said, furrowing his brow, "I don't know, breathe?"

Ford sucked a lungful through his nose, "Sorry."

"How long until the purge is complete?" Dante asked,

Scratch checked his screen, "Fifty minutes."

"That's too long." Dante grimaced,

"Purge?" Ford asked,

"We took a lot of goods from your ship. I instigated a purge of all biological matter, in case this thing somehow got on the Albacore." Dante explained.

Ford's face drained of colour, "My crew?"

"Are safe, they're still in their stasis tubes and shielded from the rays. Of course, we'll have to run medical checks before opening any of them in case they're infected."

Fords heart slowed, colour returning to his cheeks, "They won't be."

"Confidence is not fact." Dante replied, "Still, I think you're right. We shouldn't delay any longer than we need to." He paused, eyes revealing nothing of his thoughts, "Can we remote trigger the fire ball?"

"With modifications." Scratch offered,

"Then we'll keep that card up our sleeve. If the plant decides to take an interest in us we'll light it up." Dante eyed Ford up and down, "Check the crates in the back. I saw some helmets and suits."

"Thanks." Ford left to find the crates he'd pulled up from Pod Two. It seemed weeks ago now, but it had only been a matter of hours since he'd first opened the crate. Stepping over Natalie's feet, he was careful not to drag the bed sheets covering her. The crate was alone, next to her corpse. Something he found difficult to disassociate, as he tried to focus on his task at hand. Along with fresh armoured exposure suits and helmets, were the temptation of the mining lasers. The very weapon that had killed Nat... Ford shook the thought free.

"See something you like?" Dante called from across the room.

"They don't have my colour."

Dante grimaced, "I'm sure there's something there for the occasion. Just don't get any ideas on the lasers."

"I'm going to need a weapon at some point."

"That's a discussion for another time."

"Time isn't something we have a lot of." Ford snapped,

"We have forty-five minutes and counting, get dressed."

Ford grabbed the top suit, swapping it for the damaged one he was wearing, "Suit number four." He muttered to himself as he zipped himself in, then fitted the boots and gauntlets. Once in, he checked the air supply and fitted a spare canister from one of the reserve suits before carrying the helmet back to his previous position. One thing still bothered him about the plan. He was all for getting off the ship quickly. But there was still one flaw they'd not considered, "Dante."

"What now?"

It occurred then that Dante may have already thought of this eventuality, "I... well it depends...."

"Spit it out."

Ford stopped himself, knowing what he needed to say and choosing to avoid including the team. The plan as he saw it: once the purge completed, head to the loading bay and exit the ship. Once the oxygen reached target levels, they'd burn the plant on route. Should the plant take an interest in them before they left the ship, burn it. Except that was the point he had intended to make, should the plant take an interest in them it would need to open a door - or break through one. This would flood their compartment with oxygen and compromise their safety. Ford didn't know if the pirates' armour could provide the necessary protection from the fire, not for certain. But he did know his could, He shrugged, "Forget it, it's nothing."

"You sure?"

"I am." His mind travelled the route, ending in the launch bay, "No, there is something we need to consider."

"What is it?" Impatience apparent in Dante's tone.

"The launch bay, it has an emergency elevator which runs up to the infirmary deck. It opens across the way from it."

Dante closed his eyes, shaking his head, "I saw it."

"Scwatch will lock it down."

"Make sure you do, I don't fancy making it to the finish line only to find a jungle waiting for us."

Scratch raised his thumbs, giving them a little shake to emphasise his understanding.

"Because even if you do lock it down." Ford continued, "There's still a straight path to the hanger, it could already be there."

"Scwatch sees nothing of plant in hangar."

"Very well." Dante said, "Scratch, how long on the clock?"

"Forty minutes for purge. A further nineteen for O_2 levels, may be safer to wait and burn it before moving."

Ford buried his surprise at Scratch's tactical prowess, considering whether or not to dismiss his claim and force Dante into siding with his longest standing crewman.

Dante thought about it for a moment, "This plant is learning and acting once it gains a level of control. If we wait, we may no longer have the advantage. We have no option but to attempt escape as soon as it becomes available. If it thinks we're waiting on the oxygen levels, it may strike first."

"If you sure, boss."

They all fell silent, Ford guessed Dante had more to say but didn't know how to articulate it. Ford couldn't wrap his head around half of it. They were talking about a bush as if it were an enemy force. But Dante intrigued Ford. He wasn't at all like the other pirates in either his actions or the manner in which he spoke. Scratch however, who stared blankly at his screens, was a different crate of fish. While his thought process and threat analysis was up there with Mason's, he was also something of an enigma. He was someone who did '*zactly*' as he were told, but still Ford felt there was more to him, something well hidden.

"Okay." Dante finally spoke, "We wait."

***

An agonising half hour passed without Ford speaking to anyone. After the initial discussion on the monster Ford kept to himself, watching the duo banter between themselves without being able to share his own stories from the Seng. Eventually he sat himself down next to Jake Bounette's body.

Jake had wanted to die, told him precisely that and yet Ford knew the death would weigh heavy on his own mind for a long time, if Ford lived that long. He knew that if he'd refused to kill him, Dante would have killed both of them. He was certain of it. Having Bounette's blessing didn't make it easier on his soul. Even knowing Bounette may have been party to Natalie's death didn't make it easier. Ford couldn't help but think he could have done something different. He could have stood up to the pirates, they could have both gone down fighting. The word coward repeatedly ran over the cheese grater in his head. All things considered, Ford felt no better than the crew he'd signed up with and that, he was certain was the reason for the test.

"I didn't know you as much as I should have, Jake." Ford whispered, "Hell that goes for everyone on board. I guess I never expected to stay long, I only came back to make peace with Becca. Apologise to dad. I didn't get the chance with..." He stopped himself, lips quivering, "Mum. Saints save us." He grimaced at the trio of words, "Look at me, talking about myself... to myself. I'm sorry dick-head, I should have made more an effort with everyone. That's what I'm trying to say." He looked down at Bounette, he was at peace at last. *That's all you really wanted,* "Isn't it?" Ford wiped the tear from his eye before it crested his lid, "Good bye you jerk."

Ford patted the doctor's chest and stood up. A couple of metres away Scratch dragged a blanket over Xian's body. It gave Ford pause for thought. These villains were also people. Their team were their crew, their family. Two families had decimated each other over a dying vessel. All because they were in the ass end of space and desperate to survive, or make a buck. Ford didn't know what a buck was, but he'd heard the term. Mercenary. Pirate. They were scum to him and so when Scratch laid one hand on top of the sheet where Xian's head would be and touched a pendant with his other; Ford had a hard time believing what he saw and heard. The pirate muttered something which was not quite the prayer Mason had spoken at the start of all this. But even though Ford couldn't make out all the words to the pirate's poem, it was quite evident that Scratch was praying for his dead companion and a rage quickly boiled over.

"You believe she deserves an afterlife?" Ford asked the question before his filters had chance to switch on. Scratch's blue neon slits told him his filters should have come on sooner, "I didn't mean that."

"What did you mean?"

Ford expected the question from Scratch, but it had been Dante who asked it. He still sat half way across the room, but clearly hadn't been missing much. Ford became rigid at the sound of his voice; he hadn't meant what he'd said. What he'd meant, what he wanted to say was that she did deserve an afterlife, in hell.

"Ford." Dante swivelled on his stool, "What did you mean?"

"He thinks Xian deserves damnation." Scratch said; irritatingly articulate as he was accurate.

"No." Ford blurted, "I'm just shocked that Scratch believes is all."

"Of course he does, he's a damned priest."

"A priest?" Ford's words shot out the gate once again before he had chance to close it, a pirate priest?

"Pweest." Scratch asserted.

Ford was gob smacked, how could a pirate be a priest?

"Why not?" Dante nodded at Scratch, "Scratch believes in another God."

"Twu God, Kawthull."

Through the cryptic nonsense Ford could only ask, "What?" The brothers had passed into legend, all destroyed by the Trinity.

Dante looked away, "He's what your Gods call a heretic. He is a Brother of Karthull."

"They're not my Gods." Ford snarled, pushing out his chest, "And the Brothers of Karthull are all dead."

Dante smirked, "You don't believe in the Trinity?"

"I believe they exist." Ford said, not wanting to commit to anything further. Strange as it was, even with these bedfellows it was hard to admit to anyone that you were a heathen let alone a heretic. To be a heretic was to be an enemy of the Church. To be an enemy was to be hunted and in that Ford found the truth in Scratch. A hunted man would have to hide, scavenge and in the black fool's case, turn to piracy. *But a priest - a Brother of Karthull?* That was a jagged pill to swallow.

Dante on the other hand seemed comfortable to poke at both religions. He'd blasphemed the Trinity earlier with alien life and belittled Scratch's 'Kawthull'. Ford stared at Dante, trying to work him out through the veil of his stoic features.

"Don't worry; I am neither a heretic or an agent of the Church. If it pleases you, Scratch is the only crew member of the Albacore who truly believed in any religious garbage. Plus, you know the Church tolerates heathens. It's just illegal to believe in any other deity." Dante smiled, he raised his hands to the room, "But you know that. You don't get end up in a decrepit shithole like this by being a registered devout."

"I believe they exist." Ford repeated, searching for his answer, "But I don't believe in what they're selling."

"Good answer."

"Are you a heretic?"

Ford's question caused Scratch to slap his belly and laugh, "Yes he is. No one but a hewetic would take on a Saint."

Scratch's word's brought focus to the mangled halo hanging from Dante's belt. A trophy which Dante was quick to conceal by swivelling further on his stool, "Despite what Scratch believes, I'm no heretic." Ford wondered if the reluctance to admit such a thing worked both ways, "But I know the Church."

"More than anyone." Scratch said, but quickly shuffled away when Dante's glare hit him.

"You know what this is?" Dante scratched into the top of the operations table with a dagger, Ford stepped closer seeing the three moon phases.

"Nimrod, Etana and Ninus." He raised an impatient eyebrow, "It's the three phases of their eternal life."

"Just like your opinion on Karthull, you know exactly what they want you to know. Do you know that Nimrod, Etana and Ninus are ancient names?"

"So the scriptures tell us."

"Their names predate the scriptures." Dante corrected, then looked to Scratch, "Show Ford your pendant."

Scratch rubbed his head quizzically, "Huh?"

"I was perfectly clear, show him your pendant." Scratch held up the crimson trinket, a straight vertical line with a crossing bar near the top, "I doubt you recognise this symbol, its story is supposed to be..."

"It is." Scratch corrected,

"...at least according to their scriptures." Dante repeated, "Is Karthull's sword, which he used to defeat the darkness. But Karthull's sword predates the scripture. Each dominant religion of human history stole from its predecessors. The Trinity are no different. The symbol which you believe to represent them is actually the triple moon, the triple goddess. Everything they are is taken from the religions that came before them."

Ford wasn't about to be lectured by a pirate, "You a theology professor?"

"I know enough to keep out of their way." Dante pressed his hands on the table and straightened, "Just like you."

Ford thought Dante knew a lot more than he on the subject but his taste of religion was as sour as his disgust in being civil with the pirate. He nodded, ending the conversation. But he now believed Scratch when he'd said Dante had been a heretic. The arrogant manner in which he'd explained the Church's lies. The whole conversation had been laden with anger. The Church had wronged him, of that Ford was certain. And with the gnarled halo hanging from Dante's waist, it appeared that he had wronged the Church also.

Then as the pirates fell back into their routine of time checks and secretive conversations Ford found he couldn't believe he'd even had the conversation. He looked back down at Bounette's uncovered body and felt the need to find a sheet. He rummaged through the boxes, bringing the eyes of his new crewmates on him as he made as little noise as possible. Where Scratch had found the sheet for Xian he'd never know. All he did know was that it was the only sheet. Bounette had to settle for the last exposure suit.

"This is all your fault." Ford muttered, laying the body of the suit over Bounette's chest, "But I hope you've found peace." He knew he hadn't had an epiphany; he wasn't born again in the Trinity's glory. He was angry. He was angry at Mason for not calling the alarm sooner, angry at himself for not acting quicker and angry at Dante for sharing his disbelief in the Trinity. By wishing his friend peace in the afterlife he had also shared a commonality with Scratch. The thought was like a poison, an acid in his mouth he needed to spit free. But no matter how long he waited here with his deceased friend, he would have to rejoin his crew.

Reluctantly, Ford stood, "What's going on?"

Dante and Scratch sat at the conference table. The oil dipped freak looked up, "Talking bout you."

Great... "Yeah?"

Dante dropped his hands on the table in front him, parting them as if flattening an unseen paper beneath them, "Yeah." He said, not looking at Ford. "We're concerned about you."

Scratch swung on his chair to face Ford, pulling an imaginary zip across his neon teeth, "Too quiet."

"Just working some things out."

"That's what concerns me. If you're making peace with a dead man, that's okay. But if you're planning on how best to take us out..." Dante's eyes locked on Ford, "...then we have a problem."

"I signed up, didn't I?" He hid his anxiety with irritation.

"You didn't like what I said about the Trinity." Dante said,

"And you like mining lasers." Scratch added,

"They're still boxed." *Last time I checked.* Dante's inhuman stare looked straight through Ford, even when he wasn't thinking subversive thoughts Ford felt under a microscope. He couldn't afford to look guilty. Not easy, as everything he did or thought became laden with self-conscious paranoia, "Is there anyone else you want me to kill?"

"Look," Dante began, unblinking, "I was speaking the truth when I said I wanted you on my crew, I just don't want you thinking everything is righteous between us. You have a lot to prove."

Ford looked to Scratch, "*Pwobation.*"

"Siseley." The word was bookended with a flash of neon, then two fingers were raised to Scratch's eyes before he pointed at Ford, "Watching you."

Ford just replied, through gritted teeth, "Noted."

"Good." Dante winked, "Because this is the last time we have this conversation."

Scratch began inputting data on his forearm computer. He'd been working steadily on this for a while now, linking the ship's systems to it via the base system on the desk. From the limited use of the vis-sen cameras, the monster had taken over most decks. It was above and below them, but their exit route was safe. Scratch maintained control of the doors, locking them with the master override and encoding that too, as it seemed to be able to work out how to use existing systems, but struggled with complicated codes. Scratch muttered, "Monkey see, monkey do." The monster still had the advantage of controlling the data core. That was an issue.

According to Scratch, he only ran into difficulty when he attempted to take back control of a system. Life Support and visual sensors being the two main ones he'd attempted on multiple occasions. He surmised the plant was working through at its own pace, as if running off some hard coded list in its DNA. Ford would have liked to have heard Bounette's thoughts on the matter, but... Well, at least it wasn't interested in their exit or the launch bay for now, and wasn't making a rush to their position. Ford hoped it was because it didn't know where they were. Dante felt the need to theorise the plant didn't require their meat suits yet. It had enough hosts for its requirements and would only attack if its needs altered or they became a threat. It also happened to be the best reason to keep the fire ball in their back pocket until it became absolutely necessary.

Scratch raised his arm, tapping on the numbers for Dante's attention. The boss nodded, "Get your act together girls, we're moving in five minutes."

"Doesn't the purge have a little longer to go?" Ford asked. *It had to have another fifteen minutes surely?*

"Yes, but by the time we get there..." Dante offered, "We thought it best to head off as soon as possible."

"But the O_2 levels won't nearly be high enough to burn the entire ship."

"I agree, it's a terrible hand."

"But if we can't burn..." They needed the last resort, *I need the last resort.*

"This isn't a democracy." Dante assured, "I'm Captain, you follow my lead or else you can walk the plank."

Not fancying being thrown out an airlock, Ford relinquished the argument, even if it did put him in a tighter spot than the thruster nacelle. Knowing the creature may not be burning quite so brightly when the fireball was released made his personal escape plan less appealing. He stewed on this thought a moment; he didn't want to continue the theology lesson so he asked the next thing that popped into his head, "So, how long you guys been pirates?" If he couldn't force his hand, he'd better try his best at becoming friends.

One by one, Dante and Scratch looked at each other. Scratch laughed hard, slapping his hand against the table, while Dante rubbed his eyes with his thumb and finger, "You civs love a label."

"So you're not?"

"We are." Scratch answered.

"And you do... this?"

"What is, *this*, exactly?" Dante asked, his black orbs were on him again, probing him. Ford knew he'd overstepped in the conversational mine field.

Still, the best way to get them to trust him was to be truthful, "Preying on people in need."

Scratch shifted his weight, leaning more toward Ford. He didn't say anything and it took a moment for Ford to realise he was waiting on Dante to reply.

"It normally goes smoother than this." Dante said, "This job has turned out to be one disaster after another and most of it can be attributed to him." He pointed to Bounette's body, while keeping his glare fixed on Ford. "You have your share of blame too."

"I do." Ford didn't deny it, but he wasn't about to back down, "But you didn't intend on rescuing us."

Dante slipped a smile, Ford wasn't sure he was doing the right thing. His arrogance may turn them against him, but he felt, on some level, Dante respected him and from that would grow trust.

Scratch's arm computer gave a satisfied bleep, "It's time."

"Everyone good with the plan?" Dante asked, finding his feet.

Scratch saluted his Captain.

The plan was to go out the far door, following the same route Ford had led Xian. Then instead of heading to the spinal corridor, they'd take the ladders down four decks, moving Starboard through the living quarters and rec rooms. Drop another deck and then it was plain sailing, a straight line into the launch bay, which shouldn't take them more than thirty minutes. Ford knew each second was going to seem like an hour and answered simply, "Aye."

Once spoken, he took stock of his fallen crew. Stowing the vengeance he felt towards Dante and co. to fuel his intent. From the launch bay, Ford would have to work out how to take out at least one of the pirates. He wagered the one to get rid of the soonest was Dante, as he didn't seem the type to be fooled twice. However, something in the back of his mind told him that if a chance did occur, it would be Scratch who would go. If Ford believed in them and the Immortal Trinity were truly listening, he'd ask them to watch his back. To see him through this, give him the chance he needed.

"Helmets." Dante reminded everyone, "Make sure you lock the door release controls Scratch, I don't want you sneezing and setting off the fireball."

"Yes, boss."

The three of them locked their helmets in place. Standing amongst an equal number of corpses didn't go unregistered with Ford. The last leg was upon him and he recognised the fear twitching in his fingers, the adrenaline drying his mouth. Breathing deep, he pressed his tongue firm against the roof of his mouth and focused on the action until the trembling subsided.

"You good Ford?" Dante asked, knocking Ford's face plate.

"Yes." He said, pursing his lips and focusing his breathing.

"Then do us the honours and open the door."

He should have seen that coming. As much as he was part of the team, he was also going to be the most expendable. Ford would take point, no doubt under the guise he knew the ship better than the rest. He still didn't carry a weapon, which in all honesty, would be as much use to him as a snow ball if he came face to face with the monster. However, not having one only made him want one more. Resigned to being bait, Ford ended his participation in the conversation and stepped to the door, keying in the command and stepping back as it lifted. "What you waiting for?" Scratch asked.

Ford raised his middle finger and marched out of the room.

Soon every step became laboured. Walls and pipes creaked and not in the usual way from heat exchanges. The corridor ached with tension. It felt as though it was being squeezed and probed by the monster unseen. Lights flickered, sending panic signals straight to Ford's gut each time it happened. The tendrils were inside the walls, under the floor, waiting for the opportune moment to strike. Ford tried his best to keep his fears at bay, but all it did was serve to set his heart clapping faster. None of them spoke; all of them were poised to jump into action.

Each corner they rounded, Ford expected tendrils dripping with mucus. But the monster was not on their path. Scratch had done good. All Ford had to fear were the creaking walls and cameras, following their every step.

"We're coming up on the galley." Ford announced, "Next corner." He led the small band of survivors around the bend to the mess hall door, what was left of it. Jagged metal bent outward, clawing into the corridor. Something big had wanted out, and badly. Tangled around the door's metal teeth were thorny, soot black shoots.

"Scratch." Dante said, "I thought you checked the doors."

"Did boss. Still showing closed. See." He raised his arm for Dante, but the Captain ignored it.

"Will the plan still work?"

As Ford worked out the logistics, Scratch answered, "Yes, boss. Galley door to mess on other side."

"If it's not *technically* closed." Ford muttered,

"Better check it out." Dante said, tapping Ford's shoulder.

"You're kidding. We'd know if the door was compromised, it would have set the oxygen off prematurely."

"Then stall the lip, because we've a bigger problem. Whatever was inside, got out and we've no way of tracking it."

Burned shoots lay crusted on the floor panels, thin soot prints decorating the walls and ceiling leading away from the door in the direction they headed, "I don't think tracking it is going to be an issue."

Dante reached for the jagged metal, fingers seconds away from being cut by the sharp foils. Then he thought better of it, "It's strong."

"You don't know the half of it."

Dante changed the subject, "We don't have any other option." Ford nodded in agreement. They had this route and no other. Contaminated or not, Dante was right.

Not waiting for the hand on his back, Ford continued. He passed the broken door, acutely aware of scorched mucus and patches of torn barbecued vegetation clinging to the walls. "Dante." Ford said, "Can I get one of those shiny guns?" *A weapon capable of disintegrating its target would be very handy right about now.*

"I'm thinking about it."

Think faster. He'd never wanted eyes in the back of his head more. To the right, after ten meters of empty corridor a bulk head, right where it was supposed to be. Right opposite, a trail of blackened entrails. A mash of human organs and plant, thin whispers of smoke still lingering, "Now would be a good time." He said, raising his hand. There wasn't enough creature to compose a full walking monster, but somehow Ford knew it wouldn't be long before they found it.

"It's dying." Dante's statement answered Ford's question.

"How can you be sure?" He turned to face the pirate, "That could be like snake skin or something? It could had torn off the burned parts and recovered"

The pirate said nothing

Ford continued, "Okay, even if you're right and I hope you are. That doesn't mean it's not dangerous. It could still make spores..."

"If it can make spores, weapons won't help you."

"This is insane you can't expect me to walk point. If nothing else, I'm in the way of your shots."

"Scratch, give young Mr. Dahl your spare."

The grip came around Dante's side and Ford wasted no time in taking it. It was a long barrelled semi-automatic, dark grey, with silver highlights and top slide. *Magnetic launching system, just like in boot camp.* Ford pulled the slide back, checking the barrel and looked down the sights. It wouldn't vaporise anything, but it brought Ford a sense of safety none the less, "Thank you."

"Just remember what you're pointing at."

"We're a team." Ford replied, arming the pistol with a click. He kept to the right side of the hall, as far from the smoking sinew as possible. Each step calculated, watching the pile of innards for movement. Behind him; Dante and Scratch fell into step. Each inch brought with it the fear of something lurching out from beneath the surface. As Ford finally past it the hilarity of it all warmed his chest, he began laughing. He couldn't believe how terrified he'd been.

"Quiet." Dante broke his chuckle, "Some of us are still back here."

Ford jumped a step ahead, turned and found himself in the centre of the corridor looking back at the disgusting trail. Waiting until both pirates had caught up with him before saying, "Let's hope the rest is that easy."

Dante stopped and pointed, "Spoke too soon." A long thin root curled round the corner. Ford swallowed, following the plant into the adjoining tunnel. It led him along the wall where it gathered; building into a burnt thicket. Scorched brambles lay waste around the blackened husk. Then with a chill, he noticed it wasn't completely dead; an eye still blinked red. *Garret...* A new white thread sprouted from the condemned carcass. Life, it appeared, always found a way.

"Going." Scratch called, as he sprinted past them and the creature before they, or it had chance to react. Once on the other side he spun around, tapping the floor with his hand, before jumping high and clapping his hands together. "Touchdown." He waved them across, "Come, come."

Dante's hand fell flat on Ford's back, "You're up."

Ford readied himself; the rising cluster snapped and popped with the heat. The white seedling grew longer and was joined by a second. Taking a deep breath, he took his first step in front of Dante. As he did so, the branches cracked and fell away, pushing out a small pulsing sack. Dante also noticed, "Keep moving." Dante ordered, pushing on Ford's shoulder.

"Don't have to tell me twice." Ford grimaced, as he caught up with Scratch. None of them took the time to investigate the burned mass further and Ford led on. They'd been lucky up until now. At some point, he knew someone was going to come and collect. He followed their intended path exactly. Slowing only to check his air supply and opting to change it early in favour of having to swap out the canister when they reached the loading bay.

Two decks later, as they travelled through the crew's living quarters, Scratch informed them the oxygen levels were nearly ready.

"Do we hit it now?" Ford asked,

"It's one deck down let's wait until we have a straight path." Dante replied,

At the end of the corridor, Ford stopped at the ladder drop and peered down to the empty deck below, Dante joined him, "Good work."

The end had arrived, "I didn't do anything."

Dante's gauntlet tapped Ford's back, "Sure you did."

Ford ignored the false praise, taking hold of the ladder he worked his way down to the corridor below. He stood at the end, two rooms branching off left and right led to the personnel airlocks. Ahead; the corridor widened and opened into the launch bay. The bay's lights were on, the room still and invitingly empty from his position. But above Ford, unnoticed, a camera lens whirred into focus.

"Watch out." Scratch muttered, climbing off the ladder and forcing Ford back a step, "Scwatch want off this boat too, you know."

Ford nodded, unable to tear his eyes from the last obstacle of their journey; the Primary Airlock at the front of the ship.

Once Dante joined them it was time to huddle. Like a coach giving his team a last pep talk, Dante said, "Scratch, set the doors to open. We have the best chance of escaping with the plant distracted by the fire."

"Yes boss."

Both pairs of eyes fell to Ford, "It hasn't attacked us. Maybe it's better to wait until we're outside?"

"I was being polite; we're not changing the plan."

Ford nodded, "Fair enough."

"Do it." Dante ordered.

Scratch raised his wrist and tapped the buttons in sequence. After a brief pause he lowered his arm, waiting in silence.

"Is that it?" Ford asked, noting nothing had changed.

"Doors open, fire ignite. Just not with us." Scratch explained, Ford's mind filling in the blanks.

With no engine, the ship was adrift. Unless something exploded they wouldn't feel anything and the only thing they were burning was the oxygen filled air supply around the ship, "I'd like to know for sure."

"I'd like to get off this boat." Dante said, stepping forward as the first rumbles vibrated the tunnel.

Ford grinned, thoughts of storage tanks rupturing, pipes bursting. The beast burning. He stepped into line after Dante, striding down the corridor and into the launch bay when Scratch interrupted his fantasy, "Not good"

Dante swung around, face obscured by his armour, "What?"

"Hold on to something." No sooner had the words passed from Scratch's mouth and into the speakers inside Ford's helmet; red warning lamps began flashing all around him. A second later the alarm klaxon, a familiar loud two second screech followed by a one second interval. Set to repeat.

"What's happening?" Dante repeated his question.

The answer was obvious Ford who knew the ship and the distinct sounders like the back of his hand. The doors weren't opening in sequence like they'd planned. They were all opening, doors, bulkheads and locks, every single one of them and they were opening at the same time.

ELEVEN

The airflow went from zero to a thousand miles an hour in a second. Ford's feet went first, hurtling upward and clipping the ceiling, throwing him into a spin through the launch bay. Dante and Scratch disappeared from view just as fast as his pistol. The bay was a rampant tornado of equipment and fixings. He slammed into a large thick cable. His gut caught the brunt of the force knocking the wind out of him. His arms wrapped around the thick orange line, thankful Natalie had urged him to install it.

One end reached back up the bay and the other locked into Louie, secure in its docking station. Ford groaned, air pulling hard on his extremities, threatening to tear him in two. Moving one limb at a time, he threaded himself along the cable. He held his place, wind whistling over his suit. A flying box slammed the line, jerking Ford before crashing against the side of the Primary Airlock, before getting sucked into oblivion.

Another piece of debris struck the cable. Ford's gloves slipped on the orange tube, forcing him to relinquish his grip and hug the cable as it thrashed around in the bluster. Another couple of hits like that and one of the connections was sure to work itself free. Unsure whether he could continue holding until all the air escaped the Seng; Ford knew that he needed to move. If he could reach Louie, he'd be safe.

Back at the entrance to the bay; Scratch clung for dear life to the door frame, his legs straight in the torrent. Dante was still nowhere to be seen. Ford's mind travelled back to the instant before the doors opened. Orange lamps were already beginning to flash. They hadn't opened the doors, so it must have been the plant. He continued to underestimate it, but somehow it knew where they were and what their plan was. The fire should have distracted it... and as his mind raced, he realised. It wasn't trying to kill them; it was trying to save itself. By The Trinity, the damned plant was extinguishing the fire by opening the doors, "Dante..."

Silence in his ear.

"Dante?" He called again, "Scratch."

"Busy." Scratch replied, flag-like in a hurricane.

"Tug boat." He pointed as quickly as he dared, not knowing if Scratch had seen his hand. There wasn't time to waste. He needed to get to the duck before anything else hit or dislodged the cables. Mimicking a caterpillar; he crawled, upended along the cable. He pulled himself two arm lengths, *almost there...* when the orange line jerked sharply. His grip floundered, weight dragged by the current. His left hand slipped, arm wrenched straight, reaching for the airlock. He gripped his thighs tight, pulling back his arm with all his strength.

Behind him, the cause of the cable's jerking: Scratch clung one handed, straining to bring his other to bear.

Cursing, Ford forced his body to realign over the cable, "Hold on." He shouted over the torrent. Scratch's large neon eyes pleaded at him through the slit in his helmet.

"Help Scwatch." He shouted in reply, voice pounding through Ford's helmet.

"I'm coming." Ford moved back along the line, toward the dip where Scratch now hung. Ford reached along the pirate's arms, fingers searching for a hook in his armour. Ford's gauntlets were too thick and cumbersome to catch hold of the shallow grooves. He couldn't pull him up by his arms, he needed to reach further. He needed to get Scratch's legs up and around, "I can't reach, pull closer." He said, hand reaching as far as he dared, "I need to get hold of your belt."

Scratch heaved himself closer, slow against the wind but eventually his chest met the cable. Ford grabbed the leather belt and pulled, screaming as lactic acid attacked his muscles. Slowly, Scratch got closer. Another violent wobble shook the both of them. Ford's attention split, his head looking along the cable as a crate bounced over Louie and clipped their life line. Scratch slipped. The pirate was a dead weight and yanked Ford's arm. Ford screamed in obscenity.

In a spinning daze, Ford caught sight of the counter. Between the agony in his arm and Scratch's yelling he'd been lucky to glimpse it; numbers descending atop of the elevator door. There had been three survivors, and all three of them were in the bay when the airlocks opened. The elevator was coming down and Ford was done with underestimating his foe.

He looked the other way, along the length separating him from Louie. The duck was too far away, even if Ford didn't have Scratch to deal with he would be hard pressed to reach it before the elevator door opened, "No."

"What?" Scratched asked, kicking widely. Like Scratch, with each deck the elevator descended, Becca and the rest of his crew were slipping from his grasp. The window for his survival was closing with each deck the elevator dropped. Ford's hand still held Scratch's belt and was just an inch from the pirate's sheath. Rebecca needed him, his father needed him and the counter slipped down to six. Two decks away, the choice had to be made. His eyes met with neon. Scratch was a man who lived with betrayal and knew Ford's intentions before he had realised them himself. Scratch slipped a hand off the cable and grabbed Ford's clinging hand instead, "You no leave Scwatch."

But he'd made his choice, *it's just mathematics.* Ford slipped his gauntlet an inch to the right and grabbed the hilt. The neon slits bulged with realisation and the red Talissian blade swung down. Ford finished the manoeuvre, exerting more strength than he needed. The blade sliced through the pirate's arms with no resistance, Ford's own arm continued its arc as Scratch yelled out in pain, body hurtling away. His head smashed against the top of the airlock, silencing his cries. Ford's wrist slapped into the cable and buckled. Slipping from his grasp the dagger fired bullet like into the wall and the elevator door slid open.

Smoke escaped first, thick and black, it streamed into the current, blown free of the ship and there it was. A devil wrapped in a web of thorns. Its hulking form smouldered, its tendrils edged along the walls. Ford turned, regaining his grip on the cable and pursued the duck once again. Arms then legs, all working their way along the orange thread. Oblivious to the encroaching beast and its smoking limbs reaching across the launch bay. There were no Saints to save him, only his determination. Inch by inch he fought the current. Red, disorienting strobe lamps flashed. The sound of his own breath filled his ears, misting his face plate. Then when he least expected it. Louie was in arm's reach.

Rebecca. Ford pulled himself closer. *Dad.* He reached for Louie's border rail. *Mason.* His hand clasped the metal ring. *Crudge.* He glanced back along the line. The creature's thin white bramble corkscrewed around the orange, budding flowers erupted along the tangled mess. It was less than a foot from his boots.

Panic raced through him, his mind washed clean. Ford let the cable go, legs taken instantly by the airflow which would have pulled him away from the tug if not for his five digit anchor. He screamed, lightning pain running up his arm, while his other fought the current. He grabbed the ring, pulling himself up against the tug. His feet clambered for a footing and found the rungs.

The bramble flowered; seedlings weaved over each other, coating the orange in white. The cable's end was still attached, a metre of orange quickly disappearing under a blanket of foliage. Ford raced against the creature, straining his arms and legs as it seemingly spread over the power line with ease. Dropping one leg into Louie, before his second and wedging himself against the interior hull he stood on the seat and decoupled the cable. The wind took it, lashing out from his hands; it slapped the mechanical arm above him before whipping across the deck.

The monster was yanked with it; bramble tearing from its roots across the bay. Ford grinned, catching his breath. Still nestled at the elevator, the beast was wary of the bay and its exit. How long that would last Ford didn't wait to see. There was only a finite amount of air in the Seng and no matter how big she was it would eventually stop and at that point, the monster would make its move. Ford had to get out of there.

Ford slipped into the pilot's chair and activated the belts. He closed the top hatch and lit up the controls. Louie's top hemisphere vanished and Ford spun his chair around to face the devil. It remained in the corner, its roots spreading and thickening. One human eye lazily locked on Ford's position. Then it too vanished, the holographic viewer fizzled and died. He was blind, "Don't fail me now." Ford told Louie, becoming more afraid that somehow the devil had worked out how to control the duck too.

Ford worked his fingers over the controls. He needn't have worried, it was a power drain. Louie had been used as a battery and was almost depleted, when he'd powered her up she'd begun drawing power back from the Jian Seng and like Louie, the Jian Seng was dying. But both of them still had some life to give. The bay's arm lifted him out of the docking station and travelled to the centre of the bay. The duck rocked in the gale but the magnetic holdings gripped tight. It rocked again, this time more violently. Ford corrected himself and disconnected Louie from the Seng's power supply.

Free, Louie ran on its own power reserves. Ford activated the external sensors and held his breath. The interior hull vanished to reveal a web of tendrils. An orbed nest of bramble encased him, flashing in silhouette as the emergency lamps blinked on and off. Louie shook, its hull groaning as the web constricted around the sphere. The arm jerked, reaching the central run before sliding toward the exit. Invisible metal buckled around him, screeching under the pressure. Ford searched the cabin for a weapon. He flung the standard rations against the floor, picking up the spare oxygen canister. It didn't fit his current suit, but it did give him an idea. He brought the necessary controls in front of him, flipping switches, pressing buttons and thanking the 'verse his dad wasn't around to see what he was about to do. Ford found the hanger's restriction controls and overrode them.

The hull dented inward, vertical cracks splitting along its joinery. The sensor feed shorted out and Ford was flung into darkness. Air rushed through the breaches, pulling trinkets with it and the tendrils were quick to enter. They hooked around the gash and pulled, wrenching the opening wide enough for Ford to see the creature's malformed face staring right at him. Ford slapped the last button and fired Louie's thrusters. The air rushing past was high in oxygen content and it didn't take a second for the perimeter ring to ignite the surrounding current. Fire ripped across the hull, an unholy scream cried out over the storm. Tendrils caught and retracted, flames licking through the cracks. Ford raised his arm, shielding his face as the creature clung to the flaming tug, engulfed in its rage. The mechanical lock disengaged, freeing Louie into the torrent.

Ford pitched forward as Louie rolled into the airlock, flaming branches whipped past the breaches as both Louie and the devil entered the tunnel. Crushed between the tug boat and the narrow airlock it tore apart, chunks racing ahead of Ford's escape. Louie bottomed out, throwing Ford up into the hatch and straining his belt. His helmet dented inward, pinching his skull and still the tug boat rolled, breaching the exterior door and leaving the Seng spinning past. The engulfing fire blew out.

Ford blinked, eyes blurred from the hit to the head, straining as he pulled on the stick. He stabilised Louie, bringing her about and searched the cracks for sign of the beast. Louie had been violated and held no atmosphere. But Ford was alive, he didn't quite believe it yet but he was alive. He tapped his arms and legs, silently counting his fingers and wriggling his toes. A grin sliced through his cheeks, eyes burning hot with life and the possibilities ahead of him, "I'm coming Becca." He said, bringing Louie's flood lights on. Ford worked the controls. He managed to bring up the sensors and the holographic hemisphere cleared, except for the cracks in the hull. Some of the flood lamps were damaged from the exit, but he had enough to reach back to the Seng and see the demon, still clinging to the airlock. Blackened branches snapped free into space, while other, more persistent foliage took root in its new sanctuary.

He brought Louie across the front, heading starboard to the Albacore and keeping his lamps on the hull. The Jian Seng looked fully operational; all of its exterior lamps shone bright on its crevices and illuminated Dante's craft. Looking more of a mosquito close up than Ford thought possible, the docking ramp its metal proboscis. Along the Seng's hull a small humanoid crawled. Its direction was obvious as it was the same path as Ford's. He swung his lamps on the figure and red armour reflected back against the beams. The son of a bitch had survived. Ford called to Dante, but had no reply from his comms. The pirate stopped and raised his thumb. Ford chuckled, nerves and nothing more. With Dante alive, boarding the Albacore had become a lot easier but he still needed a way to best the pirate. Ford steered the tug boat to the crimson armour, close enough for the pirate to climb onboard.

After a tap against the hull, Ford pulled back on the stick and ascended toward the mosquito, "Nearly there." Ford said moments before a rampant fist pounding against the hull pulled his attention away from the Albacore. Dante's arm was outstretched and pointing toward the Jian Seng.

Through the hull plating of the Seng thick horned brambles had broken free and flowered in the dead of space, spreading out in a star pattern. While they had been fighting for their lives inside the ship, it seemed the creature had been hard at work outside. The roots had stretched out in all directions, encasing thruster nacelles and launchers with indiscriminate efficiency. No not quite a star pattern, Ford corrected himself as he studied it. The plant had burst free somewhere near the infirmary near the front of the ship and the most external growth worked toward the aft. Ford swallowed, the longest tendrils crawled toward the Albacore. Somehow the plant knew it was there and coveted it. If they'd waited longer, they may not have reached the ship in time. Ford's crew would have fallen prey to the weed.

Clenching his fist, Ford banged on the inside of the hull, wanting directions. Dante replied in kind, knocking his fist against the outside but not giving him any fresh information. Frustrated he stuck his hand out the broken viewport, waving his index finger around until Dante took the hint and pointed at Albacore's thorax, just under its resting, weapon laden wing. Ford directed the tug toward it, seeing the airlock door after a minute's worth of thrust. Once at there, Dante clambered around the rail and jumped the short distance to the door as Ford settled Louie into a full stop.

Ford reached up, turning the manual lock and opening the roof hatch. He stepped up onto the chair and yelped. All across the roof and down one side of Louie was crystallised plant matter, burned and frozen to the hull. Light slid across it, causing it to glisten like frost. If it were not for its tenacious ability to ignore death, Ford may have considered it beautiful. He allowed himself to tear one eye away from it and watched as Dante entered the airlock.

Ford climbed up onto the roof and kicked off, sailing into the lock. He bumped softly against the ceiling, pushing himself to the floor as the door closed behind. He felt the assuring tug of gravity pulling him toward the floor and Ford's feet happily accepted his own weight. As clean air filled the lock, he stepped to the outer door and pressed his faceplate against the porthole. Louie was the last of the tugs and like its two siblings, she had saved his life. For such a small industrial tool, Ford owed each of them a heart-felt thank you. It was also a sad realisation that this last surviving duck was to be left behind, nothing more than space debris.

The ceiling inside the lock faded from amber to bright white illuminating the room, "You can take your helmet off." Dante said from behind him.

Rotating the helmet to the left, the catch and seal broke. Ford raised the helmet off his head and smelled the sterile air. The smell or lack of it was alien to him. Ford understood that each ship had its own distinct odour. Jian Seng, of which he'd known for almost all his life, stank of oils and grease. He would miss that, he mused. He arched his back and spread his limbs, stretching away the weight of battle. It was good to be alive.

"Come on." Dante said, "It's not over yet." reminding Ford of the fast encroaching weed.

***

Dante led them through the ship, allowing Ford to take note of the surprising cleanliness. Whatever these people were, they weren't slobs. Metal surfaces coloured white with red trims, gleamed as if recently polished. If it weren't for the lack of furnishings and the sporadic peppering of bullet holes and energy weapon scoring in the walls he would have guessed he was on a high class passenger liner. The corridors were almost perfect cylinders, except for the raised transparent flooring that covered a network of unlabelled pipes and conduits, "Scratch?" Dante asked, not turning around.

"He didn't make it." Ford replied without hesitation waited for the inevitable follow up question, but Dante just shrugged and continued leading them deeper into the ship. With each door they past, each twist and turn they took led Ford to reconsider his preconception that the mosquito was a small vessel. Instead he realised, it had been the sheer mass of his own ship, the Jian Seng which made the Albacore appear small. The Albacore was far larger than originally perceived, complete with its own warren of corridors and after a dozen turns Ford had no hope of retracing his path to the airlock.

They took an elevator up. The interior held no interest to Ford other than the numbers on the control, symbols of an unknown language or culture offered themselves to Dante. The only piece of evidence as to the number of decks, were nine symbols. Dante tapped a finger against one. A triangular outlined shape with a sweeping curl from its right most side. The shape shimmered, the door closed and the elevator began its journey. The propulsion system was quiet, as was the rest of the Albacore, Ford noted. There was no reassuring thrum, no constant reassurance that the ship's engine was keeping you alive.

A moment later the door opened onto the bridge. Ford stepped out behind Dante, noting the slope as his foot angled down toward the centre of the room. He paused just out of the door, setting his second next to his first. The bridge was circular, with a high standing domed ceiling which was home to an intricate web of wiring and nodes. Some of which were already on, illuminating the bridge in a dull blue light. At the room's centre and lowest point of the floor, sat the Captain's chair. Not too dissimilar to Ford's father's. Behind the chair, split into two quarter arches were the bridge crew terminals.

Dante strode to the Captain's chair and took no ceremony in sitting. He tapped on the chair's arms, bringing the terminal online. Above them, a dormant projector network woke. Similar to his duck's abilities the front wall shimmered and dissolved. The area was replaced by a hologram of the Jian Seng appearing in front of them.

Ford slunk into a chair at the nearest terminal, watching on as Dante disengaged the Albacore. The image retracted, revealing more and more of the hull and the brambles, continuing their search for the docked ship as they travelled backward, "Did any of them touch us?" Ford asked,

"Scans say no, I electrified the hull just in case."

The Albacore continued to impress Ford and he felt all the safer for it. For the second time, in what seemed an eternity he felt the faintest glimmer of hope, if not tainted by the sour taste of betrayal. Ford's heart thumped, pumping a litre of fear into his arteries that spread through his body and to his thoughts. They closed around his short lived glimmer and constricted. He understood that his contract with Dante was nearing an end. If he wanted to save all of his crew he needed to take the pirate down, but the man had bested a Saint and the constricting fear became ice in his veins. He wasn't sure how he could do it, and worse still, looking at the Albacore which was so alien to him; Ford couldn't help but think killing the only person who could run the ship wasn't the best idea in the first place.

The screen now showed the Seng in its entirety, growing smaller as the Albacore distanced itself from the condemned space hulk. Soon it was no more than a blip, lost in a painting of black. Dante pressed his back against his chair, bringing the remains of Ford's home to fill the screen once more, "Would you care to have the honour?" Dante asked, swinging his chair around.

"Come again?"

"I've a missile lock."

Ford considered the option for a moment. He knew his home was nothing more than an infested nest for some devilish plant monster bent on destroying anyone it came across. However, a nostalgic hesitation prevented him from answering before he could consider the question. The thought soon past, the creature could no longer harm them, but left to its own devices there was no knowing what it was capable of. Besides which Jian Seng was family, "Yes, I do." Ford stood, walking the short distance to Dante.

The chair's arm had no discernible buttons; only holographic representations with scribing similar to what had been present in the elevator and unknown to Ford's vocabulary.

"You want to say a few words?" Dante asked,

Ford shook his head; there was nothing to say, "What do I do?"

Dante's gauntlet raised and pointed a red finger to a letter, "Press that one."

Ford followed his instruction, remembering monkey see, monkey do and smirked. His finger passed through the letter, a small vibration tingled through his glove and the letter glowed red. A soft chime echoed through the room, signalling the missile's launch.

"Now watch." Dante said and Ford did so, taking in Jian Seng for the last time. All his childhood memories, good and bad were about to disappear. His thoughts travelled to his mother, walking him into the observation lounge and showing him Earth for the first time. So blue, so beautiful. Then to Becca, chasing him through the corridors and screaming obscenities as he jumped into the air vents. She had been too big to follow him. Finally he thought of his father, he'd been so proud of this ship, his home. Ford's soul ached to be free. A small light, bright enough to be a star streaked through the space between the two vessels. It collided with the Seng's most central point. There was no large explosion, just one tiny flash of white, followed by lingering moments of nothingness. Ford readied himself to question the attack's validity when the Jian Seng did something remarkable. It buckled inward.

Like a closing fist, the Jian Seng crumpled inwards. What started achingly slow, soon sped up and torn parts of the Seng raced toward the missile's collision point before disappearing. The ship imploded and it took the weed with it. If it were screaming, it would go unheard. Just as the twisting and folding of the inches thick metal plates and struts. All of it collecting into the miniature gravity well, leaving nothing behind except stars. Ford continued to watch, his mouth agape until there was nothing left. There was no threat except the one sitting next to him. It was over, he was free and yet Ford couldn't let go of the image. The blank space vista on the screen and the invisible scar left in the Seng's place.

"I don't plan on killing you." Dante interrupted, bringing Ford's attention to the elongated pistol being drawn from its holster. The same one which had claimed Bounette's life was now being placed on the floor between them. Dante's black eyes gave no indication of truth or foul intent, "I hold to my offer. But I am curious as to what you intend to do next."

"I haven't had time to think that far." He lied. He just hadn't had time to work out how to execute them. Even if he managed to kill Dante, he had crew for a ship that he wasn't sure he could operate, without guidance. On the other hand; he could let the pirate live and if Dante kept his word, at least part of his crew would be saved. Dante would become outnumbered and his choices limited. Ford couldn't understand how Dante intended to keep the crew in order should that path be taken. However, it did seem logical that Ford would be the key in keeping them under control.

"I think." Dante said, "You've considered options. You may even believe you have the upper hand."

"Are we negotiating?" Ford asked and tried his best to ignore Dante's finger, caressing his golden weaved halo.

"You could kill me, just as you killed Scratch."

Ford's eyes remained still.

"I'm sure you did what you deemed necessary. I don't believe you would have sacrificed him to gain an advantage in escape..." *Oh but I did...* "But you need to think of the consequences of future actions. You'll be on a pirate ship, with a crew of doctors and administrators. If you could crew this vessel, which I severely doubt unless you know the divine language Glosbaen, where will you go? Which port would take you in, except for those you dare not trespass?"

"Glosban?" The word peaked Ford's interest,

"Gloss - Ben." Dante repeated phonetically,

"I've not heard of it."

"You'll need to get use to that as you've not heard much at all." Dante sneered, "The Trinity, in their holy wisdom has mollycoddled our race. They've kept the majority ignorant of the universe through fear and distraction. Just as they keep the extra-terrestrials away from our door, they reap all the benefits of their technology so they can continue their charge into the heavens on their everlasting and futile crusade."

Ford couldn't stop his smile, "That's ridiculous, how can the church keep the universe at bay. I agree that this is some advanced tech. But it's human, there are no aliens. We're alone in the universe."

"The Albacore is human. However, as like Glosbaen, most of her technology was stolen from alien cultures which were far from *human*."

Ford folded his arms across his chest. He already thought Dante was a heretic and wasn't surprised at the attack against the Trinity's teachings, but this heresy sounded more like lunacy. There had never once in recorded history been a report of any complex life-form. There were fertile planets, ones which allowed agriculture or sustained life which travelled there but if there was anything Ford believed of the Trinity's scripture was that Earth was the only place in the 'verse that life began.

"I don't ask you to believe everything I say to you. But you are a survivor and I do expect you to live long enough to learn I don't lie. I don't want to kill you Ford, but if I have to, I will. I'll wake up some of your crew tell them how I rescued their abandoned pods, losing my crew during my heroics."

"They won't follow you."

"Not at first, but living out here changes a person. I think you understand that more than most."

Ford couldn't deny that he had changed, right to the bones and through his very essence. Just as he knew exactly what he had to do. Balling his left hand into a fist, he swung it into Dante's face. Ford's knuckles cracked against the pirate's jaw and he followed up by bringing his right around, but he was too slow. Dante's arm knocked his attack wide.

Wind expelled from Ford's lungs, as Dante's fist smashed into his stomach. He collapsed, grabbing the pistol while fighting for breath. A red shielded boot flashed before his eyes and Ford toppled backward, the room spinning. He lay there on the floor, wounded. Dante, as he should have remembered, was superbly strong, inhuman, altered. Each blow received had felt more like an iron girder hitting him, "I would have preferred not to have done this." Dante said, towering over him, "But you've left me no choice." A red boot rested on Ford's chest and Dante unclipped his gauntlets one by one, letting them fall, "I'd hoped you would have listened to me. I do need you Ford, tempering your crew will be difficult and I don't have the time or the energy."

The pirate's hands moved around his torso, unfastening the straps. Pieces of armour fell from him, as a distant yet familiar voice, majestic and seductive, sang out under Dante's deep and oppressive voice, "I will not reveal this truth to any others of your crew." Dante's harsh voice juxtaposed against the angel's song. Inked paragraphs of text in the same divine language he'd seen once before daubed the pirate's arms. The singing grew louder, "The halo on my belt..." Dante continued, Ford's mind raced ahead.

He knew what Dante was about to say, the song was all too clear in his ears. He'd heard the chorus before, in the wastelands of Otzu. Just as the white sun dipped behind the snow capped hills and the Church Militant flanked his militia's escape route, "...isn't a trophy. It is a memory. I did not claim it from a murdered Saint. I was presented with it at my ascension."

The paragraphs tattooed on his arms glowered white; armour fell from his chest. Dante's stature fluctuated, his cock sure pose shed from his body as effortlessly as his armour clattered at his feet. His shoulder blades sunk down and back, thrusting his chest up. With his scabby grey top removed, muscles cut from oak adorned his body and they too were laced with the same glowing scribes. Angelic scribes, painted on him by the devout of the Church Triumphant, "The creature was alien, the Centurion of divine origin. A scout vessel sent to the farthest reaches of space. I was responsible for its loss and have hunted it since."

"Pirate..." Ford struggled with breath, the boot heavy on his chest.

"Necessity makes for strange bedfellows. They did not know the truth you now face."

Ford struggled against the angels' serenade. Disembodied voices, music without instrument, the symphony could not be denied and Ford had no choice to be seduced.

"I am a Saint, no more. And I need your help. Young, Mr. Dahl." The boot lifted, setting down on the floor. Dante lowered a hand to Ford, "I will not sell one member of your crew. Should you wish to leave, then I will allow it. But I cannot crew this ship alone, I ask that you help me dock. From there, we can part ways."

"How can I trust you?" Ford asked, unable to look away from the vibrant burning text.

"You don't have to, not now. All you have to do is submit."

Just as it had done on Otzu, the enchanted ballad bound him to the floor, sapping all of his strength. The song pushed him into submission and into his past. Snow fell around him, and the screams of his comrades echoed from beneath the music. Rage bubbled up within him; he wanted nothing more than to put the pirate's head through a wall. But he was as impotent now, as he had been then.

Dante claimed to have kept this secret from his crew and had known about the beast all along. Doubts were abundant, but Dante's offer was not an option and the only way he could free himself was to oblige the man. In Dante's other hand flashed a dagger, tinted blue by the ceiling lamps. On one face of the offer; obedience to Dante, on the other was death. Ford moved his hand, free from the force of the words. His arm rose and took the Saint's invitation, such as it was.

The cold sternness in Dante's face warmed, "Thank you." His bare hand took Ford's glove and helped him to his feet, the glowing scripture on Dante's skin faded back to ink.

Ford couldn't tell what lay ahead, whether the Saint turned Pirate would double cross him or not. He had only Dante's word and through the will of the Trinity, Dante had Ford's. He would be enslaved to him, for now. And yet with the contract renewed, there was hope. He had a ship and his crew were safe. Right now all that mattered was the promise to his sister and by the Trinity he would keep it.

The End.

Acknowledgements

This book wouldn't exist without, Claudette, Haldane and Brendan. Nor the eagle eyes of my editor Steven Frost. I especially want to thank Tereza who pushed me through all the drafts and then covered them in red ink. Of course I'll take credit for all the cool stuff, but I'll share the errors and car crashes between us. But with all sincerity, this story would have remained an illegible mess on my hard-drive if not for their feedback and support.

I would also like to thank Jim Burns who captured my vision of the Jian Seng for the cover. This man is a rare talent and I'm honoured to have him be part of this book.

About the author

Leighton Dean is an indie writer of Science Fiction. He lives with his wife in South Wales, United Kingdom. Outside of writing he spends too much time playing Gwent and is part of the Science Fiction Roundtable group for Sci-Fi & Fantasy readers and writers.

As a self published author, reviews are incredibly important for visibility in a hugely competitive market. So please review the book, a line on how it made you feel is enough.

Find out more about Leighton Dean and his other novels by registering for the free newsletter at www.leightondean.co.uk

If you enjoyed

SAVE OUR SOULS

look out for

GUNBOY

by

Leighton Dean

CHAPTER ONE

Off The Record

The sunrise banished the blackness, lighting the old satellite orbiting the earth, three hundred miles above England. A veteran of Heathrow's glory days, its archaic computer had been re-tasked by MI5 for the sole purpose of watching over Britain's greatest embarrassment: the abandoned city of London.

Each night the satellite studied the prefab buildings saturating Heathrow's crumbling runways amongst other targets. Tonight however, Pil was piggy-backing the signal, leering over the once airport, now UN Station with lustful anticipation. The feed was strong and clear, worth the money he'd paid up front. Beamed straight from the satellite into his chipset, and with some digital wizardry: projected onto his contact lenses.

It was a change of pace for him. Over the years he had succumbed to the fate of most reporters, resorting to posting inflammatory accusations and opinions in the hope of gaining a share of the internet. But his only story in recent history to receive traction was on Fray International's Human and Associated Networks Database – HAND. But aside from revealing their 'lack of privacy policy' the previous month he was still regarded as a toothless terrier.

Age had not brought wisdom, but regret instead. Sure he'd made a living, enough for a nice little cottage in the Rhondda Valley, along with a couple of failed marriages and his state of the art smart contact lenses. Oakley designed, complete with retina projected Heads-up Display, 3D imaging and recording directly attuned to his chipset. He'd made his fortune with those, alongside refining his taste for vulgarity. But now, in his later years he'd found loneliness without the company of self-respect.

December 12th 2038, today it was all going to change. He could taste it. That's why he'd packed his Sony V-Slate and had rushed to Heathrow. It was a couple of years out of date, but as computer tablets went it connected to the chipset in his skull and still held its charge. Who cared if it had scuffs along its edges and hair line crack along the face - it did the job. He was chasing a story; a real story this time, a chance to reclaim a part of himself he'd lost. All it had taken to kindle that fire was a tip, why he currently lived at Gate 5 Departure lounge and why he'd drunk his fill of BullPhett and then drunk some more.

He'd stared at the satellite's green, vitreous image for three nights, with nothing to show for it except the dull ache in his rump. You'd think they'd have at least upgraded the moulded plastic chairs. At 07:03AM, he'd been watching for five hours, twenty two minutes and thirteen seconds without a break and was beginning to worry someone was wasting his time. He dismissed the time from his Heads Up Display and faded the Sat-feed out, bringing Gate Five's familiar surroundings into prominence. The departure lounge was empty, except for Alison the desk clerk of course, who had the habit of licking her front teeth after every sentence. At twenty-seven, she was thirty years his junior but Pil made a promise to himself that if nothing happened in the next hour - he'd ask her on a date.

The Sat-feed flashed twice; there was movement at last, and with a quick wink of his right eye he signalled the chip in his brain, bringing back the satellite's imagery. Nurses, volunteers and soldiers stampeded through the camp.

He dismissed the feed as United Nation soldiers jogged through the lounge, passing along the rows of empty seats, passing Alison before disappearing through a door, over which a sign read 'Authorised Personnel Only'.

He stood up, stamped the numbness out of his feet before slipping the V-Slate into his bag and followed the UN Soldiers, preparing his best smile.

Alison looked up from her work station. "No." "This is what I've been waiting for," Pil said.

"I can't let you in, so you may as well sit down."

"C'mon Ali, it's me," he pleaded.

"I know." Her words felt like a slap across his face.

His tongue protruded through tightly sealed lips; what was her problem? He just wanted in on the ground floor, she knew that.

"Don't." She ended the conversation before he could form a reasonable rebuttal. Freedom of the press wasn't as it used to be. He looked back at the empty rows of plastic seats and saw the end of his career.

"Fine," he said, "then I may as well go back to bed."

He'd have to find another way.

***

Plan B took him outside amongst the doctors and nurses. His press pass still gave him some privileges. He snaked through the manic crowd; it was bedlam, more like a department store in the January Sales than an organised response station. It was so packed he had to resort to lifting his satchel over his head to save his V-Slate from a nasty collision with the scurrying personnel. It hadn't been this busy for a long time, not since the nuke threat back in 'twenty-nine'.

The first major alert in nine years and here he was, right smack in the middle. Pil couldn't help it, it was fantastic - he felt twenty-five again. He grinned from ear to ear, bouncing between people as he made his way past the light-weight barriers and flashing amber lights to the row of Red Cross-branded helicopters.

Large hulking tactical transports with the weapon systems removed they'd become common hand me downs from private firms. Soon they would be scrapped, but today were being loaded with paramedics and supplies, they were going to save lives. Earning their part in history and Pil was going to share in their glory.

Pil dismissed the long list of vehicle registrations offered to him by his Heads Up Display, already having spied the craft he needed. Second in line, with the dark skinned Spaniard lifting a crate into its belly. He lowered his satchel and called. "Tango!"

Tango squinted in the darkness and smiled in recognition. "A little early for you, old man?"

"That sounds like a brush off."

"Depends if you're trying to bum smokes or not." Tango slid the crate into the belly of his craft and brought his right hand in for a shake.

"Gave up." Pil grabbed the man's hand. "Insurance will kill you."

"Tell me about it."

"I'd rather you tell me about it," said Pil, nodding to the chaos.

"Off the record?" The question hailed back to an era before Tango had even been born. With all today's recording options it had become a disadvantage to the reporter who upheld that bygone code. Pil was one of the few reporters who did and Tango knew it from their previous dealings.

"They won't know it's from you," placated Pil.

Tango said nothing, but Pil, being a student of human behaviour didn't need a HudAPP to pick up on his twitching eyebrow to know he was nervous. "They won't know it came from you," he repeated quietly.

"Alright." Tango broke, "An SOS came in from behind the fence. Explosion or some shit, we're taking a couple of choppers out to provide assistance."

Pil's spider-sense tingled. "SOP?"

The Special Operations Police had a string of bases on the other side of the fence, but they were privately funded and would have their own medical response teams. If they needed help...

Tango shook his head, "Don't know. Just been told to kit up and move out."

The plot thickened. An SOS from behind the fence. Someone other than the SOPs? His mind and heart raced. There'd been no negotiations with London, at least none disclosed. This was huge.

"You know what I'm going to ask," he said, hiding the desperation in his voice with a forced smile.

"You want to come with me?" Tango asked.

Pil nodded; an eight year-old's grin spread across his face. "C'mon, consider it an early Christmas present."

"The signal must be heard huh?"

Pil laughed. "I've three daughters from three wives Tango, I need the damned cash." He held Tango's eyes, silently pleading.

"Get aboard before someone sees you."

***

Seven minutes later two Red Cross transports flew at speed into Greater London. They tailed behind their escort, an AW250 Lynx Wildcat, a remote piloted weapons platform costing more than Heathrow's entire Red Cross fleet. A state-of-the-art killing machine, relieving any concerns the paramedic team harboured about being attacked.

Tango's transport held the middle position, his co-pilot Juarez a slick fly boy. Shorter than Tango, the kid looked liked he'd overcompensated for his height by spending his downtime at the gym. Sharing the passenger hold with Pil were four paramedics. He contemplated interviewing them, but they were as green as they came and he wasn't looking for a puffed up editorial piece. He wanted something else, he wanted the fabled scoop of a lifetime.

His thoughts consumed him; an SOS was unheard of, at least publicly. London was just gangland, a violent anarchist state where no-one in their right mind would live. Murderous villainy lurked at every street corner, drug factories, people factories, kidnapping, rape, murder; everything they could squeeze into the brochure and here he was about to see it firsthand. To prove or disprove, he didn't care. He was going to be the first non-military, non-private militia to see it in fourteen years. I'd like to dedicate this Pulitzer to my children and my three ex-wives, without whom I wouldn't need to work.

He was on the top of the world; ignoring the safety instructions, letting his head hang close as he dared to the open side of the chopper, he closed his eyes and let the wind straighten his silver hair. In a world of his own, oblivious to the nervous conversations going on around the cabin and of the questions directed at him.

It wasn't until he felt the tug on his sleeve that he found all four paramedics looking at him. He tapped the soft tissue behind his ear, switching to the local channel. "Sorry?"

"You're Pil?" the closest paramedic said, blond ruffled hair and pubescent face.

"Uh huh."

"I told you!" exclaimed his friend, smiling like a Cheshire cat.

Blond nodded. "Are you going to make us famous?"

"I hope so."

"What do you think is going on?" asked Cheshire.

"No idea," Pil said, perhaps too abrupt for the crew's liking as they nodded and fell silent, "I'm sure we'll find out soon enough," he assured them.

Blond shook his head, but said nothing further so Pil returned to the fuselage's door and watched the city unfold beneath him. What remained of it anyway: grass grew where roads ran and trees climbed through buildings, disfiguring them. Nevertheless he still recognised London. No city was quite as distinct, especially for those who'd grown up there.

Eight minutes in the air and they were now over Hounslow. Roofless homes and long since abandoned vehicles scattered the derelict landscape, making the stories of a gangland city seem severely exaggerated. It was nothing more than a ghost town.

Retreating back inside the hull, Pil banged the wall behind the cockpit, switching to the pilot's channel and asked if there was any new information. "Nothing since we left," Tango replied. A sigh left his mouth; if the trip was going to be this boring, he may as well start writing. He winked the record mode on his contact lenses, pulled his

V-Slate free of his bag and penned the date and time on the file. December 12th 2038, 07:32. Pil thought about his opening. He needed something dramatic, something daring to lure them in.

When the cockpit alarm system activated, he cursed at how he'd tempted fate. He gripped the handrail ignoring the fearful faces of the paramedics. "Tango?" he called, his voice lost under the thunderous roar of the helicopter's rotors. "Tango!" he posted, but still no response.

Pil leaned out the side, the streets no different from the ones he had looked out over a minute ago. "Shit!" He mouthed the word as his eye caught the jet black stream of smoke streaking toward him. Recognising it immediately he reached back and banged on the cockpit door, shouting "RPG!"

Three paramedics panicked, screaming in terror. Only Blond had the nerve to join Pil at the edge of the craft, his eyes rounding as he saw the approaching rocket, then both he and Pil were jerked back inside the craft as it banked hard.

Pil's hands scrambled for something to grab, finding the tight orange straps securing the bird's medical supplies. He locked his arm through the net as Blond, who had no such luck, screamed for his mother as he fell through the fuselage and out the opposite hatch, immediately chased by the rocket and the screams of the terrified medical crew.

Scorching black smoke spewed from the rocket's tail, filling the cabin. But with burning eyes and blackened lungs Pil felt exhilarated. Pity about blond, but he'd remember to buy Tango a bottle of the good stuff for saving their lives. Who knows, the kid may still survive the fall.

Even above the sound of the helicopter's rotors; the distinctive high pitch whine of the Wildcat's three rotary machine guns spooling caught Pil's attention. Knowing it would be over in seconds, he had to be quick. He had to get a better view of the action.

"What are you doing?" Cheshire no longer smiled, Pil didn't hear him, he was deep in the game, more focused than his eight thousand euro contact lenses. He crawled over the crates, found footing on the deck as the transport stabilised and pulled himself into the cock pit between Juarez and his friend.

Knowing better than to distract the pilots, he took his position while watching Tango as he rotated the bird around the stationary Wildcat, still hammering the buildings to their left with its guns. It was a magnificent sight and he was catching it all on his chipset. Up close and personal with a medical team under fire.

"Another bogie!" Juarez pointed to a second smoke trail racing up from the ground, coming up behind the Wildcat.

Tango yanked back on his control stick, reversing their transport from the Wildcat. Too late, the RPG clipped the tail of the Wildcat and exploded, showering the chopper with debris.

"Brace yourselves!" said Tango, forcing Pil to slide back into the crew section. He locked his arm through the orange netting once again, but couldn't help but steal another look through the cockpit doorway, glancing long enough to realise the Wildcat was out of control and spinning toward them.

He pulled his hand free of the netting, blinked a command to his chip. He wasn't going to let a little thing like death stop him from receiving the Pulitzer. If he wasn't going to report the story, he would bloody well be it. So when Cheshire and the others tucked their heads between their knees, he jumped from the transport. Turning in mid-air he saw the flaming Wildcat crash into the helicopter and witnessed a magnificent fireball burning the morning sky. Pil smiled. He was about to live forever.

Want to find out more?

Newsletters
Events
Competitions
& Upcoming Releases

Visit
www.leightondean.co.uk

@Leighton_Dean
/Leighton.Dean.Author

Printed in Great Britain
by Amazon